This is a work of fiction. All characters and events are either a product of the author's imagination or used fictitiously, and any resemblance to real people or events is entirely coincidental.

SPECTRUM BLADE

Cover art by Michelle Ong

Edited by Amanda Dimer Silva

First Edition: November 2021

ISBN-13: 978-1-952145-17-9

SPECTRUM BLADE

SPECTRUM LEGACY BOOK ONE

BETH ALVAREZ

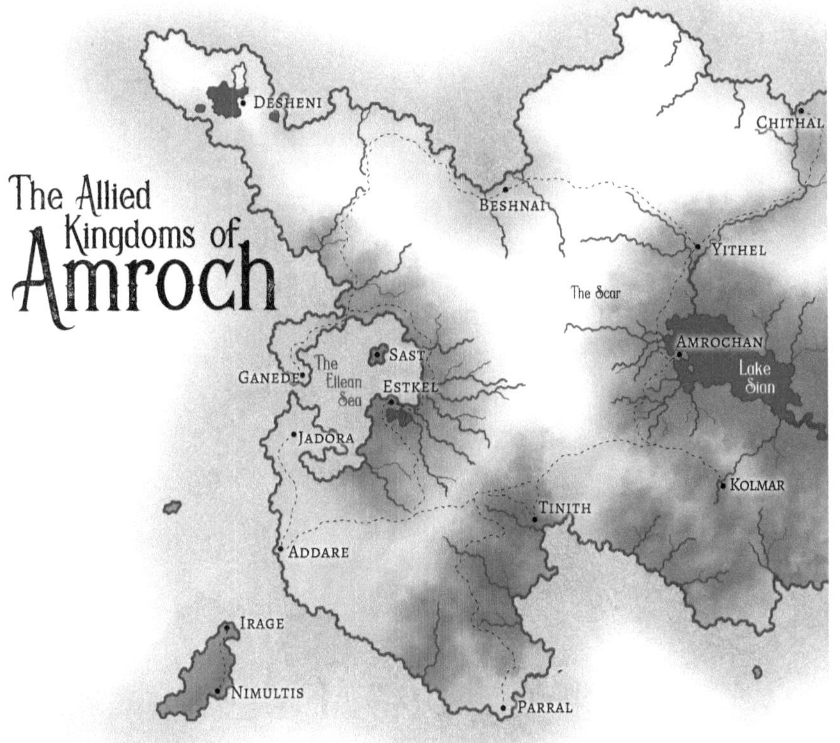

The Allied Kingdoms of Amroch
DESHENI
CHITHAL
BESHNAI
YITHEL
The Scar
AMROCHAN
Lake Sian
GANEDE
The Ellean Sea
SAST
ESTKEL
JADORA
KOLMAR
TINITH
ADDARE
IRAGE
NIMULTIS
PARRAL

CHAPTER ONE

Beyond the sprawling meadow where trainees swung longswords in the morning light, a small flash of silver among the trees caught Zaide's eye. No matter how he searched, he couldn't detect any movement in the undergrowth or the sun-dappled shadows swaying under the thick canopy, but there was no mistaking the gleam had been there. He squinted against the sun, willing the smoke from the blacksmith's forge beneath him to clear. It didn't, and no second flash came after the first.

"Sitting up there and feeling sorry for yourself again?" Resia's small, chirpy voice rose to greet him. Her presence was no surprise. He may have been staring into the far side of the woods, but Zaide had seen her coming out of the corner of his eye. His foster sister never hurried and never tried to mask herself with shadows like the trainees in the field. She was the Elder's apprentice—the favorite apprentice, to his chagrin—and had no reason to hide.

"No," he replied from the roof of the forge, still scanning the woods. "It wouldn't change anything if I was."

Resia gathered her skirts in one hand and shuffled up the angled ladder to join him. The blacksmith's roof was a common lookout point, as the forge was one of few structures built in the meadow instead of among the trees. After the fire, separating the forge from the rest of the village seemed wise.

Though Zaide expected a lecture, she sat down beside him, smoothed her green skirts and gazed out at the people in the field for a while instead. The line in which the dozen or so trainees stood flowed over the meadow hill, looking from their vantage point to be sinuous instead of even. The instructors called a steady cadence of orders and swords moved in unison, more or less.

"You ought to be out there." Resia tugged at the lock of her chin-length brown hair that hung before her pointed ear, a thoughtful habit she'd never broken. "You're better than all of them."

"Doesn't matter. The last Spring Choosing was my only chance, and you remember what the Elder said." Zaide still harbored bitterness over how his Choosing had ended, but he reined it in and kept his voice calm. It wasn't Resia's fault he'd been put out, after all. That was the Elder's doing.

Every time he looked back, Zaide wished it had been handled differently. It was an honor to be selected as one of the Elder's apprentices, but it wasn't what he'd wanted to do. As the most skilled swordsman in his year, Zaide should have been the first choice the king's advisor pulled from the candidates to become part of the king's army. Instead, the Elder had chosen the exact moment the advisor stopped before him to lay his claim, forbidding Zaide his heart's desire.

In a perfect world, Zaide would be one of the junior instructors on the field now, visiting the sleepy village of Kolmar as a service to the garrison, leading drills before the afternoon assembly where the village guardsmen made their recommendations and the king's advisor would make his picks.

"That doesn't mean you shouldn't be out there," Resia said. "At the very least, you ought to spar with some of the boys who went last year. It would be nice to see if they can hold a candle to you yet. The blade's as natural to you as breathing."

The line of trainees shifted and broke into small groups. Zaide chose to ignore the poor stance of a young man in the group closest to the forge. He let his eyes wander to the skies instead. "I can't imagine the Elder let you out of the library so you could come give me bad ideas."

Her sweet laugh lifted his spirits, if only a little. She touched a finger to her chin and grinned. "No. Actually, he wants to speak to you. He noticed your absence, though it took him a few hours."

"He doesn't have to worry. Even if I wanted to participate, you only get one Choosing. And I'll be eighteen in the fall, besides." Zaide closed his eyes, shutting out as much of the world as he could. Only the sun still demanded attention, warm on his face and putting a red glow on the inside of his eyelids. "I'll be given my piece of land then. I need to make plans for what I'll do to contribute to the village."

Resia quirked a brow. "Aside from being the Elder's apprentice?"

"You're a better apprentice than I am. Another year and I expect he'll be done with me." Zaide still couldn't fathom why he'd been chosen. Resia made sense as an apprentice, patient and studious, blessed with fine penmanship and simmering magic in her veins. Zaide was... well, Zaide. One of several children fostered in the village after war had claimed their homes. He was steadfast with a blade, competent with a bow, and skilled with little else. As far as he knew, there was no reason he shouldn't have become a soldier. That one of the other fosters had gone was still salt in the wound.

Resia shrugged and slid back toward the ladder. "Well, that's still a year you ought to be at his beck and call, then. Are you coming?"

He sighed and moved to the top of the ladder to follow her down. The moment he opened his mouth to speak, a silver gleam caught his eye. The same flash, farther into the woods, just as bright.

"Yes," he replied. He descended the first few rungs of the ladder, then hopped off the side and landed with a quiet thump. "In a minute."

She turned, her cheeks rosy with annoyance. "I thought you weren't going out there!"

Zaide raised a hand to silence her protests and sprinted across the meadow, weaving between the clusters of trainees so he was sure to lose her.

The far side of the woods was where hunters roamed. He'd been tempted to dismiss the first flicker of light as a reflection off a wayward arrowhead. It would have been a foolish mistake. Today was the Choosing; no one would venture into the woods for fresh game when the village square would hold a feast at sundown.

That left two options: someone who was sneaking off to avoid something, or someone who was sneaking off to somewhere they shouldn't.

Whether or not he'd been chosen to become a guardsman or a soldier in the king's army, Zaide was the Elder's apprentice. One of his jobs was to be eyes and ears when the Elder was not present. Curiosity couldn't hurt.

He slipped among the trees with a practiced grace, following the narrow game trails toward where he estimated that last flash had been. Someone carrying metal meant a weapon of some sort. No one in the village wore armor, and he doubted any of the visitors from the garrison would have ventured that far into the woods.

Tracking anyone equipped with a bow was of questionable safety, but he savored every opportunity to practice his woodcraft. Zaide kept his head down and worked hard to blend into the trees.

The native Kolmari were said to be made for the woods and from the woods, shaped by the Maker from the trees themselves. They were brown-skinned and brown-haired, with eyes that ranged the colors of the forests, from green to gold to earthen shades that made them almost monochromatic.

The village fosters were not so blessed, and Zaide had it worse than most. Pale-skinned, blue-eyed, and white-haired, he glowed like a beacon any time he set foot in the sun. It had driven him, though; the handicap of his appearance meant that remaining hidden was a greater challenge, and the small competitive streak in him meant he relished the opportunity to work hard and excel.

More than once, however, he'd wondered if his appearance had been one of the reasons the Elder pulled him aside. He stuck out among the Kolmari. Among most of the country's people, in fact. Though he knew little of it, his homeland had been far to the east and was among the first countries to fall when the sea of war surged toward the west. Many had fled to Amroch, the powerful Allied Kingdoms where King Sendassian's forces could stand against the tide.

Zaide's father, he understood, had gone to Amrochan—the capital city—to offer his services to the king. His mother, wounded when they fled, had stopped with tiny Zaide in Kolmar, where she could recover. But her health never returned, even after the wounds mended, and a fever had claimed her a scant few years later.

The Elder had placed Zaide with Resia's family, for which he was grateful. What had become of his father, he didn't know.

Perhaps that had been one of the things that drove him to the sword. He shared his father's spirit to serve, to fight for the safety of his people—though Zaide's people were the Kolmari, not the refugees and lost souls his father had surely fought to avenge.

The sound of rustling leaves and soft boots on hard earth made Zaide freeze.

Somewhere, not far ahead, his target followed a game trail that wound deeper into the woods. He tilted his better ear toward the sound and held his breath.

Whoever it was, they were small—smaller than him—and moving fast. He pressed forward, putting every scrap of effort he had into stealth. Silent, he stalked off the path. It curved there, swinging north before it turned back toward the east. He picked his shortcut wisely, the sound of his passing no greater than that of a squirrel or rabbit skittering through the underbrush. When the path curved east again, he hid behind a tall maple, and his target came into view.

A girl.

Her golden hair and bright eyes made her just as out of place as him, but she was no foster. And from the pack slung over her shoulder and the worried way she looked back toward Kolmar, she meant to escape fast.

Not just a girl.

A thief.

Zaide slid through the undergrowth like a viper, burst onto the trail behind her and struck out to grab her arm.

The girl yelped and spun, her silver dagger flashing toward his throat.

He jerked back, escaping to the safety of arm's length without letting her go.

She twisted in his grasp, twirled under his arm and lashed out with a kick that streaked dirt across his blue shirt but did little more than graze his side. Then she came back with the dagger, lunging close with her teeth bared.

Zaide caught her wrist and wrenched it hard, yielding a cry of pain. The dagger slid from her grip and he reeled her in. If she was a thief, she wasn't a good one. He was skilled, but not so skilled that capturing her should have been easy.

"What are you doing? What have you done?" His voice came low and dangerous, weighted with what he hoped sounded like authority.

She writhed in his arms like an eel, collapsed into her knees and slithered out of his grasp. Then she twirled back, produced a second blade as if from thin air and dove for his heart.

A quick strike to her wrist threw her off course, and he swiped the blade she'd lost moments ago from the earth.

An instant later, the blades rang together when he blocked her renewed attacks. He hadn't expected her to fight so hard. But no matter how much effort she put into it, she couldn't compare to his years of practice. He knocked her weapon aside and darted close, the long knife he'd claimed from the ground stopping only a hair's breadth from her throat.

She froze, her blue eyes wide.

"Answer me," he said, still as stone, his gaze boring into hers. "What have you done? Stolen from the village?"

"Zaide!" The Elder's gruff voice broke the still of the forest. A second later, the old man emerged from the trees and stumbled in the undergrowth. "Let her go."

Startled, Zaide turned toward his mentor.

The girl seized the opportunity and bolted up the winding trail.

Zaide started after her, but only made it a pair of steps before his feet hit the ground and stuck fast as the Elder's magic rooted him in place. He growled in frustration, glaring at the swaying foliage into which the girl had disappeared.

"I said, let her go," the Elder repeated, softer. He tugged his brown robes free of the brambles and crept closer.

Zaide pulled against the invisible force that held his feet and sighed in exasperation when he realized it was futile. He wasn't going anywhere unless the Elder released him. "She's done something, Elder, I'm sure of it. That, or she's about to do something. Why else would she attack me when I asked her a question?"

"Perhaps because you caught her off guard." His mentor spread a gnarled hand wide and passed it over the trail. The magic came loose. "What made you believe it was your place to ask her anything?"

"I thought strangers weren't to be trusted." Zaide lifted his boots one at a time, treading in place. His toes were numb after the magic's effect. Sensation came back as a thousand hot pins and needles. "We're too close to the border now. Danger comes through the woods. Isn't that what you said?"

"Yes," the Elder agreed in a slow drawl, "but she hardly seemed a danger."

"She could have stolen something. Or been on her way to do it. She kept looking back, as if she was nervous."

"Which would be why she attacked you when you surprised her, I'm certain." The Elder stroked his long, gray mustaches with a thoughtful hand. "But if she was a thief, it is better to let her go, regardless. Need, not greed, is often the precursor of theft. If she has taken from someone in the village, I shall see it is replaced. Come, now. I called for you. We shall speak in my study."

Sullen, Zaide looked up the game trail once more. The leaves were still, the sound of her footfalls long gone. His heartbeat settled and disappointment sank in. It was bad enough he'd failed to apprehend her. But for just a moment, he'd been excited to have a stroke of adventure in his life. Bowing his head, he turned to follow his mentor back to the village. "Yes, Master."

In a perfect world, Zaide would have been an instructor, or at least a guardsman. Then, he would have been in his right to pursue her into the woods. He didn't know what the girl was doing in Kolmar's forest, but he had little doubt she was up to no good.

CHAPTER TWO

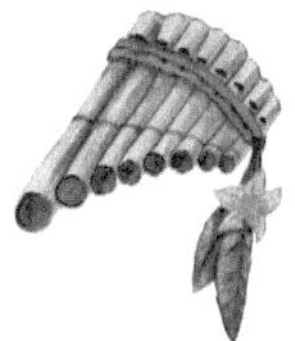

THE ELDER WAS A FAIR MAN, and that was half the problem. He was as fair to Zaide as he was to the girl, and that meant extra work as penance. Under normal circumstances, Zaide's efforts in cleaning the library took a handful of minutes; typically, he was only responsible for cleaning up after himself. But by the time he finished scouring the Elder's desk, the sun rode low in the sky and the choices for the Spring Choosing had already been made.

Zaide cleaned the ink from his fingers before he emerged from the library. The young men and women who had been chosen to serve at the garrison already stood in a line along the far side of the village square.

"I wanted to spare you from having to watch the decisions be made," the Elder remarked from the bench beside the door. He leaned against his walking stick, watching as the soldiers called orders. Tonight, they would celebrate. Tomorrow, they would leave.

Zaide grunted softly. "Is that why you wanted me to scrub the whole library?"

The old man beside him shrugged, twisting a few coarse hairs of his long beard between his fingers.

"I'm grown. I don't need your protection." Zaide's voice held no heat. His calm demeanor was one of many reasons everyone had been stunned by the Elder's choice to take him as apprentice. A cool head was invaluable on the battlefield. That coolness extended to his will toward the others, as well. He harbored no grudge against those chosen. Many were friends, as many had been the year before, and would be the year after. His misfortune was not their burden, and it would be unfair to saddle them with it.

Unruffled by the protest, the Elder chuckled. "You may need me more than you realize, boy. Do you wish to join me on the platform when I speak?"

Zaide shook his head. "Speaking isn't my specialty. I'll let Resia have that privilege." In truth, he simply didn't want the Elder's pity. Hot on the heels of his discipline, the only reason his mentor might offer him such a position of honor was out of sympathy.

"Very well." The old man rose, pressing a gnarled hand to his lower back and groaning softly as he straightened his spine. "It is a festival day. The rest of the evening is yours. If there is time to spare, perhaps the visitors from the garrison would spar with you. Maybe that would soothe your restless spirit."

There was little doubt Zaide's old comrades would want to spar. That was how they'd filled their days before and it was how he filled his free time now, when he had it. As an apprentice, free time had become scarce. Most days were filled with studies and scribe work, copying notes from endless piles of books on jumbled subjects. History and politics could be interesting, at times, but a good portion of their studies revolved around the application of magic.

And, unlike the Kolmari, Zaide had no magic.

He took the Elder's place on the bench outside the library, slouched against the cool stone wall and watched the old man's retreat. Once his mentor was a safe distance away, he drew up his foot and slid a long silver knife from his boot.

In her haste to escape, the blonde girl had left it behind. He'd avoided pulling it out while in the library, for fear the Elder might take it before he had a chance to give it a good inspection.

Now that he turned it between his hands, he couldn't fathom why it had been left behind. She could have taken it from his hand easily after the Elder's arrival, and he couldn't imagine anything stolen from Kolmar could have been worth more than that knife. It was one of the finest weapons he'd ever seen, perfectly balanced and meticulously detailed, etched with filigree down the middle of the blade. To say the edge was keen would have been an understatement. It sat perfectly still on top of his thumbnail when he rested it there, and when he lifted it, a tiny white line marked where it had been.

Had any of her attacks made contact, he wasn't sure he would have survived.

Even the blades of the men from the garrison—which were fine weapons, as the king did not skimp on his army—couldn't compare to this. Zaide rested the blade's point against the rough wood of the bench beside him and twirled it by the hilt. He hadn't meant to keep it and he supposed having it now made him something of a thief, himself. But knowing the Elder, if he mentioned having it, he would be expected to give it back. Zaide was unbothered by the idea of returning the weapon. It was the knowledge that the Elder would expect him to apologize for taking it that rankled.

Frowning, he slid the knife back into his boot, making sure his pants covered the top.

Across the village square, those chosen for the garrison assembled at the foot of the low stage. The Elder climbed the stage with Resia at his elbow, and the Kolmari began to gather.

Three were going this year, Zaide noted. Two boys and a girl, all of whom he'd trained with as they grew. He approved of all three selections. One of the young men specialized in pole arms, while the other used a sword and had been a worthy opponent in their sparring matches. The young woman was one of the best scouts Kolmar had produced in ages. They numbered few, but

Kolmar was small. Even with the few fosters and refugees, they numbered no more than two hundred.

"Our numbers dwindle," the Elder began, his voice carrying through the forest as if to finish Zaide's thoughts. "Each year the war presses near, we are fewer. And yet those who have been chosen today are vital for the safety of not only Kolmar, but all of Amroch."

"May the alliance hold true," Zaide murmured along with the rest of the village, as was customary during formal events. He didn't understand why. After thousands of years, he saw no reason the Allied Kingdoms that formed Amroch would divide.

"No matter the size of the village or the size of its defender, our importance is the same. The blight of war creeps ever nearer, yet our forest allows us to protect all others. Our forest may border the battlefield, but the blessings of the ancient temple's sages stay with us for as long as we live. Tomorrow, three Kolmari depart for the garrison, but in weeks to come, they shall patrol the border and bolster King Sendassian's armies the way only Kolmari magic can."

A roar of pride sounded from those gathered. Zaide slouched farther in his seat and tried to ignore the rest.

He bore no magic, yet he was the Elder's apprentice and they sent mages to serve. No matter how he tried to accept his fate, frustration still bubbled to the surface. It took all his strength to tamp it down.

Zaide turned his head, stared into the forest and let his thoughts return to the knife in his boot.

After so many hours, there was little chance the girl was still there. For all he knew, she could be halfway to Amrochan. But if he looked for her, he could at least say he tried. He cast one last glance over his shoulder at the ceremony and slipped from the bench.

When he'd seen her, she'd been headed east. Who knew what for. The only thing east of Kolmar was forest and the front lines, and she had certainly been no soldier. A spy was a possibility;

the notion fluttered through his head before he dismissed it. Their enemy didn't bother with spies. He chose to fight with unrelenting force, crushing and consuming the kingdoms that stood against his expanding empire.

But she could have been a messenger serving King Sendassian.

"Which would make me the antagonist, wouldn't it?" he mused.

Perhaps that was why the Elder had stopped him, though he couldn't imagine why a messenger would have been sneaking through the woods behind the backs of the guardsmen.

Finding the point in the trail where they'd fought wasn't hard. In her haste to escape, she'd left a clear path to follow, too. He tracked her eastward for some distance before the odd, orange-gold light cast on the trees caught his attention.

The evening sun had set the sky ablaze, but the light that glowed between the trees was too red. Zaide turned back toward the west to hold his hand to the horizon. He squinted and tried to count the fingers between the ground and the setting sun.

Uneasiness flowed over him, as cold as winter water from the river.

Instead of a golden sunset, he saw the sun darken.

Tongues of flame licked the sky, burning a deep red as the crawling eclipse blotted out the light.

The breeze that whispered through the trees was cold, sour. Zaide shuddered, rooted in place as if the Elder's magic had frozen him there.

The shadow of the moon.

The portent of death.

Zaide tore himself free of whatever power held him and spun on his heel.

Instead of the village, a monster filled his eyes.

Howling, the pig-faced beast lunged in, bringing a crude mace down overhead.

Zaide leaped sideways and skidded in the earth. Reflexively, his hand went to his side, grasping for a practice blade that wasn't there. He gritted his teeth, snatched the knife from his boot instead and met the goborrin head on. He couldn't hope to parry the mace with a blade so small. Reflexes saved him, letting him twist and jump aside as the heavy weapon crashed down again.

It was larger than he'd realized. He'd heard of goborrins before, knew they formed the front lines of the enemy's army as it pushed against Sendassian's borders, but the men from the garrison always made them sound smaller. This was the size of a grown man, with stout tusks curling up around its slimy, pig-like nose.

Zaide barely escaped the sweep of the mace and reevaluated his strategy the moment his boots hit the ground. He couldn't keep trying to dodge, praying the mace wouldn't connect.

The monster's second sweep went wide. Zaide lunged into the opening, driving the long knife into the goborrin's side.

Its bellow of pain was loud enough to rattle Zaide's bones. It swung back hard, its powerful arm just missing his head.

He danced backwards, bouncing the hilt of the knife a shade higher in his hand. Coppery-brown blood dripped from the blade's tip. A stab that deep would have killed a man, yet the goborrin howled and heaved its mace back for another attack.

Determined, Zaide drew a battle stance. The monster was undeterred by the injury, but it was slowed. It swung hard but staggered, its reach too shallow, and Zaide flowed in to strike. This time, he struck vitals.

Squalling like the pig it resembled, the goborrin fell.

Zaide didn't stay to see it die.

Between the trees, a ruddy glow filled the horizon. The thought of fire filled his head, scorching, consuming. The scars on the forest from the smithy fire still showed, the blistered marks on wounded trees putting fear in his heart.

He vaulted over fallen timber and crashed through the brush. Screams of pain and fear echoed in the forest, spurring him on.

On the far side of the village, flames engulfed the Elder's library. Men and women heaved buckets from the well and slapped wet burlap sacks at the crawling fire. Bodies of goborrins littered the ground, some bleeding into the earth, others blistered with what could only have been magic.

Across the square, the visitors from the garrison dispatched the last of the beasts. Zaide ran to join them. "Are there more?"

Aren, one of the young men chosen the year prior, met his eyes. "Scouts, but not many. Are you all right?" His gaze flicked to the knife in Zaide's hand, still streaked with beast blood.

Zaide knelt and wiped it in the carpet of decaying leaves. "Fine. Met one in the woods. Resia?"

"With the Elder." Aren pointed toward a house stained with soot, but otherwise unharmed, and lowered his voice. "It's bad."

Swallowing against the tightness in his throat, Zaide nodded. He slid the clean knife into his boot and jogged toward the cluster of people gathered by the door.

They parted when he approached, a clear sign of trouble. The only reason to let him through was that the Elder had requested him.

Under no circumstances did that bode well.

Grim faces turned away as he pushed through to the open doorway. Resia intercepted him before he'd gone two steps into the shadowed front room, gripping his arm and leaning close to whisper in his pointed ear. "Where were you?" Her words were harsh, accusatory, a perfect match for the lines of worry between her eyebrows.

He didn't have an answer. Instead, he pulled out of her grasp and strode between the rows of injured people and the women tending them.

At the far end of the room, the Elder lay on a cot with medics milling around him. He raised a hand and extended it toward Zaide. Resia hurried back to his side.

Zaide set his jaw and moved to take the Elder's hand.

"You saw it," the Elder breathed. "Didn't you?"

"It wasn't your death the eclipse foretold." Zaide tried not to look at the bandages that wrapped the old man's body.

"No." The Elder closed his eyes and sighed. "Not today. But I fear it is far worse than the threat of my passing. The charts said the omen would come. I believed I was prepared, but I never imagined it would herald this. The wall has fallen, my boy. The magic that kept Gadranus's beasts from the forest is gone."

Everyone in the room grew still.

"That can't be," Resia said. "The magic is anchored in the old temple by our predecessors. For the magic to fall, someone would have had to—"

"Destroy the anchor," Zaide finished. He shifted and the knife in his boot pricked at his ankle. Heat rose in his blood. "Or steal it."

The Elder squeezed his hand. "The path to the temple is forbidden to all but my apprentices. Resia must stay here. Her magic cannot be spared now. You will go. See what has happened. Return the anchor to me, so that I may replenish its power."

"What is the anchor? What am I looking for?" Zaide had never followed the narrow path, but he knew where it was. It had been pointed out to him as part of his training. Next year, the apprentices would have walked the path together.

"An instrument," the Elder said. "A set of pipes. You will know it when you see it. It was bound in the forefront of the temple, protected by magic."

"How am I supposed to retrieve it, then?" Zaide's voice faltered. "I have no magic to unbind it."

The old man chuckled, a low, wheezing sound. "I have ordered it. It will release itself to you."

One last question hovered on the tip of his tongue, dragging Zaide's spirits down until he forced himself to speak. "And what if it's not there?"

"Then, my boy," the Elder said with a small smile, "you'll have to find it, won't you?"

Zaide bowed his head. "Yes, Master."

The Elder released his hand and turned back to Resia, making it clear he was dismissed. Zaide didn't linger. He couldn't bear to, not with the fire in his chest. He'd known the Spring Choosing would be a difficult day, but something like this had never crossed his mind. Thinking again of the knife in his boot, he hurried toward the forest.

"Zaide!"

The call stopped him at the edge of the village. He turned back, frowning as Aren approached. He didn't have time to explain. They'd killed one band of goborrins, but more were sure to follow if the protective magic over the forest wasn't restored.

Instead of asking questions, Aren reached for his sword. "You've got that look on you. That one you get when you're doing something important."

"The Elder has ordered it," Zaide said.

"The Elder needs to consider your safety. I don't know where you got that nice knife of yours, but it won't do much against one of those brutes. Here." Aren held out his sheathed blade.

Zaide eyed it, hesitant. "That's king's steel. I can't—"

"We have more, and it's better than any practice blade you can take with you. Don't forget the Elder serves the king, too. If the Elder ordered it, King Sendassian won't begrudge you a proper sword."

"Thank you, Aren." Zaide closed his hands around the scabbard, the weight of the weapon in his hands sending a thrill of excitement through him at the same time it dropped a lead weight in his stomach.

That morning, he'd envied his friend's position with the garrison. Now, somehow, he had the feeling Aren envied him, instead.

He belted the sword at his side and plunged into the woods.

CHAPTER THREE

Dusk chased any lingering warmth out of the air, replacing it with a dank chill that stank of mushrooms and rot.

Zaide needed no torch despite the moonless night, relying on his other senses to find his way. His hearing was sharp despite his damaged left ear, with its pointed end severed in some injury he couldn't remember. He moved like a specter, as much a ghost in the night as he looked, passing brambles without being snared and leaving little trace behind.

More than two hours' trek from the village, he found the temple path.

It was little wider than a game trail, but the earth underfoot was hard-packed and the growth that shaded the path was young and tender. Each year, Resia and the Elder cleared the way. Zaide hadn't joined them in the year prior—he'd only just been chosen as apprentice when they made that expedition, and the Elder had insisted his studies were more important.

Now he regretted that quiet day he'd spent toying with his practice blade instead of doing his lessons. He should have insisted on helping. At least then he'd have some idea of what waited ahead.

Tips of branches brushed at him like fingertips, grasping and clinging, begging him to stop. Zaide brushed them away and followed the path in quiet wonder.

Carved stone lanterns lined the path. Long trails of pale wax traced lines down from the cage-like tops. He paused at one to look inside, but there were no candles remaining. Only wax, and charred sticks and ash from what had once been incense.

Not far ahead, a low boom sounded in the underbrush. Zaide stopped and crouched to press his fingers to the earth.

It sounded larger than a drumbird, and from the vibrations in the ground—minute, but there—he knew it wasn't one.

The forest hadn't been attacked before, but Kolmar's scouts ranged to the edge of the forest to carry news to the garrison. Part of Zaide's training before he'd been made apprentice had been learning which bird calls were used by enemy forces. The drumbird was a favorite, but its thundering call was hard to emulate in just the right tone.

Whatever they hammered on now, it was off by just a shade.

Slowly, Zaide slipped off the path to hide in the bushes. The steady, thumping vibrations he felt in the ground became the cadence of a march, the footsteps of a half-dozen men just reaching his ears.

Or, he thought it was men. More likely to be goborrins, judging from what he'd seen only hours ago. If a retinue of goborrins patrolled the path, he would have to find another way in. As grateful as he was to have a proper sword at his side, it couldn't help him against a half-dozen enemies at once. If there were any of the beasts inside the temple, he didn't know what he would do.

He sank farther into the brush, moving slow enough to keep the leaves from rustling, guiding the tender branches back to their places with his hands.

Going was much slower through the undergrowth, but he couldn't risk being seen. Now and then he caught glimpses of the patrol unit through the trees. Beastly faces and crude leather garb confirmed his suspicion. They were goborrins. And there were a lot more than six.

He hugged the trail, remaining as close to the original path as he dared, diverging only to find an easier crossing over a deep creek bed. He found it a number of horse lengths away, where the earth sloped toward a wide curve in the creek. Thick blankets of gravel sheltered shallow pools. The shape of some of those pools gave him pause.

Small footprints trapped tiny minnows. The fish darted and spun in confusion, unable to escape the imprints of sturdy heels.

Zaide crouched at the bank to examine the marks. They weren't old; silt and mud still swirled and settled, meaning he wasn't far behind the person who made them. Judging by the size and shape of the boots, he knew exactly who that was.

But these tracks were headed toward the temple, not away from it, and they were fresh, besides. Too fresh to have any bearing on the day's events. If she hadn't been the one to break the seal that kept the forest safe, who had?

He crossed the creek in three wide steps, leaving more hollow imprints for the minnows to explore. Maybe those tracks weren't fresh enough to declare her guilt, but they were fresh enough to reflect a traveler who didn't know how to navigate the woods. With the monsters lurking not far away, that was as dangerous to him as it was to her. Right now, the goborrins had no reason to suspect there was anyone in the woods. The village was cleaning, preparing defenses, sending word to the king. The soldiers from the garrison, fortunately present for the festivities, would make plans for an expedition but wait for orders from their superiors.

But if the goborrins caught that girl wandering in the woods, they would send out scouts that would find him, too.

In the moonless shadows beneath the leaves, the tracks disappeared. Though there was little reason, Zaide hoped she'd passed the temple by.

No more than the thought had entered his head than it was

proven wrong. The brush beside him crackled and silver flashed past his arm. He wheeled in place, catching her outstretched arm and twisting hard.

The girl gasped. Zaide held a finger to his lips.

Her face twisted with a scowl. "You came all this way to catch me?" Even as a fierce whisper, her voice was small, delicate. Like her. Her wrist was so small, his fingers wrapped around it and overlapped.

"Don't flatter yourself." He let go, but stayed close, his voice as low and dangerous as hers. "Your woodcraft's so clumsy that it wouldn't have taken me an hour."

Her cheeks reddened and her scowl became a look of pure indignation. "Yet here you are, hours later."

The drumbird call sounded some distance away. They both turned toward it, silent, considering. Too far off to be a threat, Zaide decided. The girl seemed to reach the same conclusion, for she turned to continue her trek toward the temple.

Zaide closed the distance between them with a few quick strides. "What are you doing?"

"I owe you no explanation." She tossed her head, her ponytail swinging.

He freed it from a branch without a thought. "You're marching toward the temple that anchored the ancients' blessing that protected my village, the very same day those protections fell and my home was set afire by monsters. I have every right to know."

She paused mid-stride. "They reached the village?" Then she shook her head and continued on at a renewed pace. "It would have happened regardless. It was only a matter of time. But if you hadn't stopped me, I could have at least reached the temple before those monsters filled it."

Zaide scoffed. "You can't blame me for this. It's your inability to navigate the forest that slowed you, not thirty seconds fighting with me. Judging by your lack of finesse, you won't be able to get past the goborrins, either."

"And you can?"

He slid past her without a sound and blocked her path. "It's my duty. If you won't tell me why you're out here, I'd thank you to not get in the way."

Her eyes fell to the sword at his hip. A spark of recognition colored her expression and she regarded him with caution. When he met her eyes without comment, she relaxed, and some of the heat left her voice. "If it's your duty, then we're on the same side. We both want those monsters out of your forest."

"I think I'm more qualified to do that on my own." Zaide slipped the dagger from his boot, flipped it in the air and caught it by the tip of the blade. He offered her the hilt. "You can't even seem to hold on to your weapons."

She snatched the knife from his grasp. "Mind your tongue. I—"

The drumbird-call echoed through the trees again, and they both quieted. When the last thump faded, she glowered at him again. "Either you're with me or you're against me, forest boy. No matter how good you think you are with that sword, you're useless against a full camp of goborrins, and I know another way in."

"What? How?" It wasn't unusual for the Kolmari Elders to make pilgrimages to the temple, but she was not an Elder, nor was she Kolmari. How could she have insight his mentor hadn't offered?

"I found a map. I copied the important parts. Help me, and I'll show you." She returned her knife to the empty sheath at her hip, then rested her hands on the matching hilts as if relieved to have them reunited.

"Help you?" Zaide could have laughed. "I don't even know you, never mind trust you." But for the moment, they were both walking the same direction.

"Well, I'm not a goborrin, so right now, I'm the best you've got. You may call me Lark."

"Zaide." They walked side by side, competing for what little clear footing there was.

"That's not a Kolmari name."

"Neither is Lark."

"No, but I never said I was Kolmari." She darted ahead and turned to the left. Away from where he thought they should go.

He hesitated. Never mind trusting her; he didn't even like her. Yet a gnawing sense of responsibility spurred him to follow. The Kolmari were guardians of the forest. If she did mean harm, the best thing he could do—as a guardian—was go after her, so long as she didn't try to keep him from reaching the temple. Grudgingly, he followed. He slipped between the trees with more grace than she possessed, earning himself a glower that he ignored.

"You saw it this afternoon, didn't you?" she asked. "The eclipse."

"Hard to miss." Under normal circumstances, the Elder tracked the celestial bodies and predicted such events, using them as history lessons. Zaide didn't understand why it hadn't been announced in advance this time. That it coincided with the Spring Choosing was an ill omen beyond compare.

The Elder had survived the village attack, ending Zaide's initial fears, but in the end that only made things worse. The omen was clear.

Somewhere, events had been put in motion that would lead to death—and that death would alter the course of history.

"That was why I came," Lark said, pausing to hold a branch for him to pass under. "I read of the prediction in the Great Library in Jadora when I was a child. It prophesied other things, too. About who would die."

Intrigued, Zaide moved closer. "What did it say?"

"That the eclipse would herald a breakthrough in the long war, and one of the two kings would die." A shudder coursed her body as she spoke.

Zaide couldn't blame her. He felt a shudder welling beneath

his skin, too.

There were only two kings left. Sendassian, King of Amroch, and Gadranus, King of the Shattered Lands. No matter which king the prophecy meant, it would be an event that would reshape the world. If Gadranus fell, Amroch would finally have peace.

If Sendassian fell, then man's last bastion of hope was doomed.

"Why are you telling me this?" he asked softly.

"To see whose side you're on." She looked back at him, her eyes narrowed, judging.

Zaide scoffed. "You have reason to doubt?"

Lark shrugged and carried on. "I've seen people like you. They filled the streets of Amrochan when I was a child. Broken-born, they call them. Fair as the snow in the north. Some of them came seeking refuge. Sendassian gave it. Those who remained in the kingdoms destroyed by Gadranus became loyal to him. They fight on his side, now. They made themselves my enemy. We're close to the border here. Can you fault me for wondering?"

"I thought you were from Jadora."

"I've been to Jadora," she corrected. "My mother wished to see the fortress walls before the wasting disease claimed her. My father sought to indulge her in anything possible."

That tugged at his heart. "I'm sorry. I lost my mother, as well."

Lark mustered a smile. "Well, that's one thing we have in common, then."

"Two," Zaide said, his blue eyes hardening to match his resolve when she looked back with a raised brow. "We both want to see this eclipse bring Gadranus to his knees."

A flicker of a grin lit her face, then she sobered. "The temple is just east of that rise ahead. We'll emerge on a cliff overlooking the ruin. I don't know what to expect there. All I know is our entry is on the western side. A small balcony. We should be able to reach it by rope."

A sound plan, assuming the goborrins were only at the front of the temple. "Do you have rope?"

She tossed her head, a gesture Zaide took to be her usual reaction to things that displeased her. "Do you think I'd come all this way from Amrochan without thinking to bring a rope?"

"I couldn't say," he said. "After all, we just met."

He expected her to snap, but instead, she sighed. "I've been preparing for this for so long. In spite of that, I still arrived a day too late. I never expected a trek through the woods would be what stopped me."

"What do you expect to find at the temple?" Zaide stopped her with a hand on her shoulder, redirecting her around a patch of blistering nettles.

"There's something in the temple," she said. "An anchor for a protective seal—"

"—Which holds unwelcome forces out of Kolmar's forests," Zaide finished. "A set of pipes in the front room."

Lark raised one fine brow. "You know of it?"

"It's why I'm here," Zaide said. "My mentor—Kolmar's Elder, that is—ordered me to find it."

She stopped in her tracks, her eyes alight. "He was the one who stopped you! I should have known. It would have saved such time. But here we are, and the Elder's apprentice is here to help me. You already know exactly what to do, I'm sure."

He wasn't sure it was what she had in mind, but he nodded anyway. So long as she was willing to help him reach his destination and return the pipes to the Elder, they were on the same side.

Lark clapped her hands together and grinned. "This will be easier than I ever imagined."

Zaide crested the hill ahead of her and peered over the cliff.

The ruined temple sat below, a dozen or more armored goborrins patrolling around it.

He swallowed hard. "Guess you spoke too soon."

CHAPTER FOUR

ZAIDE CROUCHED at the edge of the cliff and watched the patrols below. They moved without patterns, sometimes five visible and sometimes one, but each so heavily armed and armored he knew they stood little chance. On the best of days, he might take down one. But there was no doubt the clamor of battle would draw the rest.

Lark joined him, crouching and gripping a sapling to secure herself. It hadn't seemed like they'd traveled that far upward, but the drop was high enough to kill anyone who went over the edge. Glancing back the way they'd come, Zaide decided it wasn't just that they'd gone uphill, but that the temple was built in an unnatural recess in the earth.

The ruins were sheltered by a ring of high earthen walls, though now that he saw the temple, he hardly thought the word *ruins* accurate. The temple was abandoned, but it was magnificent. The weathered stone was covered in moss and lichen, the stained glass in the tall, peaked windows just as bright as it must have been the day it was set in its casements.

"There it is," Lark whispered.

Zaide's eyes followed her finger when she pointed. As she'd predicted, a railed outcropping protruded from the side of the temple. It was more a terrace than a balcony, but hosted a doorway that was as unguarded as it appeared to be unreachable. Scaling the wall wouldn't be difficult, even if they hadn't brought a rope. Numerous hand holds littered the uneven stone wall below. It was the monsters around it that would make it hard.

"Do we have a plan?" he whispered back.

"I don't know." She worried her lower lip with her teeth. "The gap's too wide for us to jump, and it's too far to fall. We're going to have to go down."

"I'm guessing that's where your rope will be useful." He thumped a palm against the tree trunk beside him. "But we have to get past those things without them chasing us."

Lark nodded toward the temple. "The hard part is getting past them. Once we get up the wall, we should be fine."

"How do you figure?"

"Goborrins can't climb." She shifted her small pack off her shoulder and removed a coiled rope from its depth. She unwound it and looped one end around Zaide's tree, fussing with the knot until he took it from her hands.

He tied it tight. "How do you know that?"

"The soldiers in Amrochan told me. Those things might be big and powerful, but they're clumsy. Maybe we can use that against them." As she untangled the rope, she stood and peered down.

Zaide drew a deep breath. "Okay. We wait until there's just one over here. It may take a bit. Then we'll drop down. You get onto the terrace, I'll keep it distracted while you climb."

"Then what?"

"Then you'd better do your part. Throw rocks at it or something, I don't care. Just make sure I get up there, too." He wasn't convinced he could hold off one of those beasts long enough for Lark to scale the wall, but if he was fortunate, one was all it would be.

They sat in tense silence, watching the pig-faced monsters tromp around the temple in the dark.

"Maybe we'll get lucky," Lark whispered as one vanished around the corner. "Maybe it's dark enough they won't see us."

Zaide resisted the urge to laugh. "Maybe."

The last goborrin passed them, marching up the beaten trail between the temple and cliff, the clank of its armor just enough to mask the sound of their descent. Lark went first, her soft boots barely a whisper when she touched the ground. Zaide followed, moving slower, watching the retreating goborrin's back and casting frequent glances the other way. The patrols moved in both directions, and their random nature meant there was no way of knowing when they'd be seen.

Lark sprinted the short distance to the temple wall and scouted out the first few handholds before she dug the toes of her boots between the stones. She crept upward, grimacing often, betraying her inexperience in climbing.

"Hurry," Zaide urged in the sharpest whisper he dared, positioning himself at the bottom of the wall and drawing his sword. The polished steel slid free of its sheath without a sound. In the dark of night, it was nothing special, but in his mind's eye, he could see the way light would gleam against its edge.

Behind him, Lark grunted in reply. The stone crackled as she climbed, pebbles and dust scattering as she wriggled her way up the wall and to the balustrade.

At the far end of the chasm between earth wall and stone, the goborrin rounded the corner and disappeared.

Zaide straightened. Now was the worst moment, knowing the monsters would come from either side, not knowing which to watch. He dragged the tip of his tongue across his dust-dry lips before letting them twitch with a silent prayer. Whichever side the patrol came from, let it only be one.

Maker, let it be one.

Lark stopped, panting softly. She hung in place for what seemed an eternity before she scrabbled over the balustrade and fell onto the terrace. "I'm up!" She couldn't have been louder than a whisper if she'd tried. She knelt, resting her hands on her thighs and struggling to catch her breath. How she'd made it all the way to Kolmar from Amrochan, Zaide could only wonder.

He turned to sheath his sword at the precise moment a goborrin rounded the corner, its small black eyes locking with Zaide's.

The creature released a bellow loud enough to split the night.

"Climb!" Lark cried.

It was faster than he'd expected, brandishing its spear and closing the distance between them with strides he'd never outpace. Zaide spun to meet the charging beast, sword ready.

The goborrin's reach left him at a disadvantage, but it was one he'd practiced against countless times. He spun to meet the first thrust, deflected the shaft and darted in. The goborrin was fast, but Zaide was faster, sweeping his borrowed blade up into a joint of the monster's armor.

The beast howled in pain as the sword twisted free. It tried to retreat, but Zaide hung close, unwilling to sacrifice the small advantage he'd gained. He ducked when the goborrin struck at him with the spear's shaft. The monster's momentum carried it around, forcing it to stagger at the end of its reach. Lark was right. They were clumsy.

He lunged in with his sword again, but the enemy's armor was crude and thick, and without striking a weak point, the attack did nothing. Zaide's heart leaped into his throat. He hadn't considered that he wouldn't even be able to hurt them.

The goborrin backpedaled, regaining distance. Zaide, too, pulled back.

"Now! Climb!" Lark shouted. Above her voice, from the far end of the temple, came the muffled beast-calls of more goborrins as they poured into the gap.

Climbing now was his only hope. Zaide flung his sword up and jumped after it, catching the handholds she'd cleared and struggling to find purchase with his boots. His sword clattered onto the terrace above and he heaved himself after it with his heart in his throat and the thunder of footsteps in his ears.

"Watch out!"

Zaide flattened his chest against the wall and craned his neck. His stomach dropped as the goborrin behind him surged forward, spear ready.

Then a stone the size of his fist struck the monster's face.

Its spear went wide, striking stone and splintering the shaft. A second rock followed, slamming into the goborrin's helmet and yielding an angry cry.

Gritting his teeth, Zaide heaved himself upward, caught hold of the balustrade and hauled himself over. He crashed into the terrace as the other monsters arrived, their spears thrusting upward through the gaps in the stone railing and missing him by inches.

Lark grabbed his arm and dragged him toward the door. Around the foot of the terrace, the goborrins milled, snorting and grunting, scratching at the stone. They were so tall they could nearly reach the edge of the terrace from the ground. Zaide got his knees under himself and half-crawled along with Lark's tugging. They collapsed against the door together, panting.

The goborrins below roared and squealed in frustration. Zaide watched their waving spears and allowed himself a single laugh of disbelief. "They really can't climb, can they?"

"One of few advantages I think we'll have," Lark said. "Now come on. Let's get inside."

Confident in their momentary safety, Zaide retrieved his sword and started to return it to its sheath, then paused when Lark pushed open the door. It groaned on ancient hinges, sagging until it scraped along the stone floor. Inside, the dark was so intense that it hurt to stare. Zaide blinked twice, then averted his eyes.

"I have a light." Lark swung her bag off her shoulder again and knelt to root around inside. "I just have to find it."

"Any idea what's in there?" He doubted the goborrins were stupid enough to stay clustered at the terrace forever. Eventually, they'd try to find another way to reach them.

"I remember the floor plan, I think. But I don't think that's what you meant." She lifted something from her bag and squinted at it in the dark before she returned it and resumed her search. At last, she produced a small black cylinder that hung from a leather strap. She let it swing a moment before she caught the bottom, twisted, and revealed a light of such brilliant white that Zaide had to shield his eyes.

"What is that thing?" he asked.

"What, you've never seen a lantern before?" Lark twisted back the other direction, shuttering the light until only thin beams escaped to illuminate an empty stone hallway on the other side of the door.

Zaide blinked hard, wishing his vision would return faster. "Not like that, I haven't."

"Oh. I suppose we are rather far south. You can buy them in Amrochan. I hear they're made by the craftsmen on the north coast. I don't imagine their trade would make it this far." She gathered her things, stood, and leaned into the hall with her lantern held at arm's length. The hall ran both directions. The goborrins still howled behind them, but inside, there wasn't a sound to be heard. Together, they stepped inside, and Zaide closed the door behind them.

He shifted his sword in hand and put out his other arm when Lark started off, effectively halting her progress. He slid past her to take the lead.

She snorted. "I don't need your chivalry."

"Oh?" Zaide stuck his sword into the hall, drawing a slow circle in the air with the tip. Spiderwebs snapped and twisted around the blade as their coin-sized inhabitant skittered up the wall. "Shall I just let you walk into that, then?"

Lark blanched.

"They're harmless," he added, "but I wouldn't want to walk into them, either."

She waved him ahead and held out the tiny lantern. "I think dealing with the goborrins is challenge enough."

The lantern's looped strap was just large enough to fit over his hand. Zaide checked before he twisted it around his fingers instead, holding it aloft with his free hand. He wouldn't risk sheathing his sword again.

Lark watched, thoughtful. "Huh."

"What?"

"I hadn't noticed." She nodded at his sword. "You're left-handed."

"To my teacher's dismay." He crept forward, not bothering to muffle his footsteps. Their voices echoed down the hall already, giving them away. "My sword instructor, that is, not the Elder. Though he has his own complaints. He makes me copy manuscripts with a piece of palimpsest under my hand while I write. Otherwise, the ink smears."

"Tragic, for a scholar's apprentice." A hint of amusement colored her voice, making it just a shade sweeter than before.

"There are worse tragedies, I'm sure."

The hallway turned left, then split. He paused at the intersection until Lark pointed down the right-hand path.

"If I recall correctly, there should be stairs this way. They'll lead to the lower floor, where we should be able to find the pipes."

"Best if we go quietly." Zaide lowered his voice. "By now I'm sure those goborrins have found a way inside. It's best if we don't let them hear us coming now."

"Maybe we'll get lucky," she whispered back. "Maybe we're alone."

Getting inside without being killed had been lucky enough. Zaide doubted that fortune would hold.

Instead of a stairway, the hall dead-ended at a door. He

gripped the ring, bracing himself for what might wait on the other side, praying they wouldn't find a nest of goborrins.

He pulled.

Nothing happened.

Flustered, he pushed. On the other side of the door, something crackled. Inch by inch, the gap grew, revealing long, thick strings of dust-filled spider silk, spun so thick it groaned and popped as it tore. Lark made a noise of pure disgust.

The sound of many scuttling feet made them both shudder.

"What about those?" Lark asked in a harsh whisper. "Are those harmless?"

"Guess we're about to find out." He sawed through the webbing with his sword, leaving sticky streaks on the polished blade. The door opened farther and he thrust the lantern into the darkness.

White spiderwebs gleamed bright in the lantern light, and sprinkled between them, a thousand round eyes flashed green.

Zaide hacked down a cluster of webs and the spider hiding inside—a monster the size of his head—fell to the floor. It landed with a thump and spun toward them, its forelegs raised in warning.

Silver streaked into the middle of the clustered eyes and the spider toppled backwards, its legs curling. Zaide stepped back, blinking in surprise.

Lark pushed past him to reclaim her knife from the spider's corpse. "I'm not taking any chances."

Farther down the hallway, a rush of tiny footsteps and a low, threatening rasp replied.

"Well, then," Zaide said. "I hope you're ready to do that a thousand more times."

The spiders surged toward them in a wave, a low hiss emanating from the sea of bristled bodies and countless eyes and legs.

Zaide grabbed Lark's arm and jerked her backwards, slamming the door shut behind them.

The door heaved as the creatures slammed into it. Wriggling legs thrust through the gap beneath the door, clawing and grasping like hands.

"Move!" Zaide shoved her hard and she stumbled, her fingertips brushing the floor before she regained her equilibrium. She stopped for only an instant, looking at the slime that coated the knife in her hand. Then she ran with Zaide close on her heels.

He glanced over his shoulder once, and almost regretted looking back.

Behind them, spiders flattened their fat bodies and squeezed under the door, little feet drumming as they raced after them.

Lark outpaced him first, then froze when she moved beyond the lantern's reach. He held the lantern out ahead of him, willing its light to go farther, silently cursing when it moved no faster than he did.

Abruptly, the spiders behind him stopped, flailing their forelegs before turning away.

Zaide crashed into Lark's back.

"What—" he started, the rest of his protest dying on his tongue the moment he looked up.

Ahead, long, slender black legs emerged from the dark, each as thick around as one of his arms. They reached, farther, farther, until the hooked claws at the end stopped only inches from the two of them, and gleaming green eyes larger than the monstrous spiders they'd run from turned their way.

They both screamed.

CHAPTER FIVE

THE RHYTHMIC CLICK of the long, jointed legs burned itself into Zaide's mind, fuel for nightmares he hoped he'd live long enough to have.

"This is your fault!" he roared, regretting the waste of breath the moment the words left his mouth. It was all they could do to keep ahead of the creature. He'd thought the spiders in the webs were large. He'd thought the goborrins were large, too. The thing chasing them was colossal, its fat, glossy body barely fitting through the halls. Its size was their saving grace; had it been even a shade smaller, it would have already been upon them.

"My fault?" Lark cried. "How do you figure it's my fault?"

A slender leg landed right beside him, spurring him to run faster. "If it weren't for you, I would have gone in the front door!"

"And been slaughtered by goborrins!" She glared when he fell in stride beside her.

The hall was longer than he remembered. They'd gained a little time when rounding a corner, but the tunnel stretched on for longer than what seemed right. In the flashing light cast off from the lantern he still held, the stones in the floor all looked the same. "I have a better chance against goborrins than against that thing." A black, clawed foot landed beside him again and he dared a glance to see how far back the spider was.

"Look out!"

There was no stone floor when Zaide's foot came down. He fell forward, his heel skidding off the edge of the top stair and sending him crashing down. His sword struck stone and escaped his hand. He couldn't stop it now. He tumbled into the wall and skidded backwards, bringing his arms up to shelter his head.

Somewhere above, Lark shrieked. Then, suddenly, she was beside him, his sword in hand and her face clouded with fear. He didn't remember reaching the bottom or coming to rest on the cool, mud-crusted floor, but he sat up on it now and rubbed his neck. Every inch of his body felt bruised, but nothing was broken, and he didn't see any blood when he touched his most tender injuries and checked his hands.

He checked them again anyway. "The spider?"

"It stopped at the top of the stairs." Lark's voice was small in the dark, weighted with the distinct sound of having not told the whole truth.

Zaide reached for his sword. "What happened?"

"You fell, idiot." She rested the blade's tip on the ground and leaned it forward for him to take.

"I meant with the spider," he snapped.

A hint of color rose in her cheeks. "I don't know. I turned back to face it and it just... stopped."

"Just like that?"

"Just like that. I didn't even draw my knives." She touched the blades, one sheathed at either hip.

His eyes narrowed. She'd had one drawn when they started running. When did she find time to put it away?

"Anyway," Lark said, eager to change the subject, "I think we're lost. I don't know where we turned upstairs, but I definitely don't remember a room like this being on the map I saw."

For the first time, he took in their surroundings. Bright as the lantern light was, it didn't travel far, filling the room with shifting shadows. Statues lurked in alcoves around the edge of the room, their faces hidden in stone hoods. Long stone benches sat in a circle in the room's center, framing an emblem on the floor he couldn't make out in the dark. Dust and cobwebs hung thick everywhere, and aside from his own labored breathing, the air was still.

"Well, this looks important," Zaide said, grimacing as he got to his knees and pushed himself up to his feet. "Why wouldn't that spider come down here, I wonder?"

"Spiders aren't aggressive by nature. Maybe once we left its nest, it didn't need to chase us anymore." Lark took the lantern, dusted it off and opened its shutters wider. The light revealed high ceilings and faded friezes on the walls. "What do you think this room is for?"

"I don't know." Zaide sheathed his sword and crept toward the emblem on the floor. It was as weathered as the rest of the temple, long forgotten and abandoned, green and gold lacquers peeling from the segmented stone. "Do you recognize this mark?"

She joined him, resting a foot on top of one of the benches and leaning forward. The lantern swung on its strap, the light playing over the cracks and recesses in the stone. Her brow furrowed. "I think so. But it doesn't make any sense."

"Neither does falling down a flight of stairs without killing myself." He stretched his aching muscles and rested a hand on the back of his neck. "I feel like I've seen it before, but I don't know what it is."

"It's his crest," Lark said. "Gadranus."

Zaide saw it now; the ram's skull with a four-pointed star on its forehead and curled tusks protruding from its jaw. He'd seen approximations of it in the Elder's books a thousand times, but somewhere like this, it was so out of place he almost didn't recognize it. "You're right. That doesn't make sense."

She paced around the emblem, rubbing her chin with her free

hand. "This place is so old. He's not come this far into Amroch since I've been alive. So unless the old legends are true—"

"After the eclipse, I'm starting to think a great deal more is true than we realized." Zaide pointed down the length of the room, to where a doorway waited in deep shadow. "We can ask the Elder when we make it back to the village. But right now, we need to keep moving. There's nothing here. Or, not what we came for, at least."

"Of course." Lark met him at the far side of the emblem and they walked side by side.

Though the doorway was dark, a light flickered at the far end of the hall to which it led. "Firelight," she whispered. "Torches, maybe?"

Zaide nodded.

She frowned. "Why do you suppose they left this room unguarded?"

"Probably because they don't expect any visitors from this direction." He wrapped his fingers around his sword's hilt as he paced into the dark. "I mean, there's not exactly a back door."

The firelight was dim compared to Lark's lantern. She stopped to shutter it after only a few steps, pressing a finger to her lips with a scowl. Zaide hadn't intended to comment, but he nodded his approval. Halfway down the hallway, he realized he should have asked what she knew about their destination. All the Elder said was the anchor they sought was inside the front room. Going in the back had never been discussed. He didn't know how many rooms there were, how many entrances might let goborrins into the temple... for that matter, after the twists and turns they'd taken upstairs to escape the giant spider, he wasn't certain they were headed toward the front.

Lark stopped near the door, pressing her back to the wall and reaching for her knives. She jerked her head toward the opening, indication she wanted him to go first.

On the other side, a trio of goborrins waited, one near enough to the door that Zaide could have prodded him in the back with his sword. The others were across the room, seemingly guarding two more doorways, through which brighter light emanated. None of them faced the shadowed hallway, which made little sense. If they were guards, why would their backs be turned to the point they were supposed to be guarding?

Unless they weren't guarding against Zaide and Lark. The faded emblem on the floor flashed through his mind, but he dismissed it quickly enough. There was nothing of importance there that Zaide had been able to see. Any further information on that room and the purpose of that painted symbol would have to come from the Elder upon their return.

He sank back, holding up fingers to warn Lark of their numbers and motioning to signify their placement. She nodded and reached for her bag. This time, instead of tools, she produced a weapon. The tiny crossbow was hardly more than a hand's span wide, but the bolts she presented to go with it were tipped with blades unlike any he'd ever seen. The three razors twisted as they tapered to a point so clean, Zaide suspected it could pierce most anything, as long as it had enough force behind it. Small as the crossbow was, it would be more than enough to deal with exposed flesh and the crude leather garments these goborrins wore.

Lark motioned to indicate her target. Zaide drew his blade, nodded, and lunged through the doorway. He plunged his sword into the near goborrin's back, sending the monster crashing to the floor. Lark spun out behind him and fired. Her razor-tipped bolt took the second goborrin in the throat. The third wheeled with its club in hand, and for a moment the fear on its pig-like face was all too human.

Zaide tore his sword free of the fallen monster and charged. Behind him, Lark reloaded her crossbow.

He met the beast head on. The previous fights had given him a small taste of what to expect; he ducked when the goborrin swung high and drove his blade into the creature's side. One of Lark's bolts thumped into its shoulder on the same side.

Squalling, the monster dropped to one knee. Muddy-looking blood gushed from its side and filled the air with the scent of dirty copper. Zaide withdrew his sword to strike again, but Lark darted in instead, sweeping her knife's keen edge across the goborrin's throat. Jubilation filled her eyes when it gurgled and dropped. Then the realization of what she'd done set in and she turned whiter than Zaide.

He caught her arm to steady her, pointing at the crossbow still in her other hand. "Why didn't you get *that* out when that thing outside was trying to skewer me?"

A rosy shade returned to her cheeks, then a flush of anger crept up her neck. "I forgot."

"You forgot you had exactly the kind of weapon that could have saved my life?"

She jerked her arm free of his grasp. "I forgot! I'm not used to having it, okay? I use a regular bow. I've trained at archery all my life. But I had to buy my supplies on the way here, and I couldn't find a bow the right size, and..." She trailed off, narrowing her eyes. "I shouldn't have to justify myself to you, besides. Can't you just be grateful we killed these? We didn't take a scratch!"

"It's too early to celebrate. The ones outside wore plate armor. These are half dressed." He pointed at the body beneath them with his sword, then knelt to wipe his blade with the leg of the monster's coarse breeches. Its chest—so similar to that of a human—was bare, though it wore a necklace of teeth and small bones. None of the three monsters were fully dressed and armored, he noted; goborrins weren't known for their modesty, but from what he knew, Gadranus did clothe his armies. Their state of half-preparedness indicated they'd been sent to guard the emblem room with little notice.

Lark turned away, busying herself with reloading her crossbow. She didn't have many bolts. With fortune, the next encounter would be better suited to blades. "They're unsettling to look at. They look as if someone stuck the head of a boar on a man's body."

"Do you think?" Zaide gave his sword another swipe, then stood back. He thought the creatures were too fleshy. Though like men in that they stood upright and moved the same way, their bodies bulged with fat and bore thick bristles of pale hair over skin that was far too pink. Flabby jowls framed tusked faces that were less of a boar's head and more like a bloated, swollen man with a jutting jaw and a blunt pig's snout in place of a nose. Hideous, and unsettling. He nudged the dead thing's leg with his boot. "They have cloven feet."

"What does that matter?"

"Little now, but it's good to remember. At least now I'll know what goborrin tracks look like."

Lark sniffed, stepping over the dead monster's splayed limbs with her head up and her eyes trained on the path ahead. "Let's keep moving."

Of the two doorways, the one she'd chosen was brighter. Zaide considered the darker one for a moment, then dismissed the idea. They'd botched their entry, alerting the enemy, and they'd just killed a trio of guards. Chances were, the light did signify where they needed to go. He followed her into the room on the other side.

This had been a prayer room at some time, or at least he thought—low benches lined the walls and basins stood in the corners that would have held water for ritual cleansing, though they held only dust now. The floor was coated with dust, too, a path down the middle showing where the monsters behind them had passed through.

Zaide put out a hand, motioning for Lark to stop. She paused with her crossbow ready.

"Slow," he whispered. "We don't know what's up ahead." After the spiders, caution seemed wise.

Nodding, she slowed until they walked side by side. The

glow ahead was farther off. Large shadows danced through the visible sliver of the space beyond.

The room ahead had to be the front entrance they'd meant to reach in the first place. The large, irregularly shaped sanctuary was lit with torches and lined with balconies. Large doors stood at the far end, looming over the space like sentinels. Yet they watched helplessly as a group of goborrins filled the space, milling around something in the center of the room. Now and then, one of the beasts stopped to inspect whatever was there, the action usually followed by some sound of malcontent.

"There," Lark breathed. "It has to be there."

Zaide felt inclined to agree. Had it been daylight outside, a squared hole in the vaulted ceiling would have allowed a single ray of light to bathe that center point. It was almost offensively obvious, yet it made sense; if the anchor for the forest's magic sat in the center of that room, it only made sense to allow part of the outside world to join it.

He pulled Lark back from the doorway. "We need to figure out how to get to it."

"I figured we'd kill the monsters and then pick it up." She tapped the blunt end of each of her remaining crossbow bolts, frowning at the count.

"Did you count the goborrins?" He doubted they'd stand a chance even if she had a bolt for every one of the monsters in the other room. They were larger than the others had been, and promised a more challenging fight.

"Eight, I think, though I'm not sure of it. More than I can handle." Sighing, Lark put a hand to the dagger at her hip on the same side. In the feeble golden torchlight, her blue eyes looked more like green glass, hazed with emotion she was still fighting. "We got lucky outside. We got lucky back there, too, and upstairs. How do we know it will hold?"

Zaide shook his head. "We don't. The best we can do is try to scatter them. If we get more than one on us at a time, we might be done for."

"Any suggestions?"

He pursed his lips and stole another glance into the sanctuary. Lark waited behind him in tense anticipation.

"If we could get you onto one of those balconies," he said at last, moving away from the door again. Their whispers were hidden under the monsters' heavy footsteps, but muffled conversation wouldn't matter if they were seen. "You could fire at them from above until you run out of bolts."

Deep lines of worry creased between her brows. "What about you?"

"Don't take this wrong, but I'd rather be able to fight without worrying about you being in the way."

The widening of her eyes and hardened set to her jaw indicated she'd taken it wrong anyway.

He sighed. "You think we should just charge in and try to take on all those monsters at once?"

"Whatever works," she muttered.

"Right. Then you get on one of those balconies while I try to split them up. I didn't see any spears, so as long as I can get them over here, the doorway should offer a choke point where I can gain some advantage." At least, that was what he hoped. Failing that, he supposed he could return to the emblem room. Maybe even the stairs—being left-handed, he could meet them in the spiral staircase without handicap. Come to think of it, the curve of the stairs was backwards. Built to defend the room against intrusion from above? That made little sense.

"I'm still not certain this is the best plan." Lark rubbed her arm, the crossbow dangling beside her knees. "What if you get injured?"

He couldn't help a smirk. "Suddenly so concerned for my safety, are you? You attacked me twice today."

"After you instigated it," she said. "Besides, I want to make it out of here alive. Right now, cooperating with you is what gives me my best shot."

That, he couldn't argue. "Then we'll have to make sure we both survive. Ready?"

"No."

"All right, let's go." He patted her arm and sucked in a breath, shifting his sword in his hand. He would have felt better with a shield. Sword and shield was his specialty, and anything he could put between him and those monsters was a boon. He didn't know how Lark was going to get to a balcony or what to expect from the fight. He didn't have enough experience to plan too far ahead. But there was one tactic he knew that worked on every enemy, both man and beast.

Zaide held his head high and strode into the sanctuary without hesitation.

A goborrin looked at him and almost glanced away. Then it startled, releasing a harsh cry that brought the others to attention, and the monsters readied their weapons.

For the first time, Zaide felt a rush of confidence.

Unlike the others, these goborrins used swords. Rough, crude blades that were only half-sharp at best, but swords, nonetheless —and sword fighting, he knew how to do.

CHAPTER SIX

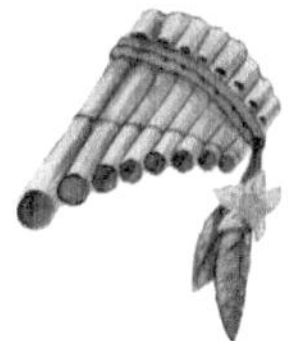

ZAIDE FLOWED in to meet an attack as if taking the first steps of a dance, meeting the first heavy downswing with the edge of his blade. The steel shuddered, but the weight of the blade kept his arm from going to jelly. He deflected the blow and twirled close to strike home.

One down. He hadn't stopped to count the goborrins on his way in the door, so he didn't know how many remained. He tried not to think about it and focused instead on twisting to strike the next beast. A cry from the others and a rush of cloven feet betrayed Lark's arrival in the sanctuary behind him. Silently, he wished her luck. He couldn't risk trying to look.

What the goborrins lacked in finesse, they made up for with strength. Zaide was the opposite, half their size and nimble enough that he darted under their arms and past their blades. He struck fast and hard, half aware of the other enemies looming behind him. Something hit one of them and the monster spun, howling in pain before falling to the floor. One of Lark's razor-tipped bolts protruded from its eye.

She'd made it onto a balcony. He saw her from the corner of his eye when he twisted to deal another blow. A pair of goborrins pulled at the rope she'd used to scale it, unable to climb, but determined to do something. The metal claw that anchored the rope to the railing groaned—or maybe the stone groaned—and the balustrade shattered, showering the goborrins beneath with debris.

Four down. There didn't seem to be any fewer. Everywhere he turned, there were more monsters, more weapons bearing down on him. His sword dug deep in a goborrin's side and resisted when he pulled back. He staggered, his battle rhythm broken. Above, two monsters swung at the same time. Their blades collided above his head, carving into the goborrin he'd just killed.

"Zaide!" Lark's voice rang high over the sound of clashing metal.

He didn't dare look. His sword came free and he ducked aside, deflecting a blow. The crude sword bounced hard and came back faster than he expected, shaving half the sleeve from his arm and a thin layer of skin with it. Zaide gasped but couldn't afford to lose focus. He gave everything to the slash that took his attacker to the ground.

Five down.

"Look out!" Lark screeched. Zaide tore himself free and spun to heed her warning. There was no goborrin behind him.

Instead, a monstrous black spider burst off Lark's balcony and slammed onto the floor.

All around him, goborrins squalled in terror. Half ran, while the other half spun to face the spider with brandished weapons. The spider raised its front legs in warning, treading sideways, circling the skirmish in the center of the sanctuary.

Zaide ran for the wall just as the spider surged forward to sink its glistening fangs into one of the goborrins. He didn't see it strike. The creature's death wail was enough.

The metal claw Lark had used lay on the floor amid the rubble, the rope still attached. He kicked broken stone aside and snatched it from the floor.

"Throw it here!" Lark called. "I'll anchor you!"

He let the hook hang a few feet and spun it hard, allowing the claw to gain momentum before he let it fly. It arced overhead and clattered onto the balcony. Lark seized it and wrapped the rope around an unbroken section of the balcony's rail before she latched the claw in place. "Come on!"

Zaide tested the rope, untrusting of the rail after the goborrins had shattered it. But he was smaller than they were, and only a fraction as strong. The stone balustrade held firm and he thrust his bloodstained sword into its sheath so he could scale the rope.

He reached the balcony, gasping for breath, and clawed his way onto the ledge. Lark caught his uninjured arm and helped him. At the far end of the balcony, a wooden door stood wide, white webs hanging behind it like curtains. "How did you know the spider was in there?"

"I didn't," Lark said.

The panicked cries below grew louder and they both turned and sat, too tired to run, too fearful to look away.

Bodies of goborrins littered the floor. More poured in from the surrounding doorways to join the battle. Their spears plunged past the spider's legs, only to be batted away. The spider's clawed feet drove every direction at once, knocking weapons aside and rending armor, slamming goborrins to the ground and tearing through flesh.

Lark shuddered. A goborrin surged toward the spider's side. Zaide leaned forward and clamped his hands over Lark's eyes.

The goborrin lunged in with his spear, slid between the spider's legs and plunged his spear deep into the beast's abdomen.

Sharp screeches filled the air and Zaide thought it was the spider screaming, until he saw the goborrin that had dealt the blow. The spider clasped its head between two massive legs, its claws digging into the goborrin's eye sockets as the spider's legs curled inward. The spear drove deeper and thick, yellow slime squelched from the wound.

The screams faded and a long, slow wheeze escaped the spider's body as it curled in on itself and died.

Still panting, Zaide stared down at the room. Nothing stirred. Lark clawed at his arm to remove his hand from her face. A sharp pain burst in his hand and Zaide jerked away from her with a shout. Dainty tooth marks marred the heel of his palm.

"I don't need you to protect me!" she snarled, but when she saw the bodies on the ground below, she paled.

"I was trying to help." Zaide rubbed his bitten hand, sullen. "You could have just asked, you know."

Lark turned her head and spat in response. Served her right; his hands were covered in grit and spatters of goborrin blood. Zaide scrubbed his palm against his trousers and stood.

"Was that all of them?" Lark asked, her voice small.

Everything had grown quiet. Zaide strained to listen for footsteps or some indicator there were more goborrins in the temple, but he heard nothing but the sound of their breath. "I think so. I hope so, anyway."

She inched to the edge of the balcony and peered down. Instead of pale, this time she looked green. But she kept hold of herself, and if she felt sick, she didn't complain. "What now?"

"I guess we climb down and see what those goborrins were guarding." Zaide hadn't bothered to pull up the rope after he'd made it onto the balcony. He checked the hook to ensure it was still secure before he sat and slid his legs over the edge, where the balustrade had broken. After the fight, he felt weak, shaky, exhausted after the adrenaline subsided. But they weren't through yet, and something told him the coming days would hold little rest.

He worked his way down the rope, wishing he'd brought gloves so he could simply slide down its length. Bare-handed as he was, the rope would have peeled the flesh right off his hands. Instead, he moved hand over hand and inched downward at a rate that would have embarrassed a snail. Climbing *up* a rope was always the easy part.

When his boots hit the floor, he fought the urge to sit and rest again. Instead he abandoned the rope to let Lark climb down on her own. He circled the spider's massive corpse and stepped over the broken bodies of dead goborrins. The stink of blood was heavy in the air. Remembering his sword, Zaide paused.

It was too good of steel to leave it dirty. He drew the blade and wiped it clean on the rough-spun clothing of a dead monster. The sheath, too, would be sullied, but he'd have to clean that later.

Lark grunted angrily behind him and he almost regretted leaving her to climb down by herself. Then he rounded the spider's body and saw what had brought them to the temple in the first place.

It seemed as though it should have glowed. The square pedestal was no more than waist-high, but the pipes floated above it, rotating lazy circles in midair. A cluster of carvings that resembled leaves and flowers hung from the band that held the wooden pipes together, but they were as still as if frozen. Zaide stared, as awed as he was confused.

"Why didn't they take it?" he murmured as he extended a hand.

"Wait!" Lark's booted footsteps echoed loudly in the still.

He froze, hand outstretched, his fingertips only inches from the instrument.

Lark grasped his wrist and wrenched his arm down. She turned to the pipes and raised both hands, a distinct look of concentration on her face. The air around the pipes rippled and for a moment, they bobbed in midair.

Realization hit him like a kick in the gut. Zaide recoiled and glared. "You're a mage?"

Panic flitted through her eyes. "I—"

"This whole time, running from monsters, running for our lives, you could have stopped them in their tracks!" Anger welled hot in his chest—anger and frustration strong enough to twist his heart. Everywhere he went, he was surrounded by those with power. Was there nothing he could simply do on his own, without magic involved?

"It's not like that!" Lark drew back, her face contorted with anguish. "My power's not... I mean, I'm not..."

"I just saw you move it!" Zaide jabbed a finger toward the pipes. "I can't feel it, but I know magic when I see it."

"Then you ought to know that's all I can do!" Her words came out like a dagger fresh from the smith's forge, rough and white-hot, but still edged. "My power has never manifested. I can't do what you think. I don't have the power to fight or even defend myself. That's all I can do!" She pointed at the pipes, too, her stance a perfect mirror of his own.

He hesitated. He'd thought she meant to break whatever enchantment held the pipes aloft. Now, he wasn't sure. "What did you do?"

"Check for traps, feel for magic someone else left behind." Lark rubbed her arms as if to warm them. Tears brimmed on her eyelashes, stirring guilt in the pit of his stomach. "I can't do anything more. But it's safe. At least I know that."

The impulse to apologize came on fast and hard. He knew what it was like to lack power, how it felt to be helpless when surrounded by mages. But it wouldn't have killed her to let him know sooner. He throttled the instinct and pushed it down as he turned back to the pipes.

Zaide paced around the pedestal to put more distance between the two of them. "Can you tell what will happen when I take them?"

Lark hesitated, extended a hand toward the pipes, and shook her head. "My power isn't great enough for that. This is old magic, much older than anything I've ever seen, but it means you no harm."

He grunted. Given everything they'd been through, he wasn't certain he believed anything in the temple meant them no harm. But this was his mission, his task, and the people of his village waited. Their safety depended on this.

Bolstering his courage, Zaide reached for the pipes.

Warmth filled him the moment his fingers brushed the wood. The pipes stilled in the air mid-turn, letting his hand wrap around them. A whisper of wind stirred in the room.

He pulled the pipes from the pedestal.

A gale erupted, swirling around him, the bodies of the dead monsters around him heaved back by its force. Lark shrieked, dropping to her knees and bracing herself against the winds. The force passed her, like a curtain brushed back, and she fell forward to her hands.

The air stilled.

Zaide turned the pipes over in his hands, studying the nicks in the wood's surface. The warmth was gone, and now he felt nothing. He swallowed bitter disappointment. "We have to get back to Kolmar."

"What?" Lark thrust herself to her feet and dusted her palms against her hips. "That belongs to the king!"

"That may be, but the Elder sent me to get it for Kolmar," Zaide said. "The Elder serves the king, and he sent me to retrieve this. We're taking it to the Elder."

Her face reddened. "I can't go back there."

The hint of fear in her voice put him on edge. Zaide gripped the pipes until his knuckles turned white. After that protest, he'd be a fool to assume she wouldn't try to wrest the artifact from him. "Why? What have you done?"

"Nothing! It's just—there are guards, and..." Her cheeks grew even more rosy and her eyes flashed blue fire. "Oh, what does it matter? Give me the flute, Zaide. I came to retrieve it for Sendassian and I won't leave without it."

"Then I suppose you'll stay here." He turned toward what he assumed was the front door.

"What?" Lark squeaked.

"You heard me." There was no way of knowing if there were goborrins outside. He could only assume there were. The fingers of his left hand curled around the hilt of his sword in preparation and he sucked in a breath to steel himself.

"But you can't—not after—where are you going? Zaide? Zaide!"

Ignoring Lark's shrill protests, he pushed out the door and into the night.

CHAPTER SEVEN

Sunrise washed the forest in a shade of red befitting of the bloodbath the new day left behind. Zaide hadn't realized how exhausted he was until he climbed the cliff outside the temple, unwilling to chance the road. There had been no goborrins outside, but that didn't mean they weren't still in the woods. Now that the sun ignited the sky and he trudged along under the shady canopy, the drumbird's call echoed back and forth in codes he didn't understand, and for the first time since he'd left the temple, he regretted leaving Lark behind.

He'd expected she would pursue him. He'd even waited outside the temple for some time, perched atop the cliff. It had been a good vantage point and a better place to rest, though he rued how much time he'd wasted.

Zaide's pace slowed as he neared the village, though urgency shot through him every time the pipes slung over his shoulder bumped against his back. Had he planned better, he would have brought something to carry them in. Lark had her satchel; he could have let her carry them. But she hadn't come after him, and his sluggish pace would have made him easy to catch. He doubted she'd stayed in the temple long, but where she'd gone after they split up, he couldn't imagine.

A soldier stood atop the blacksmith's roof, armor gleaming gold in the morning light. The intensity of the sunrise seemed to last little more than a moment. Zaide knew it had to have been longer that the sky glowed like molten metal, but fatigue blurred everything together in his head. His muscles burned, his head ached, and his throat was raw with thirst. He swallowed anyway and tried to ignore the way it hurt.

The soldier waved. Zaide waved back. Then the man descended from the roof and disappeared into the trees.

At least the Elder would know he was coming. With fortune, Resia would have a kettle over the fire. It wasn't unusual for their work to begin before sunrise. An herbal tea from the Elder's collection was exactly what he needed—he ranked it ahead of sleep and a bath, though those did not lag far behind in his thoughts.

Resia met him at the edge of the trees, a pair of soldiers at her flank. Worry darkened her eyes. He tried to smile.

She caught him by the shoulders and inspected him from head to toe. "Are you injured?" Her eyes lingered on his torn sleeve and bloodied arm.

"I'm fine." He touched her wrist with his free hand, a gentle nudge to request freedom. When she stepped back, he slid the pipes over his shoulder. How fortunate they had a strap. Whoever made them, he suspected they'd been intended as a functional instrument, rather than a mere magic artifact. The wear on the pipes certainly indicated as much.

Resia's eyes widened when the pipes swung forward and she clapped her hands to her mouth. The two soldiers braced themselves, as if they expected something to happen. Perhaps they did. Zaide had no way of knowing what the Elder had told them after his departure.

"Is the Elder awake?" Zaide's voice rasped in his throat and his thoughts turned to the herbal tea once more.

"Yes," Resia said, blinking as if she'd forgotten. "He is. You must speak to him right away. Are you sure you aren't harmed? Your clothes..."

Zaide resisted the urge to look down at himself. He was smeared with dirt, mud, and the blood of goborrins. His arm stung, but he'd deemed it little more than a scrape. "Fine," he croaked, though he hardly felt it. "Thirsty."

She nodded and spun to lead the way to the Elder's library. No doubt she'd want to inspect him for other injuries before she let him rest. So long as she did it while he had a cup of tea in his hands, he didn't feel inclined to protest.

"The Elder's health is fragile," Resia said as they reached the door, "but he will recover. I've done all my magic is capable of, and he is whole, though he tires easily. Please keep that in mind. I'm sure you will have lots to say after whatever you've been through, but he should not be overtaxed with questions."

"I understand." Zaide's tongue stuck to the roof of his mouth. Removing it was misery. "I'm a bit overtaxed, myself."

She shot him an apologetic look as she gestured for the soldiers to remain by the door. Not uncommon, he noticed; soldiers stood outside most buildings. Those they left behind positioned themselves like guards. It wasn't surprising, considering the events of the day prior, but it was a stark change in the Kolmari way of life. Zaide only hoped his mission's success meant it was a change that wouldn't remain.

The Elder's library was always dim, but now, only one of the old mage's glow stones sat among the books. Zaide looked at the stone curiously—not directly at it, of course, he didn't want to hurt his eyes—and recalled Lark's lantern. It looked to be the same luminescent material and he wondered that he'd never asked about the enchanted lamps in the library before. He supposed he'd never thought to. In the home of a mage as powerful as Kolmar's Elder, such artifacts hadn't seemed unusual or out of place. They were safer than an open flame, too, and after the previous day's fires, Zaide didn't imagine the Elder would want candles anywhere near his manuscripts. It was miraculous enough the books had escaped the blaze that had scorched the library's exterior. Miraculous or magic, he supposed.

"Master?" Resia's voice was always small, but among the crowded shelves and piled papers that muffled sound, it was even tinier than usual. She peered into the dark recesses of the back room where the Elder slept, then motioned Zaide forward.

The Elder's quarters were lit by another glow stone, even smaller than the one in the forefront of the library, and so dim it took a moment for Zaide's eyes to adjust to the darkness. He didn't recall the lamps being so weak. Or did they only seem weak now, compared to the blinding lantern Lark carried?

"You've returned so soon." The Elder's voice was low, soft, but steady and calm. "Does this bode ill for your assignment?"

Zaide slipped forward to present the pipes. "I did what was asked of me. I haven't slept." After everything he'd seen, he wasn't sure he would, either. It was one thing to desire rest and quite another to find it, when visions of monstrous spiders still burned hot and fresh in his memory.

The Elder made a small sound of approval. "Your dedication is impressive." His hand shook when he reached for the pipes, but his fingers curled around them with a surprising strength. The old man drew them close and let his fingertips travel over the wood. A small, exasperated breath escaped him.

"Master?" Resia's brows knit with worry.

"They are untouched by evil," the Elder murmured. "How could our defenses have fallen?"

"They were floating above a pedestal in what appeared to be a sanctuary when we found them," Zaide said. "It didn't look like the goborrins had touched it. But the temple itself was infested. There were dozens of goborrins, and spiders the likes of which I've never seen. They were the size of skulls. The little ones, at least." He suppressed a shudder.

The old man's brows lifted. "We?"

Zaide would have preferred to leave out her involvement,

but he didn't dare hide anything from his master. "The girl from the woods. I saw her again, on the way to the temple. She was headed there on her own. Once we saw the goborrins outside, it seemed safer for the two of us to work together. She intended to recover the artifact and take it to King Sendassian, or so she said."

A long sigh escaped the Elder's throat. He cradled the pipes to his chest, as if their presence was old and familiar, something of a comfort. "If Sendassian already seeks the artifacts, then the situation is worse than I imagined. But the presence of beasts within the temple is enough to tell me that. The corruption spreads from within."

Uneasy, Zaide tried to wet his lips with an equally dry tongue. "Master, in the temple—"

"Where is the girl now?" the Elder interrupted.

"I don't know. She refused to come to Kolmar." Her ridiculous claim she wouldn't leave the temple without the pipes came to mind, but Zaide dismissed it. No one would have chosen to stay in a sanctuary with the corpses of goborrins and giant spiders.

The old mage nodded and looked to Resia. "Child, I will need you to pull a number of volumes for me. We will speak more, Zaide, but not until you have rested. So long as the Hymnflute is in my hands, Kolmar is safe, no matter what happens outside the village. Go. Eat. Sleep. Resia shall retrieve you for the noontime meal, and we will discuss things further then."

A flicker of frustration lit in his chest, but Zaide nodded, too tired to argue. "Yes, Elder." He bowed and removed himself from the old man's presence. His questions could wait, and at least now, he could have his tea.

Zaide's home was one of those untouched by recent events, a blessing he was grateful for, though he felt no comfort when he stepped inside. The small, single-room dwelling was cozy, but the hearth was dark and the air uncomfortably cool. He struck flint to light the candle on the low table before he closed the door.

Though he had lived with Resia after his mother's passing, his fourteenth year brought the first stages of manhood and marked a point of tradition for the Kolmari. A shack had been prepared for his use and he had moved his meager belongings into it, grateful for the privacy. All Kolmari boys lived that way, eased out from family homes as they reached the threshold between childhood and manhood, expected to learn all that went into providing for one's self. Resia's family was close by and ready to help when he faltered, but it was up to him to make his own way.

The stone hearth had been built for him, the elder men of the village insisting it was too risky of a job to be left to a novice. But he had been included in its construction. Zaide scraped the cold ashes into their wooden trough and left it by the door. The size of his house left little room for storage, but there were always a few split logs and tinder inside, where they were sure to stay dry. He built a small fire and put the kettle on to heat.

The water he washed with was cold enough to make his teeth chatter, but invigorating enough that it gave him a second wind.

He should have been comforted by the Elder's reassurance the village was safe. Instead, it put a churning sense of dread in the pit of his stomach.

The corruption spreads from within. The words still made his skin crawl. The Elder couldn't have known what path Zaide had taken through the temple or what he'd seen inside, but the room that held the enemy's crest wouldn't leave his mind. There was no doubt Gadranus or his forces had tainted the temple, but the question of when pricked at Zaide like a dozen needles. The paint on the crest had been old and peeling. Whatever had happened, it wasn't recent, but it changed Zaide's perception of everything he'd just done.

He'd always assumed the protection over the forest the Elder had taught him about was meant to shelter them from forces beyond the trees. But the anchor was set in the temple, a tainted place. Gadranus and his armies threatened their borders, without doubt, but that seemed hazy and distant now. Instead, a new threat lurked in the shadows beneath the trees Zaide had always called home, and he wasn't certain it could be contained.

Zaide quenched his thirst with cold water while the kettle heated. He did not keep many herbs on hand, but he was grateful for his small stash of the mix the Elder used for soothing teas. They were useful for the nights he couldn't sleep, nights when dim, dark memories of his mother and nameless things before flitted through his head. As he thought of them, his hand drifted to his left ear. His fingertips traced the blunt end and jagged lower edge, as they often did when the vague memories played through his mind. He didn't know what happened, what violent fate he'd so narrowly escaped that it only claimed part of his ear, but he knew it had happened as his family fled their homeland. He'd always assumed the Kolmar forest had been a refuge after a harrowing journey. Now, he couldn't help but wonder if the injury had happened within the woods, caused by whatever evil he'd brushed with in the temple.

Troubled, he willed himself to think of it no more.

He sat cross-legged beside the low table and drank his tea. That was another Kolmari tradition; low tables to keep one grounded with family, tall desks to elevate one with knowledge. The forest's people had many charming traditions. Zaide only hoped the Kolmari would survive to continue them. He ate and then crawled into his pallet to sleep, the soft crackle of the fire reminding him of the tapping of a thousand spiders' feet and chasing every other nightmare from his head.

When Resia came to his door that afternoon and roused him from a fitful sleep, she wore a troubled expression.

"The Elder has called a meeting of council," she said, a cloud of worry in her eyes. "He wishes for you to attend."

Zaide brushed a hand against her shoulder, a gentle gesture of reassurance. "I'm coming. Let me find my shoes."

She mustered a smile, though faint lines of worry remained between her brows when she departed.

The Elder was in a fragile condition. That he'd seen fit to leave his library and call the village together in his state meant Resia's worry was justified. Zaide washed his face and smothered the fire with the ashes he'd left by the door. As an afterthought, he took his borrowed sword from where he'd leaned it against the wall. He strapped it to his hip with a grim sense of responsibility.

All faces were solemn when he joined the gathering in the village square. He meant only to move as close as necessary to hear, but when he reached the edge of the crowd, the people parted and the Elder's eyes fell on him.

"I hope you are refreshed," the old mage remarked, a note of sincerity in his somber voice.

Zaide nodded, but said nothing. He could have slept until the next morning and still been tired, but events would not wait.

The Elder raised the pipes for the gathered people to see. "My friends, long have I been without the Vale Hymnflute in my hands. Long have we relied on its protection. But the Vale magic is protection no longer. The Hymnflute's power has failed, and so has mine."

A low murmur of fear swept the crowd.

"I have used what power remained within both myself and the Hymnflute to restore the shielding wall of magic around Kolmar," he continued. "The village and its surrounding forest will be safe, for now. But the time has come for the Hymnflute to pass from our hands."

A soldier slid through the crowd to stand at Zaide's elbow. Aren. Zaide reached to unstrap his borrowed sword, but Aren raised a hand to stop him.

"Wait," Aren whispered. "Let's see what he has to say. I don't understand half of what he's talking about, do you?"

Zaide shook his head. Despite his place as the Elder's apprentice, the first he'd heard of this Hymnflute was when he'd been ordered to retrieve it just the day before. He wasn't certain what the Vale magic was, either, but he supposed it obvious enough that whatever it was, it encompassed Kolmar. He'd just never heard any protective magic referred to by that name.

The Elder went on without pause. "If its power is to be restored, the Hymnflute must be returned to King Sendassian, whose predecessors entrusted it to the Kolmari Elders for safekeeping. My apprentice was the one to retrieve it. Now, he will be the one to carry it to Amrochan."

Every head turned toward Zaide and for a moment, he felt faint. "Master, I—"

"The Hymnflute is forbidden from the hands of others," the old mage said. "There are few who bear the right to hold it. I cannot travel in my state, and Resia's skill with healing cannot be spared with so many injured. It must be you, Zaide. You are my apprentice, and the only other permitted to carry this burden."

Zaide's heart swelled with pride and sank with disappointment at the same time. He'd barely slept, and now it seemed half the weight of the world had been placed upon his shoulders. "When must I leave?"

"We cannot wait." Apology colored the Elder's voice. "You will depart immediately with the soldiers. They will escort you to the garrison, where you will consult with the commanding officer and determine the best route to Amrochan. I cannot guarantee an escort for you beyond that point."

His heart sank further, but Zaide bowed his head. "I understand, Master."

Aren nudged his arm and gave a slight nod of solidarity. Zaide nodded back. At least he wouldn't be alone.

"Return home and gather what you will need for this voyage," the Elder said. "Then come to my library, so that I may offer my blessing before you depart. I realize this is a great deal to ask of you, boy. But as my apprentice, this is your duty. No one can shoulder this burden for you."

Again, Zaide inclined his head. "Yes, Master. I understand."

The Elder took a single step toward the crowd and Resia appeared at his side. She offered her arm to lend him support and the old mage took it without complaint. "Go, then. I fear we have precious little time."

This time, Zaide bowed from the waist and trained his eyes on the ground. When he straightened, Aren stood before him.

"Seems you'd better keep that sword for now." Aren managed a grin, but his nerves showed in the way the corners of his mouth quivered with the effort needed to hold it. "We'll make sure you get outfitted with one of your own at the garrison."

"Thank you." Zaide touched the hilt of the sword and his fingers slid over it in a caress. He was growing fond of the blade, though he was loath to admit it. It felt good to have a real weapon at his side. Despite the weight of its burden and the weight of all he'd done with it, its presence simply felt right.

Aren's eyes brightened and his smile grew easier. "Looks like you'll get your dream of going to the garrison after all, huh?"

"I suppose." Zaide headed for his tiny cottage. Aren followed.

"You don't sound very excited."

"I mean, I'm glad for the opportunity. I really am." Zaide opened his door and gazed longingly at the rumpled bed on the floor. "I just wish it was happening at a better time."

Aren frowned and rubbed his chin. "There's no such thing as a better time. Whether or not we're at war, the intention is the same. Train for it. Be ready for it. And eventually, all of us get our time on the battlefield."

"But Kolmar's not supposed to be a battlefield," Zaide muttered. "Kolmar was supposed to be safe."

"For a long time, it was. Things change, Zaide."

As he stuffed clothing into a knapsack, Zaide saw the truth in that statement almost immediately. His possessions were so few that just the simple act of packing his clothes changed the little house. Once he packed his good boots and a handful of supplies, his home looked eerily bare.

"I can request permission to travel with you to Amrochan," Aren began.

Zaide shook his head before his friend could continue. "No. You need to stay at the garrison. The village is going to need you. I can tell that much already. I need someone here, someone close by, who can see to the Elder and Resia. They're the closest thing to family I've got. If I have to trust someone else to protect them, there's no one I'd want here more."

Aren's expression softened. "Thank you. That means a lot. After I was sent to the garrison and you stayed here, I thought..."

"That we wouldn't be friends?"

"That you would resent me," Aren finished. "And I couldn't have blamed you for it, either. It should have been you. Before any of the rest of us, it should have been you."

The same thought had crossed Zaide's mind a thousand times. "Not according to the Elder."

"No, but after what happened here last night, I'm starting to think... well, you stayed here for a reason, Zaide." Aren shrugged.

"Of course I did." Zaide swung his bag onto his shoulder and turned. "Let's go."

"To the library?"

"And then to the garrison," Zaide said.

The two of them stepped outside and as Zaide closed the door behind him, he knew the little cottage would never be home again.

CHAPTER EIGHT

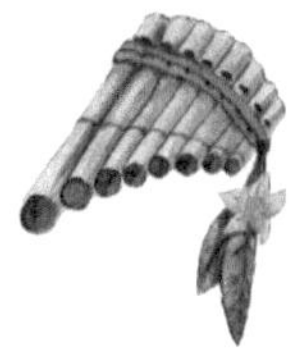

ZAIDE INTENDED to say goodbye to Resia at the library, but the Elder was alone. After the formality of the Choosing and the address to the village, their exchange was so simple that it seemed raw. The Elder pressed a wrapped parcel into Zaide's hands and curled his fingers around it. Their eyes met, and for the first time, emotion shone clear in the old man's dark eyes.

"Protect it with everything in you," the Elder said, squeezing Zaide's hands against the wrapped pipes. "Should any of the artifacts fall into the enemy's hands, all will be lost."

Every detail of the pipes stood out, even through the cloth, and Zaide marveled at how simple they seemed before he withdrew from the Elder's grasp and slipped the artifact into his bag. "I can only protect it as far as Amrochan. Once I've given the Hymnflute to Sendassian, I will have done all I can."

The Elder made a soft sound of uncertainty, but bowed his head. "May he hold the wisdom and strength to pull us from peril's jaws. Safe travels, Zaide. No matter what comes, know you will always have a home in Kolmar."

"Thank you, Master. I'll remember." Yet as the words left his tongue, Zaide doubted his own sincerity. Something had changed; something had ended. Excitement and fear mingled within him, a mix made heady by his exhaustion.

At the edge of the village square, the visiting soldiers split into two groups. They passed supplies back and forth between themselves, sorting and dividing and then stowing things in their bags. The smaller group adjusted their weapons and armor. The leader of the visiting soldiers stood among them, conversing with someone from the other group in low tones. Aren led the way toward them.

"We can't leave the village unguarded," the leader explained when the two of them joined the group. He eyed the sword at Zaide's hip, but said nothing of it. "Not in good conscience, anyway."

Zaide studied the insignia on the shoulder of the man's uniform, unsure how to address him. Visiting soldiers had always been few and far between in Kolmar.

Aren noticed. "Captain, I'd like to help escort Zaide to the garrison and then return to aid the defense of Kolmar."

The captain nodded. "I'm sure that can be arranged. Are you ready?"

"Just have to grab my bag. Give me a moment?" Aren waited for the captain's nod, then sprinted to his family's home, where he'd spent the night.

The captain scooped a pair of bags from the ground with a grunt and slung one over each shoulder. "You know how to use that, boy?" His eyes flicked to the sword again.

Zaide straightened. "Yes, sir."

"Unusual, for a mage's apprentice."

Though Zaide doubted the man meant for them to, the words needled. "Yes, sir."

The captain grunted again. "You have everything you need?"

Zaide patted his bag.

"Good. Hope you're rested, then. It's a hike."

Aren jogged back with his bag on his shoulder and another sword at his waist. Zaide wondered where it had come from, but he supposed the soldiers would have traveled with extra weaponry. The moment Aren rejoined the group, the captain turned and called for his soldiers to move.

Until that moment, Zaide hadn't realized the three youths selected in the Choosing were among them, already in uniform. The soldiers must have brought those, too.

The three looked back at the village as they walked and waved. Zaide looked back and wished he hadn't. Almost all of the village stood behind them, wearing pinched expressions and waving sad farewells. Resia's family—his family—stood among them. His adoptive parents. Two dear brothers and a sister. Only Resia was missing.

Swallowing against the lump in his throat, Zaide waved back and then tore his eyes away.

"They'll be safe," Aren said. "I promise."

"I know." Zaide stared down the shady forest road. He'd walked the twists and turns of that road a thousand times, but it felt strange underfoot. "Did you ever think you'd come back?"

"Of course I did." Aren eyed him oddly. "Why wouldn't I? I didn't know when it would be, but soldiers are given leave. They're allowed to retire, eventually. I've been to Amrochan, now. I've even been to the markets outside Tinith. I haven't liked anywhere as much as I like Kolmar, so this is where I'll come back to when my time serving is up. It'll always be home."

"Of course," Zaide murmured in a sense of agreement he didn't feel.

His friend slapped his shoulder. "Give it a little time. You'll be back to Kolmar in just a few weeks with stories about your adventure to Amrochan and your meeting with the king. Everything will be back to normal then."

Zaide hoped so.

The group moved at a steady, easy-to-follow pace. The three new recruits lagged at the back, even more reluctant to leave the forest than Zaide.

As they passed the blacksmith's forge at the edge of the

clearing, Resia's small voice piped up. "Finally found your way out the village, didn't you?"

Zaide paused and glanced toward the captain. The man nodded, and the procession drew to a halt.

Resia held her skirts close as she clambered down the ladder. Zaide moved to intercept her at the bottom.

Her arms snaked around his middle and she hugged him hard. "I always knew it would happen," she whispered. "You were always like a sapling at the edge of the trees, leaning away from the rest of the forest to find just a little more light."

"I'll come back," he promised, though he wasn't sure of it, himself.

"Maybe. But it'll never be the same." She smiled up at him with tears on her eyelashes. "Here. I found this in the library. The Elder said you could take it with you." She presented a small book on her upturned palms.

Zaide took it and spared a glance for the spine before he flipped it open. The tiny text was accompanied by illustrations and tidy bars of musical notes.

"It's a real instrument, you know." She nodded toward his bag. "The Elder said you're allowed to play it. It might remind you of home. This book will help you learn to play a little. It might help bring you comfort when you stop to camp at night."

"Thank you, Resia." He smiled and wrapped her in another hug. "That's exactly what I needed."

She beamed up at him. "Promise you'll be careful, okay?"

"Promise. But I have to go." He pulled back to leave, but she caught his arm.

"One last thing." She reached up and cradled his face in both hands. Warmth flooded into him, easing his sore muscles and restoring his strength. Zaide opened his mouth, but she cut him off before he could protest.

"It's a long trip," Resia said. "If I'm to heal everyone else, I'll heal you, too. I won't pretend to know what all the Hymnflute does, but I know what you can do, and this is the only way I can help. We're all counting on you." She stroked his cheek with a thumb.

He grasped her wrist and gave her a smile. "Thank you, Resia."

She let go and stepped back. "Be safe."

"You, too."

"All ready?" the captain called.

Zaide rejoined the group with more spring in his step. "Yes, sir."

The soldiers adjusted their bags and blades and started off again.

Though Zaide knew the forests better than he knew himself, he'd never ventured far beyond the river that was considered Kolmar's border. By nightfall, they stood at the river's edge, and he stared into the wilderness beyond with a budding sense of excitement. Worry still lurked in the pit of his stomach, but it was subdued compared to the sense of longing that came with the idea of adventure. He'd always hoped for the chance to cross the river and venture into what lay beyond, but part of him had doubted the opportunity would come. Behind him, the more experienced soldiers built a modest camp around an equally modest fire.

"Shouldn't we have crossed the bridge and built our camp on the other side?" Aren asked nearby.

Zaide turned his better ear toward the conversation.

"Not if we don't know what's on the other side," the captain replied. "We know Kolmar is secure for now, but we don't know how far the goborrins made it into the woods. It's unlikely we'd be attacked from this side, but they could be waiting for us ahead. If we're on this side, we have an easy retreat to the village, where we'll have reinforcements. On the other side, they could pin us against the river."

The idea of goborrins elsewhere had never crossed Zaide's mind, but if they were in the temple, he supposed they could be anywhere. He turned to join them. "Do you think we should expect them?"

The captain shrugged. "We should expect every possibility. I know things seem calm now, but that could change in an instant. It already did, back in Kolmar. Luck was on our side this time. If it hadn't been the Choosing, I don't know what would have happened."

An uneasy hush followed his words. The soldiers turned away, sobered.

Zaide eased himself to the ground beside the fire. "I'm not sure it has anything to do with luck."

"What do you mean?" Aren cocked his head to the side.

"The eclipse." Zaide rested his arms atop his knees. He hunched forward, gazing into the fire. "The portent of death. It surprised me, probably surprised a lot of the village, but we don't track the moon or stars. The Elder does. It's part of his job. Who decides when the Choosing takes place?"

Several soldiers looked at him, startled.

"You're saying you think the Elder knew the village would be attacked?" the captain asked.

Zaide shook his head. "I don't think he knew for certain, but I think he knew enough to be afraid. This year's was an early Choosing. Normally, the Choosing isn't held until around when the apple trees bloom. We're barely out of winter now. Several members of the village council questioned it, but he insisted it was the best time to hold it this year."

"There's no way of knowing whose life is in peril when the portent comes," Aren added.

"Except when there is." Recollection of his conversations with Lark danced through Zaide's head. "I thought it was the worst ill omen that could preside over the Choosing. But now..."

The captain studied his face. "Don't stop there, boy. If it's eating you that bad, you'd best share all your thoughts."

Aren nodded vigorously.

Zaide shifted where he sat, staring into the fire. He couldn't bring himself to look anyone in the eye. "I met a girl in the woods. She was on her way to the temple. She said she'd read a prophecy of sorts in Jadora and that the eclipse meant one of two kings will die. I think the Elder knew. And I think whatever it is he knows, he's trying to turn the tide in Sendassian's favor."

The captain snorted. "That's far-fetched, even from a mage."

Zaide shot him a hard look. "I'm a mage's apprentice. I'm not a mage."

"Strange choice of apprentices," the captain muttered.

Not for the first time, Zaide agreed. He kept the thought to himself. "How's our rate of travel?"

"It could be faster," Aren said before the captain could speak. "We should probably set a more aggressive pace in the morning. Especially if we don't know what that thing can do." His eyes fell to the bag at Zaide's side.

The Hymnflute made a strange shape against the side of the satchel. Zaide touched a hand to it and traced its longest pipe through the bag. "It can make music, according to Resia. The Elder said I could play it. I'm not sure I should try."

Conversation on the other side of the fire halted. The captain chuckled. "Not tonight. I think we've all had enough adventure for now."

"I think so, sir," Aren agreed.

A soldier brought a small bag of provisions around to divide its contents among the group, and everyone settled into a satisfied silence.

Despite Resia's healing, Zaide was exhausted again after the afternoon's trek. The others ate and lay on the ground to sleep as the captain kicked dirt over the fire.

"Captain," Zaide called softly as shadow fell.

The man turned toward him and Zaide pointed.

The captain clicked his tongue and reached for his sword.

To the east, a long row of lights threaded their way toward them, through the trees.

CHAPTER NINE

"Everybody up!" the captain roared.

The soldiers flew to their feet and tore their swords from their scabbards. The new recruits huddled closer together, startled and fearful.

Zaide rose and unsheathed his sword.

The lights amid the trees bobbed closer, snaking between and behind tree trunks. He squinted and wished he could see farther than the dark allowed. Orange light splashed onto the trees above the convoy. Torches, he decided. Fourteen of them.

A low drumming filled the air, and a chill rolled down Zaide's spine. "Goborrins."

"Orders, sir?" Aren asked, voice low.

The captain stared into the trees, his jaw tense.

"Sir?" Aren repeated.

"They're coming into view." One of the soldiers had produced a spyglass from somewhere. Had Zaide known they had one, he would have retrieved it, himself. "Fifteen of them. Fourteen bearing torches, one at the back with a standard and a drum."

Aren frowned. "There are fifteen of them and a dozen of us. I think those sound like decent odds."

From the sound of displeasure the captain made, he disagreed. "And only eight of us who are ready to fight. We left most of our extra gear behind. The new recruits don't even have swords."

"Nine," Zaide said with a twitch of the sword in his hand.

The captain looked to the weapon and then met his eye.

Irritated, Zaide straightened and met his stare. "How many goborrins have you and your men killed, Captain?"

Silence.

"How many attacked Kolmar?"

"Two dozen, maybe," the man said. A few soldiers nodded in agreement, but no one hurried to claim any kills. Were they ashamed of the small number? Or had some been spared from the fight altogether?

"Then it sounds like I'm the most experienced one out of the group." A small hint of satisfaction flared inside him and Zaide tamped it down immediately. It wasn't like him to gloat. But he'd never had his skill so blatantly challenged, either. "I'll tell you this much—they're strong. The best way to kill them is to take them by surprise, but I think it's too late for that."

"Across the river," the captain said.

The soldiers turned toward him in an unspoken question.

"Now!" he snarled.

The new recruits were the first ones to turn toward the bridge.

"But Captain," Aren said. "I thought you said we shouldn't—"

"I know what I said. But our best option is outrunning those things. Move!" The captain scooped his things from the ground and the other soldiers followed suit.

Zaide collected his bag, but stayed rooted in place. "They're strong, but they're also fast. I don't think we can outrun them as a group. Do you think we can choke them off at the bridge?"

"I think that's our best chance right now." The captain herded the group toward the river, taking up the back alongside Zaide and Aren.

A pair of soldiers flanked the new recruits and rushed them across the bridge, weapons ready. There was no way of knowing what waited in the forest ahead. They wore wariness on their faces like masks—not fearful, but not eager. The rest of the group filed over as fast as they could.

The bridge was narrow, scarcely wide enough for a small wagon. The ancient wood creaked beneath Zaide's feet as he crossed. He paused at the far end of the bridge and bounced on the balls of his feet, the wood squeaking loud enough to draw the captain's attention. The wood was spongy, springy. "Rotten," Zaide said.

"We can use that." The captain motioned him across and they fell into position at the mouth of the bridge, Zaide and Aren on either side of the captain.

Part of Zaide felt he should have been in the middle, but the position he took wasn't bad. Were he right-handed, the bridge's rail would be in the way.

"I'm not sure how many you saw up close," the captain said, glancing toward Aren, "but these things are big."

A hint of nervousness flitted across Aren's face. "How big?"

"The biggest man you've ever seen." Zaide adjusted his footing. "Some are bigger. Like a horse on two legs." The ground was soft, but not dangerously so. If the goborrins made it across, there was little chance of it giving way to cast them into the water.

The captain nodded. "If we can lure enough of them onto the bridge, they might break through."

"Which leads to my next question," Aren said. "Are they smart?"

A low chuckle escaped the captain's throat. "Smarter than we'd like."

The lights emerged from the forest's edge, spilling grotesque shadows across ugly, man-like bodies. Zaide braced for the fight. "Here they come!"

The drumbeats shifted. No longer a mimicry of a drumbird's call, they settled into the steady throb of war beats as the procession neared the bridge.

But they didn't rush onto the bridge. The fifteen goborrins fell into ranks on the other side of the river, three deep, thumping the ends of their spears against the ground in rhythm with the drums.

The soldiers shifted at Zaide's back.

"Steady," the captain breathed.

The goborrins didn't move, their tusked faces emotionless, their beady eyes cold and dark. They held their torches aloft as they drummed along.

"What are they doing?" Aren asked.

Zaide locked eyes with one of the beasts. Something passed between them—a heated instinct that begged for violence. It set Zaide's heart to thundering. His fingers tightened on his sword and he cast his bag aside.

The captain wet his lips, his nerves showing through that tiny crack in his resolve. "It's a challenge. They do this to the border camps. It's a sport to them."

The staring goborrin licked his greasy snout and huffed.

Zaide raised his chin and stepped forward.

"Hey!" Aren protested.

"Trust me." Zaide strode onto the bridge and gripped his sword in both hands. He met the monster's eye and willed it to feel his challenge.

Delighted squalls erupted from the goborrin ranks. The beast he'd met eyes with stepped forward, twirling his spear in a grand display.

Zaide did not move any nearer.

The old bridge groaned as the monster set foot on it.

He didn't give it a chance to prepare. Zaide surged forward, flipping his blade and bringing it up in a powerful upward jab.

The sword raked up the goborrin's partially-armored chest, cutting deep into sickly yellow flesh and then bouncing off a plate of boiled leather.

The goborrin howled in pain. Behind it, the rest of the ranks jeered.

Angered, the goborrin reacted—overreacted, its spear smashing into the bridge where Zaide had been a moment before.

He was small and fast, and the bridge was narrow. The spear stuck fast and Zaide lunged in again, slicing into the monster's side. Behind him, the soldiers booed. He could have killed it. They only saw half the plan.

Howls of rage filled the air and the goborrin jerked his spear to free it, baring rotten, peg-like teeth when it refused to budge. Both meaty hands wrapped around the spear's shaft and the monster snarled as it heaved.

The spear came free, tearing half a plank with it. The boos at Zaide's back stilled.

Sure, now they see it. Gritting his teeth, Zaide danced back just far enough that the monster couldn't reach him with its mighty swing. Then he darted in, needling, stabbing, stinging, anything to drive the goborrin into blind rage.

It roared in response, lunging with its spear. Zaide ducked and twisted and the spearhead skirted his side before it crashed into the bridge. The monsters behind it squealed in delight, cheering them on.

He went in for another strike. Too late, he saw the sweep of the goborrin's fist.

It plowed into his stomach and smashed him into the railing, chasing the air from his lungs. Zaide fell to his knees, gasping.

Aren started forward, but the captain put an arm across his chest and stopped him.

"He needs help!" Aren gritted his teeth and leaned against the captain's arm.

The captain held him fast. "It's one on one," he said. "He took this fight, he can finish it."

Angry, Aren shoved his arm aside. "We should be killing them! It should be a battle, not a duel!"

Zaide sucked in a breath and dragged himself to his feet as the goborrin freed his spear from the rotting bridge. A moment too late to strike, he fell back and raised his sword against the monster's swing. The spear's shaft hit the sword and bounced, the shock of impact almost knocking the blade from his hands. The second swing, he dodged.

"Come on!" someone roared behind him. Zaide didn't appreciate the distraction. His entire body hummed with pain, his stomach eager to spill its contents after that single blow. He warred with his own constitution, wrestling it into submission.

The goborrin went right. Its mistake. Zaide launched himself into the opening. His sword punched through the brute's flesh as easily as paper. It staggered, howling in agony, and fell against the rail. Wood crunched and splintered and they fell together.

Ice-cold water hit Zaide's skin like a thousand needles, driving the breath out of him. He struggled to free his sword, but it wouldn't come loose. He released it and kicked hard off the goborrin's body.

Too late. The goborrin's fist closed around his ankle and dragged him under. Inky-black water blotted out the sky and burned in Zaide's eyes. They tumbled in the current until he couldn't tell which way was up. Something struck his ribs. His sword, still embedded in the goborrin's side. He caught it with both hands and pulled again. It came loose and the goborrin's hand vanished.

Kicking off the monster, he released the last of what was in his lungs. The bubbles raced to the surface and Zaide struggled upward.

His head broke the surface and he seized one burning gasp of air before the current dragged him under again, and the river's roar was silenced by its own forceful waters in his ears. He had to get up. He had to escape. The sword slipped from his grasp as he fought. The cold scoured sensation from his fingers, his limbs growing numb. His shoulder hit something hard, but he felt no pain.

Hands wrapped around his arm and tore him out of the water.

Zaide sucked as deep a breath as his body could hold and fell against his rescuer before coughing. His legs buckled. Another pair of arms helped drag him from the river's edge.

"Fire!" the captain barked, his voice weak in Zaide's ears.

He tilted his head and jabbed a finger into his ear to release the trapped water.

"Easy," Aren said beside him.

"I lost your sword," Zaide choked.

"Maker's mercy! Nobody cares about the sword, boy!" The captain flung a blanket around his shoulders. Zaide wasn't sure where it came from, but he didn't care. He sank to the ground, his teeth chattering hard enough to rattle his skull.

"The goborrins—" he started. His voice failed.

"Trapped on the other side of the river." Aren pulled the blanket tighter. Someone dumped wood directly in front of him and a soldier appeared beside it, striking flint and steel. Blinding sparks lit the night and Zaide twisted away to spare his eyes.

The captain knelt beside him and pressed a flask to his lips. Zaide drank, but choked. The liquid inside burned, but a thread of warmth worked its way to his belly when he swallowed.

"The bridge collapsed with the two of you," the captain said. "You did good, boy." He raised the flask again.

Zaide shook his head. Whatever the drink was, it numbed his tongue as well as the cold had numbed his fingers.

"Raddan," the captain called.

One of the soldiers hurried near.

"Check his shoulder, I can smell the blood." The captain peeled back the blanket and tucked it underneath Zaide's arm instead.

Now that he was free of the water and the warmth of the newly kindled fire hit his skin, Zaide became aware of the sting in his right shoulder.

"Good thing it wasn't your sword arm," Aren murmured.

Raddan—the group's medic, Zaide assumed from the bag the man produced—pulled at the sleeve of his shirt. "Get this off. It's better if you don't sit here in wet things, even if it's not a bad injury."

Groaning, Zaide pulled the blanket closer.

"Get his bag," the captain ordered, though Zaide did not see who ran to recover his things. Instead, his attention was focused on Aren, crouching at his side and helping Raddan peel back the blankets once more.

His shirt was shredded. Whatever he hit, it had torn the fabric wide open and the cloth hung in tatters over his equally damaged skin. The medic poked and prodded with two fingers, aggravating the injury, while his other hand fished in his bag of supplies.

Zaide closed his eyes and turned away. He didn't want to see. The pain would pass, though it was misery to sit and allow it to happen.

Judging by how long it took for a soldier to return with his bag, the river had carried him a decent distance from the bridge. Aren took the bag and rooted out a clean outfit. "You're either brave or stupid, Zaide, I'll give you that. I don't know which one it is. Guess in this case, it doesn't matter."

Salve on his shoulder stung worse than the injuries. Zaide grunted. "So long as the goborrins are on that side of the river, I don't think I need to be brave."

"Lucky for you they are, then," Aren muttered.

"Are you sure?" Zaide pointed, and his companion lifted his head.

Far in the distance, on their side of the river, lights threaded their way down the forest road.

Aren's shoulders slumped. "Oh, hang it."

CHAPTER TEN

THE SOLDIERS JUMPED at the captain's orders, though this time, fear shone in their eyes. Zaide tried to stand, but Raddan gripped him by the good shoulder and shoved him back down. The new recruits clustered around them, and the soldiers formed a line of defense some ten feet ahead. They braced themselves for combat.

"Hold!" The captain's shout made more than one soldier jump.

Not far off now, the light that led the line through the trees shuttered and then blinked in a series of patterns.

Every soldier visibly relaxed.

"At ease!"

The recruits sank to the earth in clear relief.

Raddan shook his head. "Should've brought more weapons. We'd be better off if the new blood were armed."

Zaide's guilt over losing Aren's sword strengthened. "What do those patterns mean?"

"Reinforcements," Raddan said. "One of the lieutenants, bringing the rest of the captain's company."

"I'm going to have to learn all your titles and terms." Zaide flinched when the medic pushed the tattered fabric of his shirt aside and slathered salve over the other side of his injured shoulder.

Raddan chuckled. "I'm sure you'll have plenty of opportunities along the way. But I'm surprised that wasn't covered in your training. If Kolmar's Elder expected you to replace him, he should have been preparing you for political duties, too."

Zaide bit his tongue to keep it still. He doubted the Elder had ever intended any such thing. Resia was the mage. Resia would be the one to replace the Elder, the one who had been given lessons that revolved around the outside world. He'd received a reasonable education, but it had never been so intense or demanding as hers. Instead of replying, he turned to watch the approaching soldiers.

Never had he seen so many people in armor. He could not see their faces or features in the dark, but he knew the garrison held a healthy mixture of soldiers and specialties. What they were good at didn't matter, he supposed. What mattered was that they had come.

The captain joined them a short distance away, his conversation with the lieutenant at the head of the group swallowed by the night.

When the medic released him, Zaide pulled the blanket higher around his shoulders and shimmied out of his shirt. The cold air burned enough without his skin being directly exposed. Misunderstanding his efforts, Aren snapped the sword he'd half-drawn back into its sheath and took the blanket, holding it up to create a barrier between Zaide and the soldiers nearby.

Too tired to protest, Zaide shed his wet clothing and pulled on his dry pants as fast as he could. He reached for his new shirt, but Raddan stepped in and pushed his hands down, forcing him to sit still so his shoulder could be bandaged.

"I didn't think reinforcements would get here so soon."

Aren's already low voice was muffled more by the blanket he held up in front of his face. "The captain sent a messenger as soon as the village was attacked, but the garrison is more than a day away."

"If it's that far to the garrison, what makes you think they're reinforcements?" Zaide cast Raddan a questioning look, but the man only shrugged and finished his work. He pushed the dry shirt back into Zaide's hands and left him to dress.

Aren said nothing.

His shoulder protested, but Zaide pulled on his shirt anyway. He touched the bandages through the fabric and regretted that Resia's duties kept her in the village. It was a selfish thought, he knew; Kolmar needed her more than he did. He'd grown spoiled, having both Resia and the Elder to tend injuries around the village. Though it hurt, it was the shallow sting of a bad scrape instead of a deep injury that might threaten his physical ability. The antiseptic salve Raddan had slathered on him was more than enough.

"Everyone up!" the captain called.

Zaide hadn't realized anyone else sat. He climbed to his feet without complaint, though his shoulder objected. He suspected it would until it healed. Even after it scabbed over, every motion would pull.

The soldiers shuffled into an organized line. Zaide joined them, as did the new recruits.

The captain stood before them with his hands clasped behind his back. "If any of you wish to return to Kolmar, you may accompany the lieutenant. He will be glad for the extra hands. The road ahead is clear and the garrison is on alert. It's safer to continue onward for as long as we are able to walk. We will make camp only when absolutely necessary."

A few stifled groans escaped the weary soldiers. In the dark, their identities were protected. The captain glared at all of them, instead.

"My group will break soon," the lieutenant added. "If you prefer to travel to Kolmar with us, I'll allow the captain to choose troops from those under my banner to escort his party back to the garrison."

That suggestion went over better. A handful of soldiers shuffled over to join the lieutenant's group, while the captain turned and called names to select replacements. The shuffle was brief, over in moments, and then the captain barked for all of them to get moving again.

The group gathered their bags and took to the road at a dragging pace.

"We didn't expect to run into anyone on the road," one of the newcomers said as they walked. "The lieutenants drew lots to decide who would go check on Kolmar. We encountered your messenger this morning."

Zaide's brow furrowed and he moved closer. "Why would you think Kolmar needed a whole company?"

The man blinked at him, surprised. He opened his mouth to speak, then paused, taking in Zaide's white hair and fair complexion. A guarded look touched his eyes.

Aren trotted forward and posted himself at Zaide's side. "Sorry, he was getting bandaged up so we missed what was said. He's the Kolmari Elder's apprentice. We were tasked with protecting him on the way, but he got it in his head that he was supposed to protect us."

The soldier raised a brow as curiosity filtered into his expression. "You're the one that knocked out the bridge, huh?"

"Had I known anyone was heading for it, I would have thought twice," Zaide said.

The man chuckled. "At least I'm with your group now. I guess that spared me a swim."

"What was that about checking on Kolmar?" Aren asked, redirecting the conversation.

What little mirth the soldier had shown evaporated. "The garrison was attacked during the eclipse. No casualties on our side. One of the benefits of fortifications. But we never thought we'd see goborrins that close to Amrochan."

"I never thought I'd see them in Kolmar's temple, either." Zaide paused to adjust the strap of his bag on his good shoulder. He'd have to drop it to have use of his arm, but it was better than nothing. The Hymnflute bumped his back and, oddly, he found its presence comforting.

"In the temple?" the soldier asked, startled. His dark eyes widened until they glittered in the warm light cast off from the group's torches. "Why would they be somewhere like that?"

Zaide shrugged. "I don't know." And no matter what suspicions or questions he had, it mattered little—he hadn't had a chance to ask the Elder, and he did not know who else might have answers.

"What can you tell us about the road conditions? It hasn't rained, has it?" Aren asked, and Zaide welcomed the change of subject. The soldiers chatted amongst themselves, and the subjects they discussed remained shallow.

By dawn, the group moved at little more than a shuffle. The captain finally called a halt and everyone was grateful to collapse into a fitful, if short-lived, sleep.

They rested no more than a few hours before they were on the road again. Everyone dragged their feet, bleary-eyed and irritable, but at least they made progress. At nightfall, they made camp to cook and Zaide fell asleep the moment he closed his eyes.

In the early afternoon the next day, the garrison came into view.

Zaide had often fantasized about the moment he would crest a hill and see the garrison, but what sat amid the rolling fields just beyond the forest's edge was not what he envisioned.

A series of low buildings rested atop a small rise, surrounded by a log wall with heavy, barricaded gates. Men stood guard on platforms just inside the wall, rather than at the gates, and the garrison stirred to life when the guards spotted their group on the road.

The soldiers fell into organized rows of two, Zaide and the three recruits sandwiched in the middle of the group. They marched, the renewed energy that came with seeing their destination invigorating all of them.

Nearer to the gates, Zaide saw banners hung against the log wall. One bore a tree on a green field, representing Kolmar, and the other was a rich royal blue, emblazoned with the royal crest in white. He cocked his head, trying to make sense of the geometric shapes and the way they fit together. Resia had often teased him for being unable to see the symbolism, but whatever it was supposed to represent, it still eluded him.

When they were still two dozen steps away, the gates creaked open to welcome them. A handful of guards called greetings from the watch platforms, while more stood watch beside the open gates. The wary looks they cast toward the open fields around the garrison made Zaide frown.

"So," Aren said as they filed in through the gates. "This is it, huh? You'll probably have tonight to rest, but then it's off to Amrochan."

"And you'll be headed back to Kolmar," Zaide replied with a twinge of disappointment. "I know you'll take care of everyone—"

"But we both wish I could go with you," Aren finished. "If it were anywhere other than Kolmar I was supposed to defend, I'd find a way to travel with you instead. I can think of no greater task than defending my friends. I just never thought I'd have to choose which friends I was defending."

Zaide clapped him on the back. "You're still not choosing, you know. We both know Kolmar needs you more."

His companion responded with a hesitant grin.

Instead of residing inside the large kitchens and dinner hall Zaide had always imagined, the garrison's soldiers lounged around the main yard inside the log wall. The buildings they passed were storerooms and barracks, their doors open to let the warm spring breeze circulate. A number of stone-ringed fires dotted the open space between the squat wooden building, hosting griddles and cookpots and filling the air with aromas that made Zaide's stomach grumble.

"Welcome home," the captain announced as the gates groaned shut behind them. "New recruits, you're with me. The rest of you, make yourselves comfortable. Sleep where you can. Tomorrow morning, a handful of you will escort the Elder's apprentice to Amrochan."

A number of heads swiveled toward them. Zaide stood a little straighter, attempting to look like he deserved the title. To his chagrin, most curious eyes slid from his face to the empty scabbard at his side, frowns of consternation and disapproval appearing on the soldiers' faces.

So much for first impressions.

"Zaide was the first of our party to slay a goborrin on his own," Aren announced. Frowns disappeared, replaced with intrigue. "He was the first to answer their challenge at the Kolmar bridge, as well. Raddan already saw to his injuries, but I trust everyone here will gladly assist however necessary until he regains the use of his right arm."

Intrigue melted into respect, though on some faces, it was worn like a grudge. Zaide wasn't sure why they wanted to dislike him, but he had a number of guesses. Soldiers always viewed mages as outsiders, and they had no way of knowing he bore no magic. But as far as outsiders went, with his hair, eyes, and complexion, it was hard to look any less like he belonged.

Aren nudged his arm. "Come on. Let's find you a bed." He led the way into the barracks.

Empty beds built of rough-hewn wood stood in long rows, their covers pulled tight. Aren walked past a number of them before he stopped at the foot of one that was identical to all the others, which he'd somehow identified as available. Zaide peered at it with a frown.

Chuckling, Aren tapped the frame of the neighboring bed with his booted toe. "Box under the bed. You didn't notice?"

Zaide leaned forward. Sure enough, wooden boxes sat under most of the beds, each filled with belongings. The bed Aren stopped beside lacked one.

"Huh." Zaide dropped his bag on the foot of the bed and sat beside it. His entire body ached, but worse was the itching and pulling of the scabs on his shoulder. He tugged the collar of his shirt down enough to peek beneath the bandages.

"Don't mess with it, or Raddan will get you tied up. He did that to Erena last year. She was one of the recruits from Kolmar two years ago, remember?" Aren grinned.

"I remember." It was hard not to remember. All the youths had watched that Choosing with the same eagerness, knowing their turn was next, hoping they would be one of the next people chosen. Zaide made himself stop that line of thought. He wasn't resentful that Aren had been chosen and he hadn't. But he was still bitter that he hadn't been given a chance at all.

A moment of silence passed between them before Aren drew a breath to speak. "Listen... When you leave for Amrochan tomorrow..."

"Everything's going to change," Zaide finished.

Aren nodded. "Just make sure you make it home, all right? Resia will hate me if you don't. She'll say I should have gone to protect you."

"Out of the three of us, I don't think I'm the one who needs to be protected." Though he grinned, Zaide couldn't deny the creeping shadow of uncertainty. "But I'll do my best."

"Good." Aren gave another stiff nod. "Just remember that battle changes you. And if you need time, after you get back, you'll always be welcome here at the garrison. Everyone here understands."

The ordeal at the temple had already given him a taste of that. Zaide did his best to smile. "Thank you, Aren. I appreciate that."

"Sure. Now get some sleep. You're gonna need it. The road to Amrochan is... well, you'll see." Aren grinned and turned to leave.

"I'll see?" Zaide couldn't help the concern that seeped into his voice. "See what?"

Aren laughed and removed himself from the barracks.

CHAPTER ELEVEN

BEYOND THE GARRISON, the landscape sloped downward into a river basin split with more glittering tongues of water than Zaide could count. They branched from a sliver of white in the distance, which sparkled and moved like the rivers. He lingered on the hillside as the rest of his escort began their descent.

He'd been given the smallest retinue possible; three men from the garrison walked ahead of him. The field medic Raddan had been the first volunteer, which Zaide found both reassuring and concerning. The others were less friendly and spoke to him as little as possible, though they bantered amicably with each other and with Raddan. The older of the two was a stout man who had introduced himself as Murk, which Zaide assumed was not a given name, and the other was so absolutely average that when he said his name was Plain, it had been difficult not to laugh.

"That's not unusual in the army," Raddan said when Zaide asked about the curious names. "Everyone earns a nickname sooner or later. More often than not, they're easier to remember."

Zaide frowned. "Raddan doesn't sound like a nickname."

"It's not. They call me Leech. But the captain didn't think it appropriate to introduce me that way, considering you were bleeding the first time you heard my name." Raddan slapped his back and continued down the hill.

Outside his familiar forest, Zaide felt as if the distance between things had grown. They traveled until sundown, but the rivers never seemed to be any closer. On the third day, without warning, the terrain changed. The road remained raised and dry when they stopped for the evening, but the fields nearby had turned to marshes, and all manner of wildlife buzzed and croaked protests at their passing.

"So long as you stay on the road, it'll be fine," Raddan said in a murmur as the sun sank below the horizon. "Remember that, boy. Just stay on the road."

Murk built a campfire in the middle of the road, using wood scavenged from the edges of the marshy pools. He produced rations for each of them and they sat in silence to eat.

Zaide gazed toward the north, where the wide, glittering lake waited. From the marshy bottoms, he couldn't see it, but there was a stillness in that direction that left him unsettled.

"Don't need to be looking out that way," Murk muttered. "Nothing that way but marsh and water."

"How far is it to Amrochan?" Zaide asked, turning back to his food. The jerky was tough and the water stale. The rest was so flavorless, he wondered how soldiers survived.

Plain grunted. "We're halfway from the garrison, or thereabouts. Take whatever we've traveled now and double it."

As big as the forests of Kolmar seemed, Zaide had always assumed the capital was farther off. "How long is the trip by horse?"

Murk put down his food and squinted, a sour twist to his mouth. "Don't travel no faster by horse. You just arrive less tired."

"He means alone," Raddan said. "The army travels at a walk, but a good horse could cut the trip in half."

"There are wild ones in the fields, you know." Plain nodded toward the hill they'd left behind, where swaying grasses looked silver in the moonlight. "Horses. We aren't allowed to keep them, but we catch them sometimes. Take them for a good gallop, just a bit of fun."

"They get bucked off and break bones more often," Raddan said in a conspiratorial whisper.

Zaide grinned. "I would have thought the army would keep horses."

"Oh, they do." Plain paused to take another bite, then continued as he chewed. "But most of them are needed at the front lines. Where the real war's happening. That's where the horses are."

Raddan scoffed. "Real war is everywhere. Or was our battle at the bridge not real? We faced goborrins just the same. Played by their rules and nearly lost the lad." He nodded toward Zaide. "It's a miracle he survived."

Murk shook his head and scowled in clear disapproval. "He'd better learn to do more than just survive. We need fighters. The captain might have given him a sword, but that doesn't make him one of us."

"He'll never be one of us," Plain mumbled, and the words cut deep.

Zaide turned away and let his eyes wander back toward the lake. Off in the distance, cold, blue-white glimmers of light danced across the water. "What are those?"

The soldiers turned. Murk grunted and stuffed the rest of his food into his mouth, chewing only twice before gulping it down. Raddan folded the rest of his meal into a square of cloth and tucked it inside his bag. "Just what we need." The medic stood and readied his sword.

Plain stayed on the ground, chewing. "They're a ways off yet. Don't be hasty. They may leave us be."

"But what are they?" Zaide asked again, hiding his exasperation.

"Marsh-wisps." Murk turned his head and spat.

"Mostly harmless," Plain added. "You don't see them often when the weather is this cool, though."

Zaide frowned. "You don't see goborrins this far from the border often, either."

Raddan ticked a finger at him. "Fair point. Pack up, we're not camping here. The fire may draw them. We'll make camp at sunrise, when the daylight scares them off."

The other soldiers grumbled, but they both collected their things. Zaide scooped his own bag into his arms and stood as he slid the strap onto his good shoulder. "If they're mostly harmless, why would we leave?"

"Because they're only *mostly* harmless." Murk kicked dirt over their fire and stamped out the embers. "All it takes is looking at one of them the wrong way. And in case you didn't notice, lad, there are a lot of them out there. There's only four of us."

Raddan took the lead and together, they started off.

The camp they formed at sunrise was no better than the one they'd formed at dusk. They settled in the middle of the road and rested their heads on their packs, and as the sun climbed above the trees, they slept.

Before midday, Raddan woke them and they resumed travel. By nightfall, they'd reached the edge of the marsh. The marsh-wisps still danced in the distance, but they were farther off, and the soldiers did not seem to notice their presence any longer. Zaide watched them swirl and flow like flower petals on a spring breeze. That night, the gentle sway of their lights above the water lulled him to sleep.

He lost track of how long they'd traveled. The days blended together in his head, each filled with nothing but walking. He and Raddan stayed most alert, constantly scanning the horizon for threats. They saw none, but worry lingered, digging into Zaide's thoughts and holding fast.

"We're close now," Murk announced one morning, not long

after they'd broken camp and set out. From the way their provisions had dwindled, Zaide assumed they had to be.

The walls came into view before noon. Once he saw them, Zaide realized he'd been seeing the towers beyond the parapets for some time without realizing what they were. From a distance, they reminded him of mountains, peaked and misty and blue.

"The lake's beyond the wall," Plain said as the road widened and the landscape grew more diverse. Mountains rose far to the west, their peaks dusted with white that rivaled the clouds. The foothills were a vibrant green backdrop behind scattered copses of trees, while most of the land to the east—between their party and their destination—had been settled and domesticated. Orderly rows of crops lined the countryside, the sprawling expanse dotted with thatched cottages.

"Welcome to Amrochan," Murk declared, long before they reached the city walls.

"It's huge," Zaide said. Even from a distance, the number of roofs that peeked over the walls was impressive. "Do they not worry about the marsh-wisps here?"

Raddan waved a hand in dismissal. "The wisps don't come this far up Lake Sian. Once the water is deeper than a man is tall, you don't see them anymore. Amrochan is on a peninsula, but the drop off from the shore is steep. You can sail a ship right up to the city, practically, and that's half of what makes this a perfect spot for the kingdom's capital."

Zaide remembered the trade routes from his lessons with the Elder. He hadn't thought those lessons valuable, but after his Choosing, he'd also never imagined he'd travel as far as Amrochan.

The city's outer wall loomed as they drew near. Zaide craned his neck to look past its parapets. He'd expected more of a guard presence, but no one patrolled the walls. A lone guardsman stood at the gatehouse and supervised the coming and going of what little foot traffic passed through the wide gates.

"I would have thought there would be a moat around the city," Zaide said as they walked. "If it's all on a peninsula, it seems like it would be easy to dig one."

"Perhaps, but I don't imagine it's needed." Raddan nodded to the guardsman as they passed. "The walls surround the whole city. The docks are built just outside the walls on the far side from where we are now. Everything comes through gates. Jadora's similar. Defensible cities, they are. And efficient, too. It would take an army of unfathomable strength to starve out either one, and I doubt there's any other way to make them fall."

"Jadora," Zaide murmured. "Lark mentioned the library."

Beyond the wall, the city began. Houses of stone and wood lined the cobblestone streets in carefully planned rows. People bustled between them.

"That library is why the city is so well defended," Raddan said. "They say that every last scrap of man's knowledge is preserved in Jadora. Its value is beyond what most can fathom."

They wound their way through the city, toward the palace. In some places, the road narrowed to obvious choke points that slowed their progress. The city was certainly defensible, but it was not easily navigable. "Low traffic is worth less than safety," Murk grumbled at one point, though it sounded like a lie the man told himself often.

Nearer to the castle, the road they followed narrowed until horses would have been forced to travel single-file. Zaide's eyes traveled up the sides of the tall buildings beside them. The smooth-cut stone walls had rounded pieces of wood affixed to their corners, the wood burnished from the touch of countless people as they walked by. Odd as it looked, the safety purposes behind it were clear. He let his fingers trail over each wood-trimmed corner they passed.

Eventually, they spilled out into a wide plaza outside the smaller wall that separated the castle from the city. Horse-drawn wagons rolled to and from the gate. Zaide turned his head to watch.

Raddan followed his gaze. "There are wider supply routes that lead to the castle, but they're more difficult to travel on foot due to the number of wagons. The narrow alleys are better for foot traffic."

"The whole city is laid out like they expect someone to try and raze it." Zaide glanced toward the medic, hesitant.

"The last war against Gadranus is the reason for that, lad. He's pushed this far before. All one man can do is pray he never achieves it again. It took the wall and all the city's might to hold him at bay, and we may not be so lucky a second time."

The gate into the courtyard was closed. A handful of wagons waited before it, and a handful of guards moved around the wagons with wax tablets in their hands.

"What did you think of the trip, boy?" Murk asked as they crossed the plaza.

Zaide shrugged. "It wasn't so bad. A little boring, really, after the day of the eclipse."

The stout man grunted. "May fortune favor you on the way back, then."

"If he does go back," Raddan said. "You haven't seen the boy fight. He had a hunger for the garrison, but why stay at the garrison when he's already made it to Amrochan?"

The soldiers stopped. Plain raised a brow. "You think he'll try to join Sendassian's army?"

All three of them looked at Zaide as if they expected an answer.

He took a step back. Joining the king's army in the capital had never crossed his mind, but now the possibility sparked at the edge of his thoughts, vying for his attention. "I don't know." It was the most sincere answer he could give, but they still stared. He swallowed. "I suppose it's a possibility. I'd prefer to be closer to Kolmar, but my father left the forest to serve King Sendassian. Someone in the city might know what became of him, and... well, it might be nice to know."

To his surprise, Murk gave an approving nod. "Makes for a

good legacy, that does. Father and son, both serving king and country."

They took a place at the end of the line, behind the waiting wagons. One by one, the wagons lurched through the gate with their supplies, but the inspections were thorough and they waited longer than Zaide felt they ought. Eventually, their turn came.

The half-dozen guardsmen at the gate looked at the four of them as if unsure what to make of their group. One cleared his throat. "State your business."

Raddan moved to the front. "Lieutenant-Medic Raddan of the South Garrison, Kolmar region. My party serves as escort to Zaide, apprentice to the Kolmari Elder, who comes bearing news on the Elder's behalf."

The gate guard squinted at them as he scratched out a wrong mark on his tablet. "What news?"

Zaide opened his mouth, but Raddan spoke first.

"The Apprentice Elder's message is for the king's ears only." The medic's eyes narrowed. "Or have guardsmen gained authority over the Elder?"

All six guardsmen squirmed.

"As I thought." Raddan sniffed. "We will wait however long it is necessary to gain an audience with His Majesty, but he must be the one to receive us. Such is the Elder's will."

"Of course, Lieutenant." The guard etched a few hasty notes in the wax and motioned for the gates to be opened.

Raddan ushered the group forward. "Where should we wait?"

"Just inside the doors, there is a receiving parlor. Wait there and His Majesty will call for you when it is time." The guard motioned to someone in the gatehouse and the portcullis closed behind them. It hit the ground with an echoing bang.

The medic led the way to the front stairs of the palace. Another iron gate stood before the doors, but this one split down the middle and stood open to welcome visitors. Behind it, the matched wooden doors arched high overhead. They, too, stood open, though only by a few inches.

Zaide started to enter, but Raddan caught his arm.

"This may be it, lad." The medic's face was stony, sober. "I can't say what will happen beyond these doors. We may be called together, or the king may only wish to speak to you. He may dismiss us all, or he may ask you to stay. Are you ready?"

A hint of uncertainty prickled in the back of his head, but Zaide nodded.

Raddan thumped him on the shoulder. "You're a brave lad. Don't let anyone tell you otherwise. Just know that whatever happens beyond these doors, we'd be honored to have you join us at the garrison someday. No matter what these two fools say."

Murk and Plain both frowned, but they said nothing.

"Thank you, Raddan." Zaide mustered a smile and turned. His resolve wavered and he drew a breath to reinforce it. Together, the four of them stepped inside.

The white marble hall beyond the doors gleamed, cold and sterile, devoid of decoration. The massive hall hosted dozens of plain wooden benches, all of them filled with people waiting for an audience with the king. Zaide took in their faces—some anxious and most glum—and worried a single breath to bolster his courage hadn't been enough.

Beside him, Raddan offered a reassuring nod.

Near the middle of the far left section, the most inconvenient location Zaide could imagine, the center of a bench sat empty. He considered ignoring it and circling the room to find arrangements with more space, but the room was so crowded and his legs so tired from travel that he was loath to continue. Instead, he shuffled toward the empty seats and expected the soldiers would follow. They squeezed past those seated along the narrow aisle with murmured apologies. No one protested when they sat.

As great a comfort as sitting was at first, Zaide's legs soon tingled with the unpleasant lack of circulation that went along with waiting on hard wooden benches. He stretched his legs out underneath the bench in the row ahead of them, whose occupants faced the other way. It helped, but it was far from perfect.

Hours crept by. A steward emerged from the next room at random intervals, calling names and ushering visitors into the throne room. Now and then the people returned alone, some relieved and some downtrodden as they removed themselves from the palace.

Zaide rested his elbows against his knees, his eyelids heavy and his body longing for sleep.

"You, there," an unfamiliar voice called.

He snapped from his drowsy reverie.

The steward cradled his tablet to his chest and pointed at them with the back end of his stylus. "What's your business?"

Zaide pushed himself up so he could bow in a proper greeting. "I am the apprentice of the Kolmar Elder. I come bearing urgent news from Kolmar on the Elder's behalf."

The steward raised a brow. "Is that so? Come with me." The man led them on a winding path through the room, sidestepping the legs of people on benches and the bodies of those who sat on the floor. The door he led them to was smaller, but heavy and clearly intended as another layer of defense. It was not until they stood before it that Zaide thought to look up. Arrow loops overlooked the great parlor. Somehow, he wasn't surprised.

"His Majesty will expect brevity," the steward said, looking each of them in the eye in turn. "Keep your statements simple and your requests humble. You will address him as 'Your Majesty' or 'my King' and nothing else. You will not speak unless spoken to. Do you understand?"

The soldiers nodded.

A glint caught Zaide's eye and he turned his head. Halfway across the parlor, an arrow gleamed in one of the narrow overhead slits. Did Sendassian fear an attack that much?

The steward cleared his throat and Raddan jabbed Zaide in

the side with two fingers. He jumped and spun. "Yes, sir," he blurted, earning eye-rolls from his companions. The steward remained unimpressed, but he opened the door.

The true palace, it seemed, began in the second room. Plush, rich red carpeting ran the length of the room, its color blazing in the midday sunlight that spilled through the crystal ceiling. Knights in full armor lined the room, obscuring the paintings on the walls behind them. Their heads turned with interest as the group arrived. Zaide squirmed beneath the weight of their eyes, but he returned their intense gazes with a thoughtful look of his own.

"His Majesty, King Sendassian," the steward declared. "And his daughter, Her Highness, Princess Dasienna."

Zaide's head snapped around at the announcement and, when he laid eyes on the figures that stood upon the dais, shock and indignation flared inside him. "You!"

The steward gasped and Raddan stifled a quiet groan.

Zaide didn't care.

Behind the throne, with one hand resting on her father's shoulder, Lark smirked.

CHAPTER TWELVE

"WHAT IS THE MEANING OF THIS?" King Sendassian roared, thumping the end of his scepter against the floor.

Zaide took a step toward the dais, but Raddan dug his fingers into his injured shoulder and reeled him backwards. Pain shot down his arm and through his chest and back. He almost crumpled.

"What are you thinking, boy?" the medic snarled in a whisper.

"That's her!" Zaide wrenched the man's hand from his shoulder and exhaled hard. Tingles of pain still flowed through him, even after he got free. He rubbed his injury and sucked in a breath. "The girl from the temple. She never said—" He stopped short and turned to look at her, dumbfounded. He'd guessed she was wealthy from the knives she carried, but he'd never expected this. At the same time, he couldn't be angry. Why would she have told him she was a princess? She'd doubted his allegiance.

Raddan rolled his eyes. He turned back to the king and swept into a deep bow. "Forgive him, Your Majesty. He has been through great trials for a boy his age. I am Lieutenant Raddan, medic of the Kolmar garrison, and this is Zaide, apprentice to the

Kolmari Elder. We come at the Elder's behest. Kolmar was attacked and the Elder was injured, or else he would be here, himself."

The king leaned back in his throne with a frown. "Has the garrison responded to this attack?"

"Yes, sire." Raddan bowed again. "The village is now protected by a number of our soldiers, while its inhabitants recover. I do not think it is time to evacuate yet, which is a relief, as many were wounded."

Sendassian nodded slowly. His eyes drifted back to Zaide, piercingly blue, colder than those of his daughter. "The Elder's apprentice, you say? He doesn't look Kolmari."

His senses returned, Zaide offered an appropriate bow. "I am not, Your Majesty. I was a refugee, sheltered in the forest as an infant and adopted as one of their own when my mother passed." He straightened, unsure what else to say. Lark caught his eye, a spark of challenge in her gaze.

The king's eyes narrowed. "Do you think it appropriate to stare at my daughter in such a way, boy?"

Startled, Zaide blinked and then bowed his head. "I—"

"Don't be silly, Father," Lark cooed. "Why wouldn't he stare? He's near my age."

"With unbelievably lacking manners." Sendassian lifted a hand to stroke his gray beard. Despite the silvering of his hair and beard, he didn't look old. He was still fit, with clear, alert eyes and hands that were scarred by battle instead of gnarled from arthritis. "I expect better of the Kolmari Elder's apprentices. Tell me, Lieutenant. Why have you come?"

Raddan hesitated.

Lark leaned forward over the king's shoulder. "Father, shouldn't you ask the apprentice? His manners may be dreadful, but the Elder must have sent him for a reason."

Sendassian grunted. "Fine. Speak your piece, boy, but know you already tread dangerous territory."

Zaide ducked his head and bowed at the waist, murmuring

something about graciousness he recalled from his lessons. It seemed to work; when he looked up again, the storm clouds on the king's face had given way to a subtle curiosity.

"As Lieutenant Raddan said," Zaide began, "Kolmar has suffered. We were attacked by goborrins during the eclipse. Had the garrison's men not been present for the Spring Choosing, we may not have survived. We are grateful, Your Majesty, for this protection you have provided us."

The king nodded and waved a hand as if it were a given.

Zaide continued. "The Elder believed the forest came under attack because its magical protection had failed. He tasked me with retrieving the artifact that serves as anchor for our shield, but when I reached the temple, it was overrun with goborrins and... other creatures." The memory of the spiders sent a chill down his spine.

"The Elder would have been within his right to request soldiers from the garrison clear out the beasts in the temple," Lark said with such a haughty look on her face, Zaide had half a mind to throttle her, princess or not. She'd made every effort to sneak around the garrison's soldiers, knowingly depriving them of help.

"Yes," Zaide said slowly, "but as I am his apprentice, only I was authorized to touch the artifact. According to the Elder, Your Majesty, its remaining power has been drained. He felt it was of vital importance that you see the Vale Hymnflute."

The king lifted a hand to stroke Lark's fingers, a thoughtful look on his face. "If your Elder expects protection, I can offer nothing more than the soldiers who have already found their way to Kolmar. What more can the Elder wish of me?"

Zaide stared, uncertain.

Lark squirmed behind the throne, her haughtiness evaporating. "Father, in the wake of the eclipse, the books say—"

"Old tales by superstitious men," Sendassian barked. "The Elder turned to men and manmade weapons to defend his people. If magic could end this war, was destined to end this war, why would Kolmar fail? Why would magic have vanished from the royal line?"

Lark's face twisted as if she'd been struck. Tears welled in her eyes, but she squeezed them shut and drew a breath. "Forgive me, Father. I spoke out of turn." She withdrew her hand from his shoulder and curtsied. "I shall retire to the garden to collect myself."

"See that you do," the king replied. His sharp eyes turned back to Zaide and the soldiers and he lifted his chin. "If the Elder sends you to beg for protection, you may consider his request fulfilled. I will station more troops at the garrison and ensure the forest has proper defenses established, but I want no part in the Elder's archaic rituals."

Zaide watched Lark escape out the narrow hall to the side of the throne, an odd tightness in his throat. He made himself nod and bow. "Yes, Your Majesty. Thank you. Your graciousness in Kolmar's time of need is all we hope to receive."

Sendassian grunted and waved a hand to dismiss them. His steward stepped forward and motioned the group back the way they'd come.

Murk and Plain said nothing and showed less on their faces, but Raddan walked with his jaw clenched.

The noise of the great parlor enveloped them again. Zaide shifted his bag on his good shoulder and the Hymnflute dug into his back like an accusation. "What now?"

"Now?" Raddan made a small sound that was halfway between a laugh and a scoff. "We go back to Kolmar. There's nothing else to be done here, lad."

"We came all this way for nothing?"

"We came all this way for Kolmar," the medic said. "If you view every obstacle as a failure, you'll make no progress. We've done what the Elder asked and we've secured additional protection for your village. Whether or not we are soldiers, the war is out of our hands."

Zaide's shoulders sagged.

"I know you hoped for a greater adventure, but sometimes we must accept what life gives us," Raddan said. "We'll rest tonight. In the morning, we'll set out for the garrison."

"Yes, sir." Zaide tried to keep his disappointment to himself.

Raddan nodded. "We need to restock our supplies before we go anywhere."

"Come now, Leech," Plain put in, giving the lieutenant a stern frown. "Let the boy linger a minute. He probably won't ever come back to Amrochan. Why not let him wander a bit?"

A look of uncertainty crossed Raddan's face.

"Gets him out of our hair for a drink or two," Murk added in a murmur. "He's not likely to get into trouble, so long as he knows where he ought to be when all's said and done."

"The Elder made him our responsibility," Raddan argued.

Zaide didn't like the idea of being anyone's responsibility, but he tried to appear calm when he cleared his throat and spoke. "Actually, if it's all the same, sir, I'd appreciate a little time to ask questions here. In the castle." He gestured toward one of the guards near the front door. "If my father made it to Amrochan to become part of the king's army all those years ago, someone here has to know."

"See?" Plain nudged Raddan's arm. "It won't hurt to let him chat a bit."

From the way the lieutenant frowned, he didn't agree. Zaide tried to quash what little hope had tried to blossom, but before he had it smothered, Raddan sighed and waved a hand.

"All right, all right." The medic rubbed his forehead. His face was pinched with more weariness than the trip should have caused. "We'll be staying in the city's barracks tonight. Any of the guards can point you in that direction. Ask your questions, but don't leave palace grounds without an escort, understand?"

Zaide brought his boot heels together and stood straight. "Yes, sir."

"That's the spirit." Murk flashed him a grin, then turned to trudge for the door. Plain went right behind him, but Raddan lingered, his eyes thoughtful.

"I'll stay in the palace, sir," Zaide said. "I promise." Everything he needed had to be there. If it wasn't, he could always get permission to look elsewhere later.

The lieutenant nodded and went with his men. After he disappeared through the door, Zaide deflated. As eager as he was to gather information while he could, he didn't know where to begin, and it wasn't as if he didn't have responsibilities. With the set of pipes still nestled in his pack, he still carried the weight of the assignment the Elder had given him, made no lighter by his meeting with the king. Sendassian hadn't even wanted to see them. What that meant for Kolmar, Zaide didn't know.

Sighing, he glanced toward the guards beside the front door. A slow trickle of people moved past them, coming in to seek audience or retreating after they'd had it, and he doubted the guards would appreciate a distraction. Instead, Zaide scanned the room until he spotted a lone guard in front of a small arched doorway at the side of the room. No one went that direction, and the man looked bored. That one was perfect for questions.

"Excuse me," Zaide began as he approached, holding the strap of his satchel with both hands. "Lieutenant Raddan told me we were to stay in the barracks tonight. We're to return to Kolmar's garrison tomorrow. Could you point me toward the barracks?"

The guard inspected him, the corners of his mouth twitching with disapproval. "You don't look like one of the king's men."

"I'm not." Zaide shifted on his feet. Perhaps he should have introduced himself first. "I'm one of the Kolmari Elder's apprentices. The lieutenant went to gather supplies for our return trip. He told me I should stay in the palace."

For a moment, it didn't seem as if the guard believed him. Then his shoulders moved, an almost imperceptible shrug, and he stepped to one side. "Through the cloisters, right at the far end. That'll take you to the barracks. Whichever captain is on duty will see to you there."

Zaide's face brightened. "Thank you." He slipped past the guard, willing himself to walk with confidence. The captain would be a good place to begin asking after his father, too. He could ask Raddan for advice on what to do with the Hymnflute when he returned that evening.

The hallway emptied into a wide walkway lined by columns, an ornate stone balustrade between them. On the other side, a courtyard garden filled with lush greenery and delicate flowers opened to the sky. The soft melody of running water just reached his ears and he paused to listen. At that moment, a familiar girl in a flowing pink and white gown moved into his view.

Agitation raced up the back of Zaide's neck at the sight of her. He twitched, his feet eager to carry him closer, his anger ready on the tip of his tongue. Unwilling to let it loose, he sucked in a sharp breath and set his jaw.

Lark's eyes flicked his way and she grew still. A pair of guards flanked her. They followed her gaze, and both tightened their grip on their spears.

He knew he should walk away, seek the captain and ask after his father like he'd planned, but Zaide remained rooted in place and held her gaze.

One of the guards stepped toward him, but Lark raised a hand and he halted.

"Come here, boy," she called.

More than the hair on the back of his neck prickled with annoyance. Goosebumps rose on his arms until he had to fight back a shudder.

She planted her hands on her hips. "Well? What are you waiting for?"

Zaide swept a hand toward the balustrade before him.

"As if you can't climb a fence that's knee high? Come here!"

He scoffed and stepped over it, doing his best to avoid the tender plants on the other side. Both guards tilted their spears toward him as he crept through the plantings to reach the winding flagstone path.

Lark lifted her chin as he approached. "Stand down," she ordered the guards, her tone as regal as it was commanding.

Zaide eyed their spears as they obeyed.

She sniffed. "Leave us."

"But, Your Highness—" one of the guards began.

Lark wheeled to glower at him. "I gave you an order. This boy held audience with my father. He's the Kolmari Elder's apprentice. He's no threat."

Zaide bit back a retort before it could escape. Whether or not she was wrong, he didn't *want* the king's guards to think he was threatening. Instead, he put his head down and tried to look meek. It was the last thing he felt, but it seemed to work, for the guards eased back to give the two of them space. They retreated to the garden's entrance, but did not leave.

Seeming satisfied once they were out of earshot, Lark stepped forward. "Give it here."

He blinked. "What?"

"The Hymnflute! Give it here." She planted her hands on her hips, and that gesture alone made him bristle enough that he didn't want to cooperate.

Zaide mimicked her stance. "The Elder entrusted it to me. It's not leaving my hands."

"It's not *in* your hands, you dolt."

Exasperated, he rolled his eyes. "I didn't mean literally!"

She straightened and held out her hand. "I don't care. Let me see it. You owe me that much."

A refusal sprang to the tip of his tongue, but his gaze drifted to the guards by the entrance. If he didn't cooperate, what would they do? And if he did cooperate and she refused to give the Hymnflute back, what chance was there he could seize it without getting killed? She held her hand out farther. Zaide sighed and slid his bag off his shoulder. "You can look at it. But I have to take it back to Kolmar."

Lark raised a brow as he tried to pull it from his bag without jostling his injured shoulder. "What's wrong with you?"

"Let's just say the trip to Amrochan wasn't kind." He freed the pipes from his bag's strap when they tangled in it, then turned them for Lark to see. Princess Dasienna, he told himself, with a small mental kick for the casual way he still thought of her. She'd hidden her identity and given him a false name, but that gave him no right to think of her that way any longer.

She tilted her head and reached for the cluster of carved wooden leaves and flowers that hung from the instrument. They clinked together in her hand. "It's so strange," she murmured. "It doesn't look or feel magical. Now that it's outside the temple, it seems so ordinary."

"Maybe it is," Zaide said. "The Elder says the Hymnflute lost its power. That was why the shield that protected Kolmar fell. Why the goborrins got in."

"It doesn't make sense. The Hymnflute was exactly where it should have been. The magic that protected it there was still in effect, but the temple was full of monsters. What could cause such a thing?"

The thought of their enemy's symbol on the floor flashed through his head. "How much do you know about magic?"

Lark cast him a suspicious look and a guarded expression masked her face. "Why?"

"Because I don't know anything, despite being the Elder's apprentice. If someone sufficiently powerful had been there, could they have done something to sabotage the Hymnflute's power?"

She shook her head. "Not likely. It was old magic, set in place by my ancestors. It would take someone of equal power to corrupt it, and the only person who..." Her eyes glazed as she trailed off. Before he could ask what was wrong, she shook herself and stepped back, though she stared at the Hymnflute in his hands with a frown. "There's something I need to speak with you about."

Zaide drew the wooden pipes closer to his chest, unsure he trusted her not to grab them. "Go ahead."

"Not now," she said, casting a worried glance toward the guards. "In private."

His brows climbed.

She leaned close to touch the instrument in his hands again, and he was only half convinced it was an excuse to get close enough to whisper. "Meet me here in the garden, half an hour after the first change of the guard. It'll be empty. We can speak in peace then."

Unsure what else to do, Zaide nodded. Her fingers trailed over the Hymnflute one last time, her gaze longing. Then she withdrew, lifted her skirts and returned to her guards. Together, they departed the garden, leaving him to frown and puzzle over just what sort of trouble she planned to start.

CHAPTER THIRTEEN

RADDAN and the others joined Zaide in the barracks just in time for the evening meal. All three of the garrison soldiers carried bags that bulged with supplies, which made Zaide feel worse about his injured shoulder. It would be a heavy load even if spread between the four of them, but he could hardly manage his own belongings. He tried to focus on his food instead of the sacks, promising himself he would find a way to help once they were on the road.

"I'm sorry you weren't able to find more, lad," Raddan said between spoonfuls of stew. There was still enough bite in the spring air that the hearty meal had been well-received by all of them. "Then again, I suppose it has been some time."

Zaide made himself nod in agreement. As eager as he had been to ask questions, his impending meeting with Lark—with the princess, he corrected himself—had made itself too much of a distraction to pursue his investigation with any real fervor. What officers he'd been able to waylay had offered little. No one in the barracks seemed to have heard of any broken-born who fit Zaide's description of his father, but then again, that description was second-hand. He'd been too young to recall his father when the man left, and the faint shadow of a memory the man had left behind had been colored in by his mother instead.

"I might have more luck at the garrison. Maybe we can stop there before we return to Kolmar." Zaide assumed his father would have been to the garrison, at least, and as far as he knew, the commanding officers stationed there rarely changed. That anyone had been stationed there for sixteen years might have been a stretch, but it was all he had to hope for.

The lieutenant nodded. "It's probably best we do. And I'd be happy to ask around after you're back with the Elder and everything's settled. I don't get out often, but we do see soldiers on their way to the front lines. There's bound to be someone left in the army that knows what became of him."

"Thank you," Zaide murmured as he spooned another bite into his mouth.

Part of him wanted to ask Raddan's advice regarding the princess. The man seemed level-headed and friendly, without reason to lead him astray. Having him present might offer a boon; especially if the meeting went wrong. Having a trusted soldier present would spare his hide if any misunderstandings arose. But Lark's insistence they speak privately made him suspect bringing Raddan along would earn him her wrath. Knowing who she was, he wasn't certain he was willing to risk that any longer.

Instead of asking, Zaide put his head down and ate, and the rest of the evening passed quietly.

It was after midnight before a wave of guardsmen filtered into the barracks, signaling the shift change he was waiting for. The men settled without much noise or fuss, but more than one pair of eyes turned his way when he climbed out of bed.

"Latrine," he murmured as an excuse as he rubbed his eyes and shuffled for the door. He almost stopped at the doorway, thinking of the Hymnflute and how Lark had been so eager to see it, but he left it behind and moved on with only a brief hesitation. Taking an instrument on a trip to relieve himself was a good way to appear suspicious, and anyone who stopped him with questions would either figure out what he was up to, or cost him more precious sleep. Already, his eyes burned and his muscles ached, promising a miserable trip the following day.

He crept across the practice yard, wary, but the few guards who traversed the grounds on the way to their posts or during the course of their patrols paid him no mind. Perhaps he wasn't threatening, bare-footed and disheveled, with no weapons at hand. He was almost to the cloistered hall he knew led to the garden before a man in armor raised a hand to signal him to halt.

"Where are you headed?" the man asked, his eyes skimming Zaide's rumpled clothes.

"Trouble sleeping, sir." Zaide mustered a sheepish smile with little effort. He felt silly, sneaking through the palace in yesterday's wrinkled clothes. "This is my first time away from Kolmar. I thought sitting in the garden for a while might help. Being among the plants, you know."

The guard grunted softly. Zaide wasn't sure whether it was a sound of understanding or disapproval.

Maybe he wasn't convinced. Zaide allowed his brow to furrow. "This is the way to the garden, isn't it? I thought I saw it when I came through here earlier."

"Close," the man said, though he pointed to another doorway a short distance from where they stood. "But there's no way past the rail through this hall. Take that one. Three doorways down, there's one that lets into the garden."

"Oh. Thank you." Zaide offered a nervous grin, then turned to follow the guard's directions before the man could ask any more questions. He wasn't positive sharing his destination had been wise, but disclosing his intentions did seem the best way to avoid trouble. Behind him, the guard's shadow moved into the doorway. It lingered there until Zaide opened the specified door and slipped into the garden. It was still a few minutes early for his meeting with Lark, but if he made himself present and inoffensive, perhaps the guards who would inevitably patrol the cloisters wouldn't pay him any mind.

The soft sound of the fountain was soothing in the peace of the night. The courtyard was sheltered from wind, so the leaves on the shrubs and few small ornamental trees were still. He brushed a hand over them as he passed, savoring the whisper of the leaves. It had not been his intention to seek solace there, but he found it anyway. There was a small space where the garden curved and the shrubs created a cozy nook, sheltered by plants on three sides. It would have been the perfect place for a bench or tiny table, but there was only grass. He stole into the quiet space anyway and lowered himself to the ground.

Cool fragrances from the early flowers on bushes filled his nostrils when he breathed. His eyelids grew heavy and he rested his hands on his knees. There had been more truth in his statement to the guard than he'd realized. The garden was calming, soothing, and he had little doubt he would fall asleep there if he didn't remain sitting upright.

That was a peace the Kolmari didn't have, he reminded himself. Sheltered by the towering walls of the imposing palace, there was little chance of danger. Gadranus himself had never managed to breach Amrochan's defenses, if the Elder's books were to be believed. Looking up at the gray stone that surrounded him, Zaide had little doubt they were right.

Kolmar had no such defenses, and when the time came, the forest would be the first to fall.

He didn't like to think of the war's expansion as inevitable, but it had already consumed his homeland. Sendassian's forces worked hard to repel the enemy's armies, and to a limited extent, they'd been successful. Pockets of enemies sometimes breached border defenses, but it had never been so great a threat as the group that had tried to lay siege to Kolmar—or what had swarmed the temple.

Thinking they'd cleared the forest of goborrins would have

been foolish. They'd won this time, but the beasts would be back, and probably in greater numbers than before.

Across the garden, quiet footsteps padded down the flagstone path. Zaide tore his eyes from the towers overhead. He almost expected the guard who had directed him, but instead, it was Lark.

Why wouldn't it be? He almost snorted. She was the one who had ordered him to meet her in the garden. Her blue eyes were hard and sharp when she met his gaze, like sapphires cut to dangerous facets.

She pressed a finger to her lips.

Zaide straightened where he sat, though he remained cross-legged on the ground with his hands on his knees. Lark crept forward and knelt before him. Her delicate dress was gone, replaced with the same simple travel garb she'd worn when he'd found her in the forest. She looked more like herself in it, he decided; as recognizable as she was as Princess Dasienna, he couldn't shake the notion that wasn't who she *wished* to be.

"You didn't bring the flute?" she asked in a whisper.

He shook his head. "I'm supposed to be sleeping in the barracks. There were guards all around me. I didn't want to look suspicious."

Lark nodded in grudging acceptance. "I wasn't sure you would come, to be honest."

"I wasn't under the impression I had a choice."

A smile twisted her lips, but it was grim, cold. "I need your help."

Zaide studied her face and waited for her to continue. Such an admission seemed like it should have been made grudgingly. Instead, she looked resolute.

"I know my father disagrees with me." She curled her hands to fists against the tops of her thighs. "I've tried to convince him, but he won't listen. He insists might will win this war, not magic. But I've been to Jadora. I've been to the library. I've read what the scholars have to say."

"You really believe the eclipse heralds the death of a king?"

She nodded. "And by the Maker's grace, it won't be my father's."

He nodded back.

For a moment, she was quiet. Then her face twisted, the words on her tongue evidently difficult to share. "Listen, I know you have reasons not to trust me. To not want to help me. But if you're the Kolmari Elder's apprentice, you know what our enemy is capable of."

"I do," he agreed softly. "But the Elder also said the king would be able to restore power to the Vale Hymnflute. It sounds like he doesn't even believe that power exists."

"Not the king," she murmured. "It was supposed to be me."

Zaide's brow furrowed.

She sank back on the grass and drew her knees up before her to hug them to her chest. "Magic flowed on my mother's side. The royal line has always married into power. It's supposed to manifest in its children. But it... it never manifested in me."

"You mentioned that. In the temple." He refrained from mentioning how angry it had made him. Somehow, it didn't seem like that would help.

"I did. I'm the one who's supposed to be able to restore the Vale magic, and restore power to the Hymnflute, which serves as an anchor to its protective barrier. But I don't know how. All I know is that if the Hymnflute has lost its power, we must turn to the other artifacts."

Zaide started to speak, then grew quiet as the rattle of armor reached his ears. He shrank back into the shrubbery and blinked in surprise when Lark moved close to nestle in beside him. Unwilling to be seen touching the princess, he retreated a little farther.

A guard ambled down the cloistered hall and disappeared without spotting them.

"There are two more artifacts," Lark whispered in a rush. "According to the scholars in Jadora, the three can be used together to defeat Gadranus. You have the Hymnflute. Now we just need two more."

"We?" Zaide asked, incredulous.

"My father would never allow me to seek the artifacts. I can't take any of his men with me. But you know how to fight, and you're the one who was given the Hymnflute. You have to come with me to Jadora."

Zaide shook his head, unsure he'd heard her right.

"You have to!" Lark pleaded, mistaking the gesture for refusal. "I don't have anyone else I can turn to, and the fate of Amroch and all its people hangs in the balance. The next artifact on the list is a dagger. It's somewhere in the desert, and the librarians in Jadora will know where. While we're there, we can find the location of the last artifact. You don't have to stay with me. Just take me to Jadora, get me to the library, and give me time to hire mercenaries once I'm there."

"This is a stupid plan," Zaide said.

Her face crumpled into a scowl. "The Elder ordered you to restore power to the Hymnflute and protect Kolmar, didn't he?"

His eyes narrowed.

"There's a chance the librarians might also be able to help me learn to access the magic I'm supposed to have. If you take me there, I might be able to help you. I could restore its magic, then you can go home. A trade. Your help for mine."

A tempting offer. "But you don't have any way to prove this will actually help."

Lark huffed. "What will convince you? What do I have to do?"

"Get your father's blessing for this trip. Ask to take my lieutenant and his men. Raddan, Murk, and Plain." That he didn't know the real names of the latter two was a hindrance, he decided.

Her face fell. "He'll never approve."

"Then I guess I can't go with you."

She drew herself up and stared down at him, her expression regal. "And what if I order you to take me? Would you refuse?"

Zaide hesitated. There was no good way to answer. If he refused, he could be at her mercy, punished however she saw fit; she was royalty, after all, heir to Sendassian's throne and the future ruler of Amroch. But assisting her was sure to anger her father, and he dared not think what sort of punishment might come from that.

"You can't tell me no," Lark said, reading his hesitance.

"Nothing good will come of it if I do," he agreed.

Her eyes brightened. "So you'll take me?"

"Nothing good will come of it if I do," he repeated, a hint of lament coloring his words.

Lark pushed herself back. "I know you're to leave in the morning. I'll find you on the road after you depart and we'll make for Jadora then."

The declaration put a lump of dread in the pit of his stomach. "Raddan won't go along with this."

"Then you'd better figure out how to escape your lieutenant, too." She thrust herself up from the ground and hurried for the garden door before he could protest.

Zaide scrubbed a hand through his white hair and sank to the grass, flat on his back. He didn't dare groan, lest a stray guard hear him. The last thing he wanted was for a guard to catch the princess as she escaped the garden in which he was hiding. Explaining the situation to Raddan would be hard enough.

CHAPTER FOURTEEN

MURK WAS full of complaints when the expedition began the next morning. As Zaide anticipated, Raddan insisted he should carry nothing but his own bag until his shoulder was healed, and that meant the others in the group were left to lug their supplies along on their own.

"Oh, quit bellyaching," Plain chided as he tightened the straps on his own pack and put it on. "You'd think a man your size would be happy to know you'll have enough to eat. Aren't you always fussing that your muscles will waste on garrison rations?"

"I'll need double rations to maintain all the muscle I'll need to carry all this," Murk said.

Raddan merely rolled his eyes.

The lieutenant had been sound asleep by the time Zaide had returned from the garden, and though he'd tried to seek sleep of his own, it hadn't come easily. The scant few hours of rest Zaide managed to snag left him aching with exhaustion, but the time he'd lain awake gave him an opportunity to mull over what he was to do.

He'd considered asking Raddan's advice the moment the sun rose, but the barracks were not a place he thought it wise to discuss secret meetings with princesses. Instead, he'd decided to begin the conversation once they were outside Amrochan's walls, where the risk of being overheard would disappear.

"I've heard King Sendassian means to deploy Kolmar's reinforcements today," Raddan said as he checked his sword belt. "I want to reach the garrison before them, so we'd best not dally. The king's men are not slow."

"Aren't you the king's men?" Zaide asked.

"When it's convenient for him," the lieutenant said, so glumly that Zaide made a note to investigate the subject more once they were on the road.

Whether that road would be the one to Kolmar or the one to Jadora, Zaide admittedly didn't know.

They departed the palace with little notice, halted only by the guards at the main doors. Raddan explained their destination and the guards waved them on. Before long, the palace shrank behind them, and Zaide found himself wishing they could stay in the city just one more day.

Amrochan buzzed with life, even early in the morning, and the nooks and crannies between storefronts and houses begged to be explored. Zaide searched them with his eyes only as they worked their way to the city gates and finally slipped into the sparsely inhabited farmland beyond.

"No safety outside the walls," Plain noted when he caught the way Zaide studied their surroundings. "In another time, most cities grew in two parts. The inner part was where the well-to-do lived, and the working folk lived outside the gates."

"No one out here but farmers, now," Murk added. "And even some of them live inside and only come out to tend the fields."

Zaide had occasionally wondered what the cities in the Shattered Lands looked like—or what they had looked like, before they fell. He'd come across names and descriptions of architecture, but layout had never been discussed. Perhaps they'd been like the cities Plain described. Maybe that was part of why they fell.

"Speaking of safety," Zaide said slowly, uncertain how to begin. "Raddan, there's something... I wasn't sure..." Blast it all, why was it so hard to get the words off his tongue?

The lieutenant turned his head. "What's got you flustered, boy?"

"Princess Dasienna," he blurted.

Plain covered his mouth to stifle a wheeze.

Raddan's shoulders slumped and his face contorted with exasperation. He slowed, but didn't stop. "Listen, boy—"

"I don't mean like that," Zaide added hastily. "She sought me in the middle of the night to demand I escort her to Jadora. I told her I wouldn't take her unless her father approved the trip."

This time, Raddan raised a hand in signal for everyone to halt. He turned to face Zaide fully, a furrow between his brows. "Why would the princess ask you to take her to Jadora? She has an entire legion at her beck and call, and you're..."

"Unproven," Murk added, surprisingly diplomatically.

Zaide shot him a glare. "I've more than proven myself, I don't need to impress you. She wants me to go because she said she needs some kind of artifacts. The Vale Hymnflute the Elder gave me is one of them. She said she has to return to the library in Jadora to learn where the others can be found."

Whatever amusement Plain had felt at his outburst, it faded now, replaced with a hint of worry. "Artifacts?" He glanced to the other men.

Raddan raised a finger. "Did she tell you what these artifacts were?"

"She said the second one is a dagger," Zaide said.

All three of the garrison soldiers exchanged concerned looks.

"What happened when you refused to take her?" Raddan asked, his face as grave as it had been when they'd pulled Zaide from the river.

"She ordered me to take her. She said she'd seek me on the road."

The lieutenant nodded, though it was less acceptance and

more a motion of understanding. "We need to speak with the Elder about this."

Zaide's mouth worked a moment. "Not the king?" he managed at last.

"Everyone in the army has heard stories about the princess," Raddan said. He rested a hand on Zaide's uninjured shoulder and looked him in the eye. "If she's set her mind on something, then only the Maker can keep her from it. If she finds us, we'll deal with it then. Otherwise, our job is getting you back to Kolmar, and we can take all this up with the Elder when we get there."

Seeing he had no room to argue, Zaide nodded and tucked in his chin. Travel resumed at the same pace, though the easy air that had passed between the soldiers was gone now, replaced with a subtle sense of trepidation.

Zaide scanned the landscape around them as they walked, half expecting to see Lark coming toward them at any minute. But they traveled until midday without event, halted for a simple meal, then continued through until dusk.

"We'll keep going for a time," Raddan said as the last light of the sun faded from the sky. "That's one advantage we'll have over the reinforcements headed to the garrison. They'll travel sunup to sundown. If we push a little farther each night, we'll get there with a few hours to tend business before we have to sort them out."

Zaide didn't see how it was their responsibility to sort anything, but he kept his mouth shut. Weariness tugged at him, soured his mood and made him uncharacteristically sullen. He rolled his shoulders and breathed deep as he tried to shrug it off.

"Hang in there, lad," Plain said. "You've done well for someone who's not used to all the marching."

"And the battles, and the injuries," Murk added.

The vote of confidence should have been reassuring, but Zaide couldn't bring himself to smile. Instead, he let his eyes wander. "There are more marsh-wisps out than there were before," he noted, hoping for a change of subject.

"Aye," Raddan agreed. "A bad sign."

"How so?"

Murk made a low sound in his throat. "They say that evil becomes more plentiful when the enemy's power grows."

Zaide glanced toward the lights that glowed above the swampy water. They hardly seemed threatening enough to be considered evil, but he knew enough to trust seasoned soldiers when they recommended steering clear of the tiny incandescent flickers.

"Really, lad, I thought you'd know that. What sort of things does the Elder have you studying all day?" Raddan watched the wisps for a time, himself, then increased his pace. The shift was subtle, but telling. He expected trouble.

"The Elder's library is filled with history, but it's hard to say how much of it is true." Zaide found most wasn't; history was rife with exaggerations and blended with myth.

"An unbeliever, are you?" Plain chuckled. "Wouldn't have expected that from a broken-born."

For some reason, that statement made Zaide bristle. "I'm Kolmari. I wasn't born there, but it's home."

"Of course you are. Settle." Raddan made a patting motion. "He doesn't mean any harm. He's just surprised. As I am. Know that very little of what's written of this eternal war is untrue."

"No country would fight the same enemy for a thousand years," Zaide argued.

"You're right. It's probably been longer than that. The evil we face has many names, though, boy. Gadranus is just the name it's borne for the past little while."

A thousand years was hardly a little while, but Zaide chose not to argue. It wouldn't prove fruitful, and he wasn't in the right mindset for it, either.

Many volumes in the Elder's library bore the same claim: Gadranus was a spirit of evil, born as a man and reincarnated a dozen times over. The ceaseless war had pushed against Amroch for ages, inching closer, destroying countries and forcing more refugees toward the coast, slowing only in the periods after their enemy was slain and his forces waited for him to be born again.

To Zaide, the claim was absurd. Some books—few, but enough to let him know he wasn't alone in the belief—claimed the name Gadranus was more of a title, passed to each leader who rose to renew the war.

Silly as he thought the old tales were, he couldn't fault the soldiers in the army for clinging to them. When an opponent was as relentless as Gadranus seemed to be, it had to feel like there were mystical forces at work.

"Oi, what's there?" Plain put a hand to his brow as if it would aid his vision, some force of habit gained through squinting past the sun. He peered out into the dark, his mouth drawn tight.

Raddan's hand went to his sword even before he turned to search for whatever it was the soldier saw. Despite himself, Zaide mirrored the action.

Across the marsh, glittering lights swirled in a frenzy and flashed in myriad colors. Their number grew as he watched. More marsh-wisps swept across the water to join the group, their light pulsing in a rhythm Zaide almost thought was angry.

"Maker's mercy," Raddan breathed. He dropped his bags to the dusty road, unsheathed his blade, and plunged into the knee-deep waters of the marsh.

Plain was first to follow, while Murk struggled to disentangle himself from the straps of his heavy bags. Colorful oaths sprang from the man's lips and were drowned beneath the raucous splashing as Zaide abandoned his things and went after the lieutenant.

Across the marsh, a shadow fell between the wisps. Zaide's heart leaped into his throat and he charged ahead.

"Whoa, boy!" Plain shouted, but he wasn't about to stop.

Lark had made it clear she meant to follow him. Now, out in

the swamp, a slight person ducked against the water and covered their head as the wisps sped closer.

Without knowing how to fight them, Zaide darted in and struck at one of the wisps. It exploded in a gout of flame the moment his blade touched it, hot enough to make his eyes water, but not close enough to burn.

Another wisp nearby flashed red. He spun to plunge his sword into it, tip first. Like the other, it burst. A small plume of smoke retreated from the strike, almost too faint to see in the dark.

"He's got it," Raddan called, a note of surprise in his voice.

The lights weren't hard to combat. A single strike was all it took to extinguish them, but as Zaide pushed closer to the mud-covered figure who flailed in the water, the number of wisps grew.

One darted past his ear, scorchingly hot without ever brushing his skin. He hissed and spun to whip his sword through it. More than one of the marsh-wisps burst against that single swipe and he squinted against the heat.

"More coming!" Murk roared.

Zaide's head snapped up and his heart plummeted. Hundreds more lights surged toward them across the water.

"Back to the road!" Raddan batted away a pair of flames before they came within arm's reach. The wisps swirled, agitated, and Zaide darted into the opening. The muddy girl reached for him. He grabbed her hand and hauled her to her feet.

"Run!" he gasped as he hitched her arm over his shoulders and tried to follow his own advice. Raddan and Plain posted themselves behind the two of them, but they hurried along backwards, swiping wisps out of the air.

Murk caught the girl's other arm and hurried them both along. "Go, go!"

"Zaide," the girl gasped.

"Keep going." He didn't want to hush her, but they didn't

have breath to spare for conversation. Mud sucked at their feet and from the sound of the splashes at their backs, Plain and Raddan were falling behind.

A blinding light flashed past Zaide's head. He winced. That had been too close; his cheek stung in the wake of its heat.

"Get the bags!" Murk ordered as they reached the edge of the road. The three of them scrambled up the bank and Zaide skidded to a halt beside the supply bags. His injured shoulder pulled and he felt a pop and the blossom of new heat, but he didn't have time to worry about torn scabs. He scooped the straps of his bags and half of Raddan's onto his arms. The girl grabbed more than her share, Murk took the rest, and together they lit into a run.

"Down the lane, into the trees! They won't follow under the canopy!" Raddan called from somewhere behind them.

Zaide's chest already burned and the warm, itching trickle that spilled down his back promised nothing good for his shoulder, but he didn't dare stop.

Wisps billowed all around them, swirling by like embers in the wind. The grove was close enough for Zaide to smell the leaves. He willed his aching legs to hold out just a little longer.

Murk pulled ahead, and then the three of them plunged into the shadow of the trees. Something snared Zaide's foot and he tumbled to the earth with a startled cry. When he came to a halt, he was looking back the other way.

The swarm of wisps splashed against the edge of the grove like a bucket of water pitched against a window. Raddan burst through the glowing wall and collapsed to the ground. Plain followed, beating a hand against his sleeve as if to extinguish a flame.

Zaide's throat and chest ached so he could hardly breathe. He sank back against the lumpy bags he somehow hadn't lost, gasping until the tightness in his chest and the stitch in his side subsided, replaced with a new awareness of a wrenched ankle and the throbbing pain in his shoulder.

"Everyone alive?" Murk asked between ragged breaths.

A low groan answered, and Zaide slipped off the bags so he could hurry to their rescued companion. "Are you all right?" he asked, daring to touch her arm.

She rested her hand atop his and lifted her head.

Zaide's heart skipped a beat.

It wasn't Lark.

CHAPTER FIFTEEN

"Resia?" Zaide choked. He cradled her face in his hands and forced her to look at him. "What are you doing here?"

She touched his arm and closed her eyes, still panting too hard to answer. Her warm brown skin was so spattered with mud, he almost didn't recognize her.

"Friend of yours?" Raddan asked. He sat on the ground, rubbing the back of his neck.

"My sister." Zaide swiped a strand of sopping hair away from her eyes before he glanced back to the lieutenant. Beyond the edge of the trees, the marsh-wisps still milled and swirled. "Are we safe?"

"From the wisps, yes. But there are far more dangerous things in the trees."

Comforting. Zaide exhaled hard and turned back to Resia. "Can you speak?"

She swallowed hard and nodded. A smile of relief touched her lips, but she still gripped his arms as if she feared being let go. "Yes."

"What are you doing out here?" He inspected her to the best of his ability, given the feeble moonlight that filtered through the trees, hoping to see some answer to the question he'd already asked and hadn't gotten a response for.

Resia caught his hands and gave them a squeeze. "Looking for you. The Elder said it couldn't wait."

A pang of dread sparked an ache in his chest. "What couldn't wait?"

She swallowed hard and her fingers trembled, despite how hard she held on to him. "The garrison has fallen. Goborrins have taken it over."

"What?" Raddan roared, thrusting himself to his feet.

"The soldiers are all in Kolmar, defending the village," Resia continued, as if she hadn't heard. "Aren wanted to come after you, but the Elder said every soldier was needed and that my magic would keep me safe in the forest. It did, but then I stumbled out into that marsh—"

Raddan marched toward them with such intent in his step that Resia flinched when he reached for her. But his hand was gentle when he laid it on her shoulder, and he knelt at her side. "Were you injured?"

She shook her head.

"How could the garrison have fallen?" Murk asked, his voice level and strong in spite of how hard they'd run.

"I don't know," Resia said. "The garrison's commander was with the Elder when I left, but the Elder told me I had to hurry. I didn't wait to hear what he said."

Zaide glanced up and met the lieutenant's eyes with a frown. "Should we continue to the garrison as planned, or should we wait for the reinforcements?"

From the pinched look the older man's face took, there was no good answer.

Resia stiffened. "Oh, the Hymnflute! Do you have it? Did the king see its power was restored?"

"The king doesn't believe it had any power to begin with," Zaide said. "It's no more useful now than it was when I left."

Her shoulders sagged.

Zaide didn't know what to say. He hardly knew what he felt about the matter. He'd spent most of his life watching magic be spun, yet now that he reflected on the sullen note his thoughts had carried all afternoon, the incongruence of his own beliefs was enough to put a splitting headache right behind his eyes. He rubbed them with his fingertips and sank backwards to sit on the grass.

The possibility the Vale Hymnflute wasn't magical had never crossed his mind. He'd seen it floating in the temple, had seen the Elder's magic at work so many times that he couldn't fathom a world where magic didn't exist and magical artifacts weren't a simple fact of life. But it was possible to have one without the other. If their enemy was an ordinary man, it was possible the instrument in his bag was an ordinary set of wooden pipes, left in the temple as some part of a ritual.

Sendassian had called it superstitious. The Elder believed the Hymnflute's power could change the tide of war. Zaide didn't know who was right.

"We'll get back on the road," Raddan said, changing the subject before anything else could be said. "We'll cut through the woods at an angle so the road is visible the whole time. Once we're sure the marsh-wisps aren't following us, we'll take to the road and set up camp at the fork where the trade route to Tinith begins."

Resia's eyes flicked toward the wisps still swirling beyond the trees. "Why don't we just stay in the woods?"

"Because we'd be staying a lot longer than I think you intend, miss," Plain said as he scooped a pair of bags from the heap they'd managed to lug along.

She blinked at him.

"He means we'll die," Murk added gracelessly.

Raddan glared at them both. "Hush. Everyone, get up and get your things. We're moving."

Zaide pushed himself to his feet with a grimace. His wet clothing clung uncomfortably, but it stuck worse at his shoulder.

He extended his good hand to Resia and helped her rise. At least with her nearby, he had a chance at proper healing. Raddan's ministrations were appreciated, but they paled in comparison to what magic could do. He tried not to sigh, realizing he'd have to sort out his thoughts about magic and prophecies once everything calmed down.

"What about the other guest we're expecting?" Zaide asked, turning his thoughts back to the ordeal at hand as he faced the lieutenant. "I thought Resia was her, at first."

"So did I," Raddan said, squinting at her muddy face. "Not sure why. She resembles Dasienna about as much as an acorn resembles a daisy."

The comparison put a wrinkle in Resia's forehead. Zaide pushed one of the lighter bags into her arms before she could say anything.

"Did you lose anything important in the marsh?" he asked.

"Just food for the trip," Resia said as she slung the bag over her shoulder and wiggled to get it settled. "I left too fast to take anything else."

Raddan grunted. "When the reinforcements destined for the garrison catch up to us, we're going to have to pick someone to return to the king. One batch of reinforcements won't be enough to retake the garrison." He started off and motioned for everyone else to follow.

Plain and Murk adjusted their bags and went right after him. Zaide directed Resia ahead, casting one last glance toward the marsh-wisps as they left the tiny flames behind.

His ankle protested the walk and he found himself limping after only a few steps. It didn't take long for him to fall behind.

Resia looked for him over her shoulder. Her brows rose when she saw his gait. "You're hurt? Let me see."

The lieutenant stopped.

Murk grumbled something about unproven soldiers and trudged on ahead.

"We don't have time to waste," Raddan said.

Resia planted one small hand on Zaide's shoulder and pushed him down, not seeming to care that he was taller than her. He sat obediently and held out his leg. She wiggled his boot off and pulled down his sock to touch his ankle. Immediately, a cool, soothing sense of comfort washed over him, easing the pain in his twisted ankle and shoulder at the same time.

It seemed she sensed the injury in his shoulder, because she made a soft sound of displeasure and rose to her knees to reach for it. "What did you do?"

"I'll tell you all about it on the road." Zaide grunted as she probed the injury. As badly as he'd scraped it, it was the deep bruising that hurt the most, and the joint ached after days of reduced use.

"Well, I imagine this looks worse than it is," Resia sighed. She pressed a hand to the front of his shoulder and closed her eyes. The same flood of relief flowed into him as she worked to mend the injury.

He gripped her wrist as she worked. "Thank you," he murmured.

Raddan shifted uneasily until they finished and stood.

"Sorry," Zaide said, though he wasn't certain he ought to apologize for receiving the attention of a medic.

The lieutenant nodded, but set a brisker pace when walking resumed. "Walk with me, girl," he ordered. "I want to know everything that happened before you left."

Resia ducked her head and hurried to join him, leaving Zaide to take up the rear on his own. The conversation they held was quiet, but not so low that it didn't reach his ears, and Zaide found himself staring at the ground as they walked.

Had the army of goborrins that descended on the garrison come as revenge for what occurred in the temple? Or had it been a more calculated attack, planned like the strike against Kolmar?

Why had they struck Kolmar? Zaide still couldn't figure that out. The village was far enough away from the temple that the goborrins could have gone unnoticed for some time. Instead, they'd sought the village specifically to attack it—and the Elder had most likely planned and prepared for the assault. He worked that thought over in his head. He could ask Resia about it once they settled for the night, but he doubted they'd have a chance to speak before then.

"I think we've outpaced them," Plain called back from somewhere ahead. It was hard to make him out in the shadow of the forest at night. All of them were caked in mud and crusted with the dust that clung to their wet clothing and then dried. A chance to settle in camp and change into other clothing was welcome, but from the hard pace Raddan set, Zaide doubted they'd stop any time soon.

"Back on the road," the lieutenant ordered.

They all turned to emerge onto the dusty, hard-packed road. They'd traveled several miles, and when Zaide looked back, there was no sign of the wisps behind them.

Murk went ahead on the road, examining the ground. When it seemed he didn't find anything, he went the other direction and scouted a short distance from where they stood. "Nothing amiss," he reported when he came back.

"Did you expect to see something?" Zaide didn't know how he might, considering how compacted the earth was beneath his boots.

"Everything leaves tracks," the soldier replied. "Through dust, through grass, it doesn't matter. The only way they wouldn't is if they knew how to fly, and fortunately, goborrins don't do that."

"But marsh-wisps do," Resia said.

Plain made a small noise of disagreement. "It's more like floating, really."

"Floating, flying, what does it matter? They can sneak up on you, either way." Raddan flicked his fingers in a gesture for the two soldiers to take the lead again. Plain shrugged and did as the officer bade him.

Zaide walked a little faster to catch up with the lieutenant and Resia. "Earlier, you said there were things in the trees. Is it the trees that keep the marsh-wisps away, or whatever's in there?"

Raddan scrubbed a hand through his dark hair. "A bit of both, I think. The wisps can set fire to the trees, which makes the things that live here angry. Everything's afraid of something, lad."

"What's out there?" Zaide wasn't sure he wanted to know, but it seemed wiser to be ready.

"Spiders. Big ones, the likes of which you've never seen."

Zaide couldn't help a laugh. The lieutenant raised a brow at him, and he ducked his head and forced himself to be solemn.

"I think I can deal with spiders," he said.

Raddan snorted. "Don't be so sure. Just because you're from the forest, that doesn't mean you've seen what I've seen."

A hint of a smile tugged at the corners of Zaide's mouth, and he allowed himself that small expression. "Trust me, I've seen spiders."

The lieutenant grunted, but said no more.

"There's a wider space ahead," Murk called back to the group. "Would make for a good camp."

From the way the corners of Raddan's eyes pinched, Zaide could tell he didn't want to halt, yet knew they needed rest.

Zaide inched closer to Resia. "How long do you think you can keep walking?" he asked, voice low, though he was sure the lieutenant heard him.

"I'll do my best to go as long as I have to," she replied.

Raddan nodded his thanks. "Keep going."

From the way Murk shrugged and pushed on into the darkness, he didn't care one way or another. Zaide doubted they would hold out for long. They all dragged after the excitement in the marsh, but he suspected he was more tired than all three of the garrison men. He'd hardly slept, after all.

And there was still no sign of Lark.

"Lieutenant, what if she tries to follow us and runs into those wisps?" he asked.

Raddan squinted at him over his shoulder. "Who?"

"Lark. Dasienna," Zaide corrected himself.

Resia's eyebrows shot up at the nickname.

"Well, we'd best hope she doesn't," was all Raddan had to offer.

Zaide sighed.

"Why would the princess follow you?" Resia asked in a whisper.

"It's a long story. I'll explain as much as I can when we stop to rest." Assuming he could stay awake long enough to relay the tale, that was. The farther they went, the more he wondered if it was possible to fall asleep standing up.

She gave him a puzzled frown but kept her thoughts to herself.

The road ahead was blessedly clear, and when Raddan finally called a halt, they were quick to eat and quicker to fall asleep. Even the bare ground was a blessing after a day on their feet, and Zaide was loath to rise when Resia gently shook him awake at dawn.

"My watch?" he asked groggily.

"Watch is over. We're back on the road." She patted his shoulder in sympathy, and he marveled at how much better it felt after her healing and a few hours of dreamless sleep.

They gathered their bags and resumed travel at a more leisurely pace, though Zaide expected they still made faster headway than the reinforcements that had to be marching the same road somewhere behind them. Now and then, Resia asked questions about their expedition and all that had transpired, and he did his best to answer.

"How many do you think are coming?" Resia asked when he mentioned the men Sendassian had already promised to send.

"I don't know. I just hope it's enough to retake the garrison."

"Do you think Raddan believes there are enough of them?"

She lowered her voice when she spoke, as if she relayed conspiratorial information.

Zaide considered that for a moment before he shook his head. "I don't know that, either. All I know is he thinks it's best if we keep moving forward ahead of them. I won't pretend to know why, but I'll admit he has a lot more experience than me. There has to be a strategic reason."

"Maybe," she murmured.

They pushed hard and made better time than they had on their way to Amrochan. Zaide described the city to Resia the next time they made camp, and the dozen questions she asked about fashion and architecture made him regret not staying longer.

Shortly past noon on the following day, Murk scouted ahead and returned not ten minutes later. "Fork's just ahead," he announced.

"Good," Raddan said, though he sighed. "Time to make the tough decisions."

Zaide opened his mouth to ask what he meant when they crested a hill and the fork came into view.

In the center of the road, right where the path split, stood Lark.

"About time," she called.

CHAPTER SIXTEEN

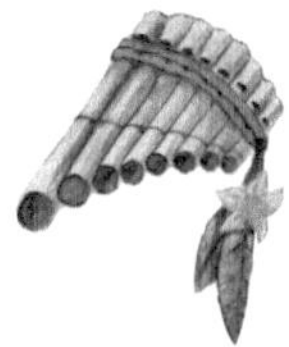

"I HAD a feeling you'd be here," Raddan shouted down the slope. He led the way toward where Lark waited, his stride easy and his pace more relaxed than it had been the whole rest of the expedition.

Zaide waited at the top of the hill and drew a breath. Resia gripped his arm, offering silent support. He'd managed to explain his meeting with the princess in the temple and her demand that he escort her to Jadora while they walked, though from the way Resia had smirked through most of the story, she found it more amusing than troubling.

Troubled was certainly all Zaide felt now.

Plain and Murk ambled toward the fork in the road to join the lieutenant, and all three men made themselves comfortable on the ground.

"Looks like we're stopping here," Resia said. She tugged Zaide toward the others.

He dug in his heels. "How did she get here before us?" If she wanted an escort, it would have made more sense for her travel to be difficult. "How did she get past the marsh-wisps?"

"Easy," Raddan said. "She left before us."

Zaide hadn't realized he'd spoken loud enough for the lieutenant to hear. Grudgingly, he let Resia draw him along, though she let go of him when they neared the others.

She spread her dusty skirt as she curtsied. "It's an honor to meet you, Princess Dasienna."

Lark crossed her arms. "Who's this?"

"My name is Resia. I'm the chief apprentice of Kolmar's Elder, set to replace him at the end of his days." She curtsied again, then swept her brown hair back behind one delicately pointed ear. "I was sent to carry news of the garrison just outside Kolmar to Amrochan, but I was intercepted by my brother." She opened a palm toward Zaide.

Lark didn't seem impressed. "You don't look broken-born to me."

"Resia's family took me in as a child," Zaide said, though he didn't know why. He didn't feel particularly charitable toward the princess. She hadn't exactly been forthcoming with him. Why should she get that sort of respect?

"I didn't reach Amrochan," Resia continued, undeterred by the princess's attitude. "But Lieutenant Raddan said we would camp here at the fork until the reinforcements your father has sent arrive. Someone will return to the capital with news from Kolmar after the officers have time to speak."

For a moment, a light of uncertainty glittered in Lark's eyes. Then she tamped it down and planted a hand on her hip. "I'm not staying here long enough for them to arrive. You'll have to forgive me, Elder-in-training, but I'm going to have to borrow your escort."

"Or at least part of it," Resia said with a secretive smile.

Zaide gave her a dirty look.

"Hm," Lark said. "So you got the response you wanted?"

Resia shook her head. "Not really. The lieutenant said we'd get reinforcements, which will help, but I'd hoped to have better news about the Hymnflute."

Though Zaide expected Lark to snap at the mention of the instrument, she appeared intrigued, instead.

"You believe in its power?" Lark asked.

A curious look drifted across Resia's face. "Of course. Why wouldn't I? The role of Kolmar's Elder has always been to ensure the Hymnflute's protection remained over the forest. I'd hoped we could use it to drive the goborrins back out of the garrison, but I guess we aren't that lucky."

"No," Lark said slowly.

Zaide would have argued everything they'd experienced was the exact opposite of luck.

Raddan sighed and motioned toward the spot he occupied on the ground in the middle of the road. "All right, everyone. Sit down. Time for us to make some hard decisions."

Resia sank to the ground carefully, spreading her skirts around her. Her dress was in sorry shape after all she'd been through, but she still managed to look proper.

Zaide locked eyes with Lark, and the two of them stared as if frozen in stone.

"Sit," Raddan barked so forcefully that both of them jumped. Both ducked their heads and sank to sit as ordered. The lieutenant sighed. "Maker's mercy, don't make this harder on me than it has to be. Your Highness, I understand you want an escort?"

Lark nodded.

He nodded back and went on. "This was why I tried to hurry ahead of the army. The reinforcements will be along soon, but you know they'd never let you venture off without your father's permission."

"By now, he's probably ordered I be returned home," she agreed. "With or without my cooperation."

"Doesn't that mean you should be returning her to Amrochan?" Zaide asked.

Raddan shrugged. "I never received that order. My orders were to see the Elder's apprentice back to Kolmar safely, then for me to report to the garrison. I can continue on to Kolmar, but there's no point in hurrying if the garrison is no longer ours."

Resia tipped her head to the side and tapped a finger against her chin. "You can't follow your orders if you're escorting Princess Dasienna elsewhere."

"Sure can't. What do you suppose I ought to do?" Raddan glanced at Zaide, and the twinkle in his eye stirred Zaide's temper.

He smothered the spark of anger and buried it so it would extinguish. Part of Zaide still wanted to please the lieutenant— maybe even impress him—and the best way to do that was to present himself as a calm and rational soldier. "What are you thinking?"

Raddan chuckled. "I'll admit my plan was a bit shaky before now. But let's back up a moment, first, because I don't think you can understand my plan without understanding what exactly is at stake."

"Kolmar being at stake isn't enough?" Zaide asked, incredulous. He already suspected the direction this was going, and the thought sent a prickle of irritation up the back of his neck.

"Kolmar being at stake is just the beginning," the lieutenant said, his tone infuriatingly level. "I was from Kolmar too, boy. I was selected in the Spring Choosing many years ago, but the forest will always be my home. I asked to be stationed at Kolmar's garrison, and I'm no happier than you to learn of its fate."

Any protest Zaide had died on his tongue. He let his shoulders sag.

"Now, the king is welcome to his beliefs, as we all are. But I grew up under the same Elder as you, and I've never had reason to doubt his magic. If the Elder says the Vale Hymnflute had power and lost it, I believe him. And if the Elder thinks restoring its power is the best way to protect Kolmar, I believe that, too." Raddan rubbed his leg as if soothing an ache.

Zaide's eyes narrowed. "Where are you going with this?"

"If the king can't—or won't—restore its power, we have no choice but to look elsewhere. Jadora's library is said to be the greatest in the world. If there's anyone else who can restore the Hymnflute's power, that library is our greatest chance at finding out who."

"You were told to take me back to Kolmar, not send me off on a hen-chase with the princess," Zaide protested, though he was now certain what the lieutenant intended.

Raddan raised a finger. "I was told to take the Elder's apprentice back to Kolmar." He opened a hand and gestured to Resia. "Well, she's right here."

It took all Zaide's strength not to groan. He allowed himself a long, slow exhale, then glanced to Lark, who had been oddly silent during their exchange. "And I suppose this works out exactly as you'd hoped?"

He'd expected her to be happy, but she frowned. "Believe me, asking you to come along for this isn't my first choice. For a while, I thought I'd be okay with going by myself if you would hand over the Hymnflute. But there was everything that happened in the temple, and... well, it just seems wiser to have someone along with me. I don't know what I would have done if I'd been alone."

The admission caught him off guard and he felt some of the tension leak out of him. "You know I can't just give it to you. Restoring its power was the job the Elder assigned me."

"That's why you should come with me," Lark said. "You can keep it in your possession, and once I get the other two artifacts and do what's needed to end this war, you can take it and go home."

"I know this isn't what you want to do," Raddan said. "But being mulish about it isn't going to help anything. Right now, I'm your commanding officer. And if Princess Dasienna says these artifacts she's after can help, I don't have much reason not to trust her on that. If I trust the Elder, I should trust the princess, especially when she agrees with him."

"Lark," she put in quietly.

The lieutenant raised a brow.

"That's the name she gave me when we met in the woods," Zaide said. "If we're on the road without a proper military escort, it's probably wiser to use a different name for her."

She shot him an appreciative look, which caught him wholly off guard. What brought about this sudden change in attitude? Was it that Raddan had removed every obstacle to what she wanted? The thought made him want to roll his eyes, but he stayed composed and perfectly still, mindful of how he presented himself.

"You're probably right," Raddan agreed. "Lark it is, then. But listen, lad. I hope you understand what I'm trusting you with, here. Word of what's happened at this crossroads will get back to King Sendassian sooner or later. If any part of this expedition ends badly, it's my head."

From the solemnity in the man's dark eyes, Zaide suspected that was no exaggeration. "I understand."

"Good. Everyone open your bags. We'll eat, then we'll repack our provisions to make sure the princess has enough rations to get her close to Tinith."

"I can hunt along the way," Zaide offered.

The lieutenant nodded as he opened his bag. "Good. You'll need to."

Plain cleared his throat. Neither he nor Murk had said a word since sitting, but now he wore a plaintive expression and it seemed he could stay silent no longer. "Oi, Leech, are you sure it's best to send them alone? If the princess needs an escort, then..." He trailed off, the suggestion not needing to be voiced.

Lark raised a hand. "I understand and appreciate your concern, but it sounds as if the front line has crossed Kolmar. The road from here to Jadora is long, but it's well inside Amroch's borders and far safer than the forest. Kolmar needs every swordsman it can get right now, and I've seen enough of Zaide's capability as a fighter to feel confident he can protect me. Besides, I'm not defenseless." She shifted and one of her long daggers appeared in her hand. Both Plain and Murk gaped.

She sheathed it. "The way to Kolmar may be dangerous. Please stay with Resia and ensure she is returned to the Elder safely."

Resia offered a timid smile.

"Lark's right," Zaide said, and the words came more easily than he expected. "Resia's no fighter. She's good with books, music, and medicine. That last part will be of vital importance to get Kolmar through this. We can handle the trip to Jadora by ourselves." The fact he'd already resigned himself to that trip was astounding, but he'd have time to marvel at that while they traveled.

"All right, then," Plain murmured, though a deep frown creased his ordinary features.

Raddan leaned forward to sit a few paper-wrapped objects in front of Lark. "We've not much to spare, but I'm sure you've packed your own. Between yours and his, that little bit extra should get the two of you to the markets outside Tinith."

"Thank you, Lieutenant." Lark worked all of it into her own bag without offering any to Zaide. Did she think he didn't have space in his admittedly bulging bag, or was she back to trying to appear independent? He supposed he would find out later.

"Eat up, everyone," Raddan ordered, "then say your goodbyes. We can dillydally all we want, but the pr—Lark and the lad better get a move on if they don't want to be seen when the army crests that hill behind us."

A few quiet grumbles answered, and Zaide let his own join them.

As everyone took their first bites, Raddan raised his waterskin. "To safe travel."

Everyone raised their food in salute.

"And to a triumphant return when all is said and done," Resia added.

Murk thumped a fist against his leg. "Hear, hear."

Zaide stared at the dry biscuit in his hand. He'd known from the moment he packed his things that his life would be upended, but somehow, he had the uneasy feeling that Jadora would only be the start.

CHAPTER SEVENTEEN

ZAIDE HAD no time to eat before Lark pushed herself to her feet and gathered her things.

"We need to move." She slung her bag over her shoulder and gave him a look that said she expected him to do the same. "If you don't know how far behind you my father's men are, we can't afford to waste a moment."

He clamped his teeth down on his piece of bread and strapped his belongings to his back. He could eat while he walked. He returned his bread to his hand and gathered the rest of his sparse meal. "I'd make the argument that these are your father's men."

Lark glanced over her shoulder at the three soldiers. Murk and Plain still sat on the ground, but Raddan stood and dusted off his legs. "I'd argue they're mine, now, since they agree we need to go."

"I wouldn't say we all agree," Murk said. "But it's Leech's head if you get caught, not mine."

"Then let's hope he gets to keep his head." Zaide stuffed the last of his bread into his mouth. He turned to Resia, but didn't know what to say. He hadn't expected to have to say goodbye to her a second time.

She stepped forward and wrapped her arms around his neck in a hug. He held what remained of his food out behind her, awkwardly squeezing her sides with his forearms while trying to hold on to his meal.

"Be careful," she said, and left it at that.

Zaide nodded once. "I will be. You too."

Her eyes grew misty as she let go and moved back, her hands clasped in front of her.

Raddan patted her shoulder. "I promise we'll do everything we can to keep her safe."

"You'd better," Zaide said.

Lark planted her hands on her hips. "Are we done with the sappy farewells? We need to be traveling. That way. Now."

"You know, I would have expected a princess would have more tact." He gave Resia one last reassuring smile, then turned west. Somewhere past the forests and rolling fields, the desert—and the fortress-like city of Jadora—waited.

"I have plenty of tact. But there's a time and place for it, and it isn't when your kingdom's at risk." Lark tossed her head and her blonde ponytail swished behind her like a banner. Instead of letting him take the lead, she hurried forward to put herself at the front.

Zaide kept from rolling his eyes as he put his leftovers away and followed. "It's not your kingdom yet."

"But it will be. Sooner or later, I will be queen." She spoke with such strength and certainty that he couldn't think of any way to tease her about it.

Instead, he stretched his arms overhead and then laced his fingers together behind his neck. His shoulder no longer pained him, and he thought a quiet thanks toward Resia. He would have turned around to shout it, but it was probably best to keep his voice down. Traveling alone meant a greater risk, and he didn't want to invite trouble in the first five minutes of the journey. "So we're headed to Tinith first, huh?" He walked at a pace just leisurely enough to irritate her, which it did after only a half-dozen steps.

She stopped to glare at him. "Yes, and it's a long enough trip without you dragging your feet."

"Do you have a map?"

"No, but there aren't that many trade routes. If we stay on this road, it'll take us right to the market. Tinith is just after that, and we can get a map there."

Zaide stretched a little farther, then let his arms drop to his sides. "I'm assuming that means you brought money."

She huffed. "Are you just going to ask stupid questions every few minutes?"

"I'm sure they'll get more intelligent as we go along. Right now, I'm a birthday shy of my rites of adulthood and I've never been outside my forest." Though he teased, he did pick up his pace, figuring it safer if he only needle at her with one method at a time.

Her ponytail swished again, a good indicator that she didn't agree.

For a while, they walked in silence. The fork in the road fell away behind them and before long, it was swallowed by the swells and dips of the landscape. Thick copses of trees framed the road in places, casting long shadows across the dusty path that made Zaide wonder about the spiders Raddan had mentioned before. He'd never seen anything like them before entering the temple, and these woods were all connected to the forest that surrounded Kolmar. If the spiders were elsewhere, was it that the Vale magic had protected Kolmar from them, or had they spawned in the corruption of the temple and spread outward from there?

"Here's a question you might not find so stupid," he said. "It's called the Vale Hymnflute, and when Kolmar was attacked, the Elder mentioned its power had failed and the Vale magic no longer offered shelter. But I've read almost every book in his library, and none of them ever mentioned any Vale magic. Do you know what it is?"

From the speculative way she glanced at him, she didn't find that question stupid at all. "Sort of."

"If sort of is all you've got, you're probably not any better off than me. I mean, I already know it's some sort of shield, something that keeps things like the goborrins out of the forest. But beyond that, I don't know what it is or how it works." He didn't like admitting his lack of knowledge, especially after being the Elder's apprentice, but he assumed there was some reason the Elder had never mentioned it before. Kolmar's people had seemed concerned when the Elder announced its protection was gone, but how much of that was because they knew what it was? Any lack of protection meant danger.

Then again, the fear on the faces of the adults was different from the uncertainty he'd seen in his peers and the village children. Perhaps he simply hadn't grown old enough to know what it was. There were many rites of passage that carried one to adulthood in the forest. Now, he wasn't sure he'd experience any of them.

Lark sighed and shifted her bag. "From my understanding, the Vale magic is two things. Both require the Hymnflute to have a..." She made a grasping motion in the air, as if searching for a word. "Charge? I don't know what else to call it. It has to hold power. A blessing of sorts, to replenish its magic. That power does two things. One is, it creates a sort of aura that discourages evil things. The other is a literal shield."

"A shield?" He shrugged, suddenly aware of the way the bulky set of pipes pressed against his back. Carrying them still felt odd, but there were times their presence pressed deeper into his consciousness than others. "Out of... wooden pipes?"

"Yes. No. Not like that." She fluttered a hand in the air, as if she didn't know how to explain. "It's magic, but it's tangible. I don't know what else to call it but a shield. A barrier, maybe. Like a dome of power that offers protection."

Which would have been useful, back in the marsh. Or when he'd fought that goborrin on the bridge. Zaide rubbed his brow as if that could wipe away his frustration. Even if he'd known how to summon it, the Hymnflute had no magic now. "So that's why the Elder needs its power restored? To push enemies out of the forest with its aura."

She shrugged. "Or maybe he intends to hunt down every last goborrin on his own, and the shield part is what he's after."

"You do realize he's something like eighty years old?"

As if it made no difference, she shrugged again.

Zaide gazed toward the horizon, turning the new information over in his head. More than ever, restoring power to the Hymnflute sounded like a necessity. He'd been frustrated at Sendassian's refusal to even look at it, but if the king had no magic with which to restore the artifact's might, perhaps it was best that he'd turned them away early.

"You really think the library will have all the answers we need?" he asked. He could still hardly believe they were walking to the desert, but there was little to do for it now.

"I hope so," Lark replied, and the subdued note in her voice gave him a chill.

After that, they both kept their tempers to themselves and walked on through the afternoon without much conversation. The sun became an annoyance in the evening and they walked with their heads bowed to keep the glare from their eyes.

They finally stopped as the sunset turned crimson, unable to continue with the sun hanging dead ahead. "I hear in the north, they make goggles that protect their eyes from the glint of the sun on the snow," Lark said.

"Maybe we can learn how to make those while we're in Jadora." Zaide sat with his back to the light, watching the bands of color in the eastern sky as the sun set. "How far do you think they made it? Resia and the others?"

"No farther than we did, I'd expect." Lark nibbled a slim wedge of cheese and squinted at the growing dusk.

Not for the first time, he wished they had a map so he could get an idea of where they were—and guess as to how far Resia's group had been able to travel. He had no doubts they would reach Kolmar before he and Lark reached Tinith, but all he could do was pray the trip would be uneventful.

Absently, he slid his hand over his bag. He'd thought of the Hymnflute so often since his departure from home, but he'd never allowed himself to sit and look at it. Curiosity had simmered within him since their conversation about what the artifact could do, but this was the first time they'd sat down. He allowed his fingers to undo the latches on his satchel and before he knew it, he had the Hymnflute in his hand.

Lark perked up as he ran his fingers over the worn wood pipes, but she said nothing.

Now that he sat and studied it closely, it seemed so unremarkable that he almost couldn't fault the king for thinking its power a myth. For a moment, Zaide thought he hardly had evidence for that power, himself. Then he recalled one irrefutable point and felt his certainty bolstered.

Kolmar had been safe when the broken-born fled the Shattered Lands. His parents had sought shelter there for a reason. Something had kept the forest safe, something that no longer did. More than ever, he felt sure the reason was in his hands.

He lowered the instrument to his lap. "Can I ask you something?"

"You just did."

"I'm being serious."

"So am I. If you have a question, lead in with your question. You can ask anything you want. It just never guarantees an answer." She licked her fingers clean.

Zaide toyed with the carvings of leaves and flowers that hung from the pipes. "Who do you think Gadranus is?"

"Our enemy," Lark said simply. "Who else would he be?"

"But who is he? Has anyone ever seen him? The war

escalated almost twenty years ago. Just before I was born. It's been a steady push since then, but all we ever hear about is his army. The goborrins, the… evil." He didn't like to use such a vague name, but it was the first thing that came to mind, no doubt because of his conversation with the soldiers in the marsh. "None of that tells us who he is. Where does he come from? Where was he born? Why does he pursue this?"

She eyed him oddly. "You don't know?"

A hint of uncertainty wormed its way into his belly. "There are stories, but—"

"There is history," Lark corrected. "Really, what are they teaching you in that forest? Gadranus is king of the Shattered Lands. They call them that because they've been destroyed. Because everything he comes upon is left a ruin in his wake."

"Men have reasons to seek destruction."

Her eyes narrowed. "Whose side are you on?"

The question mirrored doubts she'd cast upon him on their way to the temple, and a flush of anger sent heat through his limbs. "That's the second time you've implied—"

"And the first time, you weren't arguing on the enemy's side," she interrupted. "If I hadn't met the Kolmari Elder's other apprentice this morning, I'd be real uncertain you are who you claim right now. What does it matter who our enemy is? He's trying to crush our kingdom, and that's all that should matter. Why do you care?"

"Because I don't understand!" he shouted back.

Her brows drew together.

"I don't understand why someone would do this. Why they would pursue this. Why they would send wave after wave of an army against someone in this endless war. Whoever he is, if he's the leader now, he has the choice to end it." The words tumbled free like a flood of confusion and he gripped the Hymnflute with both hands, desperate for something to ground him. "The Shattered Lands encompass more than half the world. Why isn't what he has enough? All that's left to stand against him is

Amroch, and all we want to do is live. Why attack us? Why kill us?"

Lark blinked at him. "Because he must."

The statement was so simple, yet so powerful, that he didn't know how to go on. Zaide stared at her in silence.

"You really don't know?" she asked.

Slowly, he shook his head.

Her face crumpled. "Just wait until Jadora, then," she murmured. "Once we get there, you'll understand."

CHAPTER EIGHTEEN

THE CLOSER THEY got to Tinith, the more often they passed people on the road. Most of them eyed Zaide with suspicion, but they hardly gave Lark a second glance. He tried to keep his head down, to appear as inoffensive as possible. He'd heard how the broken-born were treated through the rest of Amroch, but he'd never experienced it in Kolmar. There, he was just another forest-dweller, home among the trees. But out here, he was a stranger, and it seemed many interpreted that as a threat.

"Don't be so gloomy," Lark said as another wagon rumbled past. The farmer driving stared at the two of them over his shoulder until he was too far away for his features to be clear.

"Easy for you to say," Zaide muttered. "They look at me like I'm a goborrin."

She snorted. "That's not true. If you were a goborrin, they'd scream and run."

He thought it was supposed to be a joke, but he didn't find it comforting. "I don't get it. They're farther from the front lines than Kolmar is. The forest's people had every reason to despise my family, but they took us in. They were always kind to my mother, and no one mistreated me." They'd teased him, of course; no one escaped growing up without ribbing. But even those who teased him for his snowy hair and pale eyes had been friends, and he'd been welcome at their table. Out here, he suspected most would let him starve.

Lark shrugged. "People dislike the unfamiliar. Once we're in Jadora, people will look at me funny, too. It's not like I look like I belong in the desert. Which reminds me." She stopped and spun to face him, her hands on her hips. "We're almost to the market. It should come into view just around the bend. We'll need to buy appropriate clothing for the desert, then find a ride. Leave the talking to me. You're just my bodyguard, all the business is mine. Understand?"

Zaide wanted to protest, but the steely glint in her eye gave him pause. "I understand," he said, though reluctantly.

"Good." She sniffed and started off again, her stride longer than before.

Even before they rounded the curve, the colorful awnings of market stalls and tents came into view. The shift from the sounds of nature to the sounds of business was slow enough that Zaide wasn't sure when he first noticed. He turned his better ear toward the city ahead.

"You do that a lot," Lark noted.

"Hmm?"

"Turn your head when you're listening. Is your other ear that bad?"

His hand drifted to his left ear and the damage he'd had since before he could recall. The scarring wasn't severe, since he'd been so small when the injury happened, but the ear was distinctly cropped and blunted. It had never bothered him, but no one in Kolmar had ever seemed to notice. "I wouldn't say it's bad. I can hear out of it just fine, it just isn't as sensitive as the one that's whole."

She made a soft, thoughtful sound. "Maybe you could get a prosthetic. I'd bet a jeweler could make you an earpiece that would fit over your ear and restore the shape."

"Why would I do that?"

"I don't know. So you could be like everyone else."

That drew a snort. "I don't think an artificial ear would make me like everyone else. Besides, I'm used to it. It doesn't bother me."

"If you say so." She pointed ahead. "Here we are, Tinith's market. They say it's the largest outdoor market in the world."

"I see it." He refrained from telling her he'd seen it for some time, assuming she just meant to change the subject. "They say it goes on for miles."

Her face brightened. "It does. We didn't stay long, when we passed through with my mother, but I remember seeing so many merchants and so many things for sale that it made me tired just to look."

"I would have thought we'd see more traffic between here and Amrochan, with how big this place is."

Lark shifted her bag. "The trade route runs on half-year cycles. Through late autumn, winter, and early spring, it's often too wet around the marsh for merchants to bring trade wagons through. The wheels get stuck. So when things are wet, most trade focuses on heading west, out to Addare and Jadora, and down to Parral on the southern coast. Once summer comes and things dry out, it's too hot to get through the desert easily, so trade shifts toward Amrochan instead."

"Makes sense," Zaide said. "So Tinith's market is sort of a warehouse city."

"Basically. Come on, the earlier we get there, the more time we'll have to look for a caravan to book." She picked up her pace, and Zaide jogged forward a few steps to catch up with her.

"Caravan?"

The look she gave him made him feel like an ignorant child. "You didn't think we were going to cross the desert on foot, did you? We'd never be able to carry enough water. We'll have to ride with a caravan."

Zaide said nothing, unsure how to escape embarrassment.

To his fortune, there was no need to speak once they reached the edge of the market. The bright-colored and striped tents and stalls hosted more merchants than he'd ever imagined. They shouted at passersby while holding goods aloft. People from what had to be every part of the world milled between them, and Zaide stopped with his mouth agape when he caught sight of a stranger with snowy hair.

Lark nudged his arm with her elbow. "You didn't think you were the only broken-born left in Amroch, did you?"

"No," he said slowly, though he couldn't tear his eyes away. In truth, he'd often hoped he wasn't. If there were others, then perhaps there would be someone out there who knew more about his homeland and his family's story, missing pieces of himself he'd never been able to find.

Her hand curled around his wrist. "Come on," she said, though for once it was more of a request than an order.

Reluctant, he made himself turn away and walked on in silence. Hawkers roving the crowd cried over the deep murmur of people, emphasizing how futile it was to attempt conversation anyway.

Lark tugged him along and he let himself be dragged. She seemed to know where she was going, for she wove between stalls and side streets with remarkable ease—and without ever losing her bearings. Zaide, on the other hand, found himself dizzy after the first four turns she took.

Some distance toward her intended destination, she planted her feet and halted without warning, and he collided with her back.

"Oof." She shoved him away and gave him a glare. "Watch your feet."

"You're the one who stopped." He had to shout back to make himself heard, but neither the shouting nor his words seemed to have any impact. She shifted her bags and dug in her pockets. A moment later, she produced a few bright coins with transparent, colored centers and pressed them into his hand.

Zaide blinked twice and lifted one to the light. The green crystal's facets glinted iridescent colors. "What's this?"

"Money, idiot. Buy yourself a travel cloak with a hood, would you? Traveling with the caravan will be easier if they can't see your hair."

The statement sparked his temper, but her face was apologetic when he looked her way, so he set his jaw and shoved the coins into his pocket. They were nothing like the coins used in Kolmar, but the village had little use for currency. Perhaps the coins used in Amrochan had never traveled that far.

"Fine," he agreed, though he wanted to grumble. She didn't seem to notice his annoyance before she slipped off on her own. To book the caravan by herself, he assumed. If the caravaners harbored that much ill will toward the broken-born, it was probably best they not see the two of them together at all until it was time to depart.

Zaide scanned the countless market stalls for some time before he chose a random direction and moved that way. There were easily a dozen merchants selling clothing within sight, and he made a note to compare prices at each before committing to anything. He had little experience with shopping, but there had been several books in the Elder's library that dealt with economics. He'd gathered enough from those to keep from being helpless.

Looking back, knowledge about the things he faced now seemed strangely absent from his education. He'd trained hard out of a desire to wield a sword and hadn't let that skill go slack after he'd been chosen as apprentice. There had even been books about combat and strategy in the Elder's collection. But there had been no atlases, and little history about anything except Kolmar and the few vague histories about their long-time enemy and Amroch as a whole.

The first two merchants had nothing he needed, and it didn't take more than a glance to determine the third's wares were priced too high. The next several vendors seemed more reasonable, and he noted the prices of cloaks and clothing at all of them before he returned to one to buy what he needed. Lark had only instructed him to buy a cloak, but he was short on clean clothing after his fall in the river and the fight in the marsh, and he doubted she would complain about him returning with clothing more appropriate for desert travel—and in a style less noticeable than the billowy garb that was popular in Kolmar, where the loose fabric kept one cool and the tight cuffs kept pests from crawling up sleeves or pant legs.

He selected a short cloak with a deep hood, a new pair of plain trousers, and two shirts to replace what he'd ruined between battle and blood. There were coins left in his pocket when he finished, but she hadn't specified what else would be needed, so instead of shopping further, Zaide found somewhere out of the way to sit down and wait for Lark to find him.

It wasn't long before she returned.

"I booked us passage," she announced as she came to a stop with her hands on her hips. She looked him over with an expectant set to her mouth, and it took him a moment to realize she'd expected him to already be dressed.

Holding back a sigh, he dragged his new cloak out of his bag and fastened it around his shoulders. They still hadn't even visited Tinith's city proper; his Kolmari clothing wasn't too out of place just yet. "When do we leave?"

Lark seemed placated when he pulled his hood up over his hair. Or, at least her shoulders relaxed. "They're departing as soon as they're done loading cargo. That should be some time this evening."

He blinked and looked to the darkening sky. "We're leaving at night?"

"Most travel in the desert happens at night," she said. "They like to set the schedule early, so it's easier to adjust to later on. We'll stop and camp during the day, when they can set up tents for shade, and then travel through the night."

"And when are we supposed to sleep?" Much as he hated to

admit it, Zaide had been looking forward to a real bed somewhere in the city that night. He'd never thought himself particularly soft, but his time away from home had been quick to make him aware of which comforts he enjoyed the most. A warm bed and a good down-filled pillow were at the top of the list.

"In one of the wagons. We should be able to sleep half the night, then change schedule fairly easily." She turned, beckoning him with one hand. "Come on. Did you get clothes? I need to find some for the desert."

He pushed himself up and followed as she started down the tent-lined avenue. "I did. What else do we need?"

Lark gave her head a thoughtful tilt. "More food. I've rented us one half of a wagon. It's just enough space for two people to sleep, and we should have plenty of room to take cargo with us. We'll want dry rations. We'll have to pay for water, too, but the caravaners will be the ones responsible for supplying that." A tent boasting more feminine cuts of clothing stood to the side of the road and she veered toward it without hesitation.

"Have I mentioned I'm glad you have money?"

"No, but I'm not surprised you don't. What do you do, out there in the woods? Barter with acorns?" She shot him a smirk, then ducked inside.

Zaide lingered outside the tent, unsure if he was wanted nearby—or if being in the tent while the princess shopped for women's clothing was appropriate. He stood for a long time, peering in through the large tent's open flaps, before someone nudged his shoulder none too gently. He turned and his eyes swept up to the square and scarred face of a heavily armored soldier.

"What're you staring at, broken-born?" the man growled.

"Nothing," Zaide replied. He opened his mouth to explain Lark's shopping, then clamped it shut instead. He didn't know who this soldier answered to, but every soldier in Amroch served the king. Drawing attention to Sendassian's vagrant daughter would be unwise.

The soldier grunted. "What're you buying?"

That was none of the man's business, but remaining agreeable seemed the safest choice. "Supplies."

"For?"

"A trip to Jadora, sir." Zaide hesitated before adding, "I'm on my way to the library."

Evidently, that answer wasn't satisfactory, either. The big man snorted and then rubbed his nose with a knuckle. "Empty your bags."

"What? Why?"

"Because I said so," the soldier snapped.

A figure appeared in the tent's opening and a finely-dressed woman peered out. "What is going on out here?"

Zaide took a step backwards. "Could you ask Lark to hurry up, ma'am? Please?"

The woman frowned at him, but retreated into the tent.

"Your bags," the man said, harder this time. "Empty them. Now."

"Okay, okay. Calm down." Zaide made a soothing motion with both hands, then shifted his bag forward over his shoulder. He only had one, but he supposed the man would ask to see under his cloak next to be sure.

Before he could open the top, Lark popped out of the tent with her arms full of silk clothing. "What are you doing?" She glowered at Zaide first, then at the big soldier, unperturbed by his size. "Who told you that you could harass my bodyguard?"

The soldier barked a laugh. "Bodyguard? This runt?" He shoved Zaide's shoulder, but this time, the contact was no surprise. Zaide dug in his heels and braced against it. His hand went to his sword out of reflex, rather than intimidation, but the hilt glinted and the big man froze.

"Bodyguards don't carry the king's steel," the man said, his face darkening.

"Mine does." Lark stepped forward, her jaw set and her head high. "Stand down, unless you want to explain to the king why you're interrupting my trip."

"The king—" the soldier started, but he broke off the moment he got a proper look at Lark's face. His jaw dropped and he fell to one knee. "Your Highness! Forgive me, I didn't realize—"

She made a sharp hushing sound and retreated two steps to hide in the shadows just inside the tent. "On your feet. Now."

Flustered, the man stood. Unconsciously, Zaide backed up until he stood next to Lark, his hand still on his sword. A handful of people had stopped in the street outside, and she groaned and shrank into Zaide's shadow as if she wanted to disappear.

"Forgive me," the soldier repeated, softer. "I had no idea. I just saw this—"

"Enough," Lark snapped. "Return to your duties and leave me to finish preparation in peace. If I have need of you, I will let you know, but my guard is more than enough to supervise my shopping."

The big man pressed a hand to his chest and bowed at the waist. "Of course, Your Highness. Understood."

She huffed as he retreated and a handful of curious shoppers peered into the tent.

"Your Highness," the merchant repeated from behind the sales counter. The note of breathless awe in her voice meant nothing good, Zaide was sure.

"Do not speak to Her Highness unless spoken to," he said, sounding as low and dangerous as he could. He wasn't sure it was convincing, but the woman shrank back and bowed her head.

"Of course," she murmured.

Lark's shoulders slumped and her face fell with defeat. "We'd better hurry," she whispered. "It won't take long for word I'm here to spread among the guard, and we must be on the road before that knowledge meets with the information I'm supposed to be in Amrochan."

"I'm sorry," Zaide replied, and he was surprised by the genuine remorse that knotted itself around his heart. "I shouldn't have told him anything."

"No, it was better to avoid conflict. We'll just have to see if the caravan can be hurried along." She plucked a few extra pieces of clothing off displays without taking the time to inspect them, then dropped them onto the counter and fished out a handful of coins. "You may tell people I shop here, but not until tomorrow."

The merchant nodded so hard, Zaide thought her head might fall off. "Yes, Your Highness. Thank you, Your Highness."

Lark rolled her eyes and jammed her new clothing into her bag—all save a new cloak, which she draped around her shoulders and pulled up over her golden hair. "Let's go."

Zaide fell in step behind her, assuming a stance he believed was more befitting of a bodyguard. "Should I put my hood down?" he asked as they emerged onto the street. "Maybe seeing me will make people doubt you're you. People don't seem to be fond of me, here."

"It's no wonder," she said as she cut due west. "As far as most people in Amroch are concerned, you're an enemy."

"You still seem to think I might be." He still wasn't sure if that should bother him.

"Well, of course," Lark said.

"Because my family came from the Shattered Lands?"

She paused long enough to look at him oddly. "Because Gadranus is broken-born, too."

He stopped in the middle of the street. "What?"

"You didn't know that, either?" Her voice softened.

"No," he said, and no other words would come.

Lark's face twisted with pity, but she said nothing else and continued on her way.

Zaide trailed after her, blinking as if clearing his eyes would help sort the mess in his head. That certainly explained the dirty looks he'd gotten. He'd known the people of his motherland helped fill the ranks of the enemy's army, but nothing he'd ever read mentioned Gadranus himself was one of them. Somehow, that knowledge cut deep.

His family had been driven from their homeland, his mother wounded and almost killed, at the hands of an army controlled by one of her own people. A deep, uncomfortable anger stirred within him. The Elder had to have known, yet the subject had never come up, and none of the books in the library had ever mentioned it.

At least, none Zaide had ever read.

Had the Elder hidden them? Tried to keep that knowledge from him? Frustration joined his new anger and he lifted a hand to rub his forehead as an ache sprang up behind his eyes.

"Keep your hood up," Lark said at last. "The caravan's just ahead. I'll see if I can give them a little extra and get them to buy provisions for us, too. We'll get to the wagons and hide for now."

"All right," Zaide agreed. He hardly had the energy to do anything else.

She trotted ahead and flagged down one of the caravan workers, and he trailed along silently behind her, lost in his own thoughts.

If Jadora was where she thought he'd come to understand the nature of their enemy and this war, he hated to think what else he didn't know.

The caravan did not depart until dusk, but when they left, Zaide leaned against a bulging sack of extra provisions Lark had managed to secure for them. It didn't take long for the swaying of the enclosed wagon to lull him to sleep, and for the first time since he'd left Kolmar, Zaide slept well.

He woke in mid-morning, groggy and stiff, but Lark lay curled close by, her hands tucked under her cheek. Her features were softer in sleep; with all her temper and determination gone, he thought she looked gentle and serene. Somehow, he didn't think she'd like that assessment.

He sat up and squinted out the back of the wooden wagon. It had doors, but they'd been left open through the night. The chilly breeze had roused him once, he thought, but he'd been too tired to care. Once they reached the desert, he'd probably appreciate the construction.

At some point, the caravan had stopped. They sat in a circle on a wide plain and he thought a river glittered in the distance, but it was the mountains that sat as blue shadows on the horizon that caught his attention.

"That's where we're headed," Lark said softly beside him.

Zaide twitched and turned his head. She still lay on the wagon's floor, her face soft and her eyes heavy.

"The road goes through the mountains," she continued. "We'll drive right through them. The desert's on the other side. I'm sure you'll like them. They're not that rocky, this far south. The forest is a lot like Kolmar."

"I'll look forward to seeing it," he said. Truthfully, he did.

There was little to do around the camp, but he enjoyed having a chance to stretch his legs and practice with his sword while the caravaners took their rest. When the procession started off again in the evening, he chose to walk for a time, while Lark sat at the back of the wagon and gazed wistfully back toward Tinith. Zaide regretted not seeing the city while they were so close, but their journey took precedence, and he supposed he would return along the same path when it came time to take the Hymnflute back to the Elder.

After moonrise, he climbed into the wagon to ride alongside Lark, but she remained pensive and they shared little conversation.

They camped again at the foot of the mountains, which meant they ventured onto the winding trails at sunset.

When morning broke, fog hung thick on the mountaintops

and the sun spilled long, golden rays over the peaks and into the land below.

"There it is," Lark said.

At the very edge of what Zaide could see, a patch of gold stretched the full width of the landscape and disappeared across the horizon.

The desert.

CHAPTER NINETEEN

THE DESCENT from the mountaintop to the desert was slower than the climb. Greenery gave way to rocky soil and scrubby brush, and heat swelled each day until Zaide found it all but unbearable. The parched air stole the moisture from his throat and dried his sinuses until they burned.

It only grew worse as they traveled. Cold wind gusted across the dunes at night. Zaide and Lark walked behind their wagon when they could, the cloudless sky overhead serving to drive home how vast the desert was. They camped each day with the heavy draft horses sheltered beneath tents, but the heat grew so intense, neither Lark nor Zaide could sleep. Instead, they traded shifts sleeping, and each slept half the night as the other walked.

Lark dozed throughout the period of the day she was awake, but Zaide sat upright while the rest of the camp was still, paging through the book of songs Resia had given him.

He hadn't had time to look through it before; now he was grateful to have it. He didn't dare try to play the Hymnflute while the rest of the caravan slept, but he practiced the way he held it and how to move the instrument, and tried to imagine how each song might sound.

"What do you suppose the songs are for?" Lark asked one morning, after she'd tossed and turned without finding rest.

"Rituals, it sounds like," Zaide said. He pressed the pipes to his lips and considered trying to draw a note, then lowered the Hymnflute and returned it to his bag. "Maybe we can learn more about it when we get to the library."

"Maybe," Lark agreed. "The trip will be easier once we stop in Addare to refill our water supply. With luck, we'll be there soon."

He nodded in understanding. There was little else to say.

Contrary to Lark's hopes, the first glimpse of civilization did not appear for several more days. Everyone in the caravan was weary and dehydrated, but the dunes gave way to layers of rocky earth the same shade of yellow as the desert, but with wisps of grass and even occasional wildflowers. A grove of trees beckoned them to stop, and they camped at the oasis during the peak of the day's heat. The glittering water offered welcome respite for the animals and the caravaners alike, and Zaide wasn't the only one who took the opportunity to dip his feet in the pool.

"Careful, you'll sunburn," Lark teased.

He snorted. "And you won't? You're almost as pale as me."

She eyed his legs, his pants rolled to his knees, and pretended to shield her eyes. "I doubt it. If you were any paler, I'd think you were made of milk."

"Thanks." Zaide shrugged his cloak a little farther forward and adjusted his hood. He hadn't had it down except to sleep and hated to think of how bedraggled he must look, but it was better than dealing with scorn from the rest of their transport.

He waded in peace for a time, and the caravan set off at sunset. Before sunrise the following morning, a different sort of breeze swept in, and the soft glitter of lights lit the horizon.

The city of Addare rose as blocky shapes against the lightening sky, and beyond it, a shadowy gulf threatened to swallow everything. It wasn't until dawn's light hit the shimmering waves that he realized it was the sea.

The coast was cooler, more rocky, and a shade more green, but foliage was still sparse and the heat took an unpleasant humidity during the day. The caravaners ordered the passengers to stay put while they gathered water and fresh supplies, and Zaide didn't argue. With the coastal wind that whipped through the city of tan stone, it was easier to sleep, and he rested well until travel resumed.

"It's a shame we won't get to stay and explore," Lark said when they left the city behind. "We barely saw it."

"Just like Tinith," Zaide said.

She nodded. "We're making good time so far. The road should be easier now, since we're closer to the coast and there aren't as many dunes to slog through, but it's still a long way to Jadora from here."

"Maybe we can visit the cities on the way back," Zaide suggested.

"Maybe." She didn't sound convinced.

The plunge back into the desert was not as bad as he expected, with the cooler breeze coming in from the coast, and Zaide found it easier than the first half of the journey, though every part of him was travel-weary.

Then one day, the caravan did not halt in the morning.

Lark excused herself from the wagon to ask one of the caravaners what was going on, and Zaide watched her with a sense of uncomfortable uncertainty. She returned before long, a little more spring in her step, but it did nothing to alleviate his concern.

"What's going on?" he asked as he returned the Hymnflute to his bag, having dismissed his plan to study the songbook again.

"We're here," Lark announced, a spark of excitement in her blue eyes.

Zaide blinked at her, then slid to the back of the wagon. He planted his heels against the edge and pulled himself up to look over the enclosure's top, toward a plateau that soared above the rocky desert.

Not a plateau, he realized belatedly.

A city.

"Welcome to Jadora," Lark said.

He squinted against the light and tried to make out more, but aside from splashes of color he assumed were rooftops, the city looked like a sheer cliff face. "Is that a wall?"

"Yes, but not all of it. The city's built on a natural plateau and they just extended the wall upward. It's thirty feet up from the top of the plateau. They say if you count the cliff, Jadora's fortifications are a hundred feet high." Lark clambered back into the wagon and sat with her knees drawn up. "The city's defenses are even greater than Amrochan's."

"Incredible." Zaide leaned against the wagon's roof and watched as they inched along. "I bet they can see everything from up there." He hadn't noticed their upward trajectory at first, but now he noted Jadora lay at the top of a distinct uphill slope. Somewhere to the left of the caravan, he caught a glimmer, and wasn't sure if it was sunlight glinting off the sand or the sea.

She nodded. "They call Jadora the Watcher for that exact reason. Since it's on a peninsula, uphill, and on top of that plateau, nobody can ever hope to sneak up on the city. They keep good security at the gate and everyone and everything that's allowed in is documented. They say that's why the library started. They had to have logs of everything else, so why not catalog information about the rest of the world, too?"

Zaide couldn't help his grin. "That makes sense." The sun prickled, even through his hood, and he watched until he could bear it no longer. Then he sank back into the wagon and ran a ginger hand through his hair, half expecting to feel himself burned.

"They'll inspect all our bags." She grew sober with that statement, her eyes fixed on his belongings. On the Hymnflute, no doubt.

"That shouldn't be a problem, should it? I'm not transporting anything dangerous, aside from the sword. I wouldn't think they'd be afraid of the king's steel."

"No," Lark agreed, "but I don't know if they'll recognize the artifact. If they do, they'll want us to meet with their scholars, and I'm not sure we have the time to spare."

Alone in their wagon, he felt comfortable enough to sweep back his hood and let the occasional breeze ruffle his hair. "I thought we were planning to meet with scholars."

"Librarians. They're different. They're keepers of knowledge, not deliberators over it. And if scholars get involved, I'm not positive they'll agree with us taking the dagger. If we can find it, that is."

"That sounds uncharacteristically negative of you," Zaide said. "Why wouldn't we be able to find it?"

She shrugged. "I guess we'll find out."

It sounded like she knew much more than she was willing to say, but they'd spent enough time together during the trip that he was confident pressing would get him nowhere. Instead, he tried to rest until the caravan finally arrived at Jadora's great gate.

Getting *through* the gate was a different matter. The caravan drew to a halt, one more group of wagons in a line that snaked its way up the cliff face for what had to be a mile.

Lark didn't wait. She set to gathering her things the moment the wagons stopped, and the expectant look she gave Zaide got him packing, too. They hadn't removed much from their bags and within a few minutes, they slid out of their rented wagon with their belongings slung over their shoulders.

She sought the caravan's leader and offered her thanks for the trip. Zaide nodded along, but stayed back and kept his hood drawn. He didn't know what to expect from the city, but judging by the less than warm reception he'd received since leaving Kolmar, it seemed best to avoid attention.

"Come on," Lark said when she'd finished her goodbyes. She

beckoned him with one hand and trotted up the winding cliffside trail, hugging the stone wall. He followed.

The pathway was unusually free of debris and not a single shred of green peeked out from the dust or stone. Zaide studied the trail as they walked. He couldn't think of a practical reason for such meticulous maintenance, but he supposed the maintenance itself was threatening, in a way. If the road to the gate was that pristine, the order within the city had to be intimidating.

"They'll probably split us up to search us." Lark kept her voice low as she ducked past wagons and carts. "They'll ask questions about why we're here. It's probably best if we're honest with them."

"So I tell them the princess coerced me into being her bodyguard?" Sarcasm laced his words, which only made it that much more surprising when she nodded.

"Yes. If you use my name, we'll be more likely to get in without many questions being asked."

Zaide wished she would turn around, because he was sure he looked bewildered. It would have been nice to get her to explain without having to ask, but he had no such luck. "So now we're not being secretive? I can't keep up with you."

"If you can't keep up, it just means you need to walk faster." She picked up her pace, as if to make a point. As if her conveniently missing his meaning didn't make enough of a point on its own.

"I'm starting to think you don't actually have a plan," he called as the gap between them grew.

If anything, that made her walk even faster.

"That's not inspiring any more confidence," Zaide muttered. He hunched his shoulders and hurried after her with his head bowed.

The entirety of the line was composed of wagons and carts, and once they reached the massive iron gates that barred entry to the city, the tiny person-sized portcullis beside it seemed almost laughable. A scant handful of travelers on foot waited outside it, while a pair of guards asked questions and wrote in thick logbooks before the people disappeared inside, one by one, escorted by men in armor. Taken for questioning, Zaide decided; the people veered left once they entered the gate, and there were several more iron grids between that first chamber and the outermost fringes of the walled city.

Lark planted herself in line and waited with a determined set to her jaw. Zaide settled beside her and held on to the straps of his bags as he rocked on his feet and tried to peer past the gates.

"This wall has to be twenty feet thick," he murmured. When Lark didn't reply, he fell silent and just watched. The larger grille lifted and let a wagon pass through. Like with the people on foot, it was closed in and examined before it was allowed to proceed any farther.

They crept toward the smaller gate a foot at a time, as the people ahead were called in. Eventually, they stood before the guards together.

"One at a time," one of the guards barked.

Zaide couldn't help the crease of worry that formed between his brows when he glanced at Lark.

"Head straight to the library when you're done," she murmured. "I'll meet you there." Then she stepped forward and whispered something to the guard with the logbook. His eyes darted to her face and he shared a hand gesture with his companion. A moment later, the gate opened and Lark strode inside with her head high.

Alone, Zaide felt his throat tighten. He swallowed against the thick, dry feeling and inched forward when the guards beckoned him.

"Name?" Whatever Lark had whispered to the man, it hadn't been jarring enough to throw him off, for he already sounded bored again.

"Zaide," he said, his hands tightening on the straps of his bags until his knuckles were as white as his hair.

"Full name," the guard prompted.

He hesitated. "Just Zaide."

The man squinted at him from beneath the brim of his helmet.

"I'm the Kolmari Elder's apprentice," Zaide provided, in hopes it would help. "An orphan."

The guard did not appear convinced. "We're a long way from Kolmar, boy."

"Yes, but the Elder... well, he's old. I'm supposed to visit the library on his behalf." It wasn't exactly true, but it was the fastest way to summarize all that had transpired since the eclipse.

Still unconvinced, the guard narrowed his eyes and Zaide began to fear he'd be turned away. Instead, the man scribbled several lines of notes in his logbook and motioned to the gate. "Inside, to the left. Follow the hall to the fourth holding room on the left."

Zaide released a breath and nodded. "Yes, sir. Thank you."

Something inside the wall creaked and whined as the gate rose. Zaide ducked underneath it before it was all the way up, then cut to the left as he'd been told.

The hallway wasn't dim, but he had to blink several times before his eyes adjusted to the difference. Bright lanterns with horn-plate windows cast warm light across the walls and floor. He rolled his shoulders and crept to the door he'd been instructed to find. It wasn't difficult; it was the only one that stood open.

Though he'd expected to wait inside, there was already a woman in armor sitting at a desk in the center of the room.

"Bags on the desk," she ordered without looking up from her paperwork. "Close the door behind you."

Zaide pushed the door shut with his heel and slid his things from his shoulders to deposit them for inspection.

The woman unceremoniously upended all his belongings across the desk. She rooted through them with little interest, but paused when her fingers brushed the Hymnflute. "Are you a bard?"

"No, ma'am."

She raised a brow.

"I haven't had time to learn. There's a book with instructions, but reading and doing aren't the same." In truth, he felt some guilt over that. Resia had entrusted him with the book for a reason, and he had yet to play a single note. Maybe his concern over disturbing the caravan had been unfounded. Maybe they would have liked to have some music along the way.

"Hmm." The guard opened the book and turned a few pages before she concluded it was exactly what he'd said. "Destination?"

"The library, ma'am."

This time, she lifted her head and squinted at him. "Where are you from?"

He had not yet removed his hood, he realized. Surely she didn't think he was being secretive. She hadn't asked him to take it off. "Kolmar, ma'am."

"You don't look Kolmari."

He hadn't been aware of her getting a good enough look to know. "Yes, I hear that a lot. My parents were refugees, but that was before I can remember. Kolmar is all I've ever known."

She grunted. "I don't suppose you have a passport?"

Zaide opened his mouth to speak, then closed it without a word. He didn't even know what a passport was.

"I guess I should have expected as much." She sighed and rubbed her temple. "Listen, I realize you've traveled a long way, but you can't enter Jadora without either a passport or a sponsor with a high enough station to vouch for your identity."

Everything still lay spread across the desk, and he couldn't help stepping forward to touch the carved charms that hung from the Hymnflute. "Would Princess Dasienna count as a sponsor?"

The guard snorted. "Kid, if you can get the princess to vouch for you, you could go anywhere in the world you wanted and nobody would bat an eye."

"Should I go find her, or should I wait here?"

A blank look drew itself on the woman's face.

"She came in just before me," Zaide added. "She said we'd be questioned separately and told me to meet her at the library when I was finished. I'm not sure if she'll have gone ahead."

"You're serious," the guard remarked—a statement, rather than a question, and he wasn't sure if that was good or not.

"Yes, ma'am." He slid something back into his bag, as if to test whether or not it was allowed. When the woman did nothing to indicate he shouldn't, he continued repacking.

She pushed herself up from the desk. "Stay here."

"Yes, ma'am," he repeated. She slipped into the hall and shut the door behind her. With nothing left to do, Zaide sorted his things and repacked all of them. He finished long before the woman returned.

The office lacked windows, so he had no real sense of how long he waited. He sat on the floor and ate when his stomach complained, though the dry rations from his pack were less than pleasant without a decent drink. His water skin was almost empty and he didn't want to deplete it too soon, nor did he want to drink much when he suspected there was little hope of finding a latrine.

Eventually, the door creaked open and the guard stepped inside.

Zaide climbed to his feet as she pointed down the hallway.

"Go," the woman said.

He started to ask what he was supposed to do, then closed his mouth. Soldiers rarely appreciated cluelessness, and it wasn't as if he didn't have directions. He'd find his way to the library, one way or another.

Nodding his thanks, he gathered his things and crept down the hall. It was darker than it had been, but no less busy. Someone ducked into a room just ahead, and the guard inside ordered the door be closed. When Zaide reached the series of gates where he'd first entered, he chanced a look outside. The line was no shorter than it had been. Judging by that alone, the screening of people coming and going never ceased.

"This way," a man said, and Zaide turned toward his voice. A new gate clanked open, and the guard escorted Zaide through.

As he stepped across and laid eyes on the city for the first time, the sight took his breath away.

CHAPTER TWENTY

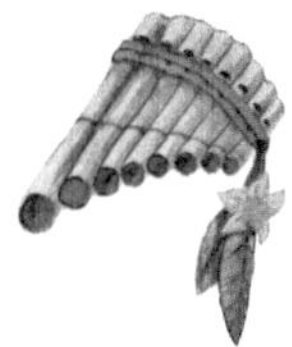

Thousands of lights glittered in the dusky city streets. They illuminated windows and were strung overhead, casting shadows in every direction. Zaide crept forward, looking at the strings of light that crisscrossed between buildings.

Though the city had appeared flat from outside the walls, he saw now that it rose in tiers. Stairways zigzagged up between levels of the city, with buildings nestled into the face of each tier. Not a bit of space appeared to be wasted. The main avenues were wide, with long ramps for carts and wagons alongside the stone staircases, but the side roads and alleys were narrow enough that he could have spread his arms and touched buildings on either side.

Tempting as it was to explore, Zaide elected to stay on the main road. He had no way of knowing which direction Lark had gone or if she had even been released, but staying in one place and waiting wouldn't be fruitful when she'd already told him to make his way to the library. He had little reason to think it would be open late at night, and the sooner he found it, the more likely he was to find somewhere to sleep, too.

Carts and foot traffic filled the road and he wove between clusters of people. He headed deeper into the city, uncertain which direction to go or what to expect from a library. Most of the buildings looked the same, built for fortification rather than beauty, but a few structures stood out, embellished with carvings or columns and accented with pots that hosted hardy desert plants. The splash of green among all the sand-colored stone drew his eye every time.

After the fourth intersection he passed, Zaide noticed etchings on the corners of some buildings. At first, he thought them decorative, but his curiosity got the better of him. A closer inspection revealed lines of text and arrows pointing different directions. Guideposts, he decided, though he didn't understand the alphabet. Somehow, he'd always assumed everyone used the same text across all of Amroch. That made little sense, now that he thought about it, and it spawned a new concern in the back of his mind. What if they got to the library and he couldn't read any of the books?

Pushing that concern aside for later, he raised a hand and flagged down a passing cart. "I'm sorry, can you read this?" He pointed to the text on one of the buildings.

The merchant steering the cart frowned at him. Though Zaide kept his hood up, it was hard to miss the strands of white that fell around his face, and he braced himself for scorn.

Instead, the merchant sighed and pushed himself from the driver's seat. He pointed to each line on the etching as he read it. "North gate. Palace. Market. South gate."

Zaide watched as the man's finger moved down the list. "Does it mention the library?"

"Library," the merchant answered, touching another word.

"Library. Thank you." Zaide put his fingertip against the end of the word as he flashed the man an appreciative smile.

The merchant grunted, offered a single nod, and returned to his cart. He hadn't been friendly, but at least he wasn't hateful.

Zaide studied the lettering for a moment longer as the merchant moved on. Had he spare paper, he would have made a rubbing to carry with him, but the symbols grew familiar after a time. When he was certain he would remember them, he turned in the appropriate direction and moved on. The next large intersection pointed him in a different direction, and bit by bit, he moved deeper into the city.

Eventually, he spotted the same symbols etched on a wide plaque above the doorway of a tall building with a long flight of shallow stairs and a half-dozen columns lining its front. The lights were dimmer here, none strung near the building's front, and he had to squint to be sure the letters were the same. He frowned to himself and lingered at the foot of the steps. If there was light inside, it was dim, and the doors were closed. But Lark had told him to meet her at the library, and she could have beaten him there. Uncertain, he climbed the stairs and tested the door.

It opened.

He stepped inside and drew the door shut behind him. His eyes adjusted easily to the soft ambience of flameless lanterns, like the one Lark carried, but warm in tone. The gentle light bathed countless rows of shelves to either side of the grand building, and curved shelves ringed each of the pillars that supported the open second floor.

Zaide's eyes traveled upward as he paced into the wide entryway, his booted footsteps loud in the empty space. More shelves waited upstairs, from the look of it. How he was supposed to find Lark in a place so big, he didn't know. He drew a breath, unsure if he should call for her.

"Can I help you?" a soft voice asked before he could decide.

He jumped and spun to face the figure that emerged from between the countless shelves.

A slim girl in a pale robe walked toward him, a lantern in her hand. Her fiery hair cascaded over her shoulders, bright against the light fabric. As she came closer, he found she was almost as tall as him.

He straightened and cleared his throat. "I'm supposed to meet someone here."

"Well, you won't find them right now," she said.

Zaide glanced at her lantern. "It's dark."

Her eyebrows lifted and she grinned. "I meant because the library is closed. Everyone is already gone."

"Oh." He shifted on his feet and looked from her lantern to her face. Her eyes sparkled with amusement, but her smile seemed genuine enough. He licked his lips and spoke again. "By any chance, did you see a girl in here? With golden hair, and blue eyes."

"No one's been in here for at least an hour," the girl said. "No one but me, anyway. You are a visitor?"

As if he hadn't made it obvious enough. "I came straight from the gates, hoping to find her."

The girl made a soft, thoughtful sound. "Well, you're welcome to wait on the stairs until she arrives." She raised her lantern a little higher, and this time, the light in her eyes was curiosity. "You must have come a long way."

Zaide blinked and looked down at himself. His clothing was dusty from travel, but he hadn't thought he looked any different from the other travelers at the gate.

"Your hair," she clarified.

"Oh." The single word felt dumb as it left his mouth a second time. Sheepish, he lowered his eyes. "I mean, yes. From... Amrochan." If Lark hadn't been to the library yet, he didn't know how open he should be.

"That is quite a distance to travel. Does your friend live near here? If not, I might be able to point you toward someplace you can rest for the night." She motioned toward the door with her lantern.

The hint was easy to take. Zaide adjusted the straps slung over his shoulders and shifted to settle his gear. "We came to Jadora together, but we were separated at the gate." And for all he knew, Lark was still there.

"Not unusual. The guards question everyone separately.

Even children. It's how they make sure no one can breach the city."

"Sounds peaceful." As intimidating as the walls were, they seemed appealing, too. Even a log barricade might have helped slow the force that tore through Kolmar.

"Usually." She grinned and opened the door.

Zaide cast one last look into the library behind him before he stepped back outside. "When is the library open? We need to, ah... my companion is supposed to be here for research, I mean. She had hoped to start right away."

Though he expected her to stay at the door, the girl stepped out onto the narrow porch and shut the door behind her. "There won't be any librarians free to assist with research for several weeks."

"We don't need assistance. Actually, she probably won't want it."

She gave him a flat look. "Only librarians are allowed to touch the books. Your companion will have to make an appointment, like everyone else."

"I doubt that," Zaide murmured.

"No exceptions," the girl said.

"There are always exceptions," Lark called from the bottom of the stairs.

Zaide and the pale-robed girl both turned to face her.

She climbed the stairs with a determined step, her eyes fixed on the girl. "By order of the crown, you will let us into the library at once."

The girl took a single step closer and glowered down at her. "Provide proof of this order, and it might be considered."

Lark's jaw tightened. "Show her the Hymnflute."

"What?" Zaide's brow furrowed. "Why—"

"Show her," she repeated, sharper.

Unwilling to question further, Zaide slid his bag from his shoulder and tugged the instrument free. He presented it in both hands, but gripped it firmly. He'd do as she ordered, but he didn't trust her not to grab it.

"We come on behalf of the Kolmari Elder, with an urgent need sanctioned by the crown," Lark said. Her crown, he assumed she meant, but he didn't interrupt, and she went on. "If you need to verify the authenticity of Kolmar's artifact, I would be happy to assist you with that. Inside. Now."

The red-haired girl stared at the Hymnflute for a time, then narrowed her eyes at Lark. She stood still, seemingly weighing her options. At last, she sighed. "Come with me."

They followed her into the library. Zaide glanced upward again as they set foot inside. Whether or not he could read anything in the library, he couldn't help but imagine what it would be like to walk between those shelves and the knowledge they had to hold.

"Give that to me," the girl ordered.

Zaide's eyes snapped to her face. She reached for the Hymnflute in his hands. Before she made contact, he pulled it away. "The Elder entrusted it to me. It stays with me until the king requests it, or until the Elder tells me otherwise."

She jabbed a finger back toward the door. "Then I must conclude your claims are false. Exit the library and do not return."

Lark's eyes darkened. "Give her the flute." Her tone was forceful, commanding.

He gritted his teeth.

"Now," she snapped. "She can't go anywhere with it. Besides, she's just a librarian. What'll she do, shelve it?"

Reluctantly, Zaide held out the Hymnflute and forced himself to let go when the red-haired girl took it from his fingers.

She turned it over, inspecting the carvings. "How did you come by this?"

"I just told you," Zaide said. "Kolmar's Elder entrusted it to me."

"He was to bring it to my father," Lark added. "But my

father's knowledge of old magic is lacking. My mother was the one who understood it. That's why we're here. Its power has been depleted. We need to know how to replenish it."

At first, the girl didn't respond. She turned one of the wooden flowers that dangled from the Hymnflute between her fingers, then peered into the pipes. She was quiet for so long, Zaide shifted in discomfort.

"Are you going to help us or not?" Lark asked at last.

A hint of disappointment fluttered over her face as she returned the instrument to Zaide's hands. "If I'm being honest, I'm not supposed to. I'm only an apprentice librarian, not a full one."

Zaide frowned. "What difference does that make?"

"I'm still in training. I don't think I have the experience you need. I don't even have the authority to have the two of you in here right now. But like I said, the librarians won't have openings for consultation for several weeks. Can you wait?"

Lark shook her head. "It took us too long to get here already. Kolmar has been overrun by the enemy's forces. Any amount of time is too long to wait. Are you certain they can't make an exception? You must know who I am."

The girl nodded. "I assume you are Princess Dasienna? Otherwise sending that artifact to your father makes no sense. I know little about the forest region, but all librarians are familiar with the sacred artifacts."

"You can tell it's real, then?" Zaide asked.

"I have no doubt about its authenticity. I do, however, have doubts that you would be able to read any books I can find on the subject of its magic." She glanced at him and paused. "You are the Elder's apprentice, were you sent to restore the magic to it yourself?"

He hesitated. His lack of magic was the last thing he wanted to discuss with a stranger.

"We don't yet know if that's possible," Lark put in smoothly, sparing him the difficulty. "I was under the impression it was a task that had to be done by a member of the royal family."

"It's possible that is the case," the girl agreed.

Zaide latched onto that opportunity to push the conversation back to the task at hand. "Isn't there anything you can do to help us? Even if I can't read any books you point us toward, she might be able to." He jerked his head toward Lark. To his relief, she nodded.

The girl pursed her lips in thought. After a time, she turned away and raised her lantern. "Come with me. And tell me your name, please. I can guess Dasienna's, but I can't fathom what a broken-born Kolmari boy might be called."

"Zaide," he replied.

She grinned at him over her shoulder. "Not one I would have guessed. My name is Tula. I am a fourth-year apprentice of the Great Library of Jadora, assigned to the third floor and... um, janitorial duty."

"Delightful," Lark said, voice flat.

Tula shrugged. "All apprentices do it. I don't expect you to understand, but Zaide might. There's a table back here, by the receiving counters. Would you wait here? I have to lock the doors and put out the rest of the lights."

They stopped by a wide wooden counter, and Tula trotted back to the front door. With her pale garb and her lantern bobbing in the dark, Zaide couldn't help but think she looked something like a ghost from afar. Up close, such a comparison never would have crossed his mind. Her fiery hair and bright eyes were the very picture of life.

"All right," Tula sighed as she returned. "I don't know how much I can help, but I will do my best. I am sorry, Your Highness, but while the senior librarians might rearrange their schedules for King Sendassian himself, they won't for anyone else."

Lark snorted. "I am sure my father would be thrilled to know I was denied aid while attending something on his behalf."

"To be fair, you've also arrived without your crown, wearing trousers, and have yet to show me any evidence of orders that come from anyone other than yourself." Despite the challenging nature of her words, Tula grinned, and Zaide took it to mean she was teasing. "Where do you wish to start? Learning of the artifact's magic, or learning of the artifact itself?"

A shadowy look crossed Lark's face. "Actually, I had hoped we could split our attention. Zaide should study its magic and see if he can determine what can be done to restore its power. I have need of other information."

The location of the other artifacts. Zaide had almost forgotten. "What makes you think I can read any of this?" He motioned toward the shelves. "She can't help two of us at once. We should start with the Hymnflute. We already have it."

"And we can't afford to waste a moment's time," Lark argued. "Tula can assist you. I only need her to point me to where I might find the location of the other artifacts."

"The other artifacts?" Tula repeated, looking between them. "If that's what you want, then you're wasting your time."

Lark frowned. "What's that supposed to mean?"

"Exactly what I said. You won't be able to reach them."

"Reach them?" Zaide looked between the two of them. "As opposed to finding them?"

Tula snorted. "We don't need to find them. I already know where they are."

A muscle twitched in Lark's jaw. "And where is that?"

"The Captured Spring rests in the waters of the northern sea," Tula said, her eyes narrowed.

"And the dagger?" Zaide asked.

The librarian girl laughed.

"Where is it?" Lark demanded.

Tula smirked. "Buried in the heart of a volcano."

CHAPTER TWENTY-ONE

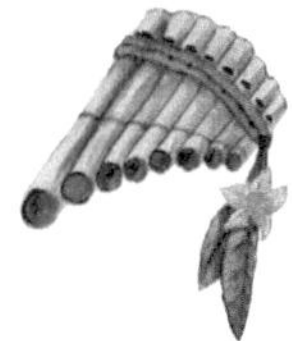

"Pᴇᴏᴘʟᴇ ᴄᴏᴍᴇ ᴛʜʀᴏᴜɢʜ ɴᴏw and then, hoping the librarians can tell them some secret that'll help them get to the dagger." Tula thumped a heavy leather-bound book onto the table and blew out a breath. "Whew, now I see why they keep these on the bottom shelf. Anyway, the librarians were able to track it down, but nobody has ever figured out how to get to it."

"How did they locate it?" Zaide watched as she opened the book and turned through the pages. She found the spot so fast, he could only assume that by *now and then,* she meant it was a regular inquiry.

Tula grinned. "Magic, of course. Isn't that how you found the Hymnflute?"

Lark crossed her arms and leaned forward to look at the open pages in front of them. If she understood anything of the strange alphabet, she gave no indication. "He found it because the Elder never lost it. Same as how I found it. Kolmar's Elders have done an excellent job of protecting their artifact. Better than Jadora's, it seems."

"You make it sound like it was an accident." Tula pointed at a passage in the middle of a page.

A frown tugged at Lark's features as she read.

Zaide shifted on his feet. As fascinating as the library was, he was useless here. The knowledge made his toes itch with a desire to pace, but he didn't want to appear nervous, even if he knew it was only restlessness. "What does it say?"

"A lot," Lark murmured.

"It's a history of the dagger, basically. It used to be held in the palace, but even a fortress city like this isn't always safe," Tula said. "We've had corrupt leaders before. Eventually, Jadora's Magister decided it was no longer wise to leave the dagger where it could be found or used. He hid it in the volcano. Or rather, in a system of caves inside it."

"And nobody's ever been able to find the dagger in the caves?" Zaide wasn't sure what a Magister was, but if the man had been in charge of the dagger's safekeeping, he assumed it was something similar to Kolmar's Elder.

Lark straightened with a sigh. "They can't get in."

He blinked at her.

Tula nodded. "The cave is sealed. No one who has visited has ever been able to open the door."

"So what do we do? Focus on the Hymnflute for now?" Zaide jostled his bag. He'd tucked it back in with his belongings so carefully it didn't make any sound when he shook it, but both Tula and Lark looked at his bag with concerned expressions. Somehow, he doubted their concern stemmed from the artifact's travel arrangements.

"Actually," Lark said slowly, "I think it might be wisest for us to split up."

He cocked his head. "In the library?"

"What good would that do? You can't read this." She waved a hand at the book. "No, I'll stay here and read. You should go look at the door to the caves. Tell me what you can gather from studying it. I don't know, maybe you'll pick up some hints and we can figure it out."

Tula snorted a laugh. "Do you have any idea how many people have tried to figure it out?"

"No, but I'm willing to guess this is the first time a member of the royal family will have been involved," Lark said. "We were the ones who entrusted the artifacts to their keepers. There may be clues that people outside the royal family wouldn't even notice."

"Fair," Zaide said. With how eager he was to move around, he wasn't opposed to venturing out to see what he could find. "Where is the cave? Is there a map?"

"No, but I could show you. I'm not really supposed to allow anyone in the library unattended, but I'm pretty sure the princess could talk her way out of trouble if it came up." Tula reached for her lantern, but Lark raised a hand to tell her to leave it. A hint of color rose in the red-haired girl's cheeks. There were no other lights in the library. Without the lantern, Lark couldn't read anything.

"Good. Take him. The sooner, the better. I can stay here and study. Maybe I'll be able to find something about the Hymnflute's power while I'm here." Lark's brow furrowed and she squinted at the book. "Can we make that lantern a little brighter?"

Tula unfastened the side and let it swing open. Inside, a small stone glowed so bright, Zaide flinched and turned away.

She giggled. "Serves you right for looking straight at it. You sure this is the guy you want to send looking for the door?"

"I don't really have many options," Lark muttered.

Zaide chose not to take it as an insult. "What do I need to take? We'll be able to move faster if I leave some of this here with Lark."

Tula raised a brow. "Lark?"

"The name I've been traveling under. It's better that we not announce my identity to everyone on the road."

"Ah," Tula said. "I suppose that makes sense. You should be armed, I suppose, since we'll need to leave the city. Bring a little food. Most other things should stay behind. I'll need a few minutes to get ready, myself. And of course, I'll need a chance to write a note for the chief librarian, because I assume the princess will be here for the next few days."

"Days?" Zaide repeated. "How far away is this cave?"

Tula scratched her forehead with her thumbnail. "That, I don't know. I don't have a firm grasp on distances, and it's not on any of our maps. But I don't know how long we're going to be down there, trying to figure this out. Travel aside, it could take a while."

"I will require sleep at some point," Lark said, though she didn't so much as blink. From the fixated expression she wore, it was a wonder she was listening at all.

"There are cots in the research rooms. That may be the best choice for sleeping arrangements. I'll show you where they are before we leave. I'll go get my things from my quarters." Tula smiled. Her teeth glittered a stark white against the rich tones of her sandy-brown skin.

"Your quarters, huh?" Zaide asked as he lowered himself to the floor and set to sorting through his things. "You live in the library?"

She shook her head, and her long hair bounced around her shoulders. "Not usually. Apprentices are assigned watch shifts. We stay here two weeks at a time, whenever it's our shift. Though I guess I'm not doing a very good job of keeping watch right now."

"Considering you're helping the princess, I'm sure your superiors will forgive you." He flashed her a grin and turned his attention to his belongings. Most choices were easy to make; most of his extra clothing wasn't likely necessary for a short expedition, and he stuck to the small, easy-to-eat travel rations. His hand returned to the Hymnflute several times before he decided to leave it and the book Resia had given him in his bag. It was his to protect. It would stay with him.

"I guess you're right. You finish preparing. I'll be back. It would be best if we leave now, it's easier to navigate the city when it's dark out. Less of a crowd to push through." Tula grinned back at him and flicked her fingers in some sort of salute he assumed was a farewell.

He committed the unfamiliar gesture to memory and finished sorting his things. He left everything he wouldn't need beside Lark's feet. "Are you sure you don't want to come with us? You'll know royal family clues and hints long before I do."

"If you truly want me to restore power to the Hymnflute, then you know this is where I need to be. We need to explore as many options as possible, and you know we don't have much time." She turned the page.

Zaide preferred not to think about what might have befallen Kolmar by now. The trip to Jadora had been long. It would be weeks before he heard anything new. "Fine. I'll let you know if I see anything unusual."

She did not reply.

By the time he climbed to his feet, Tula reappeared, clothed so differently that Zaide and Lark both started. She had pulled her flame-bright hair into a high ponytail, and her pale librarian's robe had been replaced with a colorful coat, loose-fitting pants, and a shirt that hardly deserved the name, given how it left her stomach bare. Zaide's eyes locked onto the stone in her navel that glittered when she moved into the light. An uncomfortable heat of embarrassment crept up his neck.

"Ready?" Tula asked. She hefted a bag against her shoulder and grinned. "I can show you where you can sleep now, princess."

Lark seemed reluctant to leave the book, but she straightened. "Yes. That would be best."

"I'll wait here," Zaide volunteered. He wasn't worried about leaving their things unattended in a locked and empty library, but the thought of seeing Lark's sleeping arrangements made him strangely uncomfortable.

Tula nodded. "Good plan. I'll be right back." She motioned for Lark to follow her, and the two disappeared among the shelves.

Zaide watched after them for a time, then leaned against the table to stare down at the book.

It had a few illustrations, which gave him some notion of what the text had to be about. He'd expected something about a dagger, but instead, a strange-looking pendant accompanied the unfamiliar lettering. He frowned and turned to the previous page.

There was the dagger. Or, he thought it was. It wasn't like any weapon he'd seen before, its surface depicted as rough, uneven, and black. Somewhat crude in craftsmanship, he thought. He did his best to commit it to memory anyway, then turned back one more page. An illustration decorated that one, too. It depicted an instrument, but it didn't resemble the Hymnflute all that closely. All the same, he studied it, hoping he might gain something useful from the inspection.

Quiet footsteps preceded Tula's reappearance. "All right. Let's go."

Zaide turned the book back to the page it had been on and stepped out from behind the table.

"Be careful out there." Lark's concern sounded so genuine that he stopped and blinked at her. She met his gaze with a bland expression and went on. "You're still responsible for the Hymnflute. If you lose it, you'll put us farther behind than ever."

"Thanks," he said dryly. "I'll do my best not to inconvenience you by dying." He adjusted the strap of his bag and turned to leave.

"Good luck," Lark said, softer.

Zaide paused and glanced back. The sincerity on her face caught him off guard, and all he could do was nod.

"Let's go, then!" Tula bounded a few steps ahead. She'd retrieved another lantern from somewhere in the library and it swung from her fingertips, casting strange shadows around them. "We need to hurry if we're going to get out without being noticed."

He followed her to the door. "Get out... of Jadora?"

"Yup. Well, sort of. You'll see. It's not exactly supposed to be common knowledge." She let him out and locked the library door behind them, sealing Lark inside alone. Zaide had no doubt she could take care of herself, but knowing she'd be on her own gave him a strange feeling he couldn't shake.

He'd agreed to escort her to the desert. He'd made himself responsible for her wellbeing, and leaving her by herself did not sit well.

"This way," Tula called. It wasn't until then that he noticed she'd ventured ahead and stood in the street below, waving an arm.

Embarrassment put a hint of heat in his ears. He trotted down the stairs to follow her. She'd just explained the need for speed and to move without being noticed. The last thing he needed to be doing was daydreaming.

"Try to keep quiet from here out, okay?" she murmured as she led him into a gap between buildings that was so narrow, he didn't think it counted as an alley. He ducked in after her.

The space twisted and turned, at times difficult to pass because of how angular and narrow it became. Zaide held his sword's hilt to keep it from knocking against the wall as he moved. He'd never been unnerved by tight spaces before, but the longer they were in it, the more it grated on him.

Eventually, they emerged onto a street that looked no different from the others he'd seen, but there were no familiar markings on the guide plaques. Tula hurried onward without sparing them a glance. Now and then, she stopped to peer around corners, as if to be sure they wouldn't be seen.

"Is it really so dangerous?" he asked in a murmur after the third time they stopped.

"Dangerous?" She blinked at him as if surprised he'd asked. "I never said it was dangerous. But it's going to be awkward, that's for sure."

His brow furrowed, but she held up a finger to forestall any questions. Around the next corner, she tested the door of a building with an odd number of candles lit in its front window. It swung open with a quiet creak and Tula beckoned for him to follow.

Zaide ducked inside after her, and she closed the door. More questions sprang to his lips, but when she tapped his shoulder and pointed ahead, the words scattered from his mind as quickly as all other thought.

"More adventurers, Tula?" asked a woman clothed in sheer silk and minuscule undergarments that left almost nothing unseen.

His jaw fell open before he snapped his eyes to the ceiling. The embarrassment he'd felt for being lost daydreaming was nothing compared to the flames of awkward misery that heated his cheeks now.

"Every week," Tula said, as cheerily as if nothing were out of order. She grabbed his arm and Zaide had no choice but to follow. His eyes traced the contours of the sculpted ceiling tiles as she pulled him along. The tiles bore embossed patterns of leaves and flowers, the designs so plentiful that none of them appeared the same at first glance. Somehow, he wondered if they'd made the ceiling so interesting on purpose.

"You're going to get him killed." The woman's voice was behind him now, but the soft pad of footsteps followed them as Tula dragged him through the building.

Draped fabric decorated a doorway and he swallowed as she led him into another room. A chorus of amused giggles greeted his ears. He flushed darker and kept his eyes firmly affixed to the ceiling.

Tula snorted softly. "Well, we all know you don't care, because you keep letting me bring people through. This one's different, besides."

"I noticed," the woman said, amused. "He won't look at us."

"Or where we're going," Zaide said. The collar of his shirt was uncomfortably close. He resisted the urge to tug at it. Were all the women he heard dressed the same as the one who met them at the door? He didn't want to know. "I thought we were going to—"

"We are," Tula interrupted. "And it's this way. Stay close."

He didn't have much of a choice.

She led him through another doorway, then turned and tugged him in a new direction. "Stairs," she warned, just before his foot swung out over the void. He yelped and grabbed for the walls to keep himself from going down. Blessedly, the stairway ahead was dark, empty, and devoid of near-nude women. He breathed a sigh of relief and allowed himself to watch where he was going.

"We're not cleaning up if this goes wrong," the woman called after them.

Tula harrumphed.

"I won't need cleanup," she mumbled as she pulled Zaide down to the foot of the stairs, where a plain but heavy wooden door blocked the way. A mechanism with peculiar silver wheels on it decorated the side where a lock should have been. Her fingers manipulated them faster than Zaide could see, and a moment later, the door swung open. She marched through with her chin up and an indignant look on her face.

Zaide followed with a little trepidation. She still carried the lantern, so he couldn't let her go far, but a new wave of concern rose within him. "What kind of cleanup does she mean?" And what kind of place was this? Instead of a cellar, they appeared to have stepped into a natural cavern. A clear path carved a way ahead and Tula marched along it. Even her red ponytail bounced with indignation.

"There won't be anything to clean up," Tula snapped. "It's going to work this time."

He stopped on the uneven path. "What's going to work?"

A few paces ahead, she halted. Her shoulders heaved with her sigh.

"What kind of place is this? And who are those women upstairs?" Zaide wasn't naive, but he admitted his sheltered upbringing had probably left him more innocent than his peers who'd left Kolmar. He thought of Aren, then pushed the thought away. As nice as it would have been to have a friend along for the journey, Aren couldn't help him here.

"Guards," Tula said.

He stared at her back. "Guards," he repeated. "Women in... transparent clothing."

"Yes." She spun to face him and planted her hands against her hips. The lantern clanked against her coat, betraying the presence of something solid underneath. A weapon, he guessed. "Women in transparent clothing. They guard the entrance to the tunnels, which lead to the volcano's mouth. Do you have a problem with that?"

"They're an unusual choice for guards, that's all." Zaide raised his hands, palms out. "I don't mean... I mean, I'm not from... Kolmar sends women to join the guard. They just wear more than that."

Her expression softened and she snorted a laugh. "The way they dress is exactly why they're good guards. It's a distraction. Those women are the Magister's handmaidens and some of the deadliest fighters Jadora has to offer. That's why they wear no armor or protective gear. They don't need it."

"They might be good fighters, but they're horrible guards."

Her brows crept upward. "What?"

He motioned toward the doorway behind them. "They didn't even try to stop us."

"Of course not," she said, as if the suggestion were ridiculous. "I'm a librarian. I'm allowed to come study the entrance as often as I like."

"With guests?" he asked.

"Obviously. As I said, I'm a librarian. I need protection. Just in case we get the door open." A hint of sparkle returned to her eyes and she carried on. "It's a good ways down, though. We need to keep walking if we're going to make it down there."

Zaide hurried to close the distance between them. "How

many people have you brought down here?" What had happened to the others was another question that itched in the back of his mind, but he elected not to ask, just in case he didn't like the answer.

"Not as many as it sounded like. I mean, a lot of explorers do come through wanting to see the entrance, but I'm not usually the one who brings them down. Since I'm an apprentice, technically, I'm not supposed to." Her mouth tightened and a hint of wistfulness painted her expression. "But the guards know me, and they know I want to be the one to solve the puzzle. The current Magister wants access to the volcano's sacred grounds, so he doesn't care who comes to try."

He softened his tone. "They can't get in, either?"

"Nobody can. At least, nobody's managed to yet."

"How many Magisters have there been?"

Tula shrugged. "Hundreds, probably. More than we have records of. It's an appointed position, something like your Elder, I suppose. Or, I assume so. I know a bit about the Kolmari Elder, since guardianship of the artifacts is something the librarians are supposed to track, but I don't have intimate knowledge of your history."

His history. He'd tried not to let the sidewise glances and sneers bother him, but the fact she accepted him as being Kolmari in spite of his appearance was more comforting than he'd expected. "In Kolmar, the Elder is responsible for both wielding and maintaining the Hymnflute. I don't really know why it..." He trailed off, uncertain why he'd started to share where the artifact had been. It didn't matter, in the grand scheme of things. If it was necessary to discuss the temple and its corruption, they could discuss it later.

"I don't know why he gave it to me," he said instead.

Tula shot him a funny look. "Aren't you his apprentice?"

"Yes, but he has two. There's me, and there's Resia. And it's pretty obvious she'll be the next Elder. When he entrusted the Hymnflute to me, he said Resia's healing skill was needed in

Kolmar, and so it could only be entrusted to me. But I haven't been able to do anything useful since I left."

"You escorted the princess here."

Zaide shook his head. "She would have come with or without me."

"But she wanted you to come along. That counts for something, doesn't it?" She pointed toward a tunnel that branched off in a new direction, then cut toward it.

He trailed along behind her with a sigh. "That doesn't mean I'm useful, just entertaining."

"Well, maybe you'll get a chance to be useful here," Tula said. "It's just up ahead."

His brow furrowed. "The volcano is just ahead?"

"Yes. I mean, sort of. Not exactly. We can't go to the crater, the gases would kill us. But the dagger's not in the crater, anyway. There's a network of tunnels that runs all around and through the volcano. It's hot, but you never encounter any magma or anything, so it's relatively safe."

"Relatively," he repeated.

"I mean, we are in a forbidden volcanic cave. It can't be that safe." Tula grinned at him over her shoulder, then stopped before a recess in the tunnel wall and raised her lantern. "Here it is. This is the door."

Zaide perked up at that. He crept forward to look.

When she'd said door, he'd expected metal, something easily sealed by magic or mechanisms. Instead, what lay before him was a flat expanse of stone with peculiar etchings on its surface. There were no outlines to indicate a slab had been used as a door, or to indicate there was anything separate from the wall itself.

"Huh," was all he said.

Tula's green eyes sparked. "Right? It's the weirdest thing! I know this is the door because—uh, well, it says it's the entry right there." She pointed to a set of etchings near the top of the wall. More unfamiliar markings to him; these didn't even resemble the lettering in the city above. "Right below that, there's a line that has the name of the Magister who sealed it and the date it was sealed. But the rest of these symbols don't seem to mean anything."

He stepped forward to study the rest of the markings, and she lifted her lantern to help him see. Some looked like letters, but most were patterns of circles that struck him as oddly familiar. "Are these constellations?" He raised a hand, but thought better and drew it back. "Can I touch it?"

"Sure, why not?" Tula shrugged. "And no, not constellations. At least, not any known ones."

The stone was warmer than he expected when he pressed his fingers to it, but given their location, he supposed he shouldn't have been surprised. "But it means something."

"Yeah, obviously. We just don't know what. A couple scholars have tried matching it to things like elements, magic, phases of the moon, things like that, but nothing has worked."

"Music," he murmured.

Tula nodded. "That, too. They've tried to fit it to a staff and play the notes, but it doesn't quite work. They don't fit like you'd expect, and it doesn't sound pleasant. I guess a key wouldn't have to, but they've come down here and tried to play it. Nothing happens."

His eyes narrowed and he dragged his bag around his side so he could pull it open. "No, that's not... I mean, it is what I mean. It does look like notes. Or would, if you drew in the lines between them. But maybe that's a clue, and not the answer."

She pursed her lips and watched as he pushed the Hymnflute aside in his bag and pulled out the book Resia had given him, instead. He paged through it, comparing the notes of the songs spread across its pages to the marks on the wall.

"Is that a songbook?" Tula asked. "You don't strike me as the musical type."

"I'm not. My co-apprentice thought I should have this, though." He canted his head to the side, then turned the book upside down. Some of the markings were closer to lining up, but not close enough to make a difference. "How long have the librarians been trying to open this?"

"Who knows? Longer than I've been alive." She crossed her arms and leaned back against the stone wall, blocking some of the markings from view.

Zaide sighed.

She quirked a brow. "What?"

"If they've been at it that long, I'm not sure how you expect me to do anything."

"Aren't you the Kolmari Elder's apprentice?"

"Yeah, but that doesn't mean I know how to solve these things." He waved a hand at the wall. "I'm sure your Magister has a lot more experienced scholars working on solving this."

"Probably. But sometimes an outside perspective is what's really needed for stuff like this." Tula smiled, but this time it was halting and tentative. "You're willing to try, right?"

He sank to sit on the warm stone floor and put his book aside. "Not much else I can do."

She said nothing else, and unlike with Lark, the silence that fell between them was calm and comfortable. Tula remained where she was, reclined against the wall, while he studied the shapes and markings and tried to make sense of them.

They still reminded him of stars. It didn't make sense for the marks to represent music, he decided now that he looked at them again. The circles were all different sizes; musical notes would have been uniform. Stars came in different sizes, but Tula already said they didn't seem to line up with any known constellations. He squinted at the wall for a time, then reached for his pocket.

Curious, Tula watched him with her head tipped to one side as he pulled a handful of coins from his pocket and laid them out on the floor.

"Different sizes," he said, as if that was all the explanation it needed. He had next to no money, but their travels had left him with enough coins loose in his pockets that he had them in a number of sizes. And shapes, for that matter. Most were round, but a few of the coins had numerous sides. He pushed those aside to focus on the round ones. There were none of the crystal-centered coins from Amrochan left. He doubted he would have wanted to use those.

Tula made a soft sound of encouragement.

He tried to ignore it as he slid the coins around on the floor until they mimicked the patterns on the wall. His pockets hadn't afforded enough to complete the sequence, and he pulled the many-sided coins back into play to make up for it.

The alignment revealed nothing on the floor. He maneuvered the coins into a tighter pattern and leaned back. The knowledge that he was nothing compared to the scholars who must have studied this wall before hung heavy in the back of his mind, a distraction he didn't need. Eventually, he sighed and buried his face in his hands.

"Don't rush yourself," Tula said, her voice soft and reassuring. She sank to the floor with her back against the wall and rested her elbows on her knees. "You're bound to have an idea for something we can try sooner or later."

"Maybe. Right now, I feel like my head's empty. As soon as I need a solid thought, they've all scattered like smoke." Zaide scrubbed his eyes with the heels of his palms. His eyelids were heavy. He hung his head and stared down at the coins and Resia's book. "I feel like I have to be honest. I wasn't ever a good scholar."

She flashed him a grin. "If we're being honest, I'm not, either."

"I'd think being an apprentice librarian would require a lot of scholarly prowess."

Tula laughed and flicked her hair back over her shoulder. "Yeah, you'd think that. I mean, I like the research, don't get me wrong. But I wanted to be one of the researchers that got to go out for archaeological work. Exploring the desert, having adventures, maybe sailing in search of shipwrecks. Things like that. Instead, I got assigned to the books." She waved a hand at the book on the floor. "That's why I try to get out here for things like this as often as I can. As a librarian, I'm not supposed to leave the city. Technically, we haven't left it now."

Zaide stifled his amusement. "Technically."

"Well, we haven't!" Her voice took a defensive note. "I try to take my work seriously, but... it's not me, you know? That's why I come down here so often. I can't help but feel like if I make some kind of breakthrough down here, maybe my superiors will reconsider my placement and assign me to a different group."

"If you're bringing adventurers down here to solve the door puzzle, how is that you making a breakthrough?" he asked.

She shot him a dirty look. "It counts. I'm taking initiative. Not everyone makes this much effort. Besides, I'm still part of it. I'm sitting here and thinking, too." As if to prove a point, she leaned forward and pushed a few coins closer together.

Zaide frowned. Now they were closer to resembling a melody. He snatched the book from the floor and paged through it.

Tula perked up. "You got something?"

"I feel like I've seen that before. It's nowhere near the placement of the circles on the wall, but maybe the size of the circles has to do with timing, or something like that." He scanned page after page of notes. Nothing matched.

She shifted closer and leaned in to look at the book. "Could you try playing it? If it's not in the book, maybe it's something one of us would recognize otherwise."

"I can't," Zaide said.

"Why not?"

"I can't read music. This doesn't mean anything to me. The book has a guide I can refer to, but I haven't studied it much, and I don't know what notes these are supposed to be." Despite that, he pushed the book into her hands and pulled the Hymnflute from his bag. No sooner than he had it in his hands, a wash of uncertainty flowed over him. "Uh... Also, I don't know how to play."

Tula stared at him in disbelief. "You've been traveling with that thing all the way from the Kolmar forest, with a music book in your bag, and you don't know how to play?"

He lifted the artifact to his mouth and sucked in a breath, fully intending to blow a shrill note purely out of spite. Instead, his breath caught, and his eyes locked on the symbols on the wall.

Circles.

All different sizes of circles. He lowered the Hymnflute and pushed himself up from the ground.

"What?" Tula asked. "What is it?"

"The Hymnflute," he murmured.

Her brow furrowed. "What?"

Zaide lifted a hand in signal for her to wait. He stepped over the pattern of coins laid out on the floor, raised the Hymnflute in both hands, and pressed the end of the largest pipe against the largest circle.

It fit perfectly.

"Music," he said as he touched the next circle. "But not how we thought." With the pipes all different lengths, he had to turn the artifact around to press the mouth side to the rest of the circles. One after another, he lined them up. Each circle corresponded to the diameter of one of the pipes.

"What notes are those?" Tula asked.

"I don't know. I told you, I can't read music. But I can blow notes, right? There are blank pages in the back of that book. Get something to write with out of my bag. I'll play each note, left to right, as I figure out which pipe it fits."

"Got it." She flipped the book open and leaned across the floor to grab his bag.

Zaide fixed his eyes on the first circle, the one that fit the biggest pipe, and set the flute against his lips the way he'd practiced so many times. The first note came, pure and clear, and he held it for a long moment. The placement of the circles seemed like it ought to mean something, but he couldn't fathom what. A problem for another time, he decided. Right now, all that mattered was finding each note. He fit the next pipe to the next circle, then played the single note.

Tula scratched the notes onto a hastily-drawn staff as he identified each mark. "This sounds like something. Keep going."

He hadn't planned to stop. The next circle was one he'd already identified, but he checked it against the Hymnflute to be sure.

"It's a song," she said. "It has to be!"

The seventh note started, and before him, the stone split.

CHAPTER TWENTY-TWO

Dust poured from the wall and filled the corridor until neither one of them could breathe. Zaide coughed into his sleeve and waved a hand in vain effort to clear the air. Beside him, Tula pulled her bright scarf up over her face and pressed forward with her lantern.

At first, Zaide thought the wall had collapsed, triggered by some pressure point in the circles he must have activated as he ran his fingers over the stone. Now, as she moved the light closer and the dust began to disperse farther down the hall, he saw the clear outline of a door that had retracted and swung inward.

"It's open!" Tula exclaimed, as if he couldn't see that by himself.

He opened his mouth to reply, but coughed instead. Tears tracked down his cheeks and he stepped toward the hole, hoping the space on the other side would be clear of dust.

The lantern appeared over his shoulder as Tula leaned against his back. "Nice of you to lead the way," she teased. "Should have drawn your sword first, though."

"For what?" he managed between coughs. "There's nothing in here." At least, nothing he could see. The space around them was dark, scarcely illuminated by her lantern, but small enough that he could make out four walls and what looked like doorways. At the far end of the room, a handful of jars and some sort of sculpture waited.

Tula held her scarf against her nose and trotted ahead with the light. "This looks like Fifth Age pottery. That doesn't match the... Has this place really been closed that long?"

There was less dust in the air farther into the room. He followed her toward the objects, wiped his face with his sleeve, and swallowed hard. A lungful of clean air helped. "That was a thousand years ago."

"More or less." She extended the lantern toward the sculpture to examine its face. It was humanoid, but grotesque, its squared face pinched in a perpetual scowl, with fangs jutting from its lower jaw. "This doesn't look Fifth Age."

"Older," Zaide agreed.

A sparkle lit her eyes. "What happened to you not being a good scholar?"

"I remember a few things. That thing looks like a goborrin, don't you think?"

Surprised, she turned back toward it. "Huh. It does sort of resemble the illustrations. It looks like it was supposed to be holding something." Her fingers swept over the empty space above what appeared to be carved hands, upraised before the sculpture with the palms flat.

"The dagger?" he suggested.

"I doubt it. The Magister who hid it wouldn't have made it that easy to find." She spun so fast, she almost collided with Zaide.

He put out a hand to steady her when she squeaked and teetered on her heels. "Easy, there."

"I can't relax right now. We made it inside, Zaide! Do you know how many people have tried to get in here and failed? This could change everything we know about these caverns!"

His eyes fell to the Hymnflute he still held in his other hand. "It changes a lot."

Whatever mechanism they'd activated, it was obvious the door had been sealed in a fashion that demanded the Hymnflute be present to unlock it. Part of him reasoned it made sense for the artifacts to be connected, but he couldn't recall being told anything indicating they would be.

Tula circled the room, examining the other doorways. "Well, these certainly don't seem to be locked the same way. They've got moving parts on them. I bet if you shift these rings in the right order, that's what opens them."

"No telling what that order is. You'd better leave them alone." Zaide inched closer to the strange sculpture. "Bring that light here. I can't see."

A small huff answered, but she came back and held up the lantern so he could see.

A small indentation marked the center of the statue's hands. He tapped it with a fingertip, but nothing happened.

"Not circular this time. Guess your flute trick won't work here."

"I'm surprised the flute trick worked out there. Did you see anything in here that might react to sound?"

"No, but I don't think it's unreasonable to think it might have been hidden in the wall. I don't know how exactly something like that might work, but obviously, it did." Tula squinted at the statue's hands for a moment, then sat her lantern on top of them. "Hold that, buddy."

Zaide unfastened the lantern's front and opened the horn panel to let out more light. "So do we go up and report this to your Magister?"

"Absolutely not. As soon as they find out that door is open, no one will be allowed down here anymore. I want to see a little more. Come look at this mechanism." She beckoned him toward one of the doorways.

As she'd described, a series of stone rings were inset in the door. Unlike the door that opened for the Hymnflute, this was iron, though it appeared the hinges were on the other side.

Zaide squinted at the markings on each ring. "Is this an alphabet?"

"Looks like it. It says—oh!" Tula clapped a hand to her hip, as if to feel her pocket, then spun to look the other direction. "Where's that book?"

He scanned the room and then looked back the way they'd come. It sat on the floor in the hallway, alongside his bag and scattered coins. He strode over to pick up the coins and recover the rest of his things.

When he carried them back into the small room, Tula swiped the book from his hands.

"Look how many rings there are. It's the same as the number of notes you played. I'll bet the letters on the wheels correspond with that. If we turn it to the same notes, it'll open." She flipped to the last page of the book, where she'd scrawled her notes. "Which direction does it go, though? From inside to outside, or from outside in?"

"Just try both?" Zaide touched the outermost ring, then gave it an experimental turn. It clicked into the next position with relative ease. "What's the first note?"

"Fon."

He gave her a blank stare.

Her shoulders slumped. "You don't even know the names of notes?"

"I told you, I'm not musically inclined."

"Well you're going to have to learn fast, if everything in here is connected to music. Move over." She shoved his shoulder and pressed her fingers to the ring. "Here. This symbol. Fon. We're going from the outside in?"

"Apparently."

Tula huffed. "Look. Fon, dar, sei—"

"You're just making up names. Those don't mean anything."

Her mouth puckered like she'd tasted something sour. "Fine. Let me see the flute."

Zaide held it farther away.

"Do you want to be helpful or not?"

Grudgingly, he lowered the Hymnflute back within her reach.

One by one, she tapped each of the pipes. "If you can't name them, we'll just give them numbers. This is one, this is seven. Got it?"

"Fine," he said.

"I, however, can read music, so I get to do this one." Tula sniffed and finished turning the other rings.

A low, hollow clank sounded, and the door creaked open an inch.

Zaide retreated to the statue to reclaim the lantern. "We're going deeper?"

"As long as the mechanism on the other side is the same." She pushed the door open wide enough to peek around it.

He thrust the lantern into the new hallway so she could see.

"It's the same." Tula pushed the door open wider and stepped forward. "We'll leave everything open, but just in case, it's good to know we can get back."

"Obviously. Imagine scholars spending a thousand years trying to get in here, only to get shut in and die." He stared into the darkness ahead. An odd prickle of unease crawled down the back of his neck. He thought of the spiders in Kolmar's temple and jammed the Hymnflute into his bag so he could rub the sensation away.

From the way she hurried on ahead, Tula didn't have any reservations about venturing into the dark. "I can't say I'm not worried about running into trouble, but that's also half the fun, isn't it? This is the kind of adventure I always wanted to have."

The hallway stretched on a small distance, the walls plain and featureless. Zaide couldn't shake his discomfort, but he stayed close behind her and rested a hand on his sword.

Eventually, the hall gave way to a new room. Statues like the one in the front room populated the space, some shorter, some tall.

"Huh," Tula said.

Zaide turned the open side of the lantern toward her. Something glinted among the statues.

"Metal?" she asked.

"Looks like glass." He moved closer. "Looks like a bottle of some kind. Should I get it?"

"Go ahead."

He inspected as much of the space between the statues as he could before he leaned in and wrapped his fingers around the bottle's neck. The glass was gritty with long-settled dust. Something inside clanked when he lifted it. "There's a rock in here."

Tula rose on her tiptoes to see over the top of him. "In the bottle?"

"Yeah. But it looks like it's bigger than the bottle's mouth."

"Weird. We can take that upstairs with us. Maybe the senior librarians can explain that trick."

"We should go up now," Zaide said. "We've been down here long enough. We got the door open and we figured out enough to get research started."

She retreated just far enough for him to rise. "I don't want to, though. We're here, we should look farther."

"Lark's waiting for us to bring this kind of information, though. We can't keep her waiting." Not with everything that lay on the line. This time, the thought of Kolmar made his throat tighten. He swallowed against it and stood with the bottle in hand.

Stubbornness showed in the way she thrust out her jaw, but she sighed. "Fine. Let's go up. Maybe we can ask to be part of the group that comes back down. I'm sure the Magister will want to send someone. If the Hymnflute is necessary to open that stone door again, it makes sense for you to be included. And you'll put in a good word for me, right?" The hopeful look on her face was so pitiful, it took a great deal of effort not to laugh.

"Of course," he said. "Now let's go. It's late and I'm tired, besides."

Tula trudged ahead with decidedly less spring in her step. Together, they picked their way back toward the entryway.

Halfway there, Zaide grabbed her shoulder. "Wait," he whispered.

She turned with a question on her lips, but then she saw it, too.

At the far end of the hallway, beyond the door that still stood open, light from another lantern moved across the walls.

They both froze.

"One of the Magister's guards?" Zaide asked, his voice barely above a breath.

Tula shook her head.

Slowly, he pushed the glass bottle into her hands and reached for his sword. He drew it cautiously, but couldn't prevent the soft hiss as it left its scabbard. The light ahead still moved. It grew brighter, then dimmed, as if whoever carried it walked in a circle just outside their line of sight.

After a moment of consideration, he handed her the lantern, too. "Stay here," he whispered.

She opened her mouth to protest, but he pressed a finger to his lips and she chose not to argue.

Inch by inch, he slid up the hallway. He couldn't silence his booted footsteps on the stone floor, but he kept them quiet, and the sound was buried beneath the rasp of the newcomer's movement.

More than a rasp. There was the rattle of armor and the creak of leather, the click of steps as whoever it was walked, and a strange sound that reminded Zaide of someone dragging a leafy branch along the ground. The thought of doing exactly that to hide footsteps came to mind, but he dismissed it as fast as the vision came to his mind's eye. There was no point in trying to hide anything. Even the dust left by the strange stone door's opening was already muddled with marks and prints that showed he and Tula had been there.

Or was that what was being swept away? Signs someone had found a way in? Uneasiness churned in his stomach as he eased into the doorway and looked into the first chamber.

The stone slab was closed, the exit gone, and in the middle of it all, a massive lizard in human-like armor stood on two legs, sweeping the dust left by their entry into a tidy pile.

Zaide's mouth fell open. The goborrins he'd fought in the forest had been strange enough, but a lizard?

A whisper of cloth caught his good ear, all that kept him from twitching when Tula touched his arm. He motioned toward the thing with his sword hand.

Her eyes widened and she shrugged.

No matter what it was, it stood between them and the way out. Zaide tightened his grip on his sword and stepped out into the dim room. The click of his boot heel echoed in the near-empty space.

The lizard squawked and spun toward him with its straw broom brandished like a weapon.

"Easy." Zaide made a calming motion with his free hand.

Anything but calmed, the creature flung its broom aside and drew a blade from its hip.

"Look! The other door." Tula pointed across the room to where the door opposite their hallway stood open, but Zaide didn't have time to reply. The lizard advanced on him, faster than expected, and he had no time to protest before it swung its curved blade for his head.

He met its strike and deflected it with ease.

"Get the door open!" he barked as he dropped his bag and kicked it toward her.

Tula snatched it from the floor and yanked it open. The Hymnflute sat right on top. She pulled it from the bag, and the lizard-thing squawked again.

This time, when it darted forward, it went for her. Instead of swinging, it lunged in and clamped a scaly hand around the end of the artifact in her grasp.

"Hey!" She kicked its knee and it dropped back with a squall.

Zaide struck at it from behind, but its sinuous body twisted beneath his blade and he hit nothing. It came up fast and hard with its sword in hand and it was all he could do to dodge.

The sword whistled past the side of his head and his breath caught. If he'd still had the tip of that ear, he would have lost it just then.

He twisted his wrist and brought the hilt of his sword up hard into the thing's chin.

The lizard hissed and staggered backwards.

Silver flashed for its ribs and the monster wasn't fast enough that time. Tula's blade cut into its side, yielding a blood-curdling shriek.

They both clapped hands to their ears.

A mistake.

The lizard dropped to all fours and shot past Tula's feet. It snatched the Hymnflute from the top of Zaide's bag and raced for the open door.

Zaide flowed into a downward strike, but his sword struck the stone where its tail had been a split second earlier. The lizard vanished into the dark and Zaide spat a curse.

"You put it down?" he cried.

"It attacked you! I was trying to help!" Tula pressed her fingers to her chest.

"I told you to open the door, not drop it where that thing could get it!" The monster's lantern lay on its side on the floor, having been upset at some point during their spat. He snatched it and hurried into the new hallway.

Tula's footsteps came quick behind him. "Wait!"

He didn't plan to. Anger with himself churned in the forefront of his mind. The Elder had entrusted the artifact to *him*; he shouldn't have let anyone else so much as touch it.

Ten feet from the door, the hallway transformed into stairs

that descended into shadow. Zaide gritted his teeth and ran down them. The lizard monster was fast, and he had no idea how far it might have gone. No idea what might wait ahead, either, for that matter. He slowed for half a step, then pushed for more speed instead. The way behind was closed. Even if they turned around, there was no leaving without the Hymnflute.

Which I definitely won't let anyone touch again. He mentally kicked himself and gripped his sword even tighter.

The stairs emptied into another room, similar to the one where the bottle had been. Ugly statues lined the walls to the left and right, but here, lit candles stood on their upturned hands. Maintained by the creature he chased, he could only assume. Another open door waited ahead. Zaide spared the statues a glance, just to be certain the lizard wasn't hiding among them. When he was sure, he raised his borrowed lantern a little higher and strode toward the door.

"Zaide, wait!" Tula stumbled into the room behind him, gasping for breath.

He snorted. "For what? For you to give it more things to run off with?"

"Look, I know I messed up, okay? I'm sorry. I didn't know it could move that fast."

"Fast enough I have no idea how far it's gone." He waved a hand at the space ahead. Another, almost identical room waited on the other side of the doorway. More statues, more candles, no lizard. "You know we're stuck here now, right?"

"I know." Tula leaned forward and planted her hands against her knees as she tried to catch her breath.

For a moment, he considered leaving her where she was. His legs were longer and he could walk faster, never mind going farther without needing to catch his breath. He'd barely started to run. How had she ever imagined herself fit to be an adventurer?

Before he could make up his mind, she straightened and

swallowed hard. His bag dangled against her back, and she shrugged it off to hold it out to him.

Zaide set his jaw and swiped it from her hand.

"If we keep going, there's a chance we'll run into more of those things," she said. "We're going to need to plan ahead for that. With how fast it was, do you think you can fight one on your own?"

"I don't have a choice," he spat. She'd made sure of that.

"You do have a choice. I'm right here."

He exhaled hard through his nose and looked into the room ahead.

"Neither one of us is getting out of here without those pipes," Tula said. "We may as well try to find it together, right?" She gave her own lantern a swing and pushed past him.

Zaide followed, though he allowed a comfortable distance between them. "Your sword."

"What about it?"

"You sheathed it. You're going to need to have it ready if we run into that thing again."

She paused to glance at him over her shoulder. "Fine." She drew her blade and gave her head a toss. "We just keep going forward for now, right?"

Frustration put an itch between his shoulders. He shrugged and tried to ignore it. "Not like we can do anything else."

Tula made a soft sound of agreement and forged on ahead. With nothing but a line of statue-filled rooms ahead of them, there was nowhere else to go. They passed through at least four more before she spoke again.

"Canopic jars."

He blinked and tore his eyes away from the seemingly endless row of statues and candles. "What?"

"They aren't statues. I thought they were, at first, but look. They've got a seam about three quarters of the way up. The arms are part of the jar, but the shoulders and head are the lid."

"What makes you think they've got dead stuff in them,

though?" Why anyone would want such an ugly vessel for their remains was another question that sprang to mind, but he'd seen little of Jadora beyond the external architecture. It was possible such designs were common there.

Tula waved a hand at the candles. "Because of where we are. According to some texts, goborrins revere forces of nature. A volcano would be an ideal place for a tomb if that's what you worship, don't you think?"

"Sounds blasphemous."

"To us. But they say the creatures Gadranus holds in his thrall were born from rot. They're not quite human, but they try to emulate us, so they make crude weapons and armor. Why wouldn't they make ugly jars to bury their dead? Though I suppose they could be urns, too. Maybe they hold ashes instead of embalmed remains."

Zaide grunted and hoped it didn't sound encouraging. "Maybe you can tip one over to have a look when we're done here."

"Maybe," she agreed. She lingered at the next doorway for a time, a wistful light in her eyes. Then she sighed and made herself move on. "There's more light up ahead. It doesn't look like it's just candles, too bright. What do you want to do?"

"Get there and get my artifact back." And kill the lizard creature that took it from him, though he didn't share that thought. It had attacked first, but it had also been caught off guard. They still had no way of knowing if it was an enemy, or if they'd only startled it and things had ended poorly.

Except it took the Hymnflute, he reminded himself. If it knew to seize the artifact, then it knew it had trapped them in there, and that meant the light that glowed somewhere up ahead meant nothing good.

CHAPTER TWENTY-THREE

THE LIGHT GREW as they walked, as did the heat.

"Fire," Zaide said.

"Magma." Tula stopped in the middle of the path and blocked the way.

He rolled his eyes and stepped around her. "I thought you said we'd be nowhere near the crater?"

"That was what I thought. Then that thing took off in this direction." She hesitated, but followed. "We don't want to get too close to it. There are all kinds of deadly vapors waiting for us, if that's the crater ahead."

"I doubt they're waiting for anything. They just happen to be there, and we happen to be walking in that direction." With how bright the doorway ahead had grown, the lanterns were no longer necessary. He tied his to his belt to free up his hand.

An echoing clank sounded somewhere ahead.

Tula drew a breath, then paused. Two more clanks followed. "What is that?" she murmured.

A cavern of some sort lay at the end of the corridor, and a handful of shadows loomed between the light source and them. One of the shadows moved.

The lizard.

Zaide slowed down and raised a hand in signal for her to stop.

She clasped her blade in both hands, but remained rooted in place. Good. He stalked ahead on his own, ready to strike.

The lizard had its back to them, and it hunched over a shadowy shape that looked something like a stone podium. It gripped the Hymnflute in one scaly hand and scratched at the stone with the other. Now and then, it struck the stone with the artifact. A hollow, wooden clunk sounded, loud enough to make Zaide cringe. The urge to rush forward and attack the beast was strong, but he fought it back and inched to the mouth of the cavern instead. Sweltering heat plastered his hair to his sweating face. Beyond the lizard and whatever it worked at, a chasm opened into the earth. Something below glowed; the magma and the source of light, no doubt, but that changed little. Just outside the door, a platform of stone spread to either side, hosting the entrances to new tunnels, but the lizard appeared to be alone.

Zaide raised his sword and stepped forward.

The lizard carried on without notice.

He whistled.

The Hymnflute clacked against the side of the stone and slipped from the beast's grasp. It clattered to the floor. The lizard released an angry gurgle and wheeled to face him, its blade drawn.

Zaide darted forward before it took a step. This time, it was his speed that took the monster off guard. It squeaked and chittered as it blocked a strike, but its footing was already off, and Zaide wasn't about to let it regain its balance. He slashed fast and hard, driving the monster away from the Hymnflute one step at a time.

"Tula!" he roared. He didn't dare look, but something rasped behind him and he prayed she'd picked it up.

The lizard ducked a swing and its body twisted. Recognizing

the move, Zaide slashed ahead of where he thought the beast would be and was rewarded with a sick crack as his blade struck the monster's flesh. The lizard shrieked and flailed as it collapsed against the dark stone.

Zaide jerked his sword free and plunged it forward to drive it through the lizard's throat. It flopped once, gurgled, and lay still.

"Zaide?" Tula's voice rose behind him, soft and nervous.

He squeezed his eyes closed and made himself breathe. Had she never seen battle before? Maybe the bloodshed made her ill. It might have made *him* ill, he realized. His head swam.

"Zaide, look."

A hazy sensation clouded his eyes. He rubbed them as he turned to face her.

She held the Hymnflute, and beside her, a glowing dagger hovered in midair, enclosed in a block of transparent crystal.

He turned his sword point down and leaned against it. "Is that...?"

"The dagger. It has to be." Tula leaned from side to side to inspect it, her eyes round. "It matches every description."

"So that's what we're here for, isn't it?"

"And what that thing was here for. It was trying to open this case." She traced the edge of the crystal with a fingertip.

Sweat trickled down Zaide's temples. He swiped the back of his hand across his forehead. "We need to get out of here. Let's get it and leave."

"Good idea. Look, there are circles on the front of the stand. Just like the door." Tula lifted the Hymnflute as if to play, then seemed to think better of it, for she lowered it again and then held it out at arm's length.

He took it. "How would that creature know the Hymnflute was needed to get the dagger out?"

"Beats me."

Zaide frowned, but put down his sword and crept to the front of the podium to look at the circles anyway. He wasn't confident in his ability to play, but he checked each mark to confirm they matched what he'd played before, then blew a halting, uncertain set of notes.

An odd snapping filled the air and a zigzagging crack shot up the face of the crystal. Zaide and Tula both flinched away.

A long moment passed where nothing happened. Then a chunk of crystal fell away from the case and shattered on the floor.

"Huh." Zaide pushed himself up, fighting a wave of dizziness that swept over him. He reached for the dagger.

"Wait," Tula started.

His hand closed around the hilt.

In an instant, the glow vanished, leaving a cool blade of black glass in his grasp.

Her lips parted in surprise.

"That sure was a lot easier than getting the flute," he muttered as he stepped back with the dagger in hand.

"What?"

"I'll tell you about it some time. Can we leave now? I don't feel good." He pressed a hand to his forehead as if to emphasize the statement.

Concern twisted the corners of her mouth and she stepped forward to lay her hands on his arm. "That's the vapors I was talking about. Get your sword. The sooner we get out of here, the better."

Zaide grunted in agreement. He stuck the dagger in his belt, not having anywhere else to put it, and scooped his sword off the floor.

When they stepped back into the last room with the candles and jars, it seemed darker than he remembered, and he squinted at the feeble light the lantern tied at his hip cast across the floor. Tula hurried him onward, and he was all too happy to comply. "How come you're not dizzy?" he asked.

"I don't know. Maybe you breathed more of it, since you

were the one whipping a sword around and stuff. You were definitely breathing harder than I was."

"Maybe," he conceded. There was no point in arguing, just in getting out. He kept his sword in his hand, half expecting to find more of the monsters laying in wait, but the path ahead was clear.

Tula helped him to the sealed stone door. "I think you know what to do by now."

He raised the Hymnflute in his other hand. "S'why I didn't put it away."

"Smart."

"Sometimes." Zaide managed to find the breath to play the notes he still remembered, then recoiled when the creak and crack of moving stone answered. This time, the dust was less.

Together, they emerged from the chamber. Satisfied they were safe, he sheathed his sword with a mental note to clean it later. The monster's blood still decorated the blade.

The path back to the surface seemed longer on the way out, but eventually, they reached the foot of the stairs that led into the building with the Magister's women.

The Magister's *guards*, he corrected himself silently. He still wasn't certain he believed that, but he owed the women no disrespect. With that in mind, he dug in his heels.

Tula took two steps farther, then stopped and blinked at him. "What?"

"Is there another way out?" he asked.

"Oh." A warm smile wreathed itself across her face. "No, but stay here. I'll take care of it."

She didn't give him a chance to ask how. Instead, she bounded up the stairs by threes and slipped out the door without knocking.

He hadn't realized how much he relied on her support until it was gone. Alone, he sank to sit at the foot of the stairs and cradle his head in his hands. Except he was still holding the Hymnflute in one hand. He'd never stopped to put it away. He did that now, though he found his fingers were clumsy and he had trouble rearranging things.

The book Resia had given him was in the bag, too. He didn't remember putting it back and assumed Tula had to have done it, though he couldn't recall when, and the harder he tried to recall it, the hazier everything seemed. With his hands freed, he cupped his forehead with both palms and let his shoulders sag, taking what respite he could find.

Above him, the door opened.

"Oh, Tula, he doesn't look so good," a woman's voice shared.

"I know. Help me get him up the steps?"

Hands found his arms and he didn't have the energy to fight. Instead, he let Tula and a handful of women draped in plain brown robes help him up the stairs. His knees buckled underneath him when he reached the top, and the next thing he knew, he was sinking into a pile of cushions softer than anything he'd ever felt.

Somewhere beside him, voices whispered, and he tried to make himself listen.

"What do we tell the Magister?" someone asked.

"Nothing," Tula said. "Nothing at all."

Zaide closed his eyes and exhaled as sleep took him.

"You could have killed him." Lark's voice cut through the haze. "Where would we be then?"

"It wasn't my fault. I didn't know what to expect. Nobody did." Tula sounded defensive, rather than apologetic, but there was a hint of strain, too. Or maybe worry.

Zaide sucked in a deeper breath as he roused. Shadows shifted on the other side of his eyelids and things brightened as someone moved away.

"He's waking." That voice was unfamiliar, but he had a guess as to who it might belong to. Sleep had taken him quickly, but he'd had enough of his wits about him to know where he was and where he had been.

His eyes felt gritty, but he forced them open a crack. The light was soft, but let him see Lark clearly. He'd expected she might be worried. Instead, she glowered down at him with an expression like thunderclouds.

"We got the dagger," he said, hoping the news might appease her.

It didn't. Her face darkened. "So I heard. You were supposed to report back, not go gallivanting off on some effort to kill yourself."

"I can keep it if you don't want it." His words came out hoarse and he tried to clear his throat. A moment later, Tula knelt by his side with a cup. He took it from her without hesitation. The water inside was cool and soothing, and he was thirstier than he'd realized. A sip turned into a number of swallows, and he drained the whole thing.

"The artifacts belong to the crown by right. It's mine. But you're going to need it."

Zaide scrubbed the grit from his eyes with the side of his thumb as he pushed himself upright in a pile of cushions. "What do you mean?"

Lark sat back on her heels and rested her clenched fists atop her thighs. "Tula told me what happened in the cave. If a salamander was trying to get the dagger, things are worse than I ever imagined. I must return to Amrochan to tell my father, but we need the third artifact, and the dagger will be necessary to recover it."

"Like the Hymnflute was necessary to recover this one?" His hand went to his belt, but the dagger wasn't there. His heart skipped a beat before Tula drew it from a low table nearby and held it out for him to take.

A faint crease formed between Lark's brows as he accepted the blade. "Yes. I found that information in the library's books shortly after you departed. In a way, it's good news. All this time, we've been under the impression the Hymnflute had lost its power, but if that were the case, you wouldn't have been able to unlock the door or the shield that kept the Molten Dagger locked away."

"Molten Dagger, huh?" He tilted the artifact in his hand. It was black glass that had been knapped into the form of a blade, but when he shifted it, veins of red gleamed along the edge of each chip.

Lark nodded. "Under normal circumstances, the blade is so hot that no one can touch it."

"So it's dormant?" Tula asked. "Like the flute?"

"No. If the Hymnflute were dormant, again, it wouldn't have been able to open the door. Dormancy is different for each artifact, but that's why I need to go see my father," Lark explained. "What we're seeing now isn't the artifacts going dormant. It's the artifacts waking up."

"Waking up?" Zaide repeated. He glanced between Tula and Lark before his gaze finally settled on the dagger in his hand. "What does that mean?"

A woman in a brown robe lowered a tray to the table beside them. "That the time to use them is here, and the war is about to get much uglier." The soothing fragrance of mint filled the air as she poured tea into a handful of cups. "Come. Sit. We need to discuss our plan of action."

Tula sat cross-legged on the floor beside the table. More reluctantly, Lark followed.

Zaide studied the woman's face. Her curly hair was a more subdued auburn, but she wore it in the same high ponytail as Tula. "You were the woman at the door when we came in. The naked one."

Lark's eyebrows shot up.

The woman offered a demure smile. "I was not naked. But if

you have a problem with a woman's sleeping attire, maybe you should consider that before you burst into her home."

"Regardless," Lark put in before Zaide could say anything else, "Elsanna is right. The artifacts know when they're needed. If they've made themselves available to wield, it means things are about to get much worse. Gadranus is nearing the height of his power. He must be stopped before he reaches it."

Though he was reluctant to leave the comfort of the cushion pile, Zaide moved to the side of the round table and sat. The woman, Elsanna, put a cup of tea before him and he murmured a quiet thank-you.

"The problem now is going to be keeping the Magister from finding out the dagger isn't under the city anymore." Tula lifted her cup to blow on her drink.

"Why wouldn't you want him to know? And why would you say that in front of his guards?" Zaide jerked a thumb toward Elsanna. He wasn't sure where the other women had gone. To find appropriate clothing, he hoped. The brown robe was a marked improvement over the transparent gauze she'd worn before—at least, as far as his embarrassment was concerned.

"Because the Magister is corrupt," Lark said.

Elsanna nodded. "We are the Magister's guards, but we serve the office, not the man. He put us here and ordered us to guard the entrance while the librarians worked to find a way in. There was no harm in obeying that order. But now that a librarian *has* found a way in, he's sure to hear. We can't keep other librarians from entering the tunnels, and once they see the door has been disturbed, they'll know."

"Won't that be dangerous for you?" Tula asked. "If they tell the Magister someone got in, it'll be obvious you kept that information from him."

"No, it'll be obvious that *you* kept that information from him. Not me." A twinkle lit Elsanna's green eyes. "I am supposed to guard the entrance, not investigate the tunnel on my own. I have no reason to assume the librarians under the Magister's thumb might lie to me."

Zaide cradled his tea in both hands and stifled his amusement as he listened to their back-and-forth. He hadn't expected a hot drink to be so comforting after the heat in the underground volcano's crater, but the flavor was rich and the earthenware cup bore a pleasant warmth that seeped soothingly into his fingers. He sipped the pale liquid and looked to Lark. She sat straight and proper, every bit a princess.

"No one is going to jeopardize themselves by lying," she said. "When the time comes, you will tell the Magister exactly what happened. That a broken-born sought your help in accessing the volcano, you gave it, he took the dagger and left. Of course, the story might benefit from a little exaggeration, maybe some pushing or sword fighting, but I'll leave those details up to you."

"What does me being broken-born have to do with it?" Zaide asked.

Elsanna chuckled and leaned across the table to refill his cup. "Because he'll assume you're on his side."

He thumped his cup down against the tabletop. "Why does everyone assume I'm evil?"

"It has nothing to do with you, Zaide," Lark said.

He shot her a glare. "Yes it does! Everywhere I go, people look at me like I'm their enemy."

"Because they don't know you aren't," she argued. "For all they know, your father is out there leading part of Gadranus's army—"

Zaide slammed his palms against the table and rose halfway from his seat. "My father left me and my mother in the forest so he could serve against that army!"

Lark rose to her knees, too, and met his eye with a level stare. "Then your father left because he had an axe to grind. People have no reason to assume you're different. The broken-born are an angry people, either angry at Gadranus for what he did to your homeland, or angry at my father for Amroch's failure to stop it."

"I'm not like that. I'm not angry."

"But you are yelling," Tula said quietly.

He pressed a hand to his chest. "You think I should just be quiet? Sit down and let everyone paint me as a villain at every opportunity? I sacrificed my entire life to be here!"

Lark narrowed her eyes. "Why?"

"Because of you! Because my princess ordered me to. Because you ordered me to escort you here, to assist you in this, and here I am." Zaide jabbed the table with his finger. "A thousand miles from home, sitting here, and you're trying to convince everyone to make me into the villain."

"Duty," Lark concluded.

Elsanna settled at the princess's side. "You're an honorable young man. Not many would put themselves in peril, even at the king's behest."

"I wanted to stay in Amrochan," Zaide continued, never tearing his eyes from Lark. "I wanted to ask the soldiers there about my father. Either he's still alive, or there's a grave outside Amrochan where I should have paid respects. The only reason I'm here is you."

"Peace," Elsanna said. She made a soothing, spreading motion with both hands, as if willing the tension to dissipate.

Zaide hardly felt soothed, but he sank to sit on his heels, even though he continued to glower at Lark. His chest ached, and he doubted it had anything to do with having fallen ill some hours before. He sucked in a breath and held it in hopes it would ease the discomfort. Sullen, he wrapped his hands around his cup again and squeezed his eyes closed.

He never should have agreed to help her. He should have completed his task in Amrochan, learned what he could about his father, and returned to Kolmar. The people there had never made him feel unwelcome, even if he'd always felt like something of an outsider. Had his mother lived, he doubted he would have felt even that.

"When the time comes to address the Magister, we will not tell him anything." Elsanna poured more tea into Lark's cup, though the princess had hardly touched her drink. "We knew nothing of the dagger's retrieval, and we do not know which librarian was involved."

Tula nodded. "I've already been back to the library and cleaned up our tracks. No one needs to know I wasn't there tonight. No one has any reason to believe I did anything but keep watch."

"That's dangerous for you," Lark said, though she didn't protest.

Zaide set his jaw and shifted to sit cross-legged. It hadn't seemed to bother her that retrieving the dagger was dangerous. She hadn't even thanked them for what they'd achieved.

Despite that, Tula appeared unfazed. She even went so far as to grin. "I'll be fine. I mean, if you're headed back to Amrochan, you might need to take some research materials with you, right? They're not to leave the library without an escort, but that's a task that can be assigned to an apprentice. Tomorrow, when you come to the library, I'll find you. We'll hit it off, and I'll volunteer as escort. It'll be hard for them to refuse the princess if she insists on working with me."

"Good. I like that." A hint of a smile tugged at the corner of Lark's mouth.

Zaide stifled the hint of indignation that rose within him. After aiding her in the forest's temple and escorting her all the way to the desert, she offered a near stranger more camaraderie than she'd given him. "And me?"

All her solemnity returned in an instant. "You'll be going north," Lark said. "The third artifact is called the Captured Spring. We need it. You'll have to take the dagger with you to access it. I don't know how, exactly, but it's what all the texts said. That one must unlock another."

His shoulders drooped. "How am I supposed to find it?" The words escaped before he could stop them, and when he realized how easily he'd accepted her order, he could have kicked himself.

"According to the texts I read, the spring was entrusted to the leader of Desheni, the northernmost settlement. You will have to go there and ask their leader. I suspect he will be in a position similar to what the Magister holds here, and what the Elder holds in Kolmar."

"He is." Tula pinched her lower lip in thought. "You'll need to ask to speak to Desheni's Shaman." She pushed her cup halfway across the table and pointed into it, a silent request for Elsanna to refill it. The woman leaned forward and obliged.

"And I'll be alone?" Zaide asked.

"You'll have to be." This time, true apology colored Lark's expression. "If Tula's going with me, there won't be any other options. Elsanna and the rest of the Magister's guard can't afford to leave their post."

The woman nodded. "We will cover your tracks to the best of our ability, but once you pass beyond Jadora's territory, you'll be on your own."

Zaide sighed. For what he was sure wouldn't be the last time, he regretted ever leaving Kolmar.

"The best way for you to depart will be to go north, to Jadora's docks," Elsanna said. "We can get you out of the city. From there, you'll sail to Ganede, Jadora's sister city. You will need to purchase gear for the trip. The north is unforgiving, and I am sure you did not bring clothing for the cold."

"I don't have enough money," Zaide said.

Lark waved a hand. "I'll provide funds for that leg of your journey."

Elsanna nodded in approval. "You will be able to travel the first half by road, but there is no road to Desheni. When they seek trade, they seek it by ship, and that has not been for many years."

Promising. Zaide bit back his skepticism. "How do you know they're still there?"

"Because they're the guardians of the spring," Lark said. "They have to be there."

Arguing seemed pointless, but he still gave her a hard look.

She did not so much as flinch. "I'm afraid that's all the guidance I can give you. I'll have Tula get a map before you go, but you'll have to depart tonight."

"I haven't slept!" he protested.

"You were sleeping when I got here."

"I think I was unconscious, that doesn't seem like the same thing."

"I'm going to go get that map," Tula put in. "I need to go back to the library. I'll borrow one of Elsanna's girls and send her back with it. It's not unusual for the guards to stop by the library for additional information, or to deliver new questions on behalf of the Magister. We'll make it work."

Lark waved her away. "Go."

She gave Zaide a nervous sort of smile. "Good luck."

"You too," he replied. She wasted no time in rising to leave, and his face fell as he watched her go. Despite the trouble she'd gotten them in with the lizard—salamander, Lark had called it earlier—he found himself fond of her company, and her departure was something of a disappointment.

When she disappeared from sight and he returned his attention to his table mates, Lark sent him a flat, disapproving look.

He resisted the urge to glare. "What?"

"You have to stay focused on this mission. I cannot begin to explain how vital it is."

"I am focused." More focused than he should have been, given everything he'd been through. Why he'd already agreed to this and blindly accepted a new assignment escaped him, but he couldn't think of a reason to refuse, either. No matter how he wanted to return home, Lark was the princess, and refusing her orders didn't sit well with his conscience.

"You'd better be," she said. "Once you recover the spring, I'll need you to bring it to Amrochan. It will be a long trip, and unforgiving. The northern road will be the fastest way to return to the city, but believe me when I say every ounce of haste is necessary."

Zaide shook his head and lifted a hand to rub his eyes. What was necessary was a decent rest, but it didn't sound like he'd get it unless he could sleep on the ship to Ganede. Having never been on a ship before, he had no idea how likely that was. "Why?"

"What?"

"Why do I have to hurry? Why do I need these? You still haven't told me, Your Highness." The way he spoke the title held no venom, but from the way the corners of her mouth twitched, it might as well have.

For a long time, she considered him in silence. Then she raised a hand. "Leave us, Elsanna."

The woman bowed from the shoulders and retreated from the table to pad off in silence, leaving the two of them alone.

Zaide didn't know whether to be comforted or concerned.

"When Tula told me about the salamander trying to break the dagger's case with the Hymnflute, it was worse than anything I'd imagined," the princess began. "I've tried not to share much, because I didn't know how things had progressed. I didn't know there was such urgency. The reason we need the artifacts is the same reason Gadranus wants them, and why he would have sent his creatures to recover them."

"Like the goborrins in the forest?" He'd never pieced together why the monsters might have chosen to swarm to the temple, but if the Hymnflute was the reason they were there, it was easier to understand.

Lark nodded. "Looking back, I should have recognized that

from the moment we set foot in the temple. The artifacts are a key, of sorts. They're necessary to unlock the power needed to defeat Gadranus. If he can get the artifacts—or even one of the artifacts—he can keep that power out of our grasp. Admittedly, I don't know what exactly it means by unlocking power, or how to access or use it. But we were supposed to have more time for me to learn."

"And he can't be defeated without this?" Zaide managed to keep his voice level, but asking the question made his stomach turn over.

"No," Lark said. "He cannot."

Which meant he could not fail.

"Why are you trusting me with this?" he asked, softer.

Her face twisted with something he couldn't quite decipher. Anguish, maybe. Despair.

"It was because I had the Hymnflute at first," he said. "Because the Elder gave it to me and I wouldn't let it go. But now, it's something else."

"I don't have a choice, Zaide. I have to return to Amrochan. I have to tell my father what's happening, tell him to bolster his armies and... and I don't know what else. Pray the Maker spares us, because right now, I'm not sure I see a way to get through this." Lark's voice quavered and tears brimmed on her eyelashes.

He fought the urge to brush them away.

"I know this is a mess. That this is the last thing you want to be doing, and I wish there was some other way, but there's not. You already have the flute and the dagger. The spring is a necklace. A vial as a pendant. You have to find it and bring it to me. By then, by the Maker's grace, I'll have figured out what this power we need is and how to wield it. And this..." She drew a shuddering breath. "I need you to do this. There's not anyone else."

Zaide caught her gaze and held it. All his sense and reasoning told him to refuse and go back home, but when he opened his mouth, refusal wouldn't come.

If not him, she'd do it herself; he had no doubt of that. But he'd already traveled with her to Jadora, and he still had no power to protect Kolmar. A sword, maybe, but Aren hadn't trusted him with his first blade so he could stay in the forest and try to hold back goborrin attacks. Even the garrison hadn't succeeded at that, and the soldiers there were plentiful, older, and more experienced.

He swallowed against an uncomfortable dryness in his throat and slowly inclined his head. "Yes, Your Highness."

CHAPTER TWENTY-FOUR

THE STARS HAD BEGUN to fade by the time one of Elsanna's guards returned from the library with a map in hand. Zaide took a moment to study it while Lark sorted through his gear one last time.

"You'll follow this road until here." Elsanna traced a finger across the thick paper. "I recommend crossing the river as soon as possible. The farther into the mountains you go, the more dangerous it will be to cross. Desheni sits in a region where it is always cold, and higher in the mountains, the river is deep and swift."

"Understood." Zaide folded the map and slipped it into his pocket. The hilt of the Molten Dagger bumped his hand and he adjusted the way it sat. One of the guards had provided a sheath for it that fit well enough, but he wasn't used to carrying a weapon on his left hip. He'd considered moving it to the right, but then it interfered with the way he drew his sword. The artifact would be in the way no matter what. Fitting, he decided, considering how they'd come to interfere with his life.

Lark fastened his bag. "I did my best to get everything in there. I'd feel better if you had a second bag for provisions, like we carried all the way up here, but you can get anything else you need once you make landfall. Ganede will have plenty of shopping."

"Thank you." He meant it, but did not know how sincere it sounded. He'd grown tired and frustrated, but he knew it would be some time before he had another moment's rest.

"I packed money," she went on, though she avoided his eyes as if it were awkward to say. "It should be plenty to book passage to Ganede and buy whatever you need for the expedition once you get there. If it's not, I've left a letter in your book. You can present it to any coin-changer to receive additional funding."

"Thank you," Zaide repeated, unsure what else to say.

She nodded.

Elsanna swept his bag from the low table and pressed the strap into his hands. "Best we move, then. I will get you through the city gate."

He swung the bag onto his shoulder and shifted it until it settled in a comfortable position. "All right."

Lark stood. "Zaide, before you go..."

He turned toward her, both hands on the strap of his bag.

Her mouth worked a moment before she produced words. "I know we hardly know each other, but I'm trusting you with everything I have. Please be careful. Don't make me regret this decision."

Harsh as it sounded, the honesty was easy to swallow. "You won't," he said.

Elsanna rested a hand on his shoulder. "Come. The princess must move, too, and we cannot afford any other delays."

"Good luck," Lark said.

"You, too." Zaide offered a smile, then turned to let the Magister's guard lead him from the cozy building that hid the entryway to the volcano. Her steps were swift, and he had to lengthen his stride to keep up. Blessedly, the city's streets were all but empty.

Elsanna followed the main streets instead of the winding

ways Tula had taken. Zaide studied the faces of the tall, pale buildings as they walked. Against the night sky, they struck him as paler, though the streets were no less illuminated than they had been upon his arrival.

"Pull up your hood," the guard prompted softly.

Zaide swept it up over his head. It caught on his good ear and he slid a hand between the fabric and his head to right it. "Will I need to hide in Ganede, too?"

"You will need to hide everywhere, boy." She cast him an apologetic frown. "I would say Fate has given you an unkind hand, but it is Gadranus, not Fate. He was the one who broke the Shattered Lands, who forced your people to serve him or flee. Had he not crushed your homeland within his grasp, our people would still be allies. It's easy to fault those who serve him, but it was easier to serve than to risk death in trying to cross the border."

"All the more reason to kill him, then," he said.

"All the more reason to aid the princess in her quest," Elsanna agreed.

Zaide gripped the strap of his bag until his knuckles grew pale. "Will you have to get her out of the city, too? You said the Magister—"

"I said little about the Magister," she interrupted. "I am proud to be a part of the Magister's elite guard."

A question he should have asked before they were out in the open, he assumed. "Will the princess be safe on the way back to Amrochan?"

The guard shrugged. "The road to Amrochan will be the same as it was when you traveled it. You would know better than I do. I've spent my whole life in Jadora. I expect I will die here, too."

He nodded and made himself let go of his bag. "She should be fine, then."

"You would know," Elsanna repeated, and said no more.

Before long, they reached the city's gate, where the line of people waiting to enter the city seemed no smaller than it had been the night before. That it had only been one night hardly seemed correct, but Zaide still wasn't sure how long he'd been unconscious after the guards and Tula had retrieved him from the foot of the stairs.

It couldn't have been more than an hour or two, given how incensed Lark had seemed upon his waking, but he hadn't asked, and no one had seen fit to mention it.

Elsanna flagged down one of the gate guards and pulled him off to the side. "My charge must depart with all haste. I have come to fill exit paperwork on his behalf."

The man rubbed the back of his neck. "Elsanna, I know you're in charge of the Magister's guardswomen, but—"

"Then perhaps you would like to discuss with Jadora's leadership why you're interfering with this mission by holding him at the gate?" She raised a brow.

"No, no." The guard ducked his head and crossed his hands in an X. "He will not be detained. I will gather the paperwork, just... there may be more of it. I'll need copies for my superiors."

Elsanna sighed, but waved him on. "Fine. See him through the gate. I will wait here."

"Of course, Elsanna." The guard turned to Zaide. "Wait here, please. Just one moment." He nodded to Elsanna again, then hurried on.

"Don't you have a title or something?" Zaide asked in a murmur.

She grinned. "My name frightens them enough. Now, listen. From here, travel around the foot of the plateau. One of my guards will meet you on the north side to escort you to the mouth of the bay. It should take no more than a day for you to sail across the waterway. Then you will make your way to Ganede, and from there, follow the map."

"Understood. Thank you for your help." He pressed a fist to his heart and offered a shallow bow, unsure what sort of farewell was befitting of her station. From the way her smile softened, the gesture pleased her.

"All right, we're cleared for exit," the gate guard announced as he returned. "Come with me."

Elsanna wriggled her fingers in a tiny wave good-bye. Zaide flashed her a nervous grin, then followed the guard to the gate.

Unlike the section he'd passed through with Lark—or without her, since they'd been separated—there were no guard stations or branching hallways with offices. Instead, he was taken to a small archway just large enough for a person on foot to pass through.

The guard opened the interior portcullis with a hand-cranked wheel and motioned for Zaide to cross. He strode into the small chamber and stopped just before the exterior portcullis. Beyond, the desert gleamed a pale gray.

The inner gate closed. A long, still moment passed before the grille that barred the way to the outside lifted to let him leave.

"Maker bless your travels, visitor," the guard said as the bars hit the top of their fittings.

"Maker bless your staying put, too," Zaide replied as he crossed the threshold into the desert.

The man laughed and released the portcullis. It slammed into the earth at Zaide's heels with a skull-rattling thud.

A glance toward the east showed a faint lightening of the sky. Sunrise would bring unbearable heat, and traveling along the western side of the plateau would at least put him in the shade. Without wasting a moment, he turned and started down the steep, switchbacked trail that led to the shadowy sand below.

The people in line to enter the city eyed him with mild curiosity, some with shades of distrust. Zaide ignored them and hurried onward. His boots hit the hard-packed path at the base of the trail as the sun broke over the horizon.

"Meeting to the north," he sighed to himself. There was no defined road around the city's cliffs, but small trees and scrubby bushes huddled at the foot of the rock and held firmer soil in their roots.

He stayed as close to them as he could manage, grateful for the shadow the city cast over his way. Even in the shade, the heat grew as the sun climbed into the sky, and several hours into his trek, he realized he'd sorely underestimated the size of the elevated city.

Near noon, the shadows vanished and he considered halting to rest until the worst of the day's heat subsided. But Elsanna's guard would be waiting for him, and considering that alone sounded like rebellion against the Magister he still knew nothing about, he doubted it would be prudent to keep the woman waiting.

Eventually, a bright-colored canopy strung between scraggly trees came into view. Zaide cut toward it without delay and was rewarded with the sight of a woman in sheer silks and armor that protected nothing but her modesty. She lounged against a travel pack and bedroll, a water skin in her hand. When she saw him, she took a swig.

"Took you long enough," she declared.

Zaide stopped outside the shade of her canopy. "Was I supposed to be running?"

"Might have been smart." She sealed her water skin and sat up. "Let's go."

"No introductions, huh?" He took a step forward, grateful to be out of the sun for even a moment.

She grinned at him, and he was struck by how similar all the Jadoran women he'd met were in appearance. Her ponytail was redder than Elsanna's but browner than Tula's, but her smile could have been the same as both of theirs. "I already met you while you were passed out," she said. "My name is Valla. Elsanna said I'm to get you on a boat to Ganede."

"You look like her."

"I ought to. Are you not familiar with the Magister's

guardswomen?" She stuffed a few belongings into her pack and rose to unfasten the canopy from the trees.

Zaide reached overhead to help. "Should I be? I spent less than a day in Jadora."

"Ah."

The canopy came loose and fell against his face. He shook his head and let it go.

Valla shook the fabric once and folded it into a tidy square. "The Magister's guardswomen aren't chosen. We're born. Only the women born to our bloodline are allowed to serve. The first Magister's wife was the first Magister's guard, and now we carry on her legacy."

"And Tula?" Zaide asked.

She chuckled. "We are not chosen, but we're allowed to choose. Not all of my sisters or cousins feel a need to serve."

"Explains why she's allowed to come and go from your guardhouse freely. Or whatever that place was." He adjusted his hood as she picked up her bag and draped the folded canopy over her head and shoulders. She cut a path due north, and he followed.

"A barracks of sorts, yes. It might not be what you're used to, but there's no need for guard accommodations to be uncomfortable." Valla grinned at him again, then sobered. "But that's enough talk. Come. We will put a few miles between ourselves and the city, then make camp until nightfall."

He fell in step behind her. "Lead the way."

"Of course," she laughed. "That's why I'm here."

Though Zaide expected another stretch of desert, the band of loose sand ended not far from Jadora's cliffs and gave way to stable, rocky terrain. Strange, prickly-looking plants rose from the dry earth, often with clusters of bright flowers and pockets of scraggly grass huddled at their bases. Now and then, the melody of a songbird sliced through the sound of wind, but otherwise, all was still.

"There is a road, but it hugs the coast," Valla explained when they settled in the shadow of a dead tree for rest. "It's faster to cut across the promontory like this."

Zaide allowed himself a single sip from his own water skin, then elected to conserve the rest. He didn't know how far they had to go. "Is there a large settlement where the docks are?"

"Not particularly. It's considered an offshoot of Jadora itself. We just call it Jadora's port, as the settlement on the other side is Ganede's port. Both cities sit high, overlooking the bay, but trade between the two is important." She drew a crude map in the dust with her fingertip. "We only trade with Ganede, though. Ganede is just above the docks, not separated from them like Jadora. It's easier for them to move supplies."

He leaned down to add to her drawing and marked the outline of the southwestern coast. It was little more than a wobbly outline, but it was all he remembered without pulling the map from his pocket. "Does Ganede send ships this way? Down to Addare?"

"Sometimes," Valla said. "But not often. Why do you ask?"

"For when I come back. If I could reduce the distance of the trip by sailing, I could get back to Amrochan faster." He added another line to represent the trade route they'd followed past Tinith.

Her brow crinkled. "Why would you come back south? When you are finished in Desheni, the fastest way will be to take the northern trade road. You can pass through Desheni, to the northern coast, and follow the coastline until you reach Beshnai. From there, you can ride with caravans and make your way back to Amrochan along the main trade routes. It will be faster."

"And colder," he said.

"Ah. The winters are not so severe in your forest, eh?" She grinned at him.

Zaide erased the map with his foot and leaned back against his bag. "You learned a lot about me while I was out."

"Your friends had a lot to say."

The word hit strangely and he turned it over in his head.

"Tula and Princess Dasienna," she clarified.

"I don't think we're friends."

"Hm. I think you're wrong, but you're also supposed to be sleeping, so I'll let you be wrong until another time." She winked, then pillowed her head on her bedroll.

They set out again at sunset, and before the moon had risen far into the sky, the bay came into view.

Somehow, Zaide had expected the land would slope down to the docks. Instead, the wharf and all its buildings clung to the side of the cliff, houses and shops alike built on wooden platforms that jutted out over the Ellean Sea.

Valla led him down a staircase carved into the face of the cliff and pointed toward the ships scattered across the harbor. "They often sail at night, since travel in Jadora's desert is easier at night. I'll find you a ship, but from there, you're on your own."

"Thank you, Valla. You didn't have to guide me, but I appreciate that you've taken the time to do it."

"It's a dangerous job," she sighed. "I wish it were not so. But Jadora's troubles are not yours, and I trust Elsanna to take care of things. Come, we want to stop at the third dock. You will have to sign in."

"You don't think they'll let me go if you stay to fill out the paperwork?" he asked.

She crinkled her nose and cast him a dirty look.

Zaide deflated a bit. "I was joking."

"Yes, the princess mentioned your penchant for sarcasm." She didn't sound amused. "This way."

The third dock was not the third from the staircase, as he discovered when they passed the fifth and he realized the numbers were out of order. "It seems a little counterintuitive to lay them out this way, don't you think?"

"To a visitor, maybe. They were numbered in the order they were built. Here, third dock." Valla opened the door and motioned him inside.

The office in the front of the building was so small, the two of them hardly fit with their shoulders pressed together. A shallow counter jutted from the wall with a pair of holes above it.

"Destination?" a man behind the counter asked.

Zaide leaned forward to peer through the holes. The man on the other side did not appear amused. Heat rose in his ears and Zaide straightened. "Ganede."

"Five hundred som," the man replied.

"What? That's robbery!" Valla slapped a hand down on the counter.

Zaide wasn't sure how much one som was, never mind five hundred.

The man snorted. "Five hundred for him. Less for you."

"Fifty for him. I'm not going."

"Five hundred, or no passage."

Valla leaned forward to glower through the upper hole in the wall. "You will give him passage for fifty or you will lose your job. Elsanna is sending him to Ganede. Do you really want me to send her down here?"

The man made an undignified sound. "I didn't see you, guardswoman. Forgive me. I did not know it was Magisterial business. Fifty som, of course."

She scoffed and drew a purse from her bag. "You're fortunate I pay you at all. If the boy did not need to eat while on the ship, you'd get nothing from me and be grateful for it, considering I've chosen to overlook this." Again, she slapped the counter, but this time she left a square wooden token. "Don't make me change my mind."

"Dock seven," the man replied. "The ship departs in an hour. Give them this bill of passage." He slid a folded paper across the counter.

Valla snatched it and shoved it into Zaide's hands. "Come,

boy. We've got to hurry to get you boarded if they're leaving that soon."

He pointed a thumb toward the token as the man cupped a hand over it and it disappeared behind the wooden wall. "Was that currency? Do I need some of that?"

"Walk," Valla barked.

Zaide hurried back out onto the boardwalk.

She took his arm and turned him in the direction they needed to go. "You have a smart mouth, but you seem to know nothing. Sarcastic and naive are not an ideal combination."

"Give me a few weeks, I'm sure I'll end up as jaded as the princess." He tripped on an uneven plank and stumbled a few steps before Valla managed to right him.

She planted her hands on his shoulders. "Watch yourself," she said. "And by that, I mean your mouth, not your feet."

"I'll watch those, too." Zaide shrugged her hands away.

Valla crossed her arms below her armored breasts. "I mean it, boy. You're young, you're inexperienced, and you're an obvious traveler. You've been fortunate thus far, but there are countless people like the man in there who will try to scam you or worse."

He sobered and met her eye. "Then help me before I board that ship. How much is a som, and how much is it worth compared to Amrochan currencies?"

"Five som is equal to one red-centered Amrochan rui. There are som tokens and som coins. The coins themselves are pure silver and heavy and few people carry them here. They are deposited at coin-changers and the coin-changers give us the tokens to carry instead. Does that help?"

"It would help more if I knew anything about the values of rui and what colors they came in, but I will say yes."

She scoffed and threw a hand up in defeat.

"I will speak to the coin-changers if I need further assistance," he added.

"That's a good start. They are part of a guild and held to high standards." Valla's stern expression softened. "Don't dally in the city, though. Jadora and Ganede are far from the border where war rages, but the sister cities have their own problems."

"Like the Magister?"

She inclined her head, ever so slightly. "If the princess trusts you, we shall trust you, too. But with luck, by the time your face is seen in Jadora again, both our problems will have resolved. Good luck."

Zaide stepped back onto the fourth dock in the row and double-checked the number on its post. Seven. "You, too."

The smile she gave him was sad, but she turned away and adopted a confident facade within a step. The docks were relatively empty, but the few sailors who milled about in preparation for departure or unloading moved out of her way and even offered bows of respect.

"I don't suppose I want to know what landed you a guardswoman escort," someone called from above. Zaide craned his neck to investigate. A gray-haired man leaned against the railing of the ship above him—the ship he was to board—and scratched his chin with his thumb.

"Fortune?" Zaide replied.

The man guffawed. "I wouldn't call it that, lad. Those women are terrifying. You're the last of the passengers I think I'll get. Come on up, we'll get you settled in a berth."

The gangplank was just ahead. Zaide trotted up it without hesitation. "We sail soon?"

"A matter of minutes. Fair weather for sailing today. We'll get you across the bay before sunset tomorrow." The man waved for Zaide to follow him belowdecks.

He followed, but paused at the top of the ladder to cast one last look in the direction of Jadora. News from Kolmar would have been welcome and probably would have done him good, but he outpaced it farther every day. *No different tonight,* he told himself as he plunged into the shadow of the ship's hold, his lips moving in a silent prayer that whenever word came, it would bear more hope than he held.

CHAPTER TWENTY-FIVE

ZAIDE HAD NOT BEEN AWAKE LONG before someone delved into the passenger accommodations and announced they had docked and were ready for travelers to disembark. If the voyage by sea had been rough, he'd missed it, too exhausted to do anything but sleep through the entirety of the jaunt across the bay.

He pushed himself from his berth and gathered his things, a task which had grown simple with Lark's consolidation of his supplies. The dagger hadn't left his hip and he'd kept his bag beside him as he slept, but he strapped on his sword, pulled up his cloak's hood, and jammed his feet into his boots before he concluded himself ready.

When he climbed to the ship's main deck, a handful of other passengers already stood in an orderly line to file their way down to the docks.

Unlike Jadora, there were no cliffs here, which struck him as odd until he took the time to scan the horizon and gain his bearings. Ganede's docks were nestled just inside the bay, instead of in the narrow gap that opened to the greater sea.

The cliffs rose to the west of the city, which sprawled up a slope like a climbing vine. Tendrils and branches of light emerged from the landscape as the sun dipped below the horizon, higher in the west than it was in the east.

He took his place in the line and crept down to the docks as he put his thoughts in order. He should have woken earlier and tried to plan what he had to do. Instead, he'd slept deeper than he had since he'd departed from Kolmar. Part of him suspected he was still recovering from whatever illness had come over him during his expedition with Tula. Something about dangerous gases drifted to mind, but the general sense of unwellness that had hovered over him had dissipated after a good rest, and it was of little consequence now.

What *was* of consequence was purchasing supplies for his trip to the north. The evening breeze was cool and pleasant, which made it hard to imagine what the weather would be like in Desheni, but he'd already decided he wouldn't question what he'd been told to get. Heavy winter gear was bound to be in low demand in a coastal desert town. The difficulty would be finding someplace that sold it.

The hard-packed dirt streets bustled with life and business, and for the first time since his travels began, Zaide felt more like just another traveler than an unwelcome outsider. He kept his hood up and his head bowed, but people jostled past him the same as they did any other as they hurried between destinations.

Low, wood-walled buildings with angled slate roofs boasted their wares with colorful signs written in a language he couldn't read, though he recognized a few words and symbols from the signs he'd seen in Jadora. For all that the two were called sister cities, he didn't think they could be more different. Jadora was bright, pale, and scraped the sky, while Ganede was all heavy wood and dark stone, with plants in wooden containers sitting everywhere there was space. The city glowed with soft light from windows, flames captured in glass lamps bathing passersby in warm tones.

Zaide paused beside shops with their doors open wide. Appealing scents rose from somewhere in the city, provoking his stomach until it grumbled, but he tried to focus on the task at hand. He'd find somewhere that sold what he needed, then visit a coin-changer for advice before he tried to buy anything.

Halfway through the city, he located a coin-changer who explained exchange rates in terms he understood and pointed him toward a shop for travel apparel. The moment he left, his stomach's complaints won precedence, and he followed his nose to a roadside stand where he traded a few copper pennies for a bowl made of bread that had been stuffed with roasted vegetables and wedges of half-melted cheese. He ate while he walked, and by the time he found the shop he needed, he licked the last crumbs from his fingers.

Don't dally, Zaide reminded himself as he selected thick leather garb and fur-lined gloves.

Moving on and moving fast was the smartest thing to do, but leaving without ensuring he had everything he needed would be unwise, too.

The winter gear he gathered was too bulky to fit in his bag, which was stuffed to the gills with everything Lark had deemed necessary for the trip. He bought a second bag for the new supplies, then returned to the food vendor for a second bread bowl that he wrapped in a handkerchief and tucked in the middle of the new cold-weather clothing to keep it warm. He wouldn't likely have another decent meal for some time.

Any time he stopped, he asked for news, but word from Kolmar had not yet reached as far as the coast. Little surprise there, he reasoned, though the lack of information was still disappointing. He and Lark had to have been the first travelers from that region to reach the bay.

By midnight, the city had grown quiet, though travelers still milled about and merchant caravans lined the roads, taking inventory and preparing for their next expedition. Zaide stopped beside a pool of lantern light to retrieve his map from his pocket and study the path one last time. There was a lantern in his main bag, nestled beside the Hymnflute, but he didn't want to pull it out and then be unable to put it back. The moon was still high and the landscape was pale, though it bore more greenery than Jadora's desert. He would walk by moonlight for as long as he could.

No one disturbed him as he set out from the sprawling town. The road was wide and easy to follow. It curved around the bay, letting pleasant, salty air sweep in from the water and glide up the landscape toward the higher western ridge. The going was easy, and he walked until the sun rose.

Though the bread bowl felt somewhat warm when Zaide pulled it from its wrappings, its contents had cooled into an unpleasant mass of squishy vegetables and melted cheese that wept oils from its surface. He silently hoped it would not set the tone for the rest of the trip, but he ate it anyway.

As hot as Jadora had been, he'd expected Ganede to be the same, but the way the land dipped toward the water made it considerably more pleasant. After he stole a few hours of sleep hidden in the brush a short distance from the road, he opted to continue on in daylight and camp at night.

Now and then, he passed merchants on the road, their lumbering carts and burden animals slow, but the sound of hoofbeats and creaking wheels brought a small sense of comfort through the day. It was almost ordinary; the sort of journey he'd expected he might take if he'd ever convinced the Elder to let him join the garrison.

Zaide tried to chase that thought away as soon as it landed. Worrying about home wouldn't aid his trip at all, and he still hadn't devoted much thought to what he would do when he reached his destination.

Find Desheni's Shaman and inquire after the Captured Spring, that much was obvious. But he hadn't stopped to consider what he'd have to say, or how he would present himself. The artifacts he already had were sure to help, especially if the dagger was needed to retrieve the spring from... wherever it was. All things considered, he had precious little information to work with, and all he could do was hope the Shaman would know more.

By the third day of travel, vineyards stretched across the landscape and Zaide stopped to pay for another fresh meal and borrow a hayloft to sleep in.

The day after that, the novelty wore off, and he realized something that left him both frustrated and annoyed.

He missed Lark.

Her sharp tongue and frosty demeanor had hardly been endearing, but she'd provided companionship on a long and monotonous journey. Traveling the countryside on his own could only stay novel for so long.

By the time he stood on a hilltop and looked down into a river basin, he'd grown tired of the quiet.

The first river he'd crossed had boasted a bridge. Here, the road turned to run parallel to the water, and the river itself wound farther off than he could see. Distant mountains promised chilly air, their peaks capped with snow despite the rapid approach of summer.

"So we go off the trail here," he concluded with a sigh. It wasn't hard to locate himself on the map, given the landscape, but knowing the hardest—and longest—part of the journey still lay ahead was anything but reassuring. Zaide studied the map for as long as he felt he could put off a decision.

Elsanna had told him to cross the river as soon as possible, and Valla had indicated sticking close to the coast would make travel easier. But a little farther north from where he stood, the road dipped into the river basin until it touched the line that depicted water. If there was a chance he could find a bridge and not have to swim, it would be worth it. His last dip into a river had been anything but pleasant, and though the injury was long healed, his shoulder still throbbed at the thought.

"Farther north," he concluded. He tore his eyes away from the river below and pressed on.

What he found when he reached the meeting of road and river was less than encouraging. The road bordered a steep ravine with the river glittering somewhere below, hidden by a thick tangle of trees. There were no bridges in sight, and no easy way down. The way ahead looked no better. He grumbled at himself for not listening to the guardswomen, but backtracked until sunset, when he made camp at the edge of the road. The land still fell away from the road in a sharp slope, but it was better than the ravine.

As the last rays of sun faded from the sky, lights appeared in a cluster down below, right at the edge of the river. Zaide squinted at them, uncertain. He'd not noticed any settlements when he'd looked earlier, but he supposed it was possible the trees in the river basin would make one hard to see. If there was a settlement anywhere, it made sense for it to be on the river.

But the guardswomen hadn't mentioned anyone living there, and there were no roads carved into the hillside. Would they not have reason to trade with the people in Ganede?

"Maybe there was a trail, and you missed it," he murmured to himself as he stared.

From the way the largest light flickered, he assumed it was a fire. "Which means no fire for you tonight, unless you want to be seen by potentially unfriendly strangers and asked what you're doing out here." He sighed and scrubbed his face with one hand. Why couldn't Desheni have a trade route like every other city in Amroch?

Zaide shook his head. Coming up on a camp or settlement in the wilds after dark sounded like a good way to get one's self loaded with arrows, and if Lark's reaction to his illness after the trip into Jadora's caves was any indication, she wouldn't have any pity for his plight. He settled at the side of the road with his cloak for a blanket and chose to sleep.

Ashes still smoldered in the fire pit when he reached the campsite at the river's edge. Whoever camped there was long gone, but the riverbank was so heavily marked with the hoofprints of elk, deer, and wild boar that Zaide couldn't tell which direction they might have gone. The land was surprisingly rocky, and his descent from the road to the river had taken long enough that whoever it was, they'd had plenty of time to depart.

"Would've been nice to learn if there were trails around here, though," he murmured to himself. He crouched beside the fire to warm his hands. The night had been cooler than he expected, and his muscles had been stiff when he woke. The day promised to be warm, though, and he doubted he'd need any extra layers until he chose to sleep again.

As he wriggled his fingers above the warm ashes, he glanced out across the river. It was wider than he'd expected, and the waters were murky, leaving him with no idea how deep it was. The smartest thing would have been to abandon the road the moment he'd stepped off the last bridge, he decided. Now that was more than a full day behind him, and he couldn't see an easy way to work back to the coast, where the river might branch and leave shallow spaces that would be easier to cross. Before he'd been right beside it, he'd hoped he might find a downed tree spanning the water, or something along those lines. It had been a foolish idea, and he'd woefully underestimated how wide the river really was.

"So do we swim across now, or try to find somewhere the river is more narrow?" He prodded at the coals with a stick from nearby. Judging by the charred end of it, someone else had used it for the same thing. The stick exposed a few glowing coals, and he hung close to them while he consumed a dull breakfast of dry rations.

"Going to have to cross soon. No avoiding that." The

landscape swelled with mountains farther ahead. Even if the river were more narrow farther up, both the water and air would be too cold for comfort or safety.

He studied the mountains for a time before he looked back to the river, sighed, and dusted his hands.

A short way back up the slope, he found a long stick that seemed suitably sturdy. He carried it back to the river and stuck it into the water, as far out as he could reach, to probe the depths and see how far down the bottom was. The bank fell away almost immediately after the water's edge. The stick sank to three feet, then four feet, and then he crouched and leaned out with the stick in his fingertips.

The water snagged it and carried it away.

"So we're not wading," he concluded. Most of his supplies would tolerate water and could be spread out to dry on the other side, but getting wet would ruin a good portion of his rations and the book he'd gotten from Resia. He'd have to figure out how to keep everything dry.

Behind him, a crunch sounded in the brush. Zaide glanced over his shoulder, expecting a rabbit or maybe a curious deer.

Instead, a flat-faced, gray-skinned creature no taller than his hip launched itself at him with a screech.

Zaide shouted and leaped aside. The creature's stone knife plunged into the muddy riverbank and it squawked in anger.

Mud squelched beneath his hands as Zaide rolled himself to the side and scrambled to his feet. He swiped his left hand against his hip to dry it before he swept his sword from its scabbard. The end of the steel was grungy and dark and he grimaced. He'd completely forgotten it hadn't been cleaned after his fight with the salamander.

Still squawking, the ugly, long-armed creature jerked its knife from the ground and leaped after Zaide again.

He struck it hard and his blade cleaved its stubby body in two.

Cries of anger went up from the hillside. More of the

creatures popped up from the brush, wielding crude knives, spears, and axes.

Zaide took a half step back. Even if they were easy to kill, there were more of them than he could hope to best on his own.

He swallowed hard and dove for his bags.

One strap caught on his arm and he hauled the bag up onto his shoulder. His eyes snapped up as one of the creatures landed right in front of him with its spear pulled back. Zaide ducked and stabbed at the same time. The spear whistled past his shoulder and his stab was rewarded with an ungainly screech that only enraged the other monsters more.

He grabbed the other bag and jerked the strap over his head. Both bags bounced against his back as he leaped to his feet and ran, his sword still in hand.

A pair of the gray beasts bounded into his path and he struck them down hard, but more sprang up to replace them on the hillside, howling and jeering.

A spear thumped into the path, narrowly missing his foot. He grabbed the haft and jerked it out of the dirt.

"What are you things?" he shouted.

More howls answered.

He rolled his eyes at himself and sprinted up the riverbank. Brush closed in around him and kept him close to the water's edge. The bank wasn't steep, but one wrong step could break his ankle and send him tumbling into the river. *No pressure*, he growled at himself.

A gray head popped up above a thorn bush and snarled. He flung the spear at it without looking back to see if it landed. Each thump of his heavy bags against his back threatened to bruise, but he didn't let up.

The creatures were faster than he expected, given their size. Another appeared in his path and he slashed at it. The strike missed, but the monster slipped and fell into the river. The spray of water droplets that hit his side was cold, warning of the weather ahead.

The water would be frigid farther north, but he couldn't spare time for crossing now. If he tried to swim, the things with spears would get him, and for all he knew, they could be more nimble in the water.

His chest began to burn and he tried to breathe deeper, get enough air to chase the fire from his lungs. The aching heat in his legs wasn't far behind.

The hillside narrowed and grew more steep. He was back to the ravine, but just ahead, the musical notes of tinkling water promised a rescue.

Rocks.

The river tumbled down the uneven face of a shallow cliff. Rocks protruded from its top.

"Thank you, thank you," Zaide panted. He vaulted up the stony ridge and spun to climb the rocks. They were slick with algae growth and water spray, but there were enough of them he might make it all the way across.

As soon as his boots landed on the top of a stone, he leaped to the next.

Behind him, the ugly gray creatures crashed through the undergrowth. Something splashed into the water next to him and he almost lost his balance.

Another hurled stone cracked against the rock beneath his feet.

Zaide hissed and spread his arms to steady himself before he hopped to the next rock.

A shower of stones followed, pelting his back and the water around him. One thudded into the back of his head. Zaide lost his footing and crashed into the water.

Cold shot through him like a lance. He broke the surface with a gasp and flung himself into a forward stroke. The water was just barely too deep for his feet to touch the bottom. The current fought to push him over the edge. He hit a submerged rock and it chased the air out of him, but a new barrage of stones kept him moving. He didn't realize he'd gone under until he broke through the surface again.

A sharp scrabbling behind him had the distinct sound of the monsters climbing the same rocks he'd tried to hop. He pushed harder, swam harder, but it wasn't enough.

The river spilled him over the edge and he tumbled into the rapid waters below the short falls.

By some miracle, there were no stones at the bottom, just a deeper basin where the water crashed down from above. Angry jeers chased him, but as he found a rhythm and struggled to swim for the bank, they faded, left behind.

The monsters couldn't swim.

Zaide's boot bumped something. He found his footing and dragged himself toward the shore. It took every ounce of strength he had left to haul himself up the bank.

Water poured from his clothing and ran down his face. His muscles burned, but his jaw clattered with cold. On the other side of the river, the monsters screamed and threw more stones. Their flat, smash-nosed faces were little more than a blur from this far away, but he expected they would join the spiders in his nightmares.

He sat on the riverbank and grimaced when his bags sloshed. One after the other, he upended them and poured out murky river water. His rations toppled out on the dirt, their waxed paper wrappings saturated. Resia's book was, too. He ran his thumb over the edge of the waterlogged pages and heaved a sigh. "I hate water," he groaned as he flopped back against the dirt.

A spear swung over him to point at his throat and his heart skipped a beat.

Above him stood a hunting party.

CHAPTER TWENTY-SIX

"Rest," Zaide gasped. His legs buckled beneath him a second later and he tumbled to the path.

The fur-clad hunters paused, but when one grabbed his shoulders and dragged him back to his feet, it was none too gentle.

They'd marched for two full days. Zaide's clothing had long since dried out, but the hunters had investigated his bags and apparently concluded there was little to salvage, since they'd thrown out all his provisions. They'd let him keep his water skin and had provided a sort of hard, bland bread for a meal in the morning and evening, but it was difficult to eat or drink with his hands bound.

Once he was standing, the hunter made a sound of frustration and pulled the lead rope that tied his wrists.

Zaide had no choice but to comply.

The hunters spoke amongst themselves, but not in any language Zaide had ever heard. From the responses he sometimes got to his requests for water or breaks, he suspected they understood him fine and chose to speak another tongue solely so he couldn't listen in.

They made sure he couldn't see them, either. They wore deep

hoods and face coverings that hid all but their eyes, and half of them had strange wooden pieces with slit openings for the eyes that kept him from seeing even that much. During meals, they took shifts watching him, and he wasn't allowed near the fire until everyone else had eaten.

At least they'd allowed him to pull on his cold weather gear over the top of his regular clothes. With how far they'd already traveled into the mountains, he suspected anything less and he would have frozen.

"I need to rest," Zaide said, more firmly.

This time, their conversation paused.

The hunter who led him pointed toward a rotting tree stump not far off the narrow trail they followed. Someone else made a sound of agreement, and the group stopped while Zaide's captor directed him to sit.

He was allowed to remove his water skin from his belt and drink, but the hunter who towered over him watched, unblinking.

Zaide found himself glaring up into those dark eyes. The man had taken his sword and the Molten Dagger, but they had allowed him to carry his own bags, though they were considerably lighter with his food supply gone. He dreaded what Resia's book would look like when he finally got it out, but at least they hadn't seemed interested in the Hymnflute.

They hadn't been interested in the dagger either, beyond that it was a weapon. The man hadn't even unsheathed it.

Another swallow of his cool water soothed the scratchiness of his throat, but Zaide still frowned when he plugged the skin and returned it to his belt. Everything was awkward with his hands tied, but they hadn't unbound him for anything but the few minutes when they allowed him to don his leather gear.

"It would be nice if one of you would tell me where we're going at some point," he said, knowing he wouldn't get any response. "Or maybe an acknowledgment you understand me. I know you do."

The hunter stared down at him as if made of stone. Unmoving, unblinking, unreadable without his face exposed.

A moment later, the hunter tugged the rope in indication for Zaide to get back on his feet.

He sighed and rose. Sooner or later, they'd have to reach a destination, and thus far, they'd headed north. It wasn't how he'd planned to travel to Desheni, but after the ambush beside the river, he assumed it was safer to travel in a group—whether or not he was free.

Now and then, a handful of hunters would break off from the main party. They came and went in cycles, so Zaide was never sure how many there were, but he'd identified eleven by the differences in their clothing. They came back eventually, always with some sort of catch they'd clean and cook for one of their two meals. The only one who never departed with the others was the one who led Zaide.

The others seemed more human. They laughed and chatted in their own tongue, their words sometimes accompanied by grand gestures or playful shoves. But the hunter with the rope rarely spoke and was anything but animated. Serious to a fault, judging by how the others regarded him, but they did not act as if the man was unwelcome. Zaide puzzled over that as they worked ever deeper into the mountains, unsure how he would bend it to his favor, but positive he could.

When one of the smaller parties broke away one morning and returned with an elk, Zaide knew they were close to wherever they were headed. Four men carried the beast on a pole, while another party ventured out and soon returned with a boar.

Near midday, they rounded a bend on the mountain trail and a valley opened before them.

A wide lake waited at the bottom, a village nestled at its side. Smoke rose from stone chimneys on snow-covered houses, and the steady chop of an axe echoed up the mountainside. As far as Zaide had seen, there were no other settlements in the mountains. He stared down at it for a time before he hazarded a guess. "Desheni?"

His captor glanced at him, a shade too fast for it to be casual interest.

"I'll take that as my answer." Zaide hadn't dared hope they might travel that far north and was glad they had, but arrival presented a new problem. He was supposed to reach the village and seek aid from the Shaman, prove himself trustworthy and deserving of help. With his wrists tied and his weapons taken, he wasn't sure how he was supposed to prove himself anything but helpless.

The rest of the group perked up as they worked down the winding trail. It was steep in places and Zaide slid more than once, but never lost his balance for more than a moment. The hunter leading him exchanged quiet words with the others. They waved him off, and he split away from the group with Zaide in tow. The others made their way toward what looked to be a butchering shed, while they headed into the heart of the village.

The houses were built of logs and chinked with mud, a style that reminded Zaide all too much of Kolmar. The soft fragrance of pine wafted on the air, along with scents of baking bread and roasting meat. His stomach responded eagerly to the smells and he held his hands a little closer to his middle. He could do little to silence it and didn't know why he felt he should, but the impulse was there.

"Where are we going?" he asked, not expecting a response, not disappointed when he didn't get one.

Still silent, the hunter led him to a cabin near the edge of the water, this one built on stone stilts. So it wouldn't flood when the lake was high, Zaide assumed. They climbed the stairs and the hunter pushed open the door without knocking.

Inside, the warm fragrance of incense greeted them. Smoke, too, but Zaide already couldn't see, blinded by the snow outside. He alternated between squinting and blinking in an effort to restore his vision.

A man's voice rose from the other end of the room. A shape moved in the dark, and the room grew brighter as it slid away from a hearth where a fire roared. Zaide tried not to look at the flames, either. Instead, he focused on that shadowy shape, the source of the voice and the words in the unfamiliar language of the hunters who had captured him.

The hunter replied. He touched Zaide's sword, sheathed at his own side, then reached for something else. Zaide squinted harder to make it out.

The dagger. Of course.

The shadowy shape moved closer and resolved into the form of a man bundled in dark fur. His long white mustaches were tied with beads and made a stark contrast to his garb. The beads clacked together when he tilted his head. "You bring war to Desheni."

Zaide arched a brow at him. "You speak a language I understand."

"We separate ourselves from the outer world. That does not mean we do not know it." The old man sniffed and came closer. The furs he wore dragged on the floor behind him.

The hunter held out the dagger. The old man plucked it from his hand. "You know what this is?"

"An artifact," Zaide replied. "One of three. Dasienna, Princess of Amroch, ordered me to find it and come here."

"Dasienna," the man repeated, drawing out each syllable. "She has wasted your time."

"She told me to seek Desheni's Shaman. Is that you?" Considering the size and location of the house they stood in, Zaide assumed the man held some position of respect. If he was not the Shaman, he had to be some sort of governor or clan chief.

Again, the man sniffed. "I am Athradan, and I lead Desheni. My father was Shaman, but the line of Shamans is no more. Magic has left our people."

Zaide tried not to frown. "It sounds like you're who I was supposed to look for, though, magic or no magic. I've come to recover the Captured Spring. The princess wanted to be here, but had to return to Amrochan. She sent me in her place."

"Again," Athradan said, "the princess has wasted your time. We bear no magic, and we bear no spring."

No spring. Countless hours of travel, a loss of his supplies and his book, capture and discomfort, and they didn't have the spring. Zaide stared at the Desheni leader, unsure what to say.

"Remove his hood," Athradan ordered.

The hunter jerked it back.

Zaide set his jaw and waited for a snide remark, but none came.

Instead, the old man snorted, returned to the hearth and extended his hands toward the warm fire. "You shall be fed, and then you shall be imprisoned. Tonight, our council will decide what is to become of you."

"Imprisoned? I haven't done anything!"

"You have trespassed in Desheni's mountains, bearing a weapon meant to break the world. Your fate will be discussed and decided by the council." Athradan glanced over his shoulder. "Take him. Go."

The hunter pressed a fist to his heart and pulled Zaide back toward the door.

"At least let me speak to this council!" Zaide protested. "Let me tell them what the princess said, let me explain why she sent me to—"

"Go!" the old man barked.

The hunter dragged Zaide out the door and started down a new path.

Silent as the man had been, Zaide doubted there was any reason for the hunter to answer him, but he tried anyway. "I haven't done anything to deserve imprisonment. Please, tell the council I want to speak to them. Lark—Princess Dasienna insists the fate of Amroch hangs in the balance. They need to know."

No response came. The hunter dragged Zaide into a shack

and thrust him into a cell with wooden bars and a chain to lock it.

"Please," Zaide insisted.

The hunter snapped the lock closed and slammed the door, cutting off all light.

CHAPTER TWENTY-SEVEN

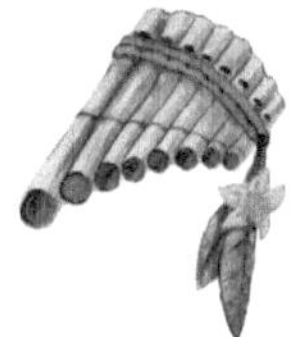

THE HOURS that dragged by could have been days. Zaide had fished his lantern from his bag and tried to open it, but the stone inside was lightless. He hadn't thought the lantern susceptible to water, but admittedly, he knew little about them. Alone in near-complete darkness, he could do nothing but sit and wait.

The sliver of light that seeped in under the doorway was no comfort. It grew golden, then ruddy, then faded to nothing, and every change deepened his despair.

Nothing had gone according to plan. Not one single thing, not since the soldiers had arrived from the garrison to hold the Spring Choosing. Zaide pulled up his knees, planted his elbows atop them, and leaned forward to rest his forehead against his arms. He couldn't even make himself sleep.

Long after the last light disappeared, a soft creak announced the opening of the door. A shadow moved against the backdrop of snow and a starry sky. Then the door closed, and quiet steps moved closer. A warm, savory smell filled the small shack and Zaide's stomach grumbled in response.

A thump of wood against wood followed, and then light pierced the darkness.

Zaide flinched and turned away.

"Sorry," his visitor said, his words softly accented. The light dimmed as he shuttered the lantern partway. "I am Andriun. I have brought you food."

Slowly, Zaide turned to look at him.

A young man stared at him from the other side of the wooden bars. He still wore his hunting garb.

"You," Zaide said.

"Yes." Andriun pushed a wooden bowl across the floor, slid it between the bars and into the cell. Stew. "I am sorry. As the Shaman's son, it was my duty to bring you here. As it is my duty to see you are fed."

Distrust crawled up his spine, but his stomach's protests were too loud to ignore. Zaide stared at the bowl, then glanced at his hands. His wrists were still bound.

"Put your hands through the bars," Andriun instructed.

Zaide frowned, but slid his hands out between the wooden bars. The Desheni hunter produced a knife and severed the ropes.

"Thank you," Zaide muttered as he picked up the bowl and brought it to his nose. The aroma would have been rich and mouth-watering even to a man who wasn't starving. "You said the Shaman. Your father... Athradan?"

Andriun nodded.

"He made it sound like there isn't a Shaman."

"The title is his, whether he wants it or not. As it will be mine, whether I have magic or not."

Zaide stared at him through the bars.

For all that he was serious and stoic, the hunter who knelt before him couldn't have been more than a few years his senior. Barely a man, without so much as a whisker on his chin. With the way he hunched forward, his dark hair hung almost to the floor, and his eyes burned with intensity. Such intensity, in fact, that Zaide almost missed the most stark difference between the two of them.

"You're blue," he exclaimed.

Andriun blinked. "Yes. I... Have you not... You do not know about the Desheni?"

Zaide shook his head.

"We are people of the sea. It is why we live beside the water. We lived on the coast, but our enemy's taint touches even the water." The hunter cocked his head. "Where have you traveled from? Northeast? South?"

"From Jadora," Zaide said. "Kolmar, before that."

"Huh. I am surprised you did not hear stories in the sister cities. There are jokes they make. Because the desert's people, they have red hair, and we are blue, so..." Andriun drew his hands together, then separated them. "Ah... Purple. They are not appropriate jokes. I do not know why I am sharing this."

Zaide snorted a laugh. "At least purple looks nice. I look like a ghost."

"Ghosts are transparent. I am reasonably certain you are solid. I tied your hands."

"You did." Zaide's amusement faded. For all that Andriun had been stony and silent on their days-long journey through the picturesque mountains, he was warm and perfectly personable when he spoke. Zaide didn't know why it was so comfortable to speak to the Desheni hunter, given the situations they'd already been through, and he tempered his emotions. "And I'm still a prisoner. Which makes me wonder, why are you here? It doesn't seem like you just came to deliver food." He put his stew aside.

Andriun sobered. He put down his lantern and sat cross-legged on the floor. "I did not. I came to speak. The dagger—the one you carried when I found you—it is the artifact from the heart of Jadora's volcano, yes?"

"I'm surprised you'd know that, being all the way out here."

"We keep to ourselves, but we are careful in our study of histories and the world." A hint of a smile tugged at the corner of Andriun's mouth. He rested his hands on his knees and Zaide saw for the first time that his fingers were webbed to the midfinger knuckle. Given the blue skin and what he'd shared about water, it came as little surprise.

When he realized Andriun expected an answer, Zaide made himself nod. "I imagine you have a lot of responsibility in that area, being the Shaman's son."

"Yes. I... well, first, there is another artifact. An instrument. It is the one in your bag, is it not? You hold them both?"

"I do," Zaide said slowly.

Andriun exhaled in relief. "There is the third, as you have said. The Captured Spring was entrusted to the Desheni, as the Molten Dagger was entrusted to the Jadorans, and the Hymnflute to the Kolmari. You say the princess has sent you. I will help you to find it."

Of all the directions their meeting could have taken, Zaide hadn't expected that one. "Why?"

"It is difficult to explain. I will try, but not now. The council will meet soon, but we will depart before they finish. Eat. I will gather supplies, and I will explain when we leave." Andriun pushed himself up from the floor in one quick, fluid movement.

"What?" Zaide stood, too. "But why—"

"You still have your bags," the Desheni interrupted. "Eat. Be ready. When I return, we leave." With that, he retreated through the door and closed it without a sound.

The lantern still sat on the floor. Zaide stared at it for a moment before he sank to the floorboards and took his bowl of stew into his hands once more. The wooden bowl was warm and comforting. When he finally made himself take a bite, he found the flavor of the stew was comforting, too. Before long, his spoon scraped the bottom and he regretted there wasn't more.

Unsure how long he had to prepare, he checked his bags. Without his rations, the second was unnecessary. He folded it and stuffed it into the first, strapped the remaining bag to his back, then adjusted his cloak and sat to wait. His wrists were raw after having been bound for so long, and he rubbed at them with chilly fingers. He considered trying to reach the lantern, too, but decided against it. If someone other than Andriun returned, he could at least pretend he was just trying to keep warm, instead of preparing to leave. If they found him with all his gear on and a lantern in his hands, it would be harder to explain.

The door rattled on its hinges and something bumped against it. A moment later, Andriun slipped inside, dressed in his full hunting gear with a spear in his mittened hand and a bag on his back. "We must hurry," he said as he fit a key to the cell's lock.

Zaide hopped to his feet. The cell's wooden door swung open and he slipped out to join his new friend.

Is he, though? The small, sour thought was little more than a whisper in the back of his mind, some distrustful part of him that lacked all spirit of adventure. There was always a possibility he was being set up, and he wouldn't deny that risk, but the way Andriun peeked out the door struck Zaide as anxious enough to be legitimate.

"Come," the Desheni hunter whispered.

Zaide swiped the lantern from the floor and shuttered it. Then, together, they emerged into the night.

Thick, fat snowflakes drifted from a hazy gray sky. A blessing, Zaide concluded, as they would cover their tracks in no time. Andriun made for the northern edge of the village and Zaide followed close on his heels. The night was silent, save for the crunch of their boots on the snow and the soft patter of the fat snowflakes as they landed in the dark. The air felt still, tense, like the uneasy moment of peace before a wild storm front pushed through.

Andriun led the way to the lake's edge, then skirted along it toward the northeast. Eventually, the lights of the village faded behind them, lost in the snowy dark.

"I'd like to know why you're helping me," Zaide asked when he judged them a safe distance from the village.

Andriun glanced over his shoulder and stared into the dark

behind them for a time, but the landscape bore nothing but snow. Not even a lantern light marred the shadow of night. He sighed. "Because I do not trust my father's judgment in this. In truth, I do not trust my father at all." Though they were alone, he kept his voice low.

Zaide lowered his, too. "About the spring?"

"About anything. I will tell you more, but first, we must reach the ice."

If the snow and the crust of ice at the lake's edge didn't count, Zaide couldn't fathom what he meant.

They trekked onward until the sky grew pale, and when it grew light enough to see, he understood.

Not far ahead, a thick, snow-covered sheet of ice stretched across the lake beside them.

"Here is where we stop for now." Andriun turned to face him and reached for something beneath his fur-lined cape. He fussed with it a moment, then cleared his throat as he presented it in one hand.

Zaide's sword.

He looked at it, then lifted his eyes to meet the hunter's gaze.

"From here, I give you two choices," Andriun said. "You can take your sword and try to best me, or you can take your sword and leave the north, abandon your mission and depart with your life."

Zaide shook his head. "I don't want to fight you."

"If you wish to recover the spring, you will. Give me a reason, broken-born. Prove you are the one I should trust with this task." The hunter held the sword out farther.

Still reluctant, Zaide took his sword and belted the sheath at his side. "My name is Zaide."

Andriun stepped back and held his spear at the ready. "Will you prove it is an honor to know you?"

From the way the hunter stood, he was no stranger to conflict. Zaide curled his left hand around the hilt of his sword and considered his options. There were precious few. "If I win, you give back the Molten Dagger, too."

"If you win, you will need it," Andriun replied with a grin.

Zaide drew his blade.

The next moment, the hunter struck at him with such force that parrying almost knocked the sword from his hands. Zaide shook off the shock and recovered with a jab of his own.

Andriun was fast, long-legged and agile. He moved like a dancer across the snow, his footing sure and steady despite the layer of ice that crackled under every step. As he moved, wind whipped up, and a swirl of snow obscured him from view.

A moment later, the spear came at him from a new side.

Zaide spat an oath as he ducked aside. Before he could retaliate, the snow swallowed his opponent again.

Fine, he thought. *We'll find you another way.* He squeezed his eyes closed and listened for the crunch of the snow.

It came on his right, the side of his good ear, and he spun so fast that it was Andriun's turn to curse. His blade shaved fur from the hunter's collar.

"You adapt fast," the hunter said as he retreated a handful of steps. For a split second, Zaide thought the fight was over. Then the whirling snow fell, all at once, and Andriun twirled his spear like a staff. He swung in fast and hard, his style of attack changed in an instant.

It took Zaide a moment to change his mindset. He'd trained for situations where an opponent might know how to wield multiple weapons, but the difference between them was usually more broad. A staff and a spear were similar, and as long as he did not allow Andriun to put distance between them again, the hunter would have no advantage.

He charged in, blade ready.

Andriun took a step backwards.

Instead of swinging, Zaide dropped low, slid on the ice, and kicked the hunter's feet out from under him.

The Desheni hunter stifled a shout as he went down. He

twisted to soften his landing, but it was too late to change the tide of their fight. Zaide stopped above him, the tip of his sword aimed at Andriun's throat.

"You are experienced," Andriun said with a grin. "I should have expected, from the princess's champion."

Champion? The very suggestion tore a laugh from Zaide's throat. He shook his head, lowered his sword, and offered his hand. "I think *errand boy* is a more appropriate title, given how she treats me."

"Perhaps. But there must be some reason that she has chosen you." Andriun accepted the hand up and dusted himself off. "Our fight was short-lived. I hope you are not offended by my quick surrender, but I have seen all that I needed to see."

"In sparring matches, you stop when your opponent is down. I wasn't under the impression I should try to kill you, just best you." The sword felt good in his hand, but it couldn't have looked much worse. He'd meant to clean it before the flat-faced, gray-skinned monsters caught him at the river. After he'd been captured by the Desheni hunting party, he'd never had a chance. He tipped the blade up to inspect the filth crusted on it. By now, it had to have rusted underneath the grime.

Andriun studied the sword, too. "Your fight with the bugraks was likely our fault. I apologize for your trouble, and the state of your weapon."

"Bugraks, huh?" Zaide reluctantly returned his sword to its sheath. "I've never heard of them. It wasn't them, though. I killed a salamander when I recovered the Molten Dagger, but the fumes in the cave made me ill and I forgot to clean it. I'm sure Aren would be embarrassed."

The hunter cocked his head. "Aren?"

"A friend from Kolmar. He gave me his sword because I didn't have one. I lost it. Now I've about ruined its replacement, too."

"Any sword can be cleaned," Andriun said. "I will help you before we enter the cavern. But first, I have made a promise."

He drew his cape forward over his shoulders and rummaged for a moment. Whether he was searching pockets or his bag, Zaide didn't know. A grin lit Andriun's face when he found what he was looking for, and when his cape parted again, he presented the sheathed dagger flat on his upturned and mittened palms.

Zaide claimed it without hesitation, though the moment it was in his hands, he closed his eyes and allowed himself a breath of relief. "I wasn't sure you'd actually give it back."

"I admit there is a temptation. But I am not the one who is to claim the Captured Spring from where it is hidden." Andriun pressed a fist over his heart. "I am not yet Shaman of the Desheni. For what I am doing, I may never become Shaman. But it is what is right. I feel that in my bones. You feel it, too, do you not? The shadow that creeps into Amroch."

"I wish I didn't." At first glance, the dagger looked no different when Zaide slid it from its sheath. The thin veins of red that lined each facet of its surface glinted in the early morning light. "But you are going to become Shaman, aren't you?"

The hunter tensed. "Why do you say this?"

Zaide jammed the dagger back into its sheath and fastened it at his left hip. "Because you were using magic while we fought."

Uncertainty filled Andriun's face.

"Snow doesn't blow like that naturally. Not after it's fallen. You have some power over it." The thought to reassure him came to mind, and Zaide offered a warm smile. "I was the Kolmari Elder's apprentice, you know. I might not have any magic, but I know it when I see it."

"How does one without magic become the Elder's apprentice?"

"How does one without magic become Desheni's Shaman?" Zaide retorted.

Suddenly sheepish, Andriun ducked his head. "I accept your point. But it does not change what I said. When my father learns I have aided you, I will likely be cast out from the village." The statement was simple and said calmly, as if he'd already resigned himself to that fate, but it hit Zaide like a blow to the stomach.

"I don't want to be responsible for that," he protested.

"If you are, then it would be best. I would rather be cast out for aiding Amroch's future than to be allowed to linger while the shadow swallows the Desheni. I will not be swallowed with them." Andriun's dark eyes hardened, but instead of saying more, he started off across the snow once again. "Come. We must continue to the cavern."

Zaide hastened after him. Delving into another cavern after what happened in the last one hardly sounded appealing, but neither one of them could help where the artifact had been hidden. "Where is it?"

Andriun raised his spear and pointed. As he did, the snowfall cleared just enough to let them see the craggy spire of rock that rose from the center of the frozen lake.

CHAPTER TWENTY-EIGHT

Both Zaide and Andriun were puffing and out of breath by the time they reached the mouth of the cavern.

Zaide braced his hands against his knees and sucked in air. The cold burned his lungs, but it eased the fire in his arms and shoulders. "I thought... this cave... would be... on the ground," he panted.

"I never said it was on the ground." Andriun managed not to sound breathless, which was frustrating and yet not surprising at all. No matter how badly Zaide had wanted to be a soldier, he'd been an apprentice tasked with copying texts and moving books. All the training he did in his free time hadn't prepared him for things like cliff climbing, and he was embarrassed to realize how unfit he truly was. Andriun, on the other hand, clearly did this sort of thing all the time.

"Well, next time, be more specific." Zaide put effort into sounding as collected as his companion, though he still breathed hard. "Maker's mercy, how do you climb in those mittens?" More than once, his gloves had cost him traction. That he'd made it to the cavern at all seemed like a miracle.

Andriun blinked and then flexed one hand. "How else would I climb? Stone is cold. I value my fingers."

"Never mind," Zaide muttered. He straightened and rested a hand against the wall as he gazed into the cavern before them. The mouth of it was wide enough that he could see the first chamber with ease, but the light wouldn't reach far into the branching pathways that opened off the back. Crystals of ice decorated the walls and ceiling, and snow coated the floor. It crunched underfoot when he took a step forward. "They'll know we were here."

"Not if I..." The hunter trailed off, but he motioned at the snow. It wasn't hard to discern his meaning. Once they moved through the cavern, he could stir the snow and hide their footsteps.

"Did you do that to hide our tracks out of the village?"

Andriun nodded. "I hoped that you would not see."

"Why?" Keeping his magic a secret had given him the advantage of surprise in their sparring match, but Zaide wouldn't have fared any better if he'd known about the Desheni hunter's power.

A hint of concern creased the space between Andriun's brows, but he said nothing. Instead, he unstrapped his spear from his back and headed for the far end of the cavern.

Zaide had little choice but to follow. "You know what we're looking for?"

"In a manner of speaking. I have heard descriptions of where the spring is kept. It is said to be embedded in a prism of ice as large as a man, but no flame can harm it." Andriun gestured to indicate the size of the thing—taller than himself and almost as wide as the span of his arms. Larger than a man, but the exaggeration was amusing.

"No flame, but the dagger can, right?" The artifact was almost weightless at his hip. Zaide let his hand hover over it, as he had a dozen times during their trek across the ice. Unlike the other dozen times he'd done it, this time, a hint of warmth graced his fingers through his gloves.

He blinked and slid it from its sheath.

The blade shimmered as heat radiated off it and its veining pulsed with a cherry-red glow.

Andriun glanced back. "It has awoken."

Despite the heat of the blade, the dagger's hilt was perfectly cool. "The Hymnflute didn't do anything like this."

"Why would it? It is not a weapon."

"No, but it is an artifact, isn't it?"

"Not all artifacts are dangerous. Did the Kolmari Elder not teach you this?" Andriun's brows knit again, but this time it was with concern.

Zaide hated to admit he hadn't. "Now that I'm outside the forest, it seems there's a lot he didn't teach me." To an extent, it made sense—teaching two apprentices was a hefty time investment, and only one of them had potential. He could only assume Resia had learned everything he hadn't. "So the Hymnflute isn't dangerous. The Captured Spring, what does it do?"

The Desheni hunter made a soft, thoughtful sound. "It is... medicine, I suppose. Its elixir can speed the healing of wounds or illness. It replenishes itself slowly."

"Sounds awfully valuable to have hidden away."

"It is not always active. Like the dagger, the spring sleeps. Or, it has slept. I do not know for certain, but I suspect it will have awakened as well." The passageway Andriun had chosen was free of snow, and he motioned for Zaide to step into it. The moment he complied, the hunter spread one mittened hand. One slight gesture made the snow on the floor shiver and swell. It rolled like a flag in the wind, erasing their footprints and smoothing itself out again.

Zaide gave a soft whistle of appreciation.

"They might suspect we have come this way, nonetheless," Andriun said, as if to deflect the praise. "But they will not be certain. Come. Draw your weapon and be ready. There are perils in the cave, and they will not be pleased to see us."

"Perils," Zaide repeated. "Great. I certainly haven't dealt with enough of those yet. Do you care to explain what they are, or should they be a surprise, like the rest?"

Andriun appeared puzzled. "You speak very negatively. Are the people of Kolmar not fond of adventure?"

"Adventure is great, but I've had more than my fair share in the past few weeks." And taking that out on his guide was hardly fair. Zaide tried to rein in his frustration. They were close; the Captured Spring was the last artifact he needed. Once it was in his hands, he could return to Amrochan and then make his way back to Kolmar—assuming Kolmar still existed by the time he made it back.

The hunter made a sound in his throat that could only be described as an audible frown. He led the way farther into the passage before he recovered a lantern from his bag and pried open its cover. "The forces of evil awaken everywhere. They seek the artifacts, as you do. The bugraks, like those you faced at the river, have been drawn toward it. They do not usually venture down so far from the mountain caves."

"So there are bugraks in here?" Zaide measured the distance between the passage's walls with his arms. If it remained as narrow as it was, he liked his odds of fighting off the wretched little beasts. He just didn't know how well fighting would work with someone else in front of him.

Andriun shook his head. "No. There are worse."

He should have known.

"They are... ice," the hunter continued. "Of a sort. I believe. As if ice could live. I know it does not, and yet these things move and fight as surely as if they were alive. But they will not take you by surprise. They are as tall as you, and they are slow."

"What's the problem, then?" Living ice that moved slowly didn't sound like a problem to him, at least.

"Their breath." Andriun moved a hand outward from his mouth as he exhaled, indicating the size of the frosty cloud it made. "It reaches far, and long, and it bites with magic. It is dangerous. It is why so many of us now use only spears. These things, they appear around the lake. Wherever there is water, they appear."

Shadows spread around them in ways that sent uneasiness crawling down his backbone, and Zaide reached for his own lantern. Or, Andriun's other lantern, he supposed. The hunter had left it on the floor; he had merely retrieved it in case it was needed. The extra light chased away some of the odd shapes that crept along the walls. "And you don't think we should have gotten a spear for me before leaving the village?"

"No."

Zaide stared at Andriun's back until the hunter shrugged in discomfort and glanced over his shoulder.

"Do you have experience using a spear?" Andriun asked.

"I don't, but—"

"Then it is better for you to use a sword. If it is what you know, it is what will keep you safe. You are crafty, and no stranger to magic."

"Yeah, but I don't have the advantage of being able to control snow, or whatever it is you do," Zaide said.

The Desheni flashed him a grin. "This is true. Their breath cannot touch me, so long as I have the strength to wield my power. This is why I have put myself in front." He thumped the butt end of his spear against the floor.

An unpleasant crack came from a cluster of ice on the wall. They both grew still and stared as a line inched up the sheet of ice and came to a stop a hair's breadth from the ceiling.

Andriun sniffed and adjusted his gear so his mouth was covered again. "We should be silent." He fastened his lantern to his belt.

Zaide nodded and tugged the high collar of his winter leathers closer to his chin. His hood was still up, but he regretted not buying some sort of hat. His ears ached with the cold.

Slowly, they started off again. The passage split and branched and Andriun considered each path for a time before he chose a direction to go. After a time, Zaide whispered, "How do you decide where we're going?"

"I feel the ice. I do not know how to explain," Andriun whispered back. "I do not know where we are meant to go, but if the spring is trapped in ice, we should seek the place where there is lots, yes?"

Zaide nodded once. They didn't travel much farther before another strange crack reached his ears.

The way Andriun's mittened hands tightened around his spear's shaft was all the more warning he got.

A gust of air spilled into the passage, so frigid Zaide couldn't help but shudder. A split second later, something lumbered into view, and Andriun plunged his spear forward.

It struck the ice creature with a sound like shattering glass and the monster released a noise that sounded all too much like a human grunt. It didn't even resemble a man; more like a twisted tree of ice. Its branchlike limbs twisted and swung in slow motion. Twiggy tendrils that looked like icicles reached for the spear and then wrapped around it like fingers.

Andriun dug in his heels, but his boots lacked traction on the icy floor. He slid forward when the creature pulled.

"Let go," Zaide barked.

The hunter held fast.

"I said let go!"

Andriun blinked and released the spear. "I thought you were talking to it!"

The ice creature groaned and lurched backwards. Ice crawled up the spear's shaft from its body to encase the wood.

"Why would I be talking to that thing?" Zaide jerked the Molten Dagger from its sheath and darted forward.

It flared to life in his hand, its veins glowing a bright crimson in the dim light of the cave. Heat spilled off the blade in waves. He slammed it into the ice beast and an inhuman shriek pierced the air.

Steam poured from the point of impact as the dagger scorched the ice away. A second later, the ice exploded.

A shower of shards pattered uselessly against Zaide's leather gear and clattered against the walls and floor. Slowly, he rotated the blade in his hand and brought it close enough to study the pulsing light trapped inside it.

Andriun breathed something that might have been an oath or words of praise. Zaide didn't understand it, either way.

He considered returning the dagger to his hip, then changed his mind. It did them no good in its sheath, and he had no way of knowing when they might encounter one of those things again. "Did you know that would happen?"

"Why would I have known? If I had known how easy that knife would make things, I would have gone to look for it myself long ago." The hunter gave the blade an appreciative glance, but didn't hold it long. Instead, he leaned down to take his spear. The ice that had formed around the shaft dissolved into powdery snow when he brushed a hand over it. The flakes sprinkled the floor.

Zaide glanced down as he stepped over the pile of broken ice, his lantern held out in front of him. Belatedly, he blinked at the lantern and realized he'd never let go of its handle. It had taken so little effort to draw the Molten Dagger and strike with it, he'd never even considered putting the lantern down.

Andriun cast him a knowing look. "They will not all be so easy. This one, it was small. We were lucky this time."

"What are they called?" Zaide asked.

The hunter squinted at him. "What?"

"The ice things."

"They are not called anything."

"What do you say when one comes after you, then? *'Oh no, it's an ice monster thing!'* doesn't exactly roll off the tongue." The path split again just ahead, and Zaide peered down both passages. One sloped vaguely downward. He started off that direction without waiting for Andriun's input.

The hunter didn't seem bothered by the choice. "We simply say there is danger, or a threat."

"I'm calling them ice trees."

"That name is stupid."

Zaide grinned at his companion over his shoulder. "You got something better?"

The pinched look Andriun's eyes took said he didn't.

"Trees," Zaide said. "But made of ice. Ice trees. Tree... ice. Trice. We'll call them trice, is that better?"

"Trice? Is that only for one, or are multiples called trice as well?"

Zaide shrugged. "Trice and trices?"

"I cannot believe this is the kind of conversation we are having when the fate of Amroch rests on finding the artifact in this cave."

"That was your chance to object. We're calling them trice and trices."

"Tricen," Andriun grumbled.

Zaide snorted. "Oh, now you want to be part of naming them? I already—" His foot came down on ice and slid out from under him. He cut off with a yelp as he went down hard. Both his elbows impacted the ice, and shocks of pain shot up his arms as cracks spiderwebbed out from where he landed.

Andriun tried to turn his laugh into a cough too late to make a difference.

Another pop beneath him made Zaide's breath catch. He rolled onto his stomach and tried to push himself up, the dagger still in his hand.

The ice underneath him shattered and he tumbled down a dark channel to land hard on a sheet of snow. His lantern landed beside him, blindingly bright that close. He grimaced and turned away, but the sight of the other side of the new cavern was enough to make his stomach drop.

"Zaide!" Andriun called from above. "Are you all right? What is down there?"

Zaide's hard swallow did nothing to remove the rasp from his voice.

One after another, long-limbed, tree-like figures slid into view.

"Tricen," he croaked.

CHAPTER TWENTY-NINE

Tree-like monsters spread across every inch of the cavern Zaide could see. They moved slowly, as Andriun had said, sliding no faster than slugs as they crept across the icy ground.

The glacial approach gave him no comfort. Zaide thrust himself to his hands and knees. His body protested, but compared to how badly he'd hurt his shoulder in the river before, this was nothing. Shards of ice and a faint dusting of snow still sprinkled down on him from where he'd broken through the ice sheet above. The dagger had been in his hand when he fell. It had to be here now.

"I am coming down!" Andriun called from above.

Zaide released a low hiss of a breath. "I'm right under you!"

"Then move!"

He bit back a curse and tried to stand. The floor was so slick that his legs almost slid out from under him, and he gyrated his arms in effort to find his balance again. Slicker than it should be, he realized. He spun to look behind him and was rewarded with the sight of the Molten Dagger on a patch of bare, wet stone.

A moment after he moved to reclaim it, Andriun landed where he'd been. The sheet of ice on the floor split and for a moment, the advance of the tricen stopped.

"Maker's mercy," the Desheni hunter breathed.

"Yeah, you should have stayed up top." Zaide half expected the dagger would be hot when he seized it, but the hilt was still cool to the touch, and only a comfortable sense of warmth wafted from the glowing blade. Not enough to melt the ice it had landed on, that was certain. "Magic is weird," he grumbled.

"You are not wrong, my friend, but I do not think mine will be any help against these." Andriun took a step backwards, but gripped his spear and kept it pointed at the wall of monsters without so much as faltering.

Zaide stepped forward to join him, though the tiny blade in his hand seemed pitiful next to the hunter's spear.

He blinked twice, then lunged for the spear's haft.

"Hey!" Andriun held the weapon aloft. "Has your brain frozen?"

"Just trust me!" Zaide reached for it again.

Begrudgingly, Andriun handed it over.

As soon as Zaide's hand closed around it, the fine hairs on the back of his neck prickled.

The Desheni hunter cursed.

A gout of glowing blue frost poured from one of the tricen. Andriun jerked his fur-lined cloak up to shelter them both.

More streams of icy breath poured from the other creatures, all of them moving again, sliding closer as the whistling frost chilled the air until it hurt to breathe.

Zaide dropped to his knees and dug in his bag.

"What are you doing?" Andriun demanded.

"I said trust me! Can you do that for a whole minute, or only ten seconds at a time?" There was rope in there, he knew. His hand closed around it and he tore the whole coil out of his bag.

Andriun's cloak crackled. "I cannot hold this for more than a moment, if it hits you—"

"Then I'll just have to hit first." Zaide twisted the rope around the spear's shaft and the dagger's hilt until he was sure it wouldn't budge. Then he knotted it and leaped to his feet to plunge the new makeshift pole arm over his companion's cloak.

The shatter of ice and an ear-splitting shriek rewarded the strike.

"Oh." Andriun blinked at him. "That was smart."

"Yeah, just keep that magic cape up," Zaide said.

"The cape is not magic. I am the magic."

"Just cover me!" He drove the spear forward again. Tendrils of frost licked at his fingers, frigid enough to bite even through his gloves. Zaide sucked in a breath as the second monster shattered.

Andriun craned his neck to see. "You cannot hope to stab them all. We must escape."

"Any suggestions on how to get past these guys, then?" There was no way they could climb back up the way they'd come, though Zaide's eyes flicked that direction anyway. Overhead, dozens of glittering icicles refracted the light from the lantern and the crimson glow of the dagger.

"Oh no," Andriun groaned.

"What?"

"There is a gleam in your eye."

"There sure is." Zaide pulled back and launched the spear toward the ceiling.

The dagger tied to the end pierced the ice. For a second, nothing happened.

Then a sharp pop echoed through the cavern, and the tricen grew still.

Another snap.

"Get down!" Andriun barked.

Zaide dropped to the floor with his arms over his head, just as the ice collapsed.

Howls and shrieks filled the cavern as the ceiling fell. Icicles speared the monsters on the floor, splitting them into glittering shards and branch-like pieces. Sheets and chunks crushed others —and slammed into Andriun and Zaide.

A chorus of curses rose from the Desheni warrior, though he kept his cloak over them both. Whether it was the fur or Andriun's magic or some combination of both that kept them safe from the weight of the ice, Zaide didn't know, but he couldn't help but laugh.

"You are a madman," Andriun snarled.

Behind them, the cavern grew still. Only the occasional clink of falling ice interrupted the silence. Zaide pushed back the edge of the cloak to look.

A heap of broken ice was all that remained.

"But it worked," Zaide said.

Somewhere in the middle of the mess, a plume of steam and the ruddy glow of the dagger gave away its presence. He stood and hurried over to dig it out.

Begrudgingly, Andriun followed. "You also could have killed us both."

"You didn't have to jump down here. I would've figured out a way to get rid of these things, either way." Zaide kicked a trice's branch. It broke into a dozen pieces.

"Or you would have died alone. Are you always so reckless?"

"I prefer to think of myself as creative. And not give myself enough time to think at all, because my life has turned into a weird series of calamities, and I think stopping to deal with any of that right now would render me incapable of doing anything."

The grunt Andriun replied with was less than supportive.

Zaide untied the spear from the artifact and gave it back. "So where do we go next?"

"Deeper," the hunter replied as he took his weapon and ran his mittened hands over the length of it as cursory inspection.

"I figured that much, but where? We didn't have any more holes open up in the ground, and it doesn't look like going up is an option anymore." He craned his neck to look back the way they'd come, but the mouth of the tunnel they'd been in was too shadowy to tell him much. There had to be another opening somewhere, unless they'd somehow ended up in a dead end. He knelt to wind the rope and stuff it back into his bag.

The spear swung lazily over his head to point toward the far end of the cavern. "There."

On the other side of the shattered tricen, a crevice opened halfway up the wall.

"You think we'll fit in there?" Zaide asked. He returned his bag to his shoulder.

"We must, because that is where we must go."

"Guess I can always melt my way in." Zaide turned the dagger, frowning at it. He considered putting it away, but kept it in his hand. It would be more useful drawn; aside from the comforting warmth that restored feeling to his chilled fingers, it was the only thing he had that offered any sort of defense.

From the way the bridge of Andriun's nose scrunched, he thought little of that plan.

Zaide started toward the narrow gap in the uneven stone. "At least it's not too high up. You want to go first?"

"I assumed that I would." Andriun's legs were longer, and it only took a few strides for him to take the lead. He climbed the heap of broken ice with a graceful ease and worked his way across it without slipping. "I do not think you have the sort of qualities one would want in a leader."

"If you're jealous, I can let you kill a few next time."

The Desheni hunter snorted. "Why do you assume they are dead? The ice has been broken, but it will reform. It always reforms. These creatures cannot be killed."

Zaide followed with a little more care. Chunks of ice shifted and slid underfoot. "Nothing is immortal."

"No, but tricen are not living things, not like you and I live. They are... magic, I believe. Malevolent, but magic, all the same." Andriun scaled the wall and slid into the crack. The passage was scarcely wider than his chest was deep, but he still managed to crouch and offer a hand.

For a moment, Zaide considered shunning the assistance. Then he thought better of it and accepted his companion's hand. "How long have they been here?"

Andriun wedged his spear in the passage and pulled him up. "Since I was a child. I do not remember the first time they appeared, so I know I was small. But I remember my mother warning me to stay away from the water in winter. Her power was greater than mine is now, but even she was afraid."

His boots crunched on loose rock and Zaide dug his fingers into the ridges of the stone walls as Andriun slid farther into the crevice. Inch by inch, they worked their way deeper. After the first few feet, the path began to widen.

Zaide paused. "The lantern."

"Leave it," Andriun said gruffly. "Mine is in my bag, but the dagger is enough light for now. I will get it out when we are farther from those things."

"Are you afraid?" Though he meant nothing condescending by it, Zaide still softened his voice as he asked, mindful it not be taken the wrong way.

"No. But their magic, it makes me..." The hunter shook his head. "I do not like it. We will leave it at that."

The passage grew wide enough that they could turn to walk without their shoulders brushing the walls, though it was still too cramped for weapons to be held with any comfort. Andriun held his spear at an awkward angle, and Zaide held the glowing dagger aloft in hopes it would provide enough light. There was no ice, nothing to reflect it, and the dark stone seemed to swallow every hint of the obsidian blade's incandescence.

"The air smells wet," Andriun whispered.

Zaide sniffed. Instead of biting cold, a hint of mustiness and humidity met his nostrils. It tingled. He fought not to sneeze. "Is that good or bad?"

"I do not know."

Unsettled by the information, Zaide reached for his bag. He still had his own lantern in there, and if Andriun was going to lead the way, then it was up to him to make himself useful. Perhaps by now, it had dried enough to work.

As if sensing his thoughts, Andriun held up a hand. "No light."

"I don't want to walk into any more surprises," Zaide argued.

"There is more ice ahead. Great ice. I sense it, and something else. It—ah!" He cut off with a shout as his foot slipped off the edge in the dark and he went down.

"Andriun!" Zaide lunged after him and caught him by the coat. The hunter scrabbled against the edge of the cliff, desperate to find a handhold. His mittens slipped against the stone more than once. Somewhere below, his spear clattered down the incline.

Zaide gritted his teeth and cast the dagger to the ground behind him. With his newly freed hand, he tried to catch his friend. Andriun's mitten slid in his grasp instead, and the covering came off.

The sound of the spear faded. Either it had landed, or it had fallen beyond where they could hear.

Andriun set his jaw and grabbed for Zaide's wrist. His grip was desperate, firm, and tight enough to hurt. "Pull me up!"

"I'm trying," Zaide replied through clenched teeth. He heaved back, transferring his other hand from Andriun's cloak to his arm. Pebbles crunched under his boots and the startling thought of the cliff's edge giving way came to mind. He pulled harder.

All at once, Andriun came over the edge and Zaide spilled backwards onto the stone. The hunter clambered up farther from the edge before he laid on the floor, panting and pulling at the collar of his heavy gear.

"Still want... to be in the lead?" Zaide got out between breaths.

"By all means, fall off the next cliff." Andriun fanned himself with his bare hand a moment before he twisted to scan the floor. "Where is my mitten?"

Zaide patted the ground around him to find it. His hand bumped the dagger twice before he did. "It's over..." He trailed off, staring at his friend's hand.

Concerned, Andriun turned it over to inspect his knuckles. When he saw nothing, his brow furrowed. "What?"

"You have webbed fingers." The observation sounded stupid the moment it left his lips, but Zaide couldn't manage to regret it. "Sorry. It's just... I mean, I saw it before, but I'd forgotten. It caught me off guard."

Andriun blinked several times before he pushed himself upright. "You truly know nothing about the Desheni, do you?" Instead of being offended, he sounded amused. He slid one blue finger under the collar of his coat and pulled it down enough to expose a series of strange folds on the side of his neck.

Unable to see, Zaide lifted the dagger and held it closer. It cast a warm glow against Andriun's skin.

Gills.

He blinked in surprise.

"We are fish," Andriun said with a grin. He let go of his collar and smoothed it out.

"Fish," Zaide repeated. He sat back and stared.

The grin didn't leave Andriun's face. "Are you bothered?"

"No, just a little surprised, I guess. The longer I'm out of the forest, the more the world seems to change." Those changes meant little, in the grand picture, but they weren't comfortable, either.

The hunter shook his head. "The world is no different. Only your knowledge of it. It is hard, to live your whole life in one place. Many like it that way. My father is one."

"Are you?" Zaide asked.

Andriun's nose crinkled. "No. I have left my village as often as I am able. I do not mean to imply I dislike it. I love my home.

But the exploration of things beyond our borders benefits us all. I have never gone far, but I am often part of the group that goes to Ganede for trade. Or, I was. It has been some time since my father allowed a trip. I miss it. I feel I learn something every time I visit."

"That makes sense. Before all this started, I never left Kolmar. There's so much I still need to learn. When I got to Jadora, I didn't even know different parts of Amroch used different currencies."

"Now imagine trying to remember all of them and then add barter into the mix." Andriun's mirth faded and he rose. "We should continue. We are close and I do not know how far we can go before we will be pursued."

Zaide climbed to his feet and followed as his companion crept back to the cliff. They both peered over the edge. Wherever the bottom was, it was too far down to see.

With a soft grunt of displeasure, Andriun searched the pockets of the inside of his fur-lined cape. "We will need more light."

"You were the one who said to leave the lantern." Zaide reached for his bag.

"Yes, and I regret that now," Andriun admitted. "Mine is gone. It must have fallen."

The contents of the bag were far more jumbled now, and it took a moment to locate and produce the lantern Lark had given him. Zaide brushed it off and settled the rest of his things. "You know, I meant to ask. If you've got gills, how do you breathe outside of water?"

Andriun gave him an odd look. "Through my nose and mouth, how else?"

"Got it," Zaide muttered. "Stupid question." He flicked the lantern's shutters open and peered inside. With the help of the dagger's light, one of the odd illuminated mage stones glinted inside. Or, previously illuminated, he thought with chagrin.

"What is wrong?"

"There's a stone inside. I think it was some kind of mage stone before it got wet. It's supposed to be glowing, though. I didn't think they could go out like this." Zaide tilted the lantern and held the dagger at an awkward angle against its shutters, hopeful it would be enough to let Andriun see.

The hunter leaned forward to look at it. "Do you wish me to recharge it?"

It shouldn't have been so easy to forget he was a mage. Zaide shrugged and pretended to be indifferent as he passed the lantern over. "If that's something you know how to do." It was far outside his own capability, which left him to wonder why Lark had packed the lantern for him. By now, it wasn't as if she didn't know he couldn't recharge it on his own. Even when they were apart, the princess managed to frustrate him.

"Not a usual mage stone," Andriun said. "Where did you buy this? This is one of ours." He squinted into it, then probed past the shutters with one finger. The webbing between his digits kept him from reaching far.

"Lark mentioned something about northern craftsmen." A whisper of sound caught Zaide's attention and he scanned the shadows. When he saw nothing, he tilted his good ear toward the cliff.

For a moment, a hint of glow returned to the lantern. It faded a second later, leaving the dark more oppressive than before. Andriun grunted. "They do not come uncharged. They are supposed to work until the stone breaks. This stone is whole, but the magic... I will try again."

Another pulse of light lit the cavern, and a glint in the shadow made Zaide's spine itch.

"It will not take root. I do not understand. For this to happen, there would have to be a... I do not know, something that is magic, something greater than this, that is drawing its power away."

"Ah... Andriun?" Zaide took a step backwards.

"I am doing my best," the hunter protested.

Another step backwards put his back against the wall. Zaide raised the Molten Dagger before him and swallowed. "You said something big and magic. What about that?"

Andriun turned, just as the lantern pulsed again. "Oh," he said. "Fish guts."

CHAPTER THIRTY

"GET BACK!" Zaide shouted. He ducked into the narrow passage they'd come from, but spun back to offer a hand.

Andriun slapped it aside as he dove into the gap.

A massive beam of ice crashed against the cliff's edge where they'd been.

They both flinched away from the shower of shards and ice chips, but the low creak and groan of movement promised another strike would be quick to come. Zaide wasted no time in retreating farther up the tunnel. "What is that thing?" he demanded.

"A trice," Andriun gasped. He followed, but fumbled with the lantern under his cloak. A few paces later, it flared to life.

Zaide bit back an oath and threw up a hand to shield his eyes. "A little warning would have been nice!"

"How was I to know there would be a trice that size in there?"

"I meant the light!"

"You knew I was working on this," the Desheni hunter protested.

A snarl of frustration escaped before Zaide could stop it.

"Do not make that angry hissing sound at me! We need light if we are going to find—"

The light went out before he could finish. This time, it was Andriun who snarled.

Zaide spun back to say something, but a soft, eerie blue glow in the mouth of the tunnel behind them made him stop and stare. "The spring?"

"Yes," Andriun replied, exasperated.

"No, no. I mean, look! Is that...?"

The hunter blinked at him in the dark, his face barely illuminated by the dagger's glow. Then he turned, and his breath caught. "The ice I sensed."

"It was that thing, wasn't it?"

Andriun's shoulders sagged. "But if the spring is inside of that beast..."

"We're going to need to take it down," Zaide finished for him.

"I have already questioned your possession of sense. Please do not give me more reasons to question."

Zaide took the dark lantern from his friend's hands and pushed back toward the cliff.

Andriun snapped something he couldn't understand, but followed. "What is your plan?"

"I'm working on that." Zaide sheathed the dagger and let the blue glow lead him onward. It swelled and grew brighter, then ebbed, like a slow pulse. The closer he got, the more clearly he saw the way the light reflected on ripples and distortions on the surface of the ice. Of the trice, he corrected himself. The light moved and the groan and creak returned, paired with a soft crackle. The glow wasn't enough to see by, no matter how badly he'd hoped.

Zaide drew back a step. "Can't you break this thing with your ice powers or something?"

"If I could do that, do you think I would have stood around while you collapsed the ceiling?" Andriun whispered. "My strength is not that great. I cannot harm something so large as this." His eyes tightened at the corners, pinched with what seemed discomfort.

"What's wrong?"

"The spring. I know you are not a mage, so you cannot feel it. But it is... overpowering. My head, it aches." The hunter touched a hand to his forehead.

"Can you tell where it is?" Zaide regretted the question the moment it left. Not because he'd asked, but because his voice drew the monster's attention, and a massive branch of ice slammed against the face of the cavern wall. It exploded into pieces and the sharp, stinging daggers of ice that grazed his skin tore a cry from his throat.

Andriun, curled into his cloak, was spared. "I already told you, it is inside that thing!"

"Yeah, but *where* inside it?" The creak of ice forewarned of another strike and Zaide flattened himself into a hollow of the wall before it hit. All around them, the tunnel groaned.

The sound Andriun made could only be described as a hiss.

"Don't make that angry hissing sound at me," Zaide retorted. "I have an idea, but I need to know where—"

"Right in its core," the hunter replied before he was finished, though his voice sounded strained. "The middle of its chest. Deep."

Hard to get to. Of course. "I'm going to need your spear."

"That is unfortunate. Perhaps you should have... should... agh." Andriun cradled his head in both hands and hunched over.

Zaide slapped his back. "Snarky banter later. Got it."

"Where are you—"

"To get your spear!" Zaide ducked with his arms cradling his head as another blow rattled the stone wall. The ground underfoot trembled, the thick layer of ice fragments sliding with the vibrations. No matter how big that monster was, it didn't seem to be regenerating the branch-like limbs it shattered against the tunnel in its attempts to reach them. It could only fight that way for so long.

Zaide ducked behind a narrow outcropping of stone at the cavern's mouth and braced for another blow.

When it hit, the force of the ice against his back squeezed the air out of his lungs. Pain was quick to follow, but he couldn't succumb to it now.

The crackle that filled his ears symbolized the short span of safety where he could move. He darted out from the tunnel. Before his feet could cross the cliff's edge, hands closed on his shoulders and dragged him backwards. Zaide stifled a shout as Andriun flung him down and spread his fur-lined cape over both of them. The next swing of the monster's branches struck the wall above them. The sharp scent of ice flooded the air as the shower of fragments poured down on their backs.

"There is no sense in your head!" Andriun snapped as he leaped back to his feet and hauled Zaide along with him.

Zaide started to protest, but the glint of blue light to his left made him shut his mouth the moment he had it open. Andriun tagged his arm and darted toward the rocky wall, flattened himself against it, and shuffled sideways. The soft glow of the spring inside the monster's body glinted on an icy ledge below his feet.

A path.

Zaide followed.

"I need that spear." He pressed his back to the wall and slid a boot along the ledge as he cast a glance toward the shadowy pit where the spear had to be waiting. It hadn't fallen that far, not if one of the tree-like monsters moved around down there and was tall enough to reach them.

"You need to think for more than two seconds before you do something," Andriun said.

Slowly, the giant ice being rotated toward them.

"It's going to hit us!"

"We are going uphill. It cannot reach."

From the way the thing shifted, it shared Zaide's doubts. The creak and groan of moving branches filled the cavern. Regret over following the hunter's lead swarmed his thoughts, but when the trice struck again, only the tremble of the impact reached their legs.

Zaide didn't allow himself to exhale. Inch by inch, they worked their way upward, until the ledge widened and Andriun pulled him into an alcove. The dagger's sheath had grown oddly warm against his thigh, and he knelt as he unsheathed it. Its glow brightened, pulsing in time with that of the blue light in the ice beast below.

"Give me your pack," Andriun ordered.

The strap was already sliding off his shoulder. Zaide let it drop and pushed the bag across the ground. Before he could ask what the hunter wanted, Andriun upended the bag and dumped its contents onto the stone.

"Hey!" Zaide caught something—he couldn't make out what—before it rolled off the edge. Another rumbling impact set more things rolling and he sat, legs out in a wide V to contain his belongings.

Andriun dug through the supplies. His mouth twisted as he considered the rope, then put it back. He balanced the dark lantern on his knee. "Metal. I need something metal."

A small utility knife sat sheathed amid the dry rations Andriun had provided for the trip. Zaide scooped it up and held it out.

"Ah!" Andriun swiped it from his hand, unsheathed it, and jammed it into the lantern. An instant later, it flared to life.

Zaide stared at it, dumbfounded. What difference did metal make? He drew a breath to ask, then shook his head. *No time.* "We need to get your spear." Another thud of the angry ice monster below. This time, it shook pebbles loose from the ceiling. They pinged off the top of Zaide's skull and he shot an angry glance upward.

"Hush," the hunter said. He brushed a finger against the

edge of the knife, as if to test its sharpness, then leaned back to trace a shape against the wall with its tip. The rasp of metal against stone made Zaide shudder.

Something on the wall moved. Andriun pressed a hand over it, then drew back, his hand curled around a dark shape. Slowly, the shape grew longer. A cylinder peeled away from the wall where the dagger had outlined its edge. Not stone, Zaide realized belatedly, but ice so dark and smooth it looked like black glass.

"You will only get one throw." The last of the ice spear came free of the wall and Andriun turned to present the blunt end. He pointed at the dagger. "I suggest you exercise precision."

Zaide blinked at the end of the spear for a moment, considering the dagger in his hand. "Won't it melt?"

"It is magic. Like the dagger. It will not last long, but long is not what we need."

"Right." And the end of the spear was already perfectly cupped to fit the dagger's hilt. Zaide pressed it into the groove. The ice expanded around it and fused, holding the dagger more tightly than rope ever could. His brows shot up.

Andriun pushed the ice spear into his hands. "Be swift."

"I thought you said I need to think for more than two seconds before I do something."

"If you have not been thinking of what you will do the whole time we are up here, then thinking before you throw will not help." The ground shuddered, and Andriun clapped a hand down on top of something before it could roll past Zaide's boot. He picked it up and crammed it into the bag.

Zaide snorted and popped to his feet. "Don't lose any of that."

"If you miss, I do not think losing any of this will matter."

Though he wanted to argue, Zaide had to admit he was probably right. He hefted the spear in his hand and spun to look below.

With the lantern lit, the wash of pale light illuminated most of the cavern, and the depth of the pit before him made his stomach drop. Some forty feet below, Andriun's lost spear protruded from a mess of ice shards and stone.

Above it, the trice loomed, so large that it missed the bottom of their ledge with the next strike by no more than three feet.

A new problem sprang to mind.

"I can't see the spring!" With the way the lantern illuminated everything, it drowned out the soft glow of the artifact embedded in the ice. The moment Zaide had stood, he'd planned to throw the spear toward that pinpoint of blue. Now, he couldn't even see where it was.

"Maker's mercy," Andriun snarled.

He tore the spear from Zaide's hand and hurled it at the trice.

The dagger flared blinding crimson as it struck the monster and pierced deep. A deep, soul-grating screech echoed off the walls as the ice around the artifact cracked. Curls of red light coiled around the blade like smoke as it burrowed deeper into the beast.

The Trice lurched, more alive than ever. Its branches—dozens of them, Zaide saw now—quivered and writhed like snakes instead of ice, and one after another, it lashed them against the cavern wall beneath their ledge.

Andriun threw himself against the floor and covered his head with both webbed hands. Zaide did the same. Rocks groaned and earth slid. The rumbling grew as stone tumbled from the walls and ceiling.

"The cavern is coming down!" Zaide shouted above the roar.

"And you wanted to be down there!" The hunter shuffled backwards on his belly until he was deep enough into the alcove that his head was covered.

The provisions on the ground jittered and rolled. Most tumbled over the edge. Zaide snatched the Hymnflute and the book Resia had given him from the pile, then darted into the shelter beside his friend. "We can't stay here, we'll die!"

Andriun gave his head a firm shake. He flattened his palms

against the wall. "Ice," he called, the single word almost lost beneath the clatter of falling rock.

Swallowing his doubts, Zaide pressed his back to the wall and held the remaining artifact tight to his chest.

The cavern's ceiling came down, and debris sealed their shelter.

CHAPTER THIRTY-ONE

Dust prickled in Zaide's throat and nose, threatening to suffocate him when he took a breath. He coughed.

Though part of him expected darkness when he lowered his arms from around his head and forced his eyes open, their little hollow in the wall was bright as day. The lantern, nestled in the debris at Andriun's feet, cast their shadows as sharp outlines against the walls. He turned his eyes away and blinked hard, regretting having looked in that direction at all. Burned into his vision, the after-image of the lantern glowed in everything he looked at. He blinked faster in hopes it would disappear.

A few of his belongings lay around their feet and Zaide tried not to step on any of them as he moved closer to the new wall of rubble. Outside, he still heard the occasional slide and clatter of stone that had not yet settled into place, but the monster's thrashing had stopped. Aside from the tumbling rock, all was still.

Eventually, Andriun sank to the floor. His hands slid down the wall as he slumped against the ice in exhaustion.

"I think it's over." Zaide's voice struck him as too loud in the tiny space they occupied. He wiped his mouth, as if to take it back. When he spoke again, he did so softly. "I'll dig us out."

"Do," Andriun replied. He breathed hard, his dark eyes half-lidded. Whatever he'd done to keep their alcove from collapsing, it had pushed him to his limits.

Zaide studied the rubble for a time, unsure how to begin. If he started in the wrong place, he could just as easily bury them in stone. But there were no gaps where he could see through to the other side—or if there were, they weren't visible, since the other side was dark. He rested a hand on a rock and frowned. If he had power like Andriun's, moving the debris would be easier. More than one chunk of ice glittered in the heap. He touched one and gave it an experimental push.

"You will have to push harder than that," Andriun said.

"Yeah, well, excuse me. All I have to work with is my arms." The ice didn't move, either.

"Very little to work with at all," the hunter replied dryly.

Zaide gave him a dirty look as he turned to brace his back against the stone. Instead of his arms, he used his legs, planting his feet against the back wall of the alcove and shoving with all his might.

Just when his legs began to tremble with effort, something gave way. The rock slid outward and downward so fast, he didn't have time to right himself, and he hit the ground hard. He threw his arms over his head to protect himself, but no stone fell from above. It made no sense until he shifted his arm aside and stared up into the clear blue of the mid-afternoon sky.

"Maker's mercy," Zaide breathed.

The cavern below was mostly filled with ice, but a ring of stone surrounded the outer edges of what remained.

"You did this?" Zaide asked weakly.

Andriun snorted. "The trice did that. It was all I could do to keep this from falling." He waved a hand at their hollow. "The dagger. The spring. Do you see them?"

Zaide twisted and got his hands and knees beneath him. His legs still trembled, but he stood anyway. It was hard to see anything but ice glittering in the sunlight. He squinted against the brightness. "No. I can't... wait, no. There's something there. I think the dagger's melting through the ice above it."

"Good," Andriun said. "We will wait a minute. Let the artifact do some of the work for us."

"It did all the work," Zaide grumbled. And he hadn't even been the one to throw the spear. Andriun had defeated the monster and saved them both. He'd done nothing but carry the dagger to Desheni, where his companion had intercepted him. His shoulders slumped.

"What?" Andriun shifted until he could sit upright. His hood had fallen back, and his hair shone glossy black in the sunlight. After everything else, the fin-like ears that protruded from the sides of his head were little surprise.

The ice in the middle of what had been the cavern shifted and a handful of large chunks slid into a slowly-forming crater. The dagger was definitely burning through the ice. Zaide stared as it sank. "Princess Dasienna sent me to get this. If you hadn't been here, I..." He shook his head. It was coming out as a complaint. The last thing he wanted to do was sound whiny or ungrateful. Andriun had risked his life in accompanying him, had earned his father's ire and would surely be punished. That assistance wasn't just appreciated, it had been vital.

"I didn't have the skill," he finished. "This was beyond what I could do alone."

Andriun raised a brow. "Lack of skill is a flaw that can be remedied."

"That doesn't change that the princess thought I could do it." Zaide picked up a stone and tossed it toward the far edge of the cavern's remains. Its clatter was distant and forlorn. There was more ice than rock in the rubble, which made little sense to him, but he supposed ice monsters also made little sense.

Slowly, Andriun tried to rise. "To be fair to both of you, she probably did not know it would be this difficult to do what she asked." He grimaced and leaned on the wall for support. By his feet, something metallic rattled and made him glance down. The lantern Lark had packed was less blinding with daylight pouring down on top of them.

Zaide picked it up and closed the shutters. "What do you mean?"

"It should not be difficult to recover the artifacts when they are needed," the hunter said as he pressed his back to the wall and sighed. "It should have been with our Shaman, my father, when it was needed. I cannot say why he chose to hide it here. Or what gave rise to the monsters in this place. But I am certain the difficulty we faced was misfortune, and not by design."

The thought of recovering the dagger from the volcano beneath Jadora seemed to oppose that reasoning, but only for a moment. Zaide tilted his head and considered it. The dagger had been locked behind a wall that was opened with the Hymnflute, sealed in a box that could only be opened by the same artifact. The chambers hidden beneath the city hadn't seemed like they were meant to be a puzzle; the lizard creature they'd run afoul of hadn't seemed like it belonged. He frowned.

"When we went to get the Hymnflute—me and the princess, I mean—the temple was full of goborrins. And spiders." He shuddered at the memory, but went on. "But the Hymnflute itself was on a pedestal in the main hall. If we hadn't had to go through the back, trying to avoid a head-on fight with the goborrins..."

Andriun nodded. "Then it would not have been hard to find. I expect your search for the dagger was similar?"

Zaide hesitated, but gave a single nod.

"I do not know why, but darkness is drawn to these things. This is why they were given protectors, those who were meant to hold them until a time of need. They should not have been hidden. But perhaps the burden of protecting them became too great. It is easier to guard something when it is under lock and key. But it is a false sense of security." The hunter waved a hand toward the rubble. A haze of fog had begun to settle over the ice, but the crater where the dagger worked on its own—diligently melting all that had buried it—was still visible. More visible, now, as it grew.

"Lark said we need them. To stop..." Zaide trailed off. To not speak the name of evil was an old superstition, one in which he'd never put stock. In his time away from Kolmar, it surprised him to see how his feelings had changed. "To stop the shadow," he finished. "Maybe that's why these monsters want them. If they stop us from getting the artifacts, we can't stop them."

"Perhaps," Andriun said. "But light finds its own way. Perhaps that is why I felt a need to be here."

"Because you'll be the next Shaman, after your father?" Zaide asked.

A line of worry formed between the hunter's brows. "Perhaps."

Zaide glanced back toward the growing pit in the ice. "I can't see how far down it's gone. I'm going to look."

Without waiting for an acknowledgment, he picked his way over the rubble and crept forward. Steam rose from the center of the hollow, indicating the dagger's location. What had looked like a crater was decidedly funnel-shaped once he was on top of it, and at the bottom, a soft, reddish glow refracted in blocks of ice. Zaide worked his way down the side of the funnel, arms out to the sides to steady him. More than once, something shifted underfoot and threatened to spill him to the bottom.

The closer he got, the clearer the color became. The light in the dagger's veins pulsed, but beside it, a soft, cool blue emanated a sense of calm. Both artifacts rested in a pool of water. Zaide tilted his head as he crouched at the edge. It couldn't have been more than ankle deep, but the chunks of ice that floated around the dagger and the curious spring promised it would be uncomfortably cold.

He wiggled his hand out of his glove, unwilling to get it wet, and reached in. The water was frigid enough to bite. He sucked in a breath as he plunged his hand in up to the wrist and curled his fingers around the spring. He removed it from the pool and gave it a shake, then dipped his hand back in for the dagger. The blade was comfortably warm in his grasp, despite the heat that radiated from its veins.

"Magic's never going to make sense to me," he said as he sheathed the dagger at his hip and stood, the spring cradled in the palm of his bare hand.

The dagger was primitive but fierce, while the Hymnflute was rustic and earthy. The spring, however, Zaide could only describe as a spectacle of craftsmanship. The slender six-sided vial was crowned with silver and gems, strung on a chain, and the blue liquid within its glass glowed with an otherworldly light.

"Is it there?" Andriun called from above. The note of anxiety that touched his voice seemed out of place.

"I got it," Zaide replied. Unsure how else to secure it, he slid the chain over his head and settled it around his neck before he started the cautious climb back up the slope. When he reached the top, he saw Andriun sitting on the floor of the alcove again.

Something dark stood out in the rocks and Zaide paused his ascent to dig it out. A packet of jerky, wrapped in waxed paper. He stuffed it into his pocket and crawled over to join his friend. "Are you all right?"

Andriun spread his fingers wide and rocked his hand. "Eh. I will survive." His eyes settled on the spring hung around Zaide's neck, and his expression grew wistful. "It is small, is it not? Such great effort for something tiny."

"I did expect something a little bigger," Zaide admitted. He rested his hand over the vial. "But that's all three."

A weary, lopsided smile tugged at the corner of Andriun's mouth. "I would ask a favor, now that your quest is complete."

Uncertainty surged in him, and Zaide gripped the spring tight. Belatedly, he realized he hadn't put his glove back on. His other hand went to his pocket to retrieve it.

"I will not take it from you," the hunter reassured him. "But I have... exerted myself. Perhaps farther than I should. The spring's waters are restorative. In return for my assistance, please, allow me to drink from it."

"I'm pretty sure the princess will be unhappy with me if I show up and the magic juice is gone."

Andriun chuckled. "The princess will not know unless you imbibe of it yourself, once we go our separate ways. Its blessing would be of little use if it could be used only once. It replenishes itself. But it will take time."

His fingers had grown too cold to wait. Zaide let go of the spring and jammed his hand into its glove. "How long?" It would take time to make it back to Amrochan, but if it took longer than that for the artifact's vial to refill itself, he wasn't sure it could be spared.

"A few days, for what I need. At most. I need but a taste." The Desheni hunter smiled, clearly trying to appear reassuring. "I will not even ask that you take it off."

A taste. Surely that was an acceptable allowance, given all Andriun had done. In truth, the spring should have been in his hand, not Zaide's. He'd been the one to turn Zaide free, to lead him there, to throw the spear. Slowly, Zaide moved closer. His gloved thumb brushed over the crown-like cap. "Do you know how to open it?"

"The top is a stopper. The chain connects to the top of the vial, below where the stopper can be removed."

Zaide plucked at the cap and frowned when it came open. "You know a lot about it, don't you?"

"Of course. My father used it when I was young. To tend the ails of our village, you see. We would benefit from having it in the Shaman's grasp again." Andriun's brows knit, and he closed his eyes. "But it was the royal family who entrusted it to the first Shaman. It is not ours to possess."

And not Zaide's, either. He glanced to the Hymnflute, still where he'd left it on the floor of the alcove. The dagger warmed his hip and the spring was cool beneath his fingers. In the end, he was nothing more than a messenger. Would Lark send him back to Kolmar empty-handed when he'd delivered the artifacts?

"Here." He held the vial out as far as it would go. The chain was not long, but he dared not take it off.

Andriun chuckled at the display. "You are reckless when it does not behoove you, and exercise caution when it is most awkward. But your heart is in the right place, broken-born. I will give you that." He leaned forward, took the vial between his fingertips, and drank a single drop from its mouth. Then he motioned for Zaide to replace the stopper and sat back.

"I'll take that as a compliment." Zaide pressed the vial's stopper with his thumb, then checked twice to make sure it was sealed. It showed no indication of leaking, so he tucked it under his thick coat, but kept it atop his shirt. Even through the spun fabric, the spring radiated cold against his skin. His hand drifted to the dagger and his gloved fingers hovered over the sheath, where a hint of warmth still seeped through.

"Yes, I expected you would." From somewhere under the rubble, Andriun produced Zaide's travel pack. It was all but flat, its supplies scattered among the ruin. He scooped a handful of stray objects into it and paused when his hand brushed the Hymnflute.

Wary, Zaide leaned forward to take it.

Andriun didn't seem to mind. "I hope you know you have been given an honor."

"If I'm being honest, it's felt more like a burden." And a harsh awakening. In Kolmar, he'd been the best swordsman the village had to offer. Beyond the forest's edge, that had turned out to mean little.

"But it is a noble burden to bear. You have done your people a great honor."

"My people are the Kolmari," Zaide replied, annoyed.

A grin split the Desheni hunter's face. "I did not say that they were not."

Voices rose in the still air. Andriun sobered and grabbed

more supplies from the ground. There was little still within reach, the rest buried or scattered somewhere farther down the slope. "You must go."

"Me?" Zaide knelt beside him and crammed as many things as he could find back into the bag. He wedged the book in, then the Hymnflute, and took the strap.

"You," Andriun repeated. "I have committed a grave crime against my people by assisting you. I must answer for it. If they find you, they will take the spring." He offered a few final objects, which Zaide reclaimed and shoved into the bag before he fastened it closed.

Confusion and puzzlement twisted his face, but the voices were growing closer, and Zaide knew he had little time to ask. "Then why'd you help me? If you didn't intend to run?"

A distant look came to the hunter's dark eyes. "Because I felt I must."

"You'll have to explain what that means some time." Zaide yanked the bag's strap over his head and turned to leave, then froze.

Somewhere behind him was the remnant of the tunnel they'd come through, but that was where the voices stemmed from. Ahead, there was nothing but the ruins of the cavern.

As if sensing his hesitation, Andriun flattened a palm against the floor, then tilted his head toward the far end of the ruined cavern and pointed. "The ice is thin," he whispered. "There. Use the dagger. Climb through the wall. Find the road and head east."

Zaide nodded. "Thank you," he whispered back.

The hunter pressed a finger to his lips and shook his head.

With his heartbeat pounding in his ears, Zaide hurried across the ice and rock to find the thin point. It wasn't hard to locate; daylight glowed on the other side of the clouded block of ice.

He snatched the dagger from its sheath and plunged it into the wall.

It hissed and crackled as the blade sank into it and thick

plumes of steam rolled forth to mingle with the fog. As shards of ice fell away to leave a hole in the cavern wall, Zaide turned to look back. He couldn't see Andriun through the haze in the air— it was thicker here, where he'd just melted a gap for his escape— but he still warred with himself.

Andriun told him to leave. Honor told him to stay and aid his friend. Duty said his task was complete and urged him to return to Lark with the artifacts he'd been ordered to collect.

Gripping the dagger tight in his hand, Zaide swallowed hard and nodded toward the smudge of shadow that represented the alcove where Andriun remained. "Thank you," he murmured again.

Then he plunged into the gap.

CHAPTER THIRTY-TWO

Sharp ridges of ice snagged Zaide's coat as he clung to the edge of the narrow gap. Wind whipped his white hair against his face as he leaned forward and squinted against the glare. The ice-covered lake was farther down than he remembered, which made little sense, considering how far he thought they'd delved into the caverns.

But then, the ceiling being ice hadn't made sense, and the monsters hadn't made sense, and sending him on a mission to retrieve the artifacts alone hadn't made much sense, either.

"Why would it make sense? At this point, you're not even sure why you agreed to be here," he muttered to himself as he sheathed the dagger and exhaled hard. The only way down was to climb. As much as he liked the idea of having the blade ready, it would only slow him down. Besides, it wasn't as if there would be any of the tricen on the craggy wall of the ice-riddled stone. If anything, they'd be at the bottom, waiting for him when his feet touched the ground.

He sank to his knees and slid a leg over the edge to scout for a foothold. "Better tricen than angry Desheni."

Zaide didn't know why he was talking to himself, but in the

still that festered in the absence of Andriun's cheerful banter, his own voice was better than silence. "Which means you'll have a new habit to break by the time you make it back to Amrochan, won't you?"

From where he was, he couldn't hear any voices, but he had no doubt whoever had come after them would have found Andriun in the ruined cavern by now. He could only hope the young hunter was able to distract them. Getting back to the road he'd followed from Ganede to where the Desheni intercepted him would be difficult enough without having to run from the Shaman or one of his hunting parties.

But the climb was slow and precarious, and the longer it took for Zaide to descend, the more he dreaded what might wait at the bottom.

"Just keep moving," he reassured himself as he shimmied down the stone spire. The sooner he got the artifacts back to Lark, the sooner he'd be free to return to Kolmar. The forest needed him, he was certain—for all that he dreaded what might be there.

For all he knew, the whole village could be gone.

"And you'll find where everyone's gone if it is. You won't know until you get there." And right now, all that mattered was getting the three artifacts into the princess's hands. After that, he could worry about Kolmar. He shook thoughts of Resia, her family, and the Elder from his head and made himself focus.

Eventually, the thick shield of ice that coated the lake crunched beneath his boots.

Zaide paused to right his gloves, his clothing, and his gear before he turned his eyes skyward. With the haze of fog and a sheet of gray that had settled over the sky, it was difficult to pick out the bright spot of the sun in all the ambient glow. He oriented himself to its position with his best guess and started out across the ice.

He hadn't gone far before a now-familiar creak reached his ears. His left hand shot to the sheathed dagger at his belt.

Underfoot, the ice groaned.

Zaide's heart sank. Without knowing how far it was to shore, he lit off in a sprint.

"Don't crack, don't crack," he chanted as he ran. The snow on the ice kept his boots from slipping, but he still grimaced with every footfall. He could swim, but not in frigid waters, and not in heavy gear made for cold weather. If he went through the ice, that was the end.

Around him, fog thickened until he could hardly see ten paces ahead. The crackle of tricen branches came from somewhere in the mist, beyond where he could see. They were slow, unlikely to pursue him, but with the fog growing deeper, he could just as easily run straight into one of the monsters. Without Andriun's magic to protect them, their burning-cold breath would be enough to scorch his nose off his face.

His foot hit solid ground. Rocks shifted underfoot and he stumbled, but regained his footing a moment later with his arms spread to either side. "Land," he wheezed.

To his left, a surge of icy air billowed through the fog.

Zaide stifled a shout as he spun away from the trice, one arm up to shield his face. The magic-chilled air bit through his lined leathers so severely it stung. When the blowing ceased, he chanced a look over his shoulder. The fog only grew thicker. He couldn't see, but the crackle of unnatural ice promised the creature was there.

He bit back an oath and ran.

Behind him, the crackle became a whine, and he looked again.

Somewhere in the fog, a shimmer of ice caught his eye as the trice twisted on itself and began to change shape.

Unwilling to wait to see what it was doing, he turned away from the monster and bolted across the snow. His footprints were deep, impossible to hide, but he couldn't worry about that now. With any fortune at all, the tricen weren't clever enough to follow footprints—and with the Maker's mercy, anyone who was clever enough was still up on that tall, frigid rock with Andriun.

The whine swelled into a howl, and the sharp keening sound made his stomach drop. Another howl answered from somewhere on the lake. Then another.

Zaide gritted his teeth and ran harder. He had no sense of direction, no idea where he was going, but the ice monsters could only travel so far from the frozen part of the lake.

The thumping footfalls of a galloping beast erupted behind him.

Maybe not, he told himself with a grim smile. If the tricen were magic, what could stop them? Zaide had none of his own, but he'd been around it—and studied it—enough to know it depended on the location of the magic's source, not the element that formed the creatures. But were the tricen themselves the source of magic, or were they tied to something else?

Thoughts of the spring surged into his mind. Could they sense it? Were they following it? Was *it* what gave the monsters life?

"Better hope it's not," he muttered through clenched teeth. His hand went back to the dagger at his belt. Already, his chest ached and his thighs burned. He couldn't hope to keep going, not with the snow deeper than his ankles.

A heartbeat later, an ice creature lunged out of the fog. Zaide skidded to a halt and the beast sailed past him to light in the snow. It spun and bared icicle fangs in a snarl, though the only sound it made was a low crackle and crunch as quill-like protrusions that formed its mane rose in a bristle.

Tricewolf, he decided as he tore the dagger from its sheath. The veins in the obsidian blade flared and for a moment, Zaide thought it shed embers.

The wolf shuddered and moved back a step.

Zaide started to follow, but the snow crunched on the side of his blunt ear. He whirled around and plunged the dagger forward as another tricewolf sprang at him.

The dagger pierced its face and the ice exploded.

Behind him, the first wolf leaped forward, snapping at his legs. He brought the dagger around and slashed where its eyes should have been, where a flat sheet of ice was, instead. The blade's edge skirted the surface of the ice and the tricewolf let out a shriek. It stumbled back until it disappeared into the fog, but more howls came from nearby.

Zaide stole a glance at his tracks and oriented himself to the same direction he'd been going, then lit off across the snow. The cold made his throat raw and he knew he couldn't continue for long, but every step he put between himself and the monsters bettered his chance of survival.

A shape moved to his right, then disappeared again. A moment later, he caught the same thing on his left. Two separate wolves. It had to be. Otherwise, he couldn't imagine they'd move that fast, whether or not they were magic. He gripped the dagger a little tighter and slowed a hair in preparation for them to strike.

The wolf on the left came first.

It launched toward him and he ducked to one side, aiming a strike to take it down the same way he'd shattered the first. But the tricewolf twisted in midair and the swing fell short. With his arm still wide, he was vulnerable. The other wolf sprang at him and hard, cold paws slammed into his back. Zaide spilled forward onto the ground and the monster's weight came down on him full force.

He snarled and twisted his arm back to swipe at the wolf's legs with the dagger. The blade caught with a pop and a hiss. A shrill yelp like ice screeching against itself filled the air and the weight lifted.

Zaide rolled onto his back before the next tricewolf lunged for his throat.

He slammed the dagger into its neck and the beast exploded into glittering fragments.

Glitter.

Sun.

The tiniest laugh of relief escaped as he thrust himself to his knees. If the fog burned off, he'd see what he was up against. The injured tricewolf had already vanished into the fog, but its uneven gait thumped distinctly in the mists.

"Keep going," Zaide breathed to himself. He couldn't afford to stay rooted in one place. Making sense of his tracks to determine which way to go was harder after his spill, but anywhere had to be better than where he'd come from.

His boots crunched on the ice of broken wolves as he pushed himself up, took a step and stumbled. A wave of blackness encroached on his vision. He was out of breath and had stood too fast, but even knowing what he'd done, a surge of panic gripped his chest and the memory of blacking out in Jadora's cavern rushed to mind.

Breathe, he reassured himself. *Just breathe, and keep moving.*

The second step was more steady. He forced air into his lungs, which forced the constriction of fear to loosen.

Another howl reached his ears, but this time, it was distant. He trotted through the snow as steadily as he could as the sun peeked out from behind the cloud cover. Bit by bit, the cloak of fog began to recede, though when he glanced over his shoulder, it was as thick over the lake as ever.

Maybe it's meant to be, he reasoned. *Maybe whoever made those wolves and the regular tricen made the fog, too.* And maybe whoever made it was out there on the lake with Andriun. That thought unsettled him more than it ought and for a moment, he slowed, fighting the urge to return to his companion's aid once again.

"No," he muttered with a firm shake of his head. Andriun told him to go; Lark expected him back. The Desheni hunter would be fine on his own, and Zaide would have the princess send a reward befitting the Shaman's son.

He took another step and the mists abruptly cleared, leaving Zaide to gape.

Ahead, the rocky landscape sloped down until it met with a glittering sea.

Behind him, a tricewolf howled.

"Sea it is," Zaide said.

He hurried down the slope.

CHAPTER THIRTY-THREE

THE NORTHERN COAST WAS LONG, winding, and bleak. The air that swept in from the ocean was bitter, both with salt and with cold, and crystals of ice clung to the edges of Zaide's hood. His ears had long since gone numb, but there was little he could do. Now and then, he raised the Molten Dagger and held it close beside one ear and then the other, warming them enough to ensure they wouldn't freeze. The longer of his ears was worse off, and ached more whenever he warmed it. He rubbed it vigorously between warming sessions to keep the blood flowing. Having one docked ear was hard enough, and while the injury had happened so early in his life that he knew nothing else, he often wondered what it would have been like for his hearing to be level from one side to the other.

When night fell and he could no longer see, he dug the lantern from his pack and pried it open with frigid fingers. The light was gone again, and without Andriun there, he had no way to relight it on his own. Instead, he scrounged driftwood from the shore and found a handful of dry grasses with which to light it. There had been flint in his bag when the expedition started, but he couldn't see well enough to find it, and everything small was indistinguishable to his gloved fingers.

Instead, he shoved the glowing dagger into the tinder and waited for embers to form. When they did, he leaned close and blew on them to coax a fire to life.

There was no telling how far he'd gone or how likely it was he'd been followed, but he couldn't continue onward in a moonless night.

Once the fire burned steadily, Zaide warmed his hands and feet, both his ears, and regained feeling in his nose.

In the ruddy light, he sorted the belongings he and Andriun had managed to stuff back in his bag. His flint was there, but only the smaller of the two pieces. A few stray coins were all that remained of the purse Lark had given him, the purse itself gone. His utility knife was gone, as were a good three quarters of the food provisions Andriun had brought for them, but a tin cup remained. Between the lost food and the lost money, the trip back to Amrochan would be lean. But he still had Resia's book and the three artifacts, and that was all that mattered.

"Foraging will be an option once we're out of this cold," he said, though he no longer knew why he spoke aloud. It was safer to be quiet, but he supposed with a fire lit like a beacon on the sand, a little noise made no difference. His eyes drifted back the way he'd come, and he released a quiet sigh.

Rocky though their meeting had been, he'd found Andriun amiable enough once they'd been on their own, away from the eyes of the other hunters. In his haste to leave and evade those hunters, he'd hardly had a chance to thank his new friend for the help.

Zaide rested a hand on his chest, above where the spring lay hidden between his layers of clothes. "Better get the princess to send a proper thank-you of her own, when all is said and done." He doubted trying to return to voice it himself would go over well.

Once his fingers and toes were comfortable, he stripped off his gloves and took closer inventory of his rations. If he restricted his meals only to what was absolutely necessary, he could make it two days.

Discouraged, he took a small piece of dense nut bread from its waxed cloth wrapping and ate. With snow everywhere, water was easier to come by. He scooped some into his lonely cup, left it close to the fire, and ate while it melted. With the edge taken off his appetite, it would be easier to sleep.

He melted another cup of water, stoked the fire, and settled on the cold sand to let the roar of the ocean lull him to sleep. When morning came, he would decide how to hunt along the way.

Hunting, Zaide decided as he ate his last piece of bread, was easier when one had tools to hunt with.

Traps were useless when he had to keep moving, the surf was too cold for him to wade out in search of fish to catch, and with only a sword and a magical dagger, he wasn't likely to take down any game. Had he any rope left, he might have tried to make a primitive spear using a sharp piece of stone and a decent stick. A sling came to mind, too, but he didn't have anything with which to make one, and it would take practice to be able to hit anything with it.

Desheni's frozen lake was now three days behind him, and while the forests had grown denser, it had yet to get warm enough for him to forgo a fire. He toasted his toes and frowned at his stale bread. He'd have to leave the shoreline, come morning. His water skin was gone, lost with who knew what else; he couldn't even recall what all had been in his bag, but there were some supplies he would have traded half of what he still carried to have back. A water skin instead of a useless lantern, to begin with.

The bread left his mouth dry, but he found a smooth pebble

on the sand and popped the salty thing into his mouth to suck on in hopes it would help moisten his tongue.

With the forest closer to the water's edge, it was harder to sleep, too. The sounds of the night woke him repeatedly, and when the sky began to lighten and he pried his eyes open, he was more tired than he'd been when he'd settled to sleep.

Groggy and disheartened, he scattered the ashes of his fire and trudged on, clinging to the memory of his map—another useful thing lost in the cavern's collapse—and its promise of an eastbound road that brushed the northern coast.

Mercy came in the form of a river in his path.

The delta was wide, but the water shallow and less cold than he expected. He drank his fill where it ran clear over a bed of sand, observed the fish that milled in the deeper pools, then revisited the plan of making a spear. Without rope, he had to improvise, but soft bark peeled off a sturdy sapling he hacked down let him braid a cord that worked almost as well. He stripped the branches, lashed the glowing dagger to the end of the sapling, and gave it an experimental toss toward the sand.

The ties held.

Zaide grinned to himself as he plucked the spear from the ground and made his way to one of the shallow pools to find a fish.

The next blessing arrived the moment he speared one, when the dagger flared and its heat cooked the fish from the inside out.

A handful of cooked fish in the bread's waxed wrappings was all the food Zaide took when he crossed the delta and continued along the coast. The temperatures grew more pleasant and he shed his cold-weather gear long before the northern road finally came into view.

The wide lane of hard-packed earth was welcoming, yet brought its own set of challenges, with sparse opportunities for hunting, foraging, or places to refill the tin cup that was all but useless for transporting water. He still tried, since it was all he had.

By the time settlements dotted the landscape and the lights of a city glinted beyond a winding river ahead, Zaide was worn, exhausted, and his clothes hung loose on his frame.

The city of Beshnai had never been anything more than a dot on the maps in the Elder's study. None of the books had mentioned it and none of the people in Kolmar had traveled that far, and so the tall, reddish-brown buildings that rose from the terraced earth were like nothing Zaide had ever imagined.

He'd seen brickwork in the smithy before, but that entire buildings might be made from what the smith reserved for parts of the hearth and furnace had never crossed his mind. His eyes traveled up one of the tall structures and across its strangely domed roof, where thick thatching shone bright yellow-gold in the morning light.

Eventually, even the dirt road gave way to brick, and the hooves of horses clopped merrily on the pavement as wagons trundled down the wide avenue.

Zaide stayed as far to one side of the road as he could. He'd expected merchant stalls, like what he'd seen in Ganede and the market outside Tinith, but instead, he found himself scanning the half-familiar lettering on signs outside of buildings that had to be shops. Some buildings sported tall windows with glistening glass panes set in delicate brickwork frames, wares bright and attractive in displays on the other side, while others were shuttered tight and offered no hints as to what might wait in the dim spaces beyond the open front doors.

Above it all, spicy scents wafted on the breeze and made his empty stomach ache, but Zaide swallowed against its grumbling and tried to focus his thoughts. Provisions fit for travel came first, and after that, a new map. Despite his appetite's protests, he scraped the coins from the bottom of his bag and found his way to a supply store, where he purchased dry rations from a woman in bright silks.

"Those won't get you far," the woman cautioned as she added a new water skin to his meager pile of supplies.

"They're all I can afford, unless you know someone who might want a broken Desheni lantern."

She hummed thoughtfully. "Come from Desheni, have you?" The way she studied him struck him as too interested.

For a moment, he thought the spring felt colder against his chest. Tucking it underneath his shirt hadn't been pleasant, but it had seemed wise to put the artifacts out of sight. "From Ganede. I fell into the river on the mountainside, halfway between here and there. I lost most of my things."

Her eyes narrowed, but he met her gaze levelly. That he'd left out everything that happened between escaping the river and escaping the tricewolves outside of Desheni didn't change that what he *did* share was true.

After a time, she took the water skin back and strode to a barrel in the corner, beside what seemed to be a terra cotta washbasin. She dunked the skin into the barrel. Air bubbled back to the surface as it filled. "Where are you going?" Her tone was lighter now, conversational.

"Amrochan," Zaide replied.

"Mmm. We all get back to where we've come from eventually."

His brow furrowed. "What?"

A hint of a smile pulled at the corners of her mouth, but it was devoid of joy. "Your sword. Guard issue, is it not?"

Zaide had never given the blade much thought. His hand went to the hilt and his mouth worked a moment before he made himself answer. "Yes."

The woman nodded as she plugged the water skin and wiped its surface dry. "There are lots of us, scattered across the Allied Kingdoms. Families with an heirloom like that. Mine was one, too." She put the water skin back on the counter and held out her hand for coins.

Zaide deposited them in her palm.

"Bag up your things, boy." She curled her fingers around the coins and stepped out from behind the counter. "I'll be just a moment."

A sense of uneasiness stole through him and he turned to watch as she slipped out the front door.

"Just pack and get out of here," he told himself as he fastened the water skin at his hip and jammed his new dry rations into his bag. He'd bought so little that he didn't even have to rearrange things to make it all fit.

It took no more than a minute, but when he turned to leave, the woman's silhouette darkened the door. "Come with me, boy."

Zaide stared at her a moment before he nodded. Getting outside was exactly what he wanted to do. His sword bumped against his right leg as he turned, an uncomfortable reminder it had been recognized. But if she thought he was off to Amrochan because of some family legacy, he supposed there was no harm in that. Better than if she'd recognized the hilt of the Molten Dagger on his other hip.

She stepped down from the doorway and motioned for him to exit, then closed the door behind him. "Have you more errands?"

"I can't really afford any more." He couldn't help the sarcastic note his voice took, but the woman wasn't offended. She shot him a wry smile, instead.

"Good. You'd miss your chance if you had anywhere else to be." She picked up her colorful skirts and motioned for him to follow.

He hefted his bag higher on his shoulder and trailed after her. After Andriun's party dragged him off to Desheni, Zaide couldn't help but regard the woman's back with suspicion. But she didn't veer into any alleys or shadowy buildings and instead stopped two streets away, where an old man chewed the end of a mint leaf and adjusted the harness that strapped two donkeys to a wagon.

The man spared them a glance and his mouth twisted downward.

"Ah, Marden," the woman sighed. "He's headed to Amrochan."

Marden grunted and gave Zaide a second, longer look. Then he shook his head and tugged the buckle on a strap one notch tighter. "Sending more after him won't bring your boy back, Orla. You know that."

Her hands bunched in her skirt. "But everyone we send betters his chances."

"Or sends more to the slaughter. Front lines move every day, and it's not been in our favor."

Orla gripped her skirt tighter. "Just take him. Please."

The old man squinted at her, then at Zaide, and grunted softly again. "Get in the back."

A sigh of relief escaped Orla's lips and she cast a weary smile in Zaide's direction, then hurried back to her shop without another word.

Zaide hesitated. "What?"

"In the back," Marden growled. "You don't hear?"

Instead of answering, Zaide craned his neck to watch Orla leave. When she disappeared into her shop and he looked back, Marden stared at him with a hint of guilt.

The old man cleared his throat and waved toward the wagon.

It took a moment for Zaide to realize the direction he'd turned. The man had seen his cut ear. A hint of warmth rose into his cheeks and Zaide turned to climb into the back of the wagon as he'd been told. "The front lines are moving?" he asked, hoping the change of subject would keep the man from asking questions.

"They always are." Marden rounded the wagon and motioned for Zaide to move to one side, then pitched in a few more bags. Wool, from the look of them. The most comfortable cargo anyone could have asked for. "Where've you come from?"

"Ganede." Zaide helped shift the bags until they were steady, then pulled up his feet when Marden slid a board into the tail of the wagon.

"Long way to go by foot."

"I'm gonna need new boots," Zaide agreed.

Marden made a gruff sound and nodded. "I'm not going as far as Amrochan, though. Hope Orla didn't get your hopes up. I only go as far as Yithel, and only once each harvest and again at shearing, but that'll get you more than halfway there."

"Thank you," Zaide said, as earnestly as he could.

The old man waved a hand, signaling the end of the conversation. He clambered onto the wagon's tongue and clicked to his donkeys.

For the moment, Zaide was content to ride in silence, but he reclined against the bags of wool and tried to put the questions that sprang to mind into order. No news from Kolmar would have reached the western coast by now, but surely it had reached Beshnai.

He'd give the old man a little peace, but before they reached Yithel, he'd have every bit of information he could twist free.

None of what the old man shared was good news. King Sendassian's army had mobilized to reclaim the garrison near Kolmar, but no word of their success had reached Beshnai, leaving everyone to assume the battle continued. As far as Marden was concerned, Kolmar's forest was lost, and the garrison represented the new front line. That brought the war closer to Amrochan than it had been since the city rose as a bastion against Gadranus and his armies, information that made both of them shake their heads while Marden shared the news.

Whether the people of Kolmar had escaped the village, the

old man didn't know. Zaide supposed he'd learn the answer soon enough, but he didn't look forward to asking.

He shared bits and pieces of information about himself in exchange; that his family had been refugees during the Breaking, driven from the Shattered Lands just after he'd been born, and that his father had departed to join the war effort not long after that. Marden nodded his approval at that, though he chanced a look at the sword that rested against the bag of wool which served as Zaide's pillow. It wasn't hard to infer the old man believed that sword had belonged to Zaide's father, returned to his widow after the war claimed his life. Zaide saw no need to disabuse him of the belief. His mother had never received a sword, but the chances the man had survived this long were as thin as one of the white hairs on his head.

That he wasn't the only youth headed to Amrochan with a sword in his hand had come as no surprise, either. Zaide wasn't even the first Marden had transported to Yithel. The migration of young would-be soldiers had started in the autumn, when the old man traveled for the last round of trade each year.

The last one had been Orla's son.

"I don't envy your youth, these days," Marden said as the city came into view, days after travel began. "I won't be surprised if Sendassian orders a draft before long. The closer fighting comes to Amrochan, the more dire things become."

"Aren't the swamps outside Amrochan an advantage?" Zaide asked.

"Aye, but they say the swamps have enough spooks of their own. I'll stick to dry land." The old man chuckled to himself. "But I wish you the best of luck, all the same. Might as well have the fighting be all your idea, and... well, who knows. Maybe if enough young ones like you show up with a sword in hand, it'll turn the tide."

Zaide brushed his fingers over the hilt of the Molten Dagger, its sheath having never left his belt. "Hopefully, it will."

He had little to gather when the wagon finally stopped, but

he left it all on the seat while Marden rested and he unloaded the wool. The sparse provisions he'd purchased from Orla were still untouched, substituted with fare from Marden's supply box under the wagon's bench. The old man had suggested Zaide could work it off. He was determined to make the transaction fair.

When Marden had his money and Zaide retrieved his things, the old man added a few extra parcels of dried meat and half a loaf of crusty bread to the bag before he handed it over.

"It's south from here," Marden said with a pinched look to his eyes. "No swamp spooks to the north of Amrochan, and the road's well-traveled by good folk. Stay on the road and not much can go wrong."

"Thank you," Zaide said as he swung the bag's strap over his shoulder. He belted on his sword and rested a hand on its hilt.

The old man cocked his head to one side. "Huh."

Simple as the sound was, it was packed with enough thoughtfulness that Zaide raised an eyebrow. "What?"

"You belt it on the right. I hadn't noticed. Left-handed, are you? In Beshnai, that's good luck."

"Hopefully it'll be good luck in Amrochan, too." And south, where battle had consumed the only home he'd ever known. One way or another, Zaide would get there and join the others. He closed his eyes for half a second, just long enough to recite a prayer in his head for the safety of Aren and the others.

Their goodbye was brief, but warm, and after a long rest in the wool wagon, Zaide felt properly rejuvenated. He refilled his water skin at one of Yithel's many shallow wells, then headed south. With everyone who had to be waiting for his help, he didn't dare dally, but he took some relief in knowing Amrochan was no longer far off.

CHAPTER THIRTY-FOUR

SMOKE DRIFTED from the horizon in thick, lazy plumes. At first, Zaide thought it some illusion caused by the humidity of the marshes, but the farther south he went, the more clear the clouds became. Despite his weariness, he picked up his pace.

The road south of Yithel had been blessedly dull. He'd managed to catch a few fish in the shallows of the river just outside the city, which had lessened the strain on his limited provisions. That luck didn't hold in the marshes, but the dried meats, fruits, and dense bread he'd gotten from Orla were enough sustenance when paired with extra water. That, at least, was easy to come by in the marshes.

Yet it couldn't douse what had to be wood fires rising from the swampy ground outside Amrochan. The plumes were too widespread to line the dry road, and too plentiful to be the work of scattered farmers or a sign of a charcoal-burner's kiln.

"Maybe the king's called an army," Zaide reasoned. Maybe the young would-be soldiers Marden had mentioned had come from all over and were preparing to go to Kolmar's aid. The thought was both sobering and exciting, and he shifted from a walk to a jog.

He'd completed his task. When Amrochan's army moved

against the forces of Gadranus, he would be with them, sword in hand.

Zaide crested a hill and stumbled to a halt.

From the city walls to the edge of the marshes, the fields outside Amrochan were ablaze. More fires dotted the marshes, bright pinpricks of orange that spat thick clouds of smoke into the air. Shapes moved across the water, toward the burning crops and grass.

His stomach lurched.

Goborrins.

It was supposed to be Sendassian's army outside the city! Zaide stood as if his feet had been rooted to the road as his eyes swept the scene. For an instant, he didn't know how he was supposed to reach the city's gates. Then a glint of armor caught his attention.

Bands of soldiers swept between patches of fire, striking against goborrins that loomed at almost twice their size.

Despite the blaze, the goborrins moved alone. They carried a torch in one hand and a weapon in the other, swinging alternately at the ground and those who tried to stop them. The bands were small, no more than five soldiers in each, but they pressed forward to meet each goborrin head on. Sounds of battle rang above the roar of flames.

Without thought, Zaide moved down the slope to join the nearest group.

They were already locked in battle by the time he reached them, their strikes quick and efficient, a few distracting the monster while the others circled to strike it down. The goborrin's pig-like shrieks rang in Zaide's ears and he forced himself to pry his fingers from his sword. These people were allies, but unlikely to recognize him. Approaching with his sword drawn would only get him killed.

One of the men silenced the goborrin with his blade, planted a boot on the dead beast's head, and jerked his sword free as he watched Zaide's approach. "Name yourself," he snarled.

"Zaide," he answered, raising his voice to be sure he was heard. "Apprentice to Kolmar's Elder, returning... with the Hymnflute." Where he'd been and what else he had probably mattered, but not now.

The man gave him a flat stare.

"Let me help you," Zaide added as the soldier's eyes dipped toward the sword he carried.

The soldier opened his mouth to speak, but before a single word could escape, another figure in armor emerged from between pockets of flame.

Whatever hope Zaide had for Kolmar evaporated.

"Lieutenant," he choked out.

The look on Raddan's face was a grotesque combination of relief and a grimace. Zaide expected a greeting or gentle reprimand. Instead, the lieutenant grasped him by the collar of his shirt and dragged him past the soldiers, who murmured between themselves in concern.

Zaide staggered and grabbed the lieutenant's wrist to try and pry the man's hand free. "I can walk on my own," he protested.

"You'd better." Raddan's voice was hoarse, betraying hours spent shouting orders and breathing smoke. He dragged Zaide past the end of the blaze, where nothing but charred grass remained between them and Amrochan's wall. The cottages, crops, and tidy clusters of trees were gone.

"What happened?" Zaide asked before he realized the idiocy of the question. He'd just seen the goborrins, even offered to fight them. He tried again with something more intelligent. "You're supposed to be in Kolmar."

"Aye, and I was," Raddan said as he let go and jerked the shoulder of Zaide's shirt to straighten it back out. "Until the front line swept through. Between those things holding the temple and the garrison, we didn't stand a chance. They pushed us back until we had no choice but to retreat."

Anxiety made his throat tighten, but Zaide forced the words out anyway. "Where's Resia?"

"In the city. With the princess. Where you should be." The lieutenant shoved him toward the gates, where dozens of soldiers stood guard in rows. "Where you're going now."

"I have the artifacts," Zaide blurted.

"Aye, you'd better. And if the Maker has any love for us at all, they'll be what the princess needs to drive these beasts back to the Shattered Lands." Raddan pointed, indication for him to move.

Zaide hesitated, but the lieutenant only pointed again, so he swallowed his desire to help and turned to run for the gates.

This *was* helping, he told himself. He gripped the hilt of his sword to keep it from banging against his tired legs as he sprinted across the field.

The soldiers had seen the lieutenant pointing, it seemed, for they parted to let Zaide through without comment.

Beyond the wall, the city was in turmoil.

Just inside the gates, soldiers in various states of readiness toted weapons, armor, and various supplies needed by an army between buildings that had been commandeered as makeshift barracks. Common folk moved between them with carts of things they didn't seem to know what to do with, or else tried to slip past the guards near the entry, only to be pushed back with stern reprimands.

Zaide shouldered his way past a crowd that clogged the street to hurry toward the castle. Navigating the city on his own was difficult and made worse by how congested the streets had become, but with the spires looming over the rest of Amrochan, it was impossible not to head in the right direction. How he was going to get into the palace, however, he didn't know.

"Zaide!" A tiny, familiar voice rang out above the noise of the city.

He stopped to scan the crowds nearby. The shifting sea of faces made it hard to see anything, but eventually, a tiny brown hand waving above the heads of passersby caught his attention. His brow furrowed and he pushed toward it.

Resia squeezed between two bickering soldiers and rushed to greet him. "Thank the Maker you're so easy to see." She wrapped her arms around him for a hug, which he returned with a squeeze.

"Probably the only time in my life I'll hear that," he said. "Is everyone—?"

"Here," she said with a nod. "Though not unscathed. The family's all here, though. We made it. Not everyone was so lucky."

Zaide nodded. After the disaster that had been the Spring Choosing, it would have been foolish to expect otherwise. Still, his chest ached with the thought of friends and neighbors lost, and he silently added the grief that was to come to the list of burdens he had yet to sort through. He hadn't allowed himself time to untangle his thoughts and feelings, for fear he'd find himself too paralyzed to move. Even now, in the safety of Amrochan's thick walls, it wasn't a risk he could take. "What are you doing out here?"

"Running messages as a representative of Kolmar." Resia swept a lock of her dark hair behind one delicate ear. "A lot of our people have taken up swords to help defend the capital. I'm doing my best to help keep everyone organized while settling the families, but..."

He rested a hand on top of her head. "But it's a lot to take on by yourself."

She struggled to smile.

"I'll help you, but I have to see the princess." His eyes swept toward the castle. It no longer seemed soaring and regal; instead, it struck him as ominous and stoic. "I have the artifacts."

"You'd better!" Resia removed his hand from her head and gave it a squeeze, then tugged him in the direction he'd been headed in the first place. "Come on. They've been letting me come and go from the palace since I'm a messenger. I'll get you in."

He had no doubt he'd be able to find his own way in, since

the princess was the one who had ordered him to return to Amrochan when he was done, but he wasn't about to turn down the opportunity for a moment with his foster sister. They slipped between clusters of people together, her grip so tight he couldn't have freed his hand if he wanted to.

"When we're done, I want to see everyone." Zaide raised his voice over the din of a nearby argument. She gave his hand another squeeze to assure him she'd heard, but she didn't reply. He couldn't blame her. There was a sense of urgency that hung heavy in the air, fueled by the anxious tones in the voices of all the people in the crowded streets.

He'd help, as soon as he was free. He set his jaw as he made the resolution. The moment the artifacts were in the princess's hands so he was no longer needed, he'd make himself useful in the defense of the city. For now, all he could do was pray the three artifacts he carried would be enough to let Lark drive back the war.

The guards at the castle did little more than nod to Resia as they passed, but so many people moved between the courtyards and the rest of the city that their position by the entryway seemed little more than formality. The castle's courtyards were in as much of a frenzy as the city's main gate. Soldiers ran from group to group and building to building. Others stood in formation while officers called out orders. Zaide watched them with an uncomfortable sense of longing. After everything, he still felt most at home with a sword in his hand, and he couldn't help the pangs of guilt that came from knowing he should have been in Kolmar to help when the village fell.

"This way," Resia said.

He blinked twice and shook himself from his self-pity.

The first place he'd seen Lark in the palace was the throne room, where she stood beside her father's throne. The realization of who she was had been unpleasant, even before he'd gotten himself in trouble for speaking out of turn. He'd expected she'd be in the same place, but instead, Resia led the way toward a place that had been more familiar during his short stay: the garden where he'd met the princess in secret, where she'd ordered him to help and he'd found it impossible to refuse. Fitting, he decided, that they would meet again in the same place.

Instead of the main door, Resia took him to the hallway with the balustrade. Most of the garden was visible from that point, and it wasn't hard to locate Lark.

The moment Zaide saw her, he climbed over the rail.

"Hey!" Resia put out a hand to stop him, but he was already over.

The guards that flanked the princess spun to face him with spears ready, but Lark shot to her feet from the bench where she sat and shoved the shafts of both spears downward, so they pointed instead at the ground. "You're alive!"

"For the moment," Zaide agreed. He started to reach for the Molten Dagger, then thought better of it and reached for the chain around his neck. He strode forward, mindful of the guards, and knelt a few paces away as he slid the third artifact out from under his shirt. "The Captured Spring, as you requested, Your Highness."

Lark came closer to take it when he lifted it on one palm. She flinched when her fingers curled around it. "And the dagger and flute?"

With that permission, he unfastened the dagger's sheath and presented it, too. "The flute is in my bag, Your Highness."

She took the dagger and looked between the two artifacts she held. Then, finally, her gaze settled on him. "You came straight here."

For an instant, he second-guessed his choice to hurry. He was filthy, road-weary, unshaven and couldn't have smelled pleasant, either. But with the army of goborrins right outside the city, stopping for a bath hadn't seemed appropriate, and he chose to believe he'd made the right decision. "You told me to bring you the artifacts. I have done so, with as much speed as I could."

"Not enough," she said, though there was no malice or disapproval in the words. Her fingers tightened around the artifacts until her knuckles grew pale. "If I'd been with you, maybe..."

"Your Highness," Resia called from the walkway. "If you're done with your squire, the Kolmari will want to see him."

Lark straightened. "I'm not. But I'll send him to you when I am. Leave us. All of you." She shot a dark look toward the guards, who hesitated.

She sucked in a breath, but that was all the warning they needed. The two guardsmen made for the door, though the sour expressions they wore indicated they expected to get in trouble for heeding her.

Zaide glanced back to the railed walkway.

Resia was still there, though she offered a halting smile as she turned away. "I'll wait for you outside."

Unsure what the princess expected of him, Zaide remained kneeling on the grass.

When they were alone, Lark's shoulders sagged. She unclenched her hands and studied the two artifacts she held.

The silence made Zaide's nerves itch. He wet his lips and kept his voice low. "There's an army of goborrins right outside the city."

"I know." She sounded resigned, but she didn't look at him.

"I've done everything you asked," he continued, mindful not to let any frustration color his words. Nothing that had happened to Kolmar had been her fault. "I returned with all three of the artifacts you wanted."

Her gaze settled on him.

Determined, he pulled the Hymnflute from his bag and held it out for her to take. After how possessive he'd felt over the artifact, it struck him as less important now, with his home destroyed and his family's refuge threatened. If it wasn't safe in the princess's hands, it wouldn't be safe anywhere. "Now I ask you, Your Highness, to release me from service and let me join the army in the capital's defense."

Lark plucked the Hymnflute from his hands. "No."

The answer was so simple and terse that he gaped, taken aback. "But I did everything you asked me to! The city's under attack—"

"The city has thousands of soldiers to protect it. Tens of thousands, once all my father's soldiers answer the summons they've been given. What difference will one more make? They don't need you."

Zaide thrust himself up from the ground. "My family's in this city! Resia, my foster parents, my—"

"If you want to protect them, you'll stay where you are," she snapped before he could finish.

He shut his mouth and felt his breath catch.

"It's not enough, Zaide. These... these things," she almost spat as she displayed the three artifacts, "are not enough. They aren't what we need, and we're not done."

Anger swelled inside him until he thought he might burst. "You sent me into the frozen wilds for something we don't even *need*?" He clenched his fists so hard, his nails dug into his flesh. "You sent me into the middle of a volcano. You sent me knowing I might die, and they aren't even what we *need*?"

"No!" Her brow furrowed and she transferred the artifacts to one arm, freeing a hand with which she could rub the lines that marred her forehead. "I mean yes, I did. They're just not... what I thought. I thought they were the tools that would turn away the army Gadianus sent against us, but they aren't. They aren't the tool, they're the key."

"I'm not chasing down anything else for you," he snarled.

Lark's face twisted as if pained. "You have to! I don't... I don't have anyone else to rely on, Zaide." Her voice cracked and tears glittered in her eyes. Their simple honesty blunted the edge of his anger, and he stared at her for a time without knowing what to say.

She went on without him needing to speak. "When I first read the artifacts were the key, I didn't think it was literal. I thought it merely meant that possessing them would give us power to defeat his armies, and that was why he was desperate to keep us from retrieving them. After I came back to Amrochan, I was able to find more texts based on things I learned from Tula. The power it means is a weapon. Locked away, where he can't reach it, because it's the only thing that can strike him down."

"We don't need to kill him," Zaide protested. "We need to kill the monsters trying to break down our walls!"

"And if we don't kill him, there will be more monsters," Lark fired back. "There are always more. The blade will be just as effective at killing goborrins as it will their leader."

"Then go get it! End this!"

Her shoulders slumped. "I... I can't."

"You have the artifacts."

She hugged them to her chest. "I know. And I know where it is. But I can't get there on my own."

The weight of what she'd left unsaid chased more of the fire from his temper and he wished for all the world that it hadn't. He wanted his anger; he wanted the fight to end with her dismissing him, for him to have a chance to leave and do something he thought would make a difference. But she was the princess, as she'd always been, and he didn't know how to refuse the order he dreaded was already coming.

"Where is it?" he asked cautiously. Perhaps he could recommend a handful of soldiers from those he'd met. He already knew Raddan had survived the expedition to Kolmar. Murk and Plain had to be in the field somewhere, and they were already aware of Lark and her expeditions.

"Sealed away," Lark said, her eyes locked with his. "Underneath Gadranus's crest."

Recollection of the eerie, peeling emblem of the ram's head on the temple's floor sent a chill down his spine.

She caught his faint shiver and nodded. "We were right there.

Right on top of it, and we never knew. There were three benches, do you remember?"

"You stood on one."

"They're altars," she said. "I'm afraid that was disrespectful of us."

Zaide let out a long breath through his nose. "Three altars, three artifacts."

Lark nodded again. "When the artifacts are placed, they'll open the way. Each is infused with a piece of the power needed to hold the seal shut."

"The seal on the weapon?" A blade, she'd said. He couldn't fathom what to expect.

"On Gadranus. Or... the last one." She lowered her eyes and turned her face away.

Not that long ago, they'd stood beside those altars and expressed what he'd thought was a shared disbelief of those old legends. Now, it seemed they'd both have no choice but to believe them. "You really think the man who broke the Shattered Lands is the same person?" he asked softly.

The princess gave a weak shrug. "If not the same man reborn, then the same power born into someone else. It doesn't matter, does it? Either way, what we're up against needs more power than what we have to defeat it, and that power is buried in Kolmar, in the last conqueror's tomb."

"Kolmar is lost," Zaide said.

She spread one hand in a helpless gesture. "Then hope is lost."

He scoffed. "One special sword won't change the tide of war, but more hands might. Outside the city walls, they've got teams assembled—five men to take down one goborrin. You think you stand any chance alone?"

"Then get more hands, and we'll go to the temple with them."

"No."

"That wasn't a request," Lark snapped.

"Find someone else." He scooped his bag from where he'd left it on the ground and turned toward the door.

"I gave you an order!" Her voice rose to a shout.

Everything in him wanted to walk out, leave her in the garden alone, and find Resia. He could reunite with her family—his family—and report to Lieutenant Raddan, join the war, and finally make a difference. It was all he'd wanted for himself. The chance to play to his strengths, the chance to fight for the country that had given his parents refuge, the chance to feel he had a skill that wouldn't be wasted. And yet for all that he wanted to leave, he remained where he was, stuck in one place with his heart racing, listening as she drew another breath with which to berate him.

"I don't want anyone else," she said instead.

Zaide looked at her over his shoulder.

She stared back, her face as determined as ever, though her blue eyes shone like glass.

She was the first person he'd ever met that had eyes like his. Richer, bolder, more like cut sapphires or the summer sky than the soft, chilly spring shade of his own, but still like his in a way he'd never known after his mother's death.

"I want you to do this. To take me. No one else." A small quaver broke her voice. "I've pushed for this for years, tried to make this happen so long before now. You're the only person who's ever taken me seriously. You're the only one who's ever helped."

"You didn't give me a choice."

Lark gave a small, humorless laugh. "Can you blame me? Nobody believes any of this is real. Not you, not even my father. I thought I could do this on my own, but in the temple, when I had you there, I realized how much it meant to have help. I don't want to do this alone anymore. Not when I know you've been there, able to handle everything that's come your way."

"But I'm not." The admission wounded his pride and offered a surprising respite from his frustration at the same time. He raked his fingers through his hair. "I almost drowned when trying to get the Hymnflute to Amrochan. I blacked out while trying to bring the Molten Dagger back from the crater. And if I hadn't had the Shaman's son helping me in Desheni, I would have gotten myself killed instead of getting the spring."

"But you didn't. You got through all those things, and you still came back with these." She lifted the artifacts in her arms, then cradled them to her chest with one hand so she could sweep back a strand of her hair. "You're so determined. You're capable—"

"Stop," Zaide groaned.

"You're trustworthy—"

"Why can't you just let me say no?"

She lifted her chin. "Because you won't. If you were going to refuse, you would have done so already."

"I did refuse. I said no."

"But you stopped," she said. "Instead of walking out that door."

And for the life of him, he couldn't understand why. Everything he wanted for himself waited outside the garden. Why did he hesitate?

"I want you to take me back to the temple in the forest." This time, Lark spoke softly, but it still wasn't a request. "If you think we need more hands, then go back to your sister and find some of the Kolmari who you think can help us. Visit the barracks with them and equip yourselves with whatever weapons and armor you need. I'll give you time to get something to eat and gather supplies for the journey, but we'll set out at first light."

"I never said I'd do this."

If she heard his protest, she gave no indication. "I'll find you in the morning."

As if her words released him, he made for the door, silently cursing that he knew that meant he had no choice.

CHAPTER THIRTY-FIVE

"You're right," Resia said as she guided him through the narrow back streets, where things were more calm. "There doesn't seem to be any way to get out of it."

"But why me?" Zaide twisted to move through the tight space between a wall and a pile of crates without his bag or his sword getting caught. More than once, his hand had gone to his belt as if to check the dagger he'd grown used to having sheathed there. That it was no longer his to use meant he'd need time to adjust.

She frowned at him, but continued on ahead. "She already told you why. She trusts you."

"There are a thousand soldiers out there better qualified to help her than I am. She has to trust some of them just as much."

"And how many of them have been in Kolmar? How many saw the inside of the temple and know where they need to go?" She made a sharp turn and beckoned him with one hand. "Right here."

The door they stopped at looked no different to him than any others they'd passed in the alleyway, but he looked around anyway and tried to orient himself. "It's a giant temple in the forest, and the seal she's looking for is a massive painting on the floor in an enormous room that has nothing else in it. It's going to be hard to miss."

For whatever reason, Resia rolled her eyes. Then she opened the door and stepped inside.

"Resi!" Her father's voice was both welcome and comforting, as was the sound of her shortened name. "What are you doing back here? I thought you—" He stopped short when Zaide stepped in behind her.

Across the room, her mother dropped a ladle into the soup pot with a clang. "Zaide!"

A handful of heads popped up around the room—his other foster siblings and several neighbors from Kolmar. Before any of them could react, his foster mother had crossed the space between them and swept him into her arms.

"Thank the Maker you're safe!" she gasped.

He tentatively returned the hug, then grimaced as she caught his face between her hands. "I'm fine, Sarma."

"You're most certainly not! Look at you, you're almost bones. You hadn't any weight on you to lose. Oh, Resia, where did you find him?" She hurried back to the pot, produced a bowl from somewhere, and wasted no time in filling it. If retrieving the ladle from the boiling soup burned her fingers, it didn't show.

"I saw him as he came into Amrochan. He'd just come back from the mission the princess sent him on." Resia pulled a low stool up to the table and motioned for Zaide to sit.

"Well, I don't mean to speak ill of the princess, but she ought to have sent you with more supplies!" Sarma thunked a bowl down in front of him and thick soup sloshed over its rim. Before he could thank her, his stomach growled. She threw up her hands, clearly vindicated. "You see? Starving! Sit and eat, boy. Tell us where you've been."

"Tell us!" one of Resia's younger brothers cried as he clambered onto a stool.

Zaide sighed and sat down. "I don't even know where to start."

"At the top," his foster father, Verlin, said as he and everyone else clustered around the table. "Everything that happened since you and Resia parted ways, after she was sent to seek help in reclaiming the garrison."

"That's not really the top, but I'll do my best." He blew on a spoonful of soup until he could eat it, then began his story.

Everyone—Resia included—listened as he recounted the trip to Jadora and the exploration of the volcanic tunnels underneath, the short journey to Ganede, and the misfortune and blessings he encountered on the lonely expedition to Desheni. Their faces morphed from wonder to surprise to concern as he shared everything he could, then filled in more information about the first half of his trip, from before he'd encountered Resia in the marsh.

Sarma refilled his bowl so many times while he spoke and others asked questions that he lost track of how much he ate. Eventually, he pushed the bowl aside to signal he could eat no more. The conversation had shifted to Princess Dasienna's order that he help her return to Kolmar.

"Well, there's nothing for it, then," Resia's father said. "Aren would be a good one to take. He's here, made it with the rest of us."

"I can't just take an army into enemy territory," Zaide protested.

"The Elder would want it," Resia said.

"Then maybe he should take her."

Her parents exchanged looks. The burden of something left unspoken took the wind out of his sails.

Resia touched his arm. "My father is acting Elder now, until I complete my training. The Elder didn't..." She couldn't finish.

Zaide stared at her in disbelief. "The goborrins—"

"No," her father put in. "It wasn't violent, thank the Maker. His power sheltered us until we reached Amrochan. But he was old, Zaide. The oldest person in Kolmar, and that power took a lot from him."

Sarma rested a hand on her husband's shoulder. "He faded away peacefully, two nights after the Kolmari reached Amrochan. The other Kolmari have been given quarters nearby. We all held a vote, and they chose Verlin to lead us until Resia comes into her power."

"I'm sorry," Verlin added. "I'm sure there's a lot you wished to discuss with him, after all you've been through."

"Of course," Zaide murmured, though he slumped on his stool. There were a hundred things he thought he might ask. Out of everything, a confirmation of whether or not the sword Lark wanted even existed sprang to the forefront of his mind. He sighed and rubbed his brow with one hand. "I guess I'll just have to ask you, then. The forest temple—how much do you know about it?"

Sarma made a displeasured sound and pressed her hands to her chest. Not a favorable sign.

"That good, huh?" He tried to inject a little humor into his words, but failed.

Verlin sighed and drummed his fingers on the table. "There's a reason none of the Kolmari visited the temple. It was our holy place once, where we went to worship the Maker, but that was hundreds of years ago. The fact it was a sacred site was why it was chosen to hold what it does."

"The remains of Gadranus?"

Resia nodded. "Which you would have known, I'd like to add, if you'd ever done your studies like you were supposed to."

"I read enough," Zaide said, irritated. "The same books as you. You know they're written like myths."

"And we wish they were." Verlin rubbed the back of his neck.

Sarma reached over to smooth Zaide's hair. "No one's unhappy with you, boy, there's no need to be defensive. If that was the conclusion you reached, then it was our failing. The Rise came late, and the later it got, the more it became our way to simply not talk about it."

Her husband nodded his agreement. "A superstition, I

suppose you could say. A belief that if we simply didn't speak of it, it wouldn't come to be."

Resia leaned closer. "But really, the point is, you've done everything you could and there's no point in dwelling on things you'd do differently now. What you've learned or studied doesn't change that there's an army out there, flattening the southern part of Amroch and knocking on our door again, even in one of the most defensible cities in the country. If they're trying to burn Amrochan, they're attacking Tinith, too, and it'll only be a matter of time before that wave spreads everywhere and everyone is at risk."

"Which is why if the princess believes there's something in Kolmar that will change the outcome of all this, it's important for you to do what you can to get her there," Verlin said.

Zaide resisted the urge to snort. "What about what I believe?"

"You're welcome to it, lad, but it doesn't change much. Whether you believe there's a weapon or not, it doesn't change that there's a man out there ready to crush our homeland, the same way he crushed yours." The steady, level way the man delivered the statement was a balm to Zaide's nerves, and he found himself nodding before he realized he agreed.

"I'll go with you," Resia said.

Zaide expected her parents to object, but instead, their solemn faces showed approval.

"As heir to the Elder, your power may be needed." Sarma smoothed Resia's hair the same way as she'd done with Zaide. "Your father and I can take care of the Kolmarı here."

"I'll let Aren know he's needed," Verlin added.

Somehow, the task was easier to palate with his foster parents supporting it. Zaide wiped a hand over his face, relieved, but weary. "We need to leave by sunrise, and I still need to get equipment. When you find Aren, can you also send someone to ask if Lieutenant Raddan would be allowed to join us?"

"I'll see to it."

"Thank you."

Across the table, Resia's youngest brother stared with wide eyes. "Zaide's gonna be a hero."

"By the Maker's mercy, he'll be alive. I'll settle for that." Sarma clucked at the boy as she shooed him away from the table. "Come on, now! We need to pack some proper food so he and your sister can get on the move, and he'll need a bed made up. Go fetch a nice pillow, he's sure to be exhausted."

"Thank you," Zaide repeated as she and the boy hurried into another room.

Verlin slipped away to fetch his boots and set out, while the others at the table launched into excited murmurs about the voyage to come. Zaide wished he could be half as excited as they sounded.

"Chin up," Resia whispered beside his bad ear. "We'll get there all right. Everything will be fine in the end."

"You know what's waiting there as well as I do," he murmured in reply. "You didn't even see the temple. The goborrins, the spiders—"

"But that was before. They're frightening, but you'll have more people with you. You and the princess already know what to expect, and besides, you'll have more tools at your disposal. You said the dagger you got in Jadora was powerful, right?"

He frowned. As useful as the Molten Dagger had been in the ice cavern north of Desheni, he didn't see how it would help with brutish pig-beasts that were nearly twice his size.

"It'll work out," Resia said, patting his shoulder as she spoke, as if he was a child in need of soothing. "Just you wait and see."

In the small hours of the morning, Zaide woke to Verlin shaking him by the shoulder. He fought back a groan. The simple straw-filled mattress felt like heaven after all his time traveling, and every inch of him craved more sleep.

"Come on, lad." Verlin's voice was soft, coaxing, like it had been a hundred times when the man had roused a young Zaide for early-morning hunting trips. "First light's coming soon, and we've still got to get your equipment."

Exhausted as he still was, Zaide pushed himself from his bed and gathered his things.

Sarma was awake in the other room when he emerged, bags for him and Resia already packed and waiting on the table. She sat a plate of fruit-filled pastries at one end of the table and motioned for him to sit. "Resia's getting ready. She'll be out soon."

"Thank you," he murmured, mindful of the others in the cozy house. Both side rooms were filled with straw mattresses; aside from Resia's family, a half-dozen other Kolmari now called the place home. All of them were familiar faces, people he'd been happy to see, but the more people who knew about the new mission he'd been assigned, the more he worried he wouldn't meet their expectations.

He ate while Sarma filled another bag with extra provisions. Resia appeared before he finished. She tip-toed through the room, mindful not to wake anyone.

Verlin sat and took a pastry of his own while the two of them ate. "I'll take the two of you to the castle barracks. Aren's to meet us there. You can all get whatever you need, and I assume that's where the princess will find you."

"What about Lieutenant Raddan?" Zaide asked.

"I found him, and I was able to relay your request he be there. But whether or not he will be, I don't know."

It was probably the best they could hope for. If nothing else, Raddan was unlikely to tell anyone what the princess had requested. Zaide doubted her father would take kindly to her determination to get behind enemy lines.

"I'm ready," Resia said as she licked her fingers clean. She took two of the bags from the table and gave her mother a hug.

"Be careful." Sarma squeezed her eyes shut as she hugged Resia close.

Resia patted her arm and extricated herself with a little wiggling. "I will be."

Before Zaide could escape, his foster mother rounded the table and wrapped him in a hug, too. "Both of you."

The show of affection was embarrassing, but Zaide couldn't bring himself to shrug it off. "I'll do my best." He didn't dare promise more than that.

Verlin opened the door as Zaide grabbed his bags and the sword he'd grown used to carrying. Outside, the narrow alleyways were still shrouded in dark, but the haze of smoke over the city carried a faint ruddy glow.

"The fires are still burning." Though Verlin was usually steadfast, he seemed resigned. "It's been this way for a week, now. Maybe more."

"Maybe this will be what changes that," Resia said.

Her father looked doubtful, but he still nodded as he led them toward the castle. "I hope so."

Soldiers came and went from the barracks at all hours of the day and night now, it seemed. Aren met them at the castle gate and escorted them across the barracks grounds. He was already outfitted in steel armor and had a bag over either shoulder, but he guided Zaide to the armory all the same.

"Best choose your own gear, boy," a familiar voice chimed in from nearby. "Don't pick what your friend has just because it looks good on him. You're light on your feet. Consider something that suits it."

Zaide twisted one direction and then the other before he found the man sitting at a table at the far end of the armory. "Murk?"

The soldier offered a stiff nod. "Here to escort your party. The lieutenant sends his regards, but the king can't spare him now. Nor was he willing to ask, given the nature of the request." A hint of amusement pulled at the corner of his normally stern mouth, but it didn't last long.

"I'm glad to have anyone familiar." Zaide regarded the armor racks with a thoughtful frown. He'd planned on doing exactly what Murk recommended against; Aren's armor promised to withstand a battering. But every time Zaide had fought a goborrin, it had been his speed and dexterity that worked in his favor. He chose lightweight leather armor instead, though he had to try on several pieces before he found anything comfortable.

Murk nodded his approval.

"I'll leave the lot of you now," Verlin said, a wistful glint in his eye as he looked between the Kolmari youths. His gaze lingered on Resia, but he didn't treat her any differently. Whether that was because of their mission or his role as acting Kolmari Elder, Zaide didn't know, but he supposed it didn't matter. "Maker's blessings on your journey."

"Are they ready, then?" Lark asked from the doorway.

Verlin spun to face her, mouth agape.

Zaide belted his sword to his hip, his new armor tightened. "We're ready if you are. If we make it out before sunup, all the better."

"Aye." Murk levered himself up from the table and swung a bag over his shoulder. "The less we're seen, the better."

Resia took advantage of her father's momentary surprise and leaned up to kiss his cheek. "We'll be back."

Right behind her, Aren gaped at the princess, too.

"Well, come along, then. The last thing I wanted was a gaggle of children instead of soldiers, but I guess we'd best make do." Murk offered a stern nod of goodbye to Resia's father and slipped into the barracks yard.

"Be safe," was all Verlin had time to get out before Lark hurried them all along.

They trailed behind Murk like a row of ducklings, far from

the powerful strike force Zaide had hoped for, but the best he'd be able to get.

Instead of cutting toward the city's main gates, Murk led them north through the city.

"Where are we going?" Resia asked as they trotted along. The sky had already begun to lighten. Sunrise wouldn't be far off.

"Across Lake Sian," Murk said.

"Sailing?" The single word escaped Aren like a mouthful of dread.

"Aye. The lieutenant's orders. Safer and faster than a trek on foot."

"And gives us more time to rest and think of a solid plan," Zaide said.

Lark lifted her chin, pleased by the suggestion. "Have any of you sailed before?"

"To Ganede," Zaide replied, at the same time Aren and Resia shook their heads.

The princess flashed the two of them a smile. "Don't worry. You're going to love it."

CHAPTER THIRTY-SIX

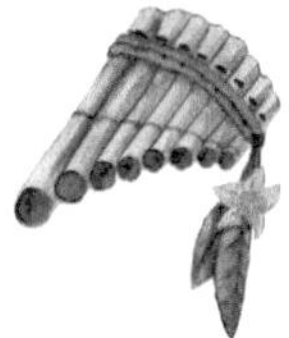

EVEN THE ROAR of water couldn't drown out the howling wind. Zaide pressed his hands to his ears and wished for a pillow or something else to muffle the noise, but with the speed at which the ship had been loaded, he had to be grateful his bunk had bedding at all.

The tiny cabin was stifling, and the constant creaking and lurching made everyone tense. The storm had swelled not long after they'd set sail. Black clouds blotted out the sun and harsh winds whipped Lake Sian into a churning mass that seemed alive.

"Not bad luck," Murk had assured them as soon as the first fat, stinging raindrops fell. "The winds will be harsh, but the rains are what we need to settle the fires outside Amrochan. It'll slow us down, but the ship will get us there fast enough."

The schooner boasted a full crew and the captain kept all of them on deck through the storm, manning a tangle of rigging and sails Zaide could never hope to understand. The woman had seemed unconcerned about the storm and remained convinced the trip to Kolmar's river would be brief.

Zaide couldn't help but wonder what she'd been paid to abandon the trade route on the river that trailed from Lake Sian to the northern coast, but with the princess on board, he assumed it had been a handsome fee. He'd spared only the briefest glance for the cost of passage to Amrochan by boat before he left Yithel on foot. That kind of travel would have taken every coin he'd lost in Desheni. He shifted to see Lark, nestled in her bunk on the other side of the cabin. She lay with her hands folded together on her stomach and her eyes fixed on the ceiling, as she had since Murk had banished them to the cabin in the same breath he'd volunteered to aid the ship's crew.

She hadn't asked about his expedition. She hadn't seemed concerned with how he'd obtained the Captured Spring or what he'd endured. He wasn't eager to recount the story, rife with his failings as it was, but her silence grew concerning.

On the bunk below hers, Resia groaned and rolled over. "I have to admit, I am not enjoying this trip."

"None of us are," Aren replied from Zaide's side of the cabin.

"The ship from Jadora to Ganede definitely made it easier to sleep." Zaide turned onto his side and tucked an arm beneath his head. It was no more comfortable than the flat mattress on its own, but there was no helping that. There would be time for comfort when their work was done.

"Maybe I'll ask for a post out there when this is finished. Going somewhere it rarely rains sounds like a great idea right now." Aren's sense of humor hadn't suffered, despite the number of hours he'd spent heaving over a bucket the captain had helpfully provided when she shut them inside the ship. The cabin door wasn't locked, but it may as well have been. They all knew they weren't welcome on the deck.

"You'd like it. The lights in the city are beautiful at night." Zaide leaned over the edge to peer into the lower bunk. "Feeling better?"

Aren grimaced. "I wouldn't say that, but I'm... acclimating. I won't be eager to get on a boat ever again."

"That reminds me," Resia said. "We haven't talked about

how we're getting back from Kolmar. Are we taking the ship back to Amrochan?"

"I don't think it'll be safe for the ship to stay. She probably won't even be able to get us all the way there. There's that tight bend in the river north of the village, where the water gets shallow. If we get that far, I'll be impressed." It wasn't far from the temple, either. If they landed that close, Zaide figured they'd reach their destination a scant few hours later—assuming they weren't met with a host of goborrins in the forest, that was.

Resia rubbed her chin in thought. "So we'll walk from there, and walk back to Amrochan? We'll have to go past the garrison, won't we?"

"We should have brought a bigger team," Aren muttered.

"A bigger team would be harder to move through the forest undetected. Remember, we've got Resia's way with nature on our side. We should be able to evade notice, if we're careful." Zaide flashed his foster sister a smile, one she returned half-heartedly.

After a moment of silence, Aren reached for his bucket. "Sneaking in and out, huh?"

Zaide shrugged. "Unless the princess has a better idea."

Lark said nothing at all, and a sober silence fell over the cabin. After long seconds dragged by and no one spoke, Zaide turned onto his back and stared at the ceiling above his bunk. He wasn't sure it sounded like a good idea, himself, but going to Kolmar at all hadn't struck him as wise. Rain still thundered against the deck above, and he shut his eyes and silently prayed it had extinguished the fires in the fields outside Amrochan. Kolmar, he feared, was beyond praying for.

The morose attitude that had fallen in Lark's silence persisted until they reached the river, at which point it morphed into a new, sharper anxiety. The ship hovered in the lake at the mouth of the river until the storm dwindled. The captain poked her head into the cabin once to declare the Maker favored their trip, and that everyone could exit the cabin as long as they stayed out of the way.

Aren and Zaide raced for the door, but Aren escaped first. At Zaide's heels, Resia followed at a more sedate pace, though she looked back at Lark twice. The princess had no interest in seeing how they'd get upriver, it seemed.

"She'll be fine," Zaide murmured as he led the way to the deck.

There were few places out of the way, but Murk jabbed a finger at a specific spot and the three of them posted themselves there to watch. The crew worked the sails hard and fast to take advantage of the wind that blew—somewhat unexpectedly— from their back. The schooner zigzagged its way up the river, against the current, and the snail's pace at which they progressed made pressure wrap Zaide's chest in uncomfortable bands.

"This could take days," Aren whispered.

Resia gave him a hard look. "It isn't that bad."

Slow as progress was, Zaide was inclined to agree with her. The trees moved by at a steady pace. Considering the density of the undergrowth, they would have been hard pressed to move anywhere near the same speed by foot.

"It'll get better," Murk offered as he passed with an armful of rope. "Right now, we're south of the meeting of two branches. Once we pass the fork, it'll be easier going."

Whether or not it did, they were just along for the ride.

After a time, watching grew dull and someone retrieved food from the galley. The three of them sat and ate, and then sat and watched, and then ate again when evening fell.

Just as the sun dipped beneath the tree line, Lark appeared on deck. "It's time," she announced, earning herself more than a few concerned looks from sailors.

"How do you know?" Zaide hoped she wouldn't take the question as an affront, but she didn't even have to answer him.

The moment she turned to face him, he saw the artifacts she carried, each surrounded by a soft aura of colored light. He stared at the Vale Hymnflute, which now hung from her neck by a strap she must have crafted after everyone else had left the cabin. "It's never done that before."

"It's because the other two are with it." Lark shrugged, then made her way across the deck to seek the captain.

The crew had long since quieted, something about the dark and the forest that loomed to either side of the river oppressive enough that it made everyone wish to be still. The captain called out orders for the ship to be drawn close to the bank on the port side. With what little Zaide knew about ships, he found himself standing in the doorway to the cabin, looking down at his hands and trying to figure out which side that meant.

"Left, genius," Aren said as he shouldered past to retrieve his things. "You know, the side that faces Kolmar?"

"If we're being completely fair to me, I don't have a map anymore." Zaide followed him into the cabin and fetched his bags. The journey by ship had been so brief, it almost felt like traveling to Amrochan by foot when he'd first been sent to deliver the Hymnflute to the king had been a waste of time. In some ways, he supposed it was. When he emerged, he couldn't help but seek the glow of the artifacts, and by association, Lark.

The glow still surprised him. He knew they'd been dormant, rather than depleted, but now it seemed as if they'd been waiting to be reunited—or waiting for the right person to hold them. He'd felt something in the Captured Spring, an otherworldly cold that radiated off it all the time. Likewise, the Molten Dagger shed heat, and it had worked perfectly well for shattering tricen and tricewolves in the north. But until now, the Hymnflute had never done anything. To his surprise, seeing it aglow in the princess's hand lit a small spark of jealousy in his chest.

Murk appeared by his elbow as if from nowhere. "They'll let down a plank as soon as they've got the boat settled. Hope you're ready, boy. There's something ugly out there in the woods. I can feel it."

"About to be a lot more ugly things," Zaide remarked blandly.

The older man offered a flat, unamused stare in return.

"Don't feel bad, Zaide." Aren clapped a hand on his shoulder and then pushed him toward where Lark and the captain stood watching the men heave a long wooden walkway toward the shore. "We can't all be good-looking."

Murk snorted and trudged across the deck.

The plank fell short of the bank and splashed into the water. A few of the sailors sucked air in through their teeth. The tension in the air felt something like the still before a storm, though the sky was clear enough.

A different sort of storm, Zaide concluded. He checked his sword as he stopped beside the princess.

Lark passed the captain a fat pouch; a hefty amount of money, no doubt. "Safe travels and fair winds on your way back to Amrochan."

"I thank you, Princess," the captain said as she bounced the pouch in her hand. It jingled like a fistful of brass winter bells. "I think we're headed for Yithel after this, though. Safer to run the trade routes between there and Chithal until the siege is over."

"Not much of a siege, what with ships still coming and going," Murk grumbled. "Come on, the lot of you. We need to move while it's easy to stay hidden." He started down the plank with one hand on the bag slung over his shoulder, but the other on his sword.

Zaide took a single step before Resia put a hand on his arm.

"I know you have a cloak in one of those bags. You should put it on. Pull up your hood, just in case." She rubbed his arm as she spoke, soothing, knowing all too well that the suggestion would needle at him. But the swell of frustration he experienced at having his appearance pointed out was less than he expected, and he nodded in return. Best to do it on the ship, in any case, rather than slow them down while he pulled out the light travel cloak and draped it around his shoulders.

Resia pulled up his hood and smoothed back his white hair. "The best ghost is the one that's not seen," she whispered. Her hand cradled his cheek for a moment, soft, gentle, and warm. He closed his eyes and leaned into that touch. It was the most grounding thing he'd felt in ages. After weeks on the road, feeling lost and adrift and uncertain what he'd gotten himself into or why, the simple reassurance his Kolmari family was still there offered more comfort than he'd realized it might.

Then she withdrew and hurried down the plank to catch up with the others, who already clustered on the shore.

Zaide was the last one off the boat. He splashed into the water and sloshed to the riverbank, the same as everyone else had. Wet to the waist, he sat on the grass and pulled off his boots to dump out the water.

"Guess we should've taken those off before jumping in," Aren said.

Murk snorted. "You're free to walk barefoot while they dry out."

Above them, the ship seemed smaller than ever before. The captain and her crew said nothing as they pulled the plank back on board, but the captain offered a stiff nod of farewell. Everyone on the ground returned it and then, even faster than they'd been to halt and unload their passengers, the schooner was back in motion, letting oars and the current carry it back downstream.

"All right. Everyone on your feet. With shoes on." Murk frowned at them. At the edge of the riverbank, the moon provided enough light to see, but traversing the forest would grow difficult fast once they were in the dark of the canopy.

Zaide squinted into the shadows as he squeezed water out of his socks and put them back on his feet. Lark stood a few paces away, staring into the forest, but the glow of the artifacts was gone. Stowed in her bag, he assumed. Left uncovered, their light would be too quick to draw attention.

Murk watched until everyone was on their feet and ready. "Which way to this temple of yours, Princess?"

Instead of answering, Lark turned to Zaide with a question in her eyes.

Of course. She had no idea where they were. Her one and only trip to Kolmar had her entering the temple from the village side, and the rest of the forest was foreign.

Zaide looked to the sky and took in the stars, then examined the shape of the river. "This way." He took the lead without prompting and was surprised by the wash of relief that came when Murk didn't object. As the oldest and most experienced soldier in the group, it made sense for Murk to lead, bowing only to the princess. But the forest was strange to soldiers from outside Kolmar, too, and that put them on unexpectedly even footing.

Young as they were, Zaide, Resia, and Aren knew the forest. Murk's experience would help him, and while the princess had authority and experience with the weapons Zaide hadn't seen but was certain she carried, the unfamiliarity of their environment meant all she had to rely on was her skill, her wits, and the strange artifacts now in her possession.

Unable to help himself, Zaide looked back at her once. She stared back, as if daring him to speak.

"When everything's over," he said, mindful not to speak too loud, "I want the Hymnflute back."

Her brows shot up. "You have no right to it. When this is over—"

"Walk," Murk barked before they could argue.

Both ducked their heads and hurried onward.

No more than a dozen paces in, the forest's shadows swallowed them, but Zaide had already located a game trail. He motioned for everyone to move single file. One by one, the others settled in a row behind him. Resia walked right at his heels, with Aren behind her, and Murk took the back so the princess would be guarded from both sides. If Lark thought anything of the arrangement, she didn't show it.

Not that Zaide would be able to see. The familiar outlines of people was all he had to tell him they were there, and ahead, there was nothing but darkness. Yet the farther they got from the river, the easier it became for him to pick shapes out of the shadows.

"There's something ahead," he whispered. He could just make out the tiny twinkle of light in the distance, but it was enough. Warm light. Firelight. "A goborrin camp."

"You're sure, lad?" Murk whispered back.

Zaide's brow furrowed. "Straight ahead, then a little to the right. Don't you see it?"

The long silence that followed put a strange uneasiness in the pit of his stomach.

"I see it." Resia leaned against his arm as she peered into the night. "We aren't close to the temple yet. Do we go around?"

"Probably best," he said. "There's a split in the trail. We'll duck that direction and loop north, just a shade. It'll take us back toward the river, but we can find another game trail from there."

She nodded and relayed instructions to the three behind her.

When everyone whispered confirmation, Zaide led the way. The trail was narrow and undergrowth brushed at their shoulders as they passed, a rustle in the dark that would be easy to mistake for the movement of a deer. Somewhere overhead, an owl hooted a warning call. He paused for half a step, but no drumbirds answered. Lark might have remembered the beats the goborrins used to communicate, but he hadn't thought to mention them to the others.

By the time the rushing sound of the river reached his ears, he'd located another game trail that took them back the direction they needed to go, but one that offered the goborrin camp a wide berth. The firelight was still visible, as were hulking shadows around it, and the silence of the group grew tense as they softened their footsteps and slipped between the trees.

Somehow, Zaide expected they'd find the temple inhabited. Instead, when they crested the hill and looked down at the ancient structure from behind, there weren't any goborrins in sight.

He crouched at the edge of the cliff and waited, counting seconds to see if they'd caught a gap in the patrol.

Lark inched forward to sit beside him. The way her brows drew together said she'd expected them, too.

"What is it?" Murk asked in a whisper.

Zaide leaned back to speak with him. "When we were here before, there was a camp out front and a handful of goborrins patrolling the perimeter. There's no firelight on the other side of the temple, and no goborrins down below." He pointed into the wide gap between the temple's walls and the earthen cliff on which they crouched.

"There's a balcony on the side of the temple over there," Lark added. "It's where we got in before. They saw us enter and almost caught us. Shouldn't they have bolstered their defenses?"

Murk grunted. "Better look again, Highness."

The princess glanced at him, brow furrowed, but her eyes followed his finger when he pointed. Zaide's did, too. He'd looked before, but he'd been looking for goborrins, not at the temple. Now, when he saw what he should have noticed right away, his shoulders slumped.

The balcony they'd climbed was gone, the doorway above it bricked in with crude stone and fresh mortar. He scanned the wall. The windows, too, had been plugged.

"Keeping us out?" Lark asked quietly. "Or trying to keep something in?"

The monstrous spider sprang to mind first, but his thoughts slipped to what they were there for a moment later. "Both, maybe."

Aren inched closer. "Think the front's blocked, too?"

"I'd bet on it." Lark rubbed her mouth and then curled her hand into a fist. "We should look, then find another way in."

Zaide nodded. The brush wasn't as dense here, and he led the way easily down the slope. He and Aren were quieter on their feet than the rest, used to striving for stealth in the forest.

When they reached the front of the temple, no one was surprised to see the entryway barricaded with massive blocks of stone. Some of them still sported moss and lichen, having been uprooted from elsewhere in the woods.

Frustrated, Zaide rubbed the back of his neck. They still hadn't seen any sign of goborrins nearby, but he kept his voice low. "I don't think we can chisel these out."

"Strong mortar," Murk confirmed. "And long dry. It's been blocked up for a few weeks, at least."

"Probably done right after we left," Lark said.

Resia's shoulders slumped. "More likely after they took Kolmar. How do we get in now?"

All eyes except Lark's turned in Zaide's direction. That they deferred to him came as no surprise, but he still found himself studying the princess and wishing she'd say something. She'd never been so taciturn while they traveled, though she'd always been cross.

"I have an idea," Zaide said when it became clear Lark would not speak. "There's one spot they probably didn't plug."

Murk crossed his arms. "I don't like the sound of that."

"I don't blame you. When we came to get the Hymnflute, it was suspended in the front hall. Chamber? I'm not sure what to call it, but the big room. Magic held it floating, but there was a hole in the ceiling above it to let in light. It won't be easy to get to, but if we can climb to the roof, we'll probably be able to lower ourselves in." Zaide tried to smile, but he hadn't even managed to reassure himself. They had rope, but that wouldn't help them scale the temple.

As if to confirm his worries, Resia glanced doubtfully up its side.

Lark rested a hand on her shoulder. "Zaide will find a way up."

"Why me?"

"Because whoever goes up first needs to be strong enough to pull up the next person. That rules me out, and Resia's smaller than I am. Out of the three of you boys, you're the one wearing the lightest armor, so the climb will be easiest for you."

Aren glanced down at his gear, then shrugged. "She's got a point."

"Fine," Zaide grumbled. He slid his bag off his shoulder to find his rope, then left the bag on the ground. "One of you will have to bring that up."

"Resia should go up the rope first," Lark said. "Then me. That leaves Aren and Murk for defense while we're climbing."

"Solid plan, Highness." Murk reached for Zaide's bag to add it to his load, but Resia snatched it out from under his hand.

She batted her eyes at him. "I'm the lightest. It'll be easier if I'm the one with the extra weight."

The soldier hitched one shoulder. "Fair enough."

Zaide scanned the front of the temple as he looped the rope over his shoulder. There were enough ridges and reliefs that it shouldn't prove too difficult to climb, as long as he found handholds between them. Satisfied, he dug his fingers into the gap between stones to begin his ascent.

As an afterthought, he paused to adjust his sword in its scabbard, so it hung behind him instead of at his side.

"I could hold that, too," Resia offered.

"I'd rather have it with me. Don't know what's at the top." He pulled himself up until he could grab hold of the ledge above the rocked-in door, which provided a nice footrest.

Below, the others waited in uneasy silence. Zaide did his best to ignore them, pretending at the same time that he didn't fear long, chitinous black legs might reach for him from above before he finished his climb.

When he reached the top, the roof was bare. After a sigh of

relief, he crept across the ridges of stone, exploring. There was little point in pulling anyone up if the hole he remembered was sealed, and he wasn't positive where it was.

He found it at the peak of a pyramid-shaped protrusion at the top of the temple's roof, still open, the room below pitch black.

"No spiders, at least," he muttered to himself as he returned to the edge. Finding somewhere to brace his feet while he pulled someone up would be a greater challenge.

Three worried faces looked up at him when he peered down to make sure all was well below. Murk just frowned and motioned for him to hurry. Zaide nodded in acknowledgment and tested a few footholds before he found a raised stone solid enough for his liking. He tossed the coils of rope over the edge and wished he had somewhere to tie it, instead of needing to loop it around his arm, grip with both hands, and hope for the best.

A few light tugs came before Resia started her ascent. He gritted his teeth and hauled back on the rope, holding fast while she climbed. A sheen of sweat decorated his brow before she reached the top.

"Made it," Resia whispered as she slid over the edge and released the rope.

Zaide exhaled hard and swiped a hand across his brow. He'd kept plenty of rope topside, but he looked down again before he pulled up a little more. Once he was sure he'd drawn up enough to ensure there was space for all the hands that would assist him, he motioned for Resia to join him. Before he had his feet braced, a sharp tug almost pulled him over.

Resia set her jaw and pulled hard while he regained his footing.

"Should've tugged to be sure we were ready," he grumbled. Resia's weight behind him made it easier to hold fast, and Lark proved a far more dextrous climber than she'd been in their first visit to the temple. The change in her ability came as a surprise, but he supposed it shouldn't have. He had no way of knowing what she'd done after they parted ways in Jadora. Training, it seemed, had filled a decent portion of her time.

Aren followed her up—a little slower, weighed down by his armor—and his hands on the rope once he reached the top meant Murk's climb was easy to manage. The four of them on the roof greatly outweighed the old soldier, and the moment he was fully on the roof, Zaide wound the rope around his arm and led the way to the opening he'd found.

The dark seemed more oppressive when Zaide peered down into the temple again. "I'll go in first."

Murk grunted. "We go down in reverse order. After we find somewhere to secure the rope."

"What? Why?"

"Because whoever goes down first can stick their foot in a loop and get lowered in. Everyone else has to climb down, and Aren and I are both in plate armor."

"Can't you just slide?" Resia asked in a whisper.

Lark patted her shoulder. "Not unless you want to strip the skin off your palms."

"There's a groove over here," Aren announced. "I think we can tie the rope to it."

Zaide descended the pyramid to investigate. "Looks solid enough. I'll tie it off. You get ready."

"Aye aye, Captain." Aren flicked his fingers against his forehead in a mock salute before he bounded back up to the opening.

The stone didn't budge when Zaide looped the rope around it and tied it off. He pulled hard to test before he joined the others. "Ready?"

"As we'll ever be, lad." Murk slid over the edge with the rope, and together, they lowered him into the darkness.

CHAPTER THIRTY-SEVEN

Zaide's boots hit the floor with a soft thump. Shadow swallowed everything around him, the hole they'd entered through little more than a blot of midnight blue that glowed faintly against the backdrop of pitch black.

"Strange," Lark said after a moment, her voice tight with frustration. "The lantern was fine when I checked it on the ship. It won't work now."

"Strong magic," Zaide replied without thinking.

A moment later, the soft, warm light of the Molten Dagger illuminated their faces. It was brighter than he recalled, strong enough for him to make out the pale square on the dirty floor where he stood. He scuffed the toe of his boot against a ridge of dirt.

Resia squinted at him. "I'm surprised you'd remember that."

He lifted his head and found her scrutinizing his face. "Remember the magic?"

"That magic-made lanterns dull in the presence of something more powerful."

The tips of his ears burned with embarrassment, but he took comfort in knowing everything was red in the dagger's light.

"It's hard to hold onto everything, since magic stuff isn't a skill set I can do anything with, but, uh, I remember a few things."

Lark nudged his shoulder and pointed at his feet. "The pillar is gone. This is where the Hymnflute was."

"Yeah, and good thing, or Murk might have hurt himself, being the first one down." Zaide kicked the crusted dirt again. "See anything else we left behind?"

The sour twist of her mouth indicated she knew exactly what he meant. She turned, holding the dagger aloft, but nothing glinted in the dark around them. If the great spider's remains were still there, its glistening body would have reflected the dagger's glow in dozens of places.

Unperturbed, or maybe just unaware of what should have perturbed him, Aren planted his fists against his hips and turned in a slow circle. "So, which way do we go? You two know where we're supposed to be, right?"

"We entered the temple from the second floor before." Lark took a few steps in a random direction, then turned. The dagger's light was definitely brighter than it had been, but it didn't reach far enough to reveal much of the vast room. "We came through a handful of rooms from there and ended up here." She paused to study a doorway when the dagger's light revealed it, nestled between two raised platforms.

Instead of the doorway, Zaide studied the balustrade on the platform above. "The rail was broken where the spider came down, wasn't it? If we can find that, I'll know which doorway we came through."

The group trailed along behind Lark as she circled the room. The spider's carcass was gone. So were the goborrins. "They must've had a time cleaning this up. Think they wanted to prevent scavengers?" she asked.

"I don't really want to think about what they wanted to prevent. Aside from us getting in here." They passed the rocked-in main entryway and Zaide trailed his fingers across the stone.

"Should we put together an exit plan? Maybe knock some of these down while we look for the right door?"

"By what light, lad?" Murk shook his head. "The princess can stand there and wait for us to move stone, or she can find where we need to go. I say we move on. This black chills me. The sooner we're out of it, the better."

"I agree." Lark raised the dagger a bit higher. "Here. This must be where it came off the balcony."

Zaide padded forward to look. "Yeah, that looks right. That means the door we came through was over here." He pointed across the room.

Murk led the way into the dark. "Let's go, then."

Everyone followed.

The doorway they reached looked little different from the others, and Zaide was sure they'd walked past it once already, but the events of that night remained so vivid in his memory that he was positive they'd chosen the right direction. His hand went to his sword and his shoulders bunched.

"Everything is empty," Lark murmured.

Aren shrugged. "It's an abandoned temple. There shouldn't be much."

"Not abandoned, you know that. The Elder's duty is to make a pilgrimage to maintain it." Resia sniffed as if he'd suggested she might abandon that responsibility.

"Well, the Elder's not here, is he?" he replied hotly.

"Enough," Zaide growled. "Be on your guard. The place was infested when Lark and I were here last. I don't want to be caught unprepared a second time."

A moment of quiet followed before Resia spoke again. "Why Lark, Your Highness?"

The princess glanced over her shoulder. "What?"

"Your alias. Why Lark?"

"I couldn't exactly go around calling myself Dasienna. But my mother always called me her meadowlark. It was the first thing that came to mind when..." Her eyes drifted to Zaide, then returned to the dark path ahead of them. "When I needed a name."

Zaide cleared his throat. "We're here."

Before them, the dagger's light was swallowed by the great expanse of the room they'd sought. Even the stone tile under their feet grew harder to make out.

Lark made a soft sound of surprise and paused mid-step to pull the spring out from under her shirt. Its blue light mingled oddly with the glow of the dagger.

"The Vale Hymnflute, too," Resia whispered.

Surprised, Lark glanced down. A pale green light peeked out from underneath her bag's flap.

"The Captured Spring was glowing when I found it," Zaide said, "but the Hymnflute's never done that. Not even when we used it to open the Molten Dagger's case."

Lark pulled the pipes from her bag. "The artifacts must be reacting to the altars, now that they're all together. They know we're here."

"They shouldn't *know* anything," Aren protested. "They're things, they can't think."

"Maybe not." The princess weighed the two artifacts in her hands thoughtfully as she peered down at the spring on its chain. "But something's happening, and I don't think we can deny that."

Murk put himself at the front of the procession. "All right, Highness. What do we do with them now, and what do we expect after we do it?"

She motioned toward the center of the room, or perhaps the far end of it. The oppressive weight of the shadows around them made the gesture seem smaller than it was. "There's an emblem on the floor that marks the seal. We place the artifacts on the three altars around it, and then it should open."

"And when it does?" Zaide asked. His hand tightened on the hilt of his sword. They'd encountered nothing in the temple, and the ease with which they'd reached their destination struck him as wrong. They'd battled hard before to get to the Hymnflute. Had the goborrins really thought rocking up the doors and windows would be enough to protect what they sought now?

Lark met his eye, her mouth set in challenge. "I guess we'll find out."

Resia brushed Zaide's arm, her fingers gentle, the touch just enough to remind him to remove his hand from his weapon. "What do you need us to do, Your Highness?" Her voice was steady, but faint lines of worry marred her forehead in the eerie glow.

"Each of us should place an artifact." The princess motioned toward herself, then the two of them. Aren opened his mouth with a question, but she turned a frown on him before he could speak. "You and Murk have the best armor. Stand ready, in case something happens when we place them. Resia, you're to become Kolmar's Elder, so you'll place the Vale Hymnflute. Zaide, you place the Molten Dagger. I'll take the Captured Spring."

"Of course, Highness." Resia took the Hymnflute the moment it was offered.

Next, Lark extended the dagger toward Zaide.

Of the three artifacts, it had proven the most useful. Even now, its glow seemed to be the brightest. Zaide supposed he should be happy to have it back in his grasp, but as he closed his fingers around it, he couldn't help a twinge of disappointment at knowing he'd have to leave it behind. "Do we get these back? After we're done with all this?"

Lark shrugged. "Who can say? We're in uncharted territory now. The records I found didn't say what happened after the seal was opened. Just that these were what opened it."

"Exactly what every soldier wants to hear," Murk said as he drew his sword. Beside him, Aren did the same, their blades glinting in the muddy combination of colored light.

"Does it matter where they go?" Resia circled the emblem on the floor. She paused to study each of the altars—which Zaide still thought looked like regular benches—but from the way she considered each with the same expression, they did not seem to be marked.

The princess positioned herself behind one altar and held the Captured Spring above it. "No. I don't think so, anyway. Zaide, get over here. We should place them at the same time."

He started to reach for his sword, but Murk shook his head. Zaide frowned, but took his place behind the third altar. "Did your book say that?"

"No, I just think we should. Considering it's my expedition, I think you can indulge me." Her tone remained light, but her eyes glittered with challenge.

Zaide sighed. "Fine. Let's just get it over with."

Lark raised her artifact. He and Resia did the same. In unison, they lowered them to their altars.

Something seized the dagger from Zaide's grasp before he touched the stone. It pulled free of his fingers and floated in place, rotating above the altar.

Long seconds drew past.

He opened his mouth to ask what came next and a ring of light shot from the circular emblem's edge.

Murk spat an oath as a low rumble began beneath their feet. The emblem split into quarters, then twelfths. More lines of light lanced to the ceiling. A section of the floor dropped. Another followed, and another.

"It's sinking!" Resia exclaimed.

"Opening," Zaide said. He shielded his eyes against the brightness and a swelling cloud of dust as the segments of the emblem cascaded into the floor, forming a circular stairwell.

The twelfth piece landed with a heavy thud and the light faded, leaving all of them blinking hard. Instead of darkness, though, a soft glow surrounded them, diffuse light filtering up from the new passage below.

Aren coughed.

"Maker's mercy." Murk swiped the back of his hand across his forehead. "What we're after is down there?"

"It better be." Zaide stepped around the altar where the Molten Dagger still floated and started down the stairs. The light came from nowhere; no lanterns or mage-made lights decorated the new hallway, where more stairs descended into the ground below the temple. It was warm, golden and welcoming, but the way it emanated from nothing made the hair on the back of his neck prickle. He reached for his sword.

Lark's hurried steps behind him made him cock his good ear back. "Wait for the rest of us!"

The padding sound of Resia's soft slippers followed, then the rattle of armor as Aren and Murk rushed to reclaim the lead position.

Zaide drew his weapon anyway. "This place is weird. Where do you think—" A stair gave way beneath his foot and he cut off with a shout as the floor opened to swallow him.

Instead of a pit, he hit a ramp and slid. The coarse stone scraped the skin from his back. His sword hit a wall and the hilt slammed into his ribs, ripping the blade from his grasp.

"Zaide!" Resia's small, panicked voice called from somewhere behind him.

He tumbled to a halt on a cold, dusty section of floor and wheezed, unable to reply. When he didn't answer, panicked voices rose in words he couldn't make out. With a grimace, he sat up and pressed a hand to his side. Probing made him wince, but he didn't think anything was broken.

"Impulsiveness," he whispered to himself with the first breath he caught. "Have to... stop that." He swallowed and waved dust away from his face.

"Zaide, stay where you are. We're coming down as soon as we figure out who has the rest of the rope," Lark called. Her voice bounced strangely, so much like the light that swelled from nowhere as the dust began to settle.

He started to turn back to answer, but a soft glint in the

passage ahead caught his attention. There shouldn't have been *anything* glinting, even in that strange light. But it did—a different color, this time, soft and cool instead of bright.

Zaide squinted past the clearing dust and pushed himself to his feet.

"Zaide, can you hear me?" Lark's question struck him as strange and distant.

Ahead, the light changed again. A soft, hot spark danced above a shape he couldn't make out. Curiosity drove him closer and slowly, the shape resolved into a heap of bones.

"Maker's mercy," he breathed.

Atop the pile sat a skull, its crown pierced by an iridescent blade.

"I found it." Zaide dropped his hand from his side. "I found it!" he called, louder.

"What?" Lark squeaked. "Don't—don't do anything! We're coming down!"

He crept forward and the space around him widened. Not a passage, but a room connected to the tunnel he'd fallen from. His back stung and his side ached, but curiosity still urged him forward. Zaide cradled his bruised ribs with his hand as he crept into the circular space.

There were no decorations. No patterns or reliefs on the wall, no painted symbols or shaped tiles on the floor. The chamber was plain, round, and held nothing but the bones and that blade. His eyes narrowed as he inched closer.

The sword itself was ordinary, so unremarkable in design that he wouldn't have thought anything of it, were it not for the colors that danced across the blade. They were soft, so faint he could have believed it a trick of the unusual light if it didn't glitter or spark from time to time. Swirls flowed across the metal like the iridescent reflections on a soap bubble, competing for precedence and then slipping away. Sometimes the lines converged, and a soft shimmer of colored light formed at their union before it vanished, too.

A soft scrabbling and a few frustrated voices rose behind him. Zaide turned back, expecting Aren or Murk, but Lark was the first one down the slope.

She glanced his way, just long enough to be sure he was in one piece, then the sword caught her attention and she grew still. "That *is* it," she whispered. "The Spectrum Blade."

"I've never seen anything like it." He moved aside as she strode forward.

Lark wet her lips as her eyes traveled down the bones that served as its pedestal. "Me neither. I didn't realize it would be so..." She trailed off and reached for the hilt.

Something sparked against her fingers and she jerked back with a yelp.

Zaide started toward her, but she raised a hand in signal for him to stop.

Beside her, the sword glittered. He reached for it instead.

"Wait—" Lark started.

His hand had already closed around the hilt. He drew it back, and the pile of bones collapsed and clattered across the floor as the sword pulled free of the skull.

Confusion and dismay played across the princess's face as he gave it an experimental swish. "It's..."

"Tiny," Zaide finished, disappointed. He tilted the sword in his hand, watching the muted colors swirl across its surface. "It's a whole foot shorter than anything I've ever trained with."

"Princess?" Resia called, her voice faint.

Lark strode toward the slanted entrance to answer.

At the foot of the slope where the rope she'd descended still lay, a stone slab rose from the floor and slammed into the ceiling, cutting off their only escape. She spat something decidedly unladylike and jumped to grasp at the tail end of the rope, which still dangled over the top of the slab.

Zaide took a single step to join her before a sharp hiss filled his ears and he spun back.

The pile of bones trembled as black mist poured from the

skull's mouth and the split in the top of its head. Shadows pooled on the ground and divided into tendrils that snaked toward him with a single-minded intent.

"Uh, Lark?" He danced backwards as a coil of black twisted around where he'd been.

"Come help me," she snapped.

More mist wrapped itself around the bones. They shifted and creaked as the shadow began to take form above them.

"Lark?" he repeated, alarmed. He backed up, almost to the wall, nothing but the iridescent sword between him and the darkness. He didn't dare tear his eyes away.

The princess gasped.

A low, deep rasp like an exhale emanated from the cloud. It twisted into a shape that was vaguely human, its hands held before it.

Something clacked on the back side of the slab that blocked the door. Muted voices announced the arrival of the rest of the party behind it, but Zaide couldn't make out anything they said. He and Lark both backed against the stone, watching as the mist-creature opened eyes of dim yellow light. Its formless head lifted and its eyes settled on the blade.

"Bearer," it wheezed, its voice like sliding sand, words indistinct and radiating from everywhere and nowhere all at once.

Zaide shifted on his feet, his pulse heavy in his ears. "Is it... a ghost? How do you fight ghosts?"

"How should I know?" Lark cried.

The shadow moved as if taking a step, mists curling and slipping away from its body as it slid across the floor. It reached out.

Zaide swung the iridescent sword at its extended arm. The black mist of its limb exploded and dissipated, and the creature shrieked and reeled backwards.

"The sword repels it? It must've been holding that thing

inside the... the..." She pointed at the shadow-shrouded bones on the floor, uncharacteristically at a loss for words.

"Then maybe it's connected to them." He swept the blade at the tendrils of darkness on the ground as he inched forward. They scattered like smoke as he progressed, parting as if the shadow feared contact.

The being itself retreated against the wall, its yellow eyes angled with distress.

Zaide plunged the sword into the front of the skull, piercing it between the eyes.

A screech like steel on stone burst from the shadows as they split into pieces. Each swirling tendril shot in a different direction, struck the walls, and sank into the crevices between the stones.

Silence settled, but Zaide's skin still crawled.

"What was that thing?" Lark asked in a hush.

He braced a boot against the skull as he pulled the sword free. It felt wrong in his hand, shorter than he was used to, lighter than he'd trained for. Repelling the shadow-being had been easy with it, but he couldn't help the dismal frown that creased his face. Weren't legendary weapons supposed to be intimidating?

"Don't know," he said as he checked to ensure the blade was clean. Not even dust marred its color-swirled surface. "But it's gone for now, so let's figure out how to get out of here. Now that we've got your sword." As he spoke, he offered the sword to her, hilt-first.

Lark studied it for a moment, then returned her attention to the slab. Soft scrabbling noises still came from the other side. "Having it doesn't mean much if we can't get out of here. There has to be some way to open this."

The sheath at his side was empty, so Zaide slid the strange sword into it. It didn't fit well, but it freed up his hands. He hadn't seen where his sword landed during his fall, but it didn't seem to be in the room with them. "See any markings?" If it was anything like the door they'd encountered in Jadora's caves, they could shout for Resia to retrieve the Vale Hymnflute from the altar above.

"No. Not on this side, anyway." She ran her hands over the surface of the stone. Dust and grit flaked away, but revealed no patterns or etchings that might have offered clues.

"Maybe on the other side, then. Resia!" Zaide shouted against the corner where the slab touched the wall.

The noise on the other side halted and he turned his head to press his right ear to the crack.

"Zaide?" His foster sister's voice was faint, but present. "We can't find a way to get it open. Murk says we should try closing and reopening the entrance with the artifacts."

"Try it," he called back. It was as good a guess as any.

When he straightened, Lark gave him an expectant look.

"They're going to use the artifacts to try to reopen the way," he explained. "It'll take them a minute to get back up there."

She nodded, but sighed. "We may as well look around, then. Maybe we'll find some other clue."

"Or maybe he's all that's in here." Zaide jerked his thumb toward the bones on the floor.

Her nose crinkled, but she padded across the floor to crouch beside the remains. "You know who this is, right?"

"Does it matter? He's dead."

Lark scoffed. "It's Gadranus. The last one. Or what's left of him, anyway." She touched a finger to the skull, just above the split he'd left between its eyes, and tilted it upward. Her gaze softened—saddened—as she did.

He glanced between the skull and her face. The change in her demeanor made no sense. "Isn't him being dead a good thing?"

"I suppose so. But to be entombed here, to be held that way, with that sword..." Her finger drifted to the split in the top of the skull. "Do you think he was killed that way? Fast, almost painless? Or did they make him suffer the way he made the people of Amroch suffer?"

"Should we care?" he asked, unsure he wanted the answer.

No answer came. Instead, Lark tilted her hand. "I feel something over here. Air."

Zaide crossed over to crouch beside her, his hands out. A soft current of air flow brushed his fingers. "Coming from the wall." He inched closer, following it to its source. "Here. A hidden door?"

"It must be." She glanced back at the slab and squinted.

"What?"

"It's getting dimmer in here. Did you notice?"

He shook his head. "I hadn't, honestly. Are they back? Go call for them. I'll see if I can find a way to open this." The crack where the draft came through was almost imperceptible, but he followed it up the stone wall and across the top of what had to be the door.

Lark pressed an ear to the side of the slab to listen for their companions. More than once, Zaide bumped the bones that lay scattered on the floor. Their clatter earned him a glare.

"Sorry," he muttered. "I'm just trying to find..." His fingers brushed something and he paused to probe around it. It was too far overhead to see clearly, barely within the reach of his arms, but its shape reminded him of a latch.

She perked up. "Did you find it?"

"Maybe." Nothing happened when he pushed it, so he dug his fingers in around its edges. It lifted. He pulled hard and, when the hidden door didn't move, gave it an experimental twist.

A low thud sounded somewhere in the walls. Dust spilled from the cracks as the door shifted, slid, and folded itself back against the wall of a new corridor. Unlike the circular room, there was no light in the hallway ahead. Zaide frowned before he caught himself. What did it matter if the hall was dark? It was no stranger than the soothing yet sourceless light that occupied the round room.

He turned to beckon Lark, but she was already coming his way.

"I can't hear them. Either they're trapped upstairs and can't get the artifacts to reopen the stairway, or they can't get back down to the ramp you fell down." She stared into the dim hall ahead, her expression unchanging.

Zaide grunted softly. "My sword's on the other side of that slab."

"Maybe you should stop losing weapons." One fine eyebrow climbed, the only indication she was teasing. "Besides, you're not unarmed."

He glanced to the iridescent blade's hilt, comically small in his longer sword's sheath.

"If you were able to fight with the Molten Dagger, you'll be fine with that. Let's go." Lark swept a lock of hair back from her face as she slid past him and started off down the hall.

It stretched on for some time, growing darker as they walked.

"Still got your lantern?" Zaide asked.

The princess paused to open her bag. "Yes, but it still isn't lit. I don't know how to fix it after it's gone out. I've never had that happen before."

"Resia's a mage, she should be able to fix it. Unless it's out because it's too close to this thing." He touched the strange sword, then glanced down. Soft light peeked out from around its hilt. "Oh."

After the glow of the artifacts, he should have known. He unsheathed the blade and held it out before him. Its glow was a soft white, despite the myriad colors that rippled across its surface.

Lark nodded her approval. "Good. You carry that."

"Don't you want it?"

"Unlike you, I still have the weapons I trained with. No sense in handicapping myself when you haven't got your sword."

"Fine. Where are we going?"

Lark shrugged. "Hopefully, up."

Instead of up, the hallway led them to a spiral staircase that descended farther into the earth below the temple.

Zaide stood at the top of the stairs for a time, wishing the light from the sword reached farther. "Do we go down?"

"I don't think we have a choice." Lark trailed her fingers over the stone wall. "We go down. And hope we don't run into any more surprises."

For a time, their footsteps were the only sound. Then the soft tinkling of water seeped into the air. Neither spoke as they traveled farther, the sound growing stronger, the air laden with cool, fresh scents.

"Underground river?" Zaide suggested.

She shook her head. "It doesn't sound that big to me."

Uncertain, he turned his better ear toward the sound.

"How did that happen, anyway?"

It wasn't until he caught her looking at his shortened left ear that he knew what she meant. He lifted his right hand to feel the blunted edge, his left hand occupied with the sword. "Not sure. It happened before I can remember. My mother never said, and I never thought to ask before she passed. When something's just the way you've always been, and it's all anyone's ever seen, nobody mentions it and it never really comes to mind."

Lark nodded, but a hint of color touched her cheeks. "Forgive me. It was rude to ask."

"Nah. It doesn't bother me." He squinted as they neared what he assumed would be the bottom of the stairs. "Light down here."

She pressed a finger to her lips as the traces of light grew and the stairs beneath their feet became more clear.

Zaide started to sheath the sword, but some nagging sense of uncertainty made him keep it in his hand. He'd expected the cavern, pool, and fountain that came into view as they reached the bottom stair.

He hadn't expected the figure that stood at its edge.

CHAPTER THIRTY-EIGHT

"At the end of each era, there is a cycle that repeats itself," the man at the water's edge said. His voice was low, hollow, yet bore a strength and calm confidence that made both Zaide and Lark remain still and listen. "How it ends determines the course civilization is to take. Whether the era will usher in new advancements and a spell of peace, or if countries will fracture and new ways of life will be born."

Zaide's hand tightened on the hilt of the iridescent sword. His fingertips tingled, an odd sensation, and the urge to move warred with the compulsion to stay put.

The man went on, as if their silence were permission. "We are part of that cycle. For a time, I believed the Paragons were reborn, as I was. I no longer believe that is so. Instead, I am the only constant. The Paragons, the crown I battle, the Bladebearer, they are new each time. Theirs is a blessed existence."

"Gadranus," Lark said, not a question, yet not a statement.

He turned toward them.

Instead of features, his face was a pool of shadow. His black cape rippled, spilling curls of mist as he moved. His body, his armor, even the sword at his side appeared solid when he was still. Now and then, a subtle shift ruined the illusion. Finery and black enameled steel, garments suitable for a king, were nothing but mist.

Zaide gripped his sword until his fingers ached. "You're supposed to be in the Shattered Lands."

"I am," Gadranus answered, the words carrying the distinct impression of a smile. "In spirit. Even the strength of the sword you carry cannot hold my power at bay when my time to rise has come."

"I cut you."

The man chuckled. "You tried."

Shadow spilled out from his cape in dark clouds, covering the floor, twisting into dark tendrils that raced toward them.

Zaide slashed each with the glowing blade, and each burst and dissipated on contact. He stepped forward into the wide cavern and settled into his favored stance.

"You're unwise to challenge me as you are, boy," the shadow warned.

Lark drew her silver knives and positioned herself at Zaide's side.

"Suit yourself." Gadranus unsheathed his sword and dissolved into thin air.

A chill ran down Zaide's spine and he spun, his sword up.

It struck the shadow-man's blade and the mists parted, rushing around Zaide's sword in two torrents of black. Gadranus materialized at the water's edge again.

Lark darted forward to strike before he'd fully formed. Her knives slid through him as if he were nothing more than smoke.

He thrust a hand toward her, struck her in the chest and sent her reeling.

Zaide sprang forward and drove his sword into the shadow's side. A sound, not quite a cry but less human than a grunt, spilled from the mists as they burst and retreated across the water to reform on the other side.

"The Spectrum Blade's the only thing that can touch him."

Lark jammed a knife back into its sheath, fire and frustration in her eyes.

"Maybe not the only thing." Zaide moved to put himself between the shadow and the princess. The water didn't look deep enough to keep Gadranus at bay. "The artifacts—"

"Might work," she finished for him as she bounded for the stairs.

Predictably, coils of darkness shot out across the water and raced toward the princess. Zaide slashed through them before they could do more than brush her heels. Then she was up the stairs and gone, leaving him with the unfamiliar sword to guard the way.

A soft hiss resolved into a chuckle as the shadows drew themselves into their humanoid shape again, this time in the center of the pool. Gadranus flowed across the surface of the water without so much as a ripple. "A strange Bladebearer, this time. How much history do you know, boy? How much have I shattered? Sendassian should be the one to wield the Spectrum Blade this time. Not you."

"The sword is Dasienna's." Zaide kept his footing firm as he adjusted his stance to compensate for the length of the blade and waited for the next strike. "She told me to hold it."

"Ignorant children," the shadow spat.

It surged again, this time like a wall of darkness that blotted out the cool light and threatened to swallow him whole.

Zaide responded out of instinct, lunged forward and drove the sword straight.

He made no contact.

Darkness wrapped around his middle and dragged him across the floor, his boots skidding to the water's edge. A shape like a hand seized him by the collar and hauled him into the pool, then plunged him beneath the surface.

Zaide clawed at the formless hand and kicked once, then cursed himself. Only the sword could touch him. He couldn't let habits lead him astray. He swung hard, severed the shadow's arm and scrambled to his feet. The water was no deeper than his knees, but it was enough to slow him down. He flipped water out of his hair and paced backwards as he coughed.

Gadranus gave him little time to recover. He returned with his sword and this time, when their blades clashed, it didn't dissolve.

The force of the blow sent a shudder through Zaide's arms, but sword fighting was one thing he could do. He ducked a second swing and went in low to drive the iridescent blade up into his opponent's chest. He'd expected the mists to burst and collect elsewhere, but instead, the blade glanced off the steel breastplate.

"You are nimble," the shadow conceded.

"And you're still talking. How many times do I have to stab you?" Zaide asked through gritted teeth. He tried to twirl away, but the water slowed him down and his feet dragged along the bottom of the pool. When Gadranus struck again, he barely deflected the shadow blade.

"You cannot defeat magic with a sword, boy. The blade sleeps, and there is no one here to waken it!" The shadow surged in with a wide swing.

A blast of shrieking wind struck his form and scattered it across the cavern.

"Zaide!" Aren splashed into the pool and grabbed him by the arm. Zaide waved him off and spun to face the stairs.

Resia held the Hymnflute ready before her mouth, her dark eyes tracking the swirls of darkness as it began to collect again.

Lark flanked her with the spring's glowing vial in hand. Murk had already pushed past them with the Molten Dagger and advanced on the shadows as if he'd known what to expect.

"Get him into the water!" Resia shouted.

Murk stabbed at the dark mist before it could shape. It fled from the dagger in his hand, not as forcefully as from Zaide's sword, but enough to keep Gadranus from assuming a form that could fight back. He swiped left and right, herding the shadows toward the pool.

Lark positioned herself directly across the water from him, with the Captured Spring held aloft. Its light swelled and shot outward to create a ring around the water. Zaide stared with his mouth open as the barrier formed. *That* was what had held the ceiling of the ice cavern. Aren gave a low whistle of appreciation.

Last of all, Resia strode to the water's edge and raised the Hymnflute again. The notes she blew were strong and sweet and as they filled the cavern, a buffeting wind churned through the black mist and spiraled it into the center of the pool.

The shadow released an animal-sounding snarl that swelled into a howl, and when it took form again above the pool's center, it was that of a hunched-over and horned beast instead of a man.

Zaide sloshed through the water, cursing the way it impaired his speed, but the wind that rushed around them hindered the beast that was Gadranus the same way. The water didn't slow his sword arm, and when Zaide slashed, the strike hit strong and true.

A streak of searing white lanced across the monster and its howl rose into a more human scream. It tried to dissipate. Before it could, a beam of light struck its side, followed by two more.

Zaide grimaced and shielded his eyes. To three sides, his companions advanced with their artifacts, each emitting a ray that burned itself into his vision.

Resia's feet touched the water and the pool itself began to glow.

"Hit him!" Lark cried.

He gathered all his strength and drove the blade through the shadow-beast.

Crackling power shot up his arm as the beams of light converged on the iridescent sword in his hand. Zaide gritted his teeth, screwed his eyes shut and pressed harder.

Deep, monstrous shrieks echoed off the walls and waves of water lapped at Zaide's knees, but he refused to lose his footing.

The light brightened until it hurt, even through his closed eyes. Then, all at once, a single, sharp note like shattering glass split his ears and the light and water waves vanished.

Zaide fell forward with a gasp. A dark purple prism splashed into the water directly in front of him, close enough that droplets spattered his face. Beneath the water's surface, the sword still in his hand shimmered and faded until its light was gone, and only a faint, sleepy swirl of colors remained. He stared at the blade until silt in the water began to settle on its surface, then lifted his head. The prism shone with a dull light of its own, a pulse of purple like the twinkle of a faint star in the night sky. His eyes traveled to Murk as the man waded into the pool. "What was that?"

"Couldn't say, lad, but I'm glad we got that stairway open when we did." The soldier helped hoist Zaide to his feet.

Lark scoffed. "What part of it are you asking about? We already know who he was."

"Yeah, but that's not him." Zaide pointed at the prism. He fought back the impulse to take it. Impulsiveness had gotten him in enough trouble for one lifetime. Instead, he touched it with the toe of his boot. It shifted in the gravel on the bottom of the pool, but its light did not change.

"It's a fragment of his power," Resia said. She waded closer, the Hymnflute still in her hands. "This was what brought the goborrins here and infested the temple. It must've gotten in using his last incarnation's remains as an avenue to breach the Vale's defenses."

Zaide turned his attention to the artifact she held. "That makes wind?"

Her brow furrowed. "I gave you the songbook. Didn't you study it?"

He carefully wiped any expression from his face.

"Zaide!" Resia cried, exasperated.

"It's nothing new for him, is it?" Lark asked as she joined them in the water. She bit her lower lip as she examined the prism at the bottom of the pool, her hand still curled tight around the spring. Eventually, curiosity won out and she hung the vial around her neck and pulled the prism from the water. Its surface was smooth, uniform, and they all stared as she turned it to inspect each side.

"What do we do with it now?" Aren asked.

Lark drew a cloth from her bag and wrapped it around the gem. "I suppose we take it to my father. He hasn't been the most supportive, and he definitely didn't condone this expedition, but maybe having something to show for it will convince him of what must be done to save Amroch."

"Two somethings to show for it." Zaide extended the sword to her, but the corners of her eyes tightened and she held up one hand, palm out.

"The Spectrum Blade chose you."

No one else said anything.

Zaide lowered his hand, unsure what to do with the blade if she wouldn't take it. "What do you mean?" They'd come to retrieve it for her. For her to take it back to Amrochan and lead the city to victory.

Lark shook her head and waded back to dry ground.

"It means we've still got to cut our way back out of here." Murk slapped his shoulder and motioned for the rest of the group to head for the stairs.

Aren pointed at the dagger in Murk's other hand as they moved. "We left the door rocked shut because we didn't have enough light. How are we going to see to do it if these things aren't glowing anymore?"

"We'll make it work. Come on, little lady," Murk called.

Zaide had lost track of Resia. He turned right and then left to spot her meandering across the pool, to where the fountain spilled from a smooth stone wall.

She spread one hand and slid it through the falling water. The fountain shimmered until a soft white light began to pour from the spout.

It flowed into the pool and enveloped her in its glow.

He took a step, but Aren caught his arm and stopped him from going after her.

"Princess Dasienna!" Aren shouted.

Lark turned back from the stairs and straightened when she saw the scene.

Aren pulled Zaide back as the ring of light in the water expanded, but they were slow, and the light wrapped harmlessly around their legs. "What's happening?"

The princess twisted the chain hung around her neck. The vial suspended from it bobbed in response. "The fountain... this must be the spring that feeds the Hymnflute's power. Each of the Paragons—"

"The what?" Zaide interrupted.

She threw up her hands. "Maker's mercy, Zaide, you were the Kolmari Elder's apprentice! Have you never opened a book in your life? The Paragons! Kolmar's Elder, Desheni's Shaman, Jadora's Magister, they're all the heads of power in their region!"

"And everyone has always called them the Elder, Shaman, and Magister," he replied, though a small voice in the back of his head warned him not to try and defend himself to the princess. "The first time I ever heard that word was ten minutes ago, when that shadow thing said—"

"Peace," Resia interrupted softly. "There's no need to argue here." The glow faded from the water as she pulled her hand from the fountain.

Lark's mouth took an unpleasant twist, but it was fast and fleeting. "The spring's magic responded to you. I take it to mean it has accepted you as Kolmar's new Elder?"

Resia nodded. "I wouldn't say it spoke, exactly, but it told me things in its own way. Before we can depart, I must complete my ascension to Elder by restoring the Vale's perimeter."

"Will that drive the goborrins out of Kolmar?" Aren asked.

"I'm afraid not," Resia said. "The monsters that are already here will remain here until they're killed or driven out."

"Oh, good."

Zaide blinked twice. *"Good?"* he repeated, hardly believing what he'd just heard.

"Oh, no!" Aren lifted his hands as if to defend himself from their stares. "I don't mean—it's just that everyone here got to do something to help, except me. I haven't done anything to help Kolmar at all. If I can chase monsters out of the Kolmari valley, it'll feel like I did something."

Resia's smile put a twinkle in her eyes. "The valley is Kolmar's physical form, while the Vale magic is its spiritual existence. For the spiritual shield to be restored properly, I'll need you to do exactly that. Once the shadow has been chased out of the valley, the Vale's barrier will settle, and the aura that keeps evil out will be replenished."

Aren's shoulders sagged with relief. "Oh. Good, then. Do we need to kill all of them for that to happen?"

She tilted her head as if listening. "No," she concluded after a moment. "If I can start by having the temple's immediate vicinity cleansed, I can plant the seeds of that magic and work to expand it over the rest of Kolmar. The Vale's shelter will grow."

"Let's go, then," Zaide said. He swung the strange blade up to rest the flat of it against his shoulder. "There have got to be some goborrins nearby to take out, and I could use some practice with this thing."

"Aye, I'd say. You were clumsy as a first year cadet in that water." Murk sniffed and pointed to the stairs. "It's a straight shot up, the rope's still hanging to help us climb to the altar room. We'll work our way back to the front and break the entry open."

"We'll need a lantern." Lark dug hers out of her bag and ran her fingers over the shutters.

Zaide glanced doubtfully at the water behind them. In the presence of the artifacts, his sword, the prism in Lark's bag, and the fountain, he couldn't fathom making the lantern work.

From the way Resia stepped from the water and held out her

hand to take it, she didn't share his concerns. "Let's go up, then. I know what I'm supposed to do now, I can do it from the sanctuary. I can perform the ritual while the rest of you clear out the forest immediately surrounding the temple."

"Good," was all Lark said in response.

She led the party back up the stairs, all of them dripping, but none as wet as Zaide. He finger-combed his hair as they scaled the staircase to the circular room, which no longer glowed as it had. The place was eerie in the dark, but the three artifacts emitted light again, as if they knew they were needed. The soft glow provided enough light to see. Each figure ahead of him was outlined by color, and Aren walked at his side. The sword, for whatever reason, remained dark. During their ascent, they found the blade he'd lost, and Zaide returned it to its sheath. Unsure what to do with the Spectrum Blade, he carried it against his shoulder.

There was no conversation until they reached the temple's sanctuary.

Behind them, the stairway that led to the hidden pool remained open. Zaide assumed that was safe; Resia seemed unconcerned. Then again, her demeanor struck him as different, and he wasn't certain if concern would have shown. She was always calm and cheerful, level-headed and good at keeping people grounded, but something about her had shifted the moment she'd touched the fountain's water. Her air was more confident—wiser, perhaps—and subtle as it was, the sudden change left him unnerved. They'd have time to talk about it on the way back to Amrochan, he was sure, but for now, all he could do was watch to be sure she was all right.

"There," Resia said as she brushed something inside the lantern and it sprang back to life. Light bounced off the walls of the sanctuary. Aren applauded, earning a laugh and bright smile from Resia. Murk looked amused, but Lark was already at the front door, examining the rocks that blocked the way.

Moving the rocks proved difficult. The mortar that held them together was easy to damage, but the stones were immense. Chipping the fragile mortar out with other rocks spared their weapons, but not their arms, and by the time the doorway stood open and the stones were scattered, everyone sat on the floor, exhausted.

"I have a request," Aren announced when they'd been settled long enough for everyone to catch their breath. "While we go out there to kill whatever goborrins are in the village, I want someone to stay here with Resia while she does her ceremony thing."

"Are you volunteering?" Zaide asked, half in jest, but his friend grew sober.

Lark rubbed the back of her neck and stared at the floor. He'd never seen her so weary, but she managed to look collected. "I think that would be wise. Aren is a capable fighter."

"Which is why we need his help clearing the forest." The tone Zaide used was harder than he should have tried with a princess, but she seemed indifferent.

"Then I'll stay. The two of us will be able to defend the temple, and I have the Captured Spring in case of emergencies." Lark's fingertips brushed the vial, which still glowed, though its light was muted in comparison to the lantern.

Murk grunted his disapproval. "Are you sure, Your Highness? I'm not here to leave you alone."

"Then you stay, too." Zaide straightened where he sat. "Give the dagger to Aren, and we'll sweep the forest. The two of us know this area better than anyone else here. The dagger's magic will give him a leg up, and I've got my sword back, so I'm at full fighting capacity."

Lark waved a hand, the simple gesture all the more permission he was likely to get. "Just don't do anything reckless. We've been through enough without having to hunt down the sword in the middle of the forest after we've already retrieved it once." She instructed Murk to pass over the Molten Dagger with a jerk of her head.

The older man frowned, but held it by the tip to present it to Aren. "It's a strange weapon, but you'll get used to it. Won't burn you, no matter how you touch it, but it'll melt anything else from the inside out."

"Why didn't we stick it in the wall, then? Instead of moving all those rocks by hand?" Aren studied the glittering glass blade before he lowered his hand. He had nowhere to sheath it in his armor. He wedged it under his belt instead.

Zaide beckoned him toward the door. "That's a good question, but I think we can assume it's just because we're all tired and it didn't cross our minds. Come on. While we're out there, I want to see what this thing can do." The Spectrum Blade was light and unfamiliar against his shoulder, but its grip was comfortable in his hand. Both hands, he noted as he transferred it from his right to his left. He'd had a little training with off-hand blades, but it was too long for that. If he used it at all, it would be as a primary weapon.

Aren followed him into the night. After all that had transpired, it seemed it should have been closer to dawn, but Zaide was grateful for the cover. It would be easier to find goborrins in the dark, their campfires and torches serving as beacons to give them away. The hardest part would be singling them out. Even with two of them, and Aren being as competent of a swordsman as Zaide knew himself to be, a lone goborrin was still strong enough to present a challenge.

"You have a plan, or are we making this up as we go?" Aren followed close at his heels, as graceful in the woods as any other Kolmari, though even his cautious footsteps couldn't mute the rattle of his armor.

"The plan is killing a bunch of monsters. Beyond that, I haven't got a lot." Zaide cut a path back the way they'd come. They'd all seen the campfire, it would be easiest to start where he knew there were goborrins and then follow their tracks to see where others might have gone.

Aren flashed him a grin, all but invisible in the dark. "Works for me."

They moved faster with just the two of them, and it wasn't long before the fire glowed between the trees. A few shadows milled around the campsite, but Zaide couldn't distinguish shapes below the brush to determine if there were any goborrins laying down. Come to think of it, he wasn't sure if the monsters slept.

"We'll go around," he whispered, "approach from the back side, the dense part of the forest. There should be a narrow trail that runs back there. We can get a better count from the undergrowth when we're closer."

Aren nodded. They skirted the camp and settled beside a thorn bush to count. Zaide held up three fingers and glanced to his companion for verification. There hadn't been time to get a good look when they'd passed through before, but he'd been confident there were more goborrins in the camp.

They both counted again, and Aren held up three fingers of his own to confirm.

Zaide rubbed his chin as he thought it through. The rest could have left on patrol, departed for another camp, or made their way toward the temple. The last of those options was the only one that concerned him, though Murk and Lark were more than capable of defending themselves and Resia. As long as the few monsters that left the group were the only ones headed that way, it wouldn't present a problem. Satisfied, he motioned for them to progress.

He slid forward through the brush, emerged behind one of the goborrins, and plunged the iridescent sword into the beast's back before it knew they were there. The blade cut through the creature's flesh like butter. When he jerked it back, it came free just as easily. The wound filled with light and the goborrin collapsed without a sound.

Both Zaide and Aren gaped, but the other two goborrins

sprang into action with bellows that would surely alert the others in the forest.

Aren moved first, his movements sure and practiced. He met one of the beasts head-on. Its club smashed into his sword, but he retained his footing and deflected a second blow.

Zaide lunged in to meet the second goborrin, went low, and caught the flesh of its exposed leg with a slash. The slice across the monster's flesh lit up as if infected with the blade's power, a pool of white with swirling colors on its surface. The goborrin howled and Zaide stabbed for its throat.

The sword crashed through and the goborrin collapsed.

Behind him, Aren grunted as he deflected another strike and landed a killing blow. His breath came heavy, but he managed not to look bewildered as he freed his blade. The bewilderment came after he wiped it clean on the monster's breeches.

"What was that?" Aren cried, pointing at the two creatures Zaide had felled.

"Magic?" Zaide guessed as he held up the Spectrum Blade. Its surface was as clean as if it hadn't been used at all.

Aren laughed. "Maker's mercy, you could cut down a whole army with something that does that! This is going to change everything!"

"That's the idea." Zaide rested the blade on his shoulder again. He'd have to have a scabbard made, something the right size. "Let's swing south, head toward the village. We can go by the temple to make sure the others are okay."

"Good plan." Aren pushed back into the underbrush.

After the howling of the first round of goborrins dispatched, there was little point in trying to remain stealthy. They sprinted down a wider path together and passed by the temple, close enough to check for trouble, but far enough off to spare them a tongue-lashing from Lark for daring to question her ability to protect herself. Once certain the temple was the same as they'd left it, they continued down the trail, toward the village proper.

There were no goborrins on the trails; whether it was a blessing or spelled trouble, Zaide couldn't decide.

Then the first fire appeared, and they slowed.

"Maker's mercy," Aren breathed, a phrase Zaide had grown tired of hearing on their short expedition, as it seemed they'd encountered little mercy at all.

Kolmar had been replaced with a fortress.

CHAPTER THIRTY-NINE

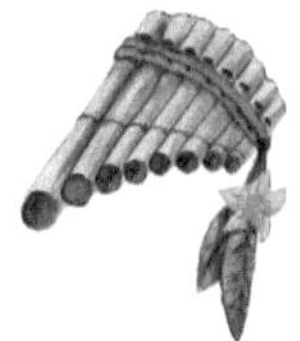

WHERE COZY HOUSES and the village square had been, crude log walls with jagged tops stood lashed together to create a barricade. Beyond its ugly facade, lights glowed in the windows of houses. New structures, as crude as the walls, had been erected between residences, and the forbidding silhouette of a watchtower loomed over the square. Smoke drifted from cook fires, or maybe campfires, as there were no scents of food on the wind—just a wet, foul stench that reminded Zaide of a dog that had been soaked and left to mildew.

He tightened his grip on his sword and started forward.

"Wait!" Aren grabbed his shoulder and reeled him back. "You can't just walk in there! Just imagine how many goborrins are waiting on the other side of that wall. Even with the others to help, we wouldn't stand a chance."

Zaide jerked free of his friend's grasp. "I didn't come all this way to do nothing! This is our home, Aren. We can't leave it this way. And even if I could just turn around and leave, Resia needs us to do this."

"Zaide—"

He didn't give him a chance to finish. Zaide retreated farther into the trees and slipped through the forest, surveying the fortifications as he walked. There had to be a weak point. If he found it, maybe found a way to use the walls to his advantage, he could lure the goborrins into a position where he could take them down while limiting how many he faced. He paused to study a gate in hopes someone might emerge.

Before long, the soft clink of armor reached him and he turned, ready to defend his decision again. Instead of questioning the wisdom of the expedition, Aren pressed a finger to his lips in a signal for silence as he approached, glowing dagger in his hand. He crouched by Zaide's side. "If we're going in, it should be from that side. Behind your cottage. It's less occupied, so it'll take longer for them to respond to the breach. That should throttle how many we face at once."

"I thought you said we wouldn't stand a chance," Zaide whispered.

"We don't. But if we're going to run in there and get ourselves killed, we might as well take out as many of them as we can, first. And besides." Aren rubbed the back of his neck. "Resia needs us to do this, right? I don't want to disappoint her."

There was a hint of doubt in the way Aren carried himself, but Zaide wouldn't refuse the assistance. "We'll circle to the back, then. We may be able to climb the barricade."

Aren nodded, and they made their way to the back of the village. The sour smoke hung low beneath the trees and put a thick feeling in Zaide's throat. He struggled to keep from coughing. Once they were in, there was no going back, but he didn't want to alert the camp to their presence just yet.

At the far side of the village, Aren motioned toward the log barricades and made a cutting motion with the Molten Dagger.

Zaide shrugged and crept toward the wall to inspect it. The logs were seated securely in the dirt, but their tops were still bound together with rope. He pointed at it, then leaned his sword against the barricade and planted his hands against his knee to offer a boost. Not his best idea, he concluded, the moment Aren and all his heavy armor accepted the lift and strained upward to slice the ropes. Plumes of smoke rose from the point of contact and each rope snapped as easily as a thread. When the last gave way, he dropped back to the earth. Zaide grunted and pressed a hand to his lower back. The only reaction he got was a quick eye roll.

"Push," Aren whispered as he planted his shoulder against the log he'd just cut free.

It didn't budge.

Zaide dug in his heels and pushed harder. The earth below his feet seemed to strain, then the log came free and crashed into the campsite.

Aren spat a curse. "They'll know we're here now, won't they?" He regarded the dagger for a moment, as if unsure whether to wield it or draw his sword.

Guessing at his thoughts, Zaide patted his own blade before he reached for the iridescent sword still propped against the wall. "You tried that on the last one. Use the artifact."

A lone goborrin trundled its way around the corner of a house to investigate. It squawked, an unbecoming sound from a monster so big, and clumsily unsheathed a rough blade.

Zaide launched himself through the gap and slammed his sword into the goborrin's chest. The impact sent a jolt up his arms and a shudder down his spine. The monster staggered and fell, pierced by the same light-filled wound as the others. Zaide stared as the glow shimmered and faded.

"Heads up." Aren smacked his shoulder and spun as a handful more appeared around the corner. He moved first this time, darting in with the dagger ready to plunge it into a goborrin's side. The beast roared and flailed, but Aren jerked the black blade free and ducked under its arm to strike it again in the back.

One of the other goborrins drew back a club to strike, but Zaide lunged in to intercept it. His sword's edge sparked at the impact and for a moment, he swore the iridescent colors on its surface swirled faster.

Aren's goborrin went down and he twirled to take on the next. Zaide tried to focus on his fight instead of his companion's. Aren had his own grudge against these monsters, and as Zaide tore through the beast he fought and moved to take on another, the frustrations he'd given himself no time to explore bubbled back to the surface.

His home—his life—had been here. They stood in the gap behind what had been his cottage, the one home that had truly been his, the only remnant of the life he'd thought he'd have. Goborrins had overrun his village, seized the garrison where he'd thought he'd serve, stolen peace from his mentor in the final years of the man's life.

He struck another down.

The camp knew they were there now. Horns blew and goborrins flowed from the stolen homes and clumsy hovels. Not far to Zaide's left, Aren fought his own handful of beasts, darting and twisting between them with a competence that betrayed how overwhelmed the garrison's forces must have been for them to lose.

But the fight was different now, Zaide reminded himself.

Now, they had the artifacts.

As if to confirm, the Spectrum Blade flashed as he raked its edge across a goborrin's chest. He stepped over the body and progressed to the next, and the next. Each kill brought him satisfaction, a sense of justice, yet he was cold, detached. The first time he'd killed one of these monsters, it had seemed a triumphant task, though he'd been given little time to celebrate. Now, dispatching them seemed shallow, mechanical, as if it made no difference.

How many were there? How many more, across the fields outside Amrochan? How far had they pushed across the Allied Kingdoms?

Zaide spared a glance for Aren as he dragged his blade free of another corpse.

"I got it," Aren called, though he never looked Zaide's way.

His own pile of monsters lay around him, their number already startling, yet nowhere near large enough.

Monsters came from everywhere. Sometimes in groups, sometimes alone, but as goborrins fell and Zaide carved a path toward the village square, some began to flee. He advanced on those who remained, breath hard but even, sword glittering in his grasp.

Horns sounded again, different, sharp. Groups of the pig-faced beasts collected between buildings and then scattered, and above the foul stench of their fires, the earthy fragrance of wood smoke scented the air.

"Zaide!" Aren appeared at his side, panting hard and spattered with monster blood. "The fires—"

"I see them," Zaide said. Already, flames licked up the sides of houses he'd known since he was a child.

In the center of the square, where the Elder had stood and ordered Zaide to carry the Hymnflute to the king, a cluster of goborrins melted into a loose circle around a tall central figure that barked orders in harsh, unfamiliar words. Zaide fixed his eyes on that goborrin. The leader. His next target.

"We need to go," Aren said, voice tight and desperate.

"Not yet." Not when felling one more could render the group leaderless and send the remaining goborrins running back the way they'd come.

The tall goborrin turned as if it had expected them, spiked club in its massive hand. It snorted and licked its slick nose.

"Keep the others back," Zaide said as he assumed a combative stance. "This one's mine."

If Aren had any more argument in him, he kept it to himself. He exhaled hard and retreated a step as Zaide beckoned the goborrin with one hand.

The monster answered with a wheeze. Behind it, a ring of goborrins thumped clubs and the ends of spears against the ground.

Zaide wasn't threatened. A vision of the fight at the bridge flashed through his mind, memory of how challenging it had been, and that goborrin had been smaller than this one. But he'd been less practiced then, too, and differently armed. Now, he brought the Spectrum Blade up and gripped the hilt with both hands. It was awkward, small in his grasp and shorter than what the stance demanded, but he would make it work.

The goborrin moved.

Their speed had surprised him in the beginning, but he'd learned to work around it. They were still clumsy, their movements visible early due to their size. This one was no different. It brought its club down hard, but Zaide dodged easily and stabbed for the monster's side. His sword hit the rough leather armor and bounced aside.

Zaide's brows shot up as the cut he'd made revealed steel.

Leather over steel was something he hadn't seen before. He slipped back to get another look at his opponent.

The massive goborrin was almost entirely covered. Only his upper arms and shoulders were bare. But that meant a gap beneath his arms was left unarmored, too, and Zaide fixed that piece of information in the forefront of his mind. A stab there could kill the thing.

Now all he had to do was reach it.

The monster strode sideways, trying to lure Zaide into the ring of goborrins behind it. He wouldn't fall for the bait. Behind him, the sound of Aren's grunt and a goborrin's squeal threatened to steal his attention. He couldn't afford distraction.

Patience, Zaide told himself. Sooner or later, his opponent would have to attack, and with so many monsters waiting to destroy him, it was better to be cautious and reactive than to rush in and leave himself vulnerable. If only the blasted thing would *move*.

The large goborrin made a low sound that was almost like laughter. It waved its club, taunting him. Around them, wood crackled as the fires grew. Heat spilled off the burning houses in waves.

Zaide clutched his sword tighter as sweat beaded on his brow. *Patience.*

It grew tired of waiting.

The goborrin lunged forward and swung hard, not the vertical swing Zaide expected from its first motion, but a hard diagonal. He darted left and the club impacted the stone of the village square. Rock shattered beneath the force. Behind the leader, goborrins howled with delight.

Zaide bit back an oath strong enough that Resia might have slapped him. If the thing knew how to feint, it would be harder to fight than he'd thought. The urge to reevaluate his plan to wait the monster out rose and he tamped it down. Switching strategy or improvising early on would change nothing. Scarce of catching a gap between pieces of the goborrin's armor, the space beneath its arm was his best chance.

Or its head. The thought sprang to mind forcefully enough that he looked the monster in the eye. It wore no helmet. No gorget. Its face and throat were exposed.

It was an option.

When he made no move, the goborrin advanced on him again. It swung left and Zaide ducked, and this time, the twist of its wrist betrayed the coming backswing. Zaide spun to the side as the monster's momentum forced it to turn with the swing. He came around the goborrin's side as it lurched and started to stab for the space under its arm. He halted almost as soon as he'd started. The thing was gargantuan. The gap in its armor was above his reach.

Instead of striking, he spun around to the monster's back and drove his sword at its knee.

Its leg buckled and it staggered forward a step. Before Zaide could react, it regained its footing and turned on him. Its second attack landed closer. The vibrations from the club's impact sent a shudder up his legs.

The smoke thickened as he backed away again to search for

another opening. Orange light bathed the village square as flames reached toward the sky.

"We need to go!" Aren shouted.

"Then go," Zaide barked back. The goborrin was on the offensive now, its swings and strikes faster and without pause between. Dodging was all Zaide could do. The creature's club was as big as he was—he had no hope of deflecting a blow like that.

"I can't leave you here!"

"Then I guess you'll have to stay." The club whooshed past and one of its spikes tore hair from Zaide's head. The proximity made his blood run cold.

The rest of the goborrins still drummed with their spears and clubs, their jeering voices filled with notes like those of squalling swine.

Zaide's eyes watered with the smoke, but he didn't dare wipe them. Instead, he glanced at the flames crawling up the side of the watchtower the monsters had erected on the far side of the stone plaza.

There.

He dove under the sweep of the great beast's arm and stabbed for its stomach. The Spectrum Blade glanced off its armor with a spark and the goborrin bellowed with laughter, but it moved. One massive booted foot shifted backwards.

Determined, Zaide hit it again. This time, his blow bounced off the goborrin's arm, but the closer he got, the more the monster was forced backwards.

It reached for him with one fat, clumsy hand, but Zaide darted to its other side to strike its leg. A sound of frustration escaped its mouth.

The watchtower wasn't far. Left of the ring of watching goborrins, who shouted and bellowed as their leader struggled to follow Zaide's darting and weaving around his trunk-like legs.

Scorching heat poured off the burning tower as he worked to

put himself between it and the goborrin leader. Sweat rolled down Zaide's spine. His shirt clung and his borrowed leather armor rubbed him raw. Only his grip on the sword and his footing remained solid and sure. Smoke choked his lungs and he fought a cough so hard it made tears track down his cheeks. He backed as close to the log structure as he could. He only had one chance.

It took the bait.

The goborrin drew back its massive club and roared as it swung.

Its club tore through the fire-weakened wall, and the watchtower fell.

CHAPTER FORTY

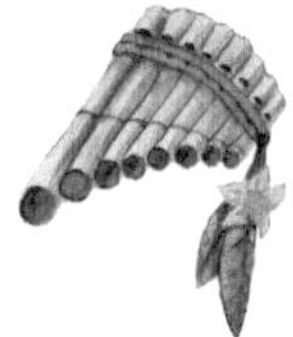

Ash and embers poured down across Zaide's back as he lunged into a roll and the watchtower crashed to the earth.

The giant goborrin howled in pain as the burning logs collapsed over him. He fell amid the wreckage, and roars of fear and anger went up from the audience of monsters.

Smoke and soot clogged the air. The cough he'd tried so desperately to hold in during the fight tore free of Zaide's throat and racked his body. He couldn't get his feet under him. All he could do was press his forehead to the cool ground and fight to suck in air.

A squall and gurgle close by forced him to lift his head. A scant few feet away, Aren jerked his blazing dagger from a smaller goborrin's throat and then stumbled over a chunk of wood in his haste to move.

"Idiot," Aren spat as he seized Zaide's arm and dragged him to his feet.

"I've killed entirely too many things by making stuff fall on them," Zaide croaked.

"You're lucky you didn't kill yourself." Aren grunted as he heaved Zaide's arm over his shoulders and hauled him away from the fire. He still carried the Molten Dagger in his hand, ready to fight, and a pang of guilt struck Zaide's chest.

He'd been eager to end things and confident Aren could manage the fight on his own with an artifact at his disposal. The disparity between the Spectrum Blade in Zaide's left hand and the Molten Dagger in Aren's right struck him as far greater now.

He pulled away from his friend's assistance.

A split second later, a goborrin rushed them from the side.

Zaide parried its primitive sword and Aren dove under its arm to plunge the dagger into its side. Instead of bouncing off the creature's armor, the dagger flared and its blade melted through. The goborrin went down in an instant.

"Hey!" Zaide protested. If he'd had *that*, his fight would have been over in a heartbeat.

The grin Aren shot him was merciless. "Maybe that'll teach you to retreat and regroup instead of trying to plow through, next time!" He motioned toward the rough front gate of the fortifications, now wide open as the surviving goborrins fled.

The sight was more disheartening than the fortifications themselves. "We can't chase them all down," Zaide said, defeated.

"I don't think we have to. They're headed east. We beat them, Zaide! Just the two of us, we wrecked their camp!" Aren's dark eyes shone with excitement, but it was a sentiment Zaide didn't share.

Together, they retreated to a hill of trees that overlooked the village and turned back to watch.

Adrenaline faded and a deep sense of loss took its place. Zaide gazed out across the only home he'd ever known as the flames consumed it. His chest constricted and his heart ached, and this time, the sting in his eyes wasn't from smoke.

"We'll rest here a bit," Aren said. He settled on the hillside with his elbows on his upraised knees.

Zaide watched a moment longer, then thrust the tip of the Spectrum Blade into the earth and flopped down flat on his back.

He didn't want to look anymore, didn't want to see the result of his failures. Smoke hazed the sky overhead and glowed with a reflection of the flames, refusing to let him escape.

He closed his eyes instead.

As his lungs cleared and his pulse settled, the first cold drop hit his face. He flinched, but didn't open his eyes.

The downpour came on slowly, but as the rain arrived, the hiss of water on the fire was audible even from where he lay.

Rain was different under the trees. The drops that worked their way down through the leaves were fat, and most of them stung when they hit his skin.

"Zaide!" Lark cried nearby.

"He's fine," Aren called back. "We both are."

Zaide opened his eyes and reluctantly sat up. Weariness consumed every inch of him now. His hands shook when he grasped the sword beside him, but he removed it from the earth, wiped its tip clean, and rested the blade across his lap as Lark trekked up the hill. Murk followed, but Resia stayed on the trail below, watching the blaze. Her posture revealed little with her back to them, but she clasped her hands before her chest and Zaide could picture the way she unconsciously cradled her broken heart.

His didn't feel much better.

Lark came to a stop and planted her fists against her hips as she inspected the two of them. She looked at Aren a little longer, but it wasn't hard to see why. Blood and dirt spattered his armor, while Zaide sported dirt and soot and not much else.

"What happened here?" she asked.

"Well, Your Highness, we were supposed to kill the goborrins in the Kolmari valley so the Vale magic could be restored," Aren said.

"So we did it," Zaide finished for him. The statement should have been triumphant, but with his foster sister silhouetted against the ruins of the home they'd shared, victory felt more distant than ever.

Murk surveyed them, then the village, and grunted. "I spotted a few stragglers on our way down the trail. They were headed east, but I'll go scout to be sure. We might be able to mow them down before they get to the border."

"Be safe." Lark's expression remained cool and neutral as her eyes drifted to Resia.

Aren pushed himself up. "I'm going to check on her. You stay here and rest, and try not to have anything fall on you."

The princess raised a brow, but said nothing.

Slowly, Zaide climbed to his feet. Part of him thought he ought to see Resia too, offer some comfort and explain what he'd done. That the goborrins occupying the village had set it afire was far from his fault, but guilt still gnawed at him like an irritable beast.

Instead of joining his childhood companions, he went the other way. The field beyond the blacksmith's hut wasn't far off, and as he stepped from the trees and let the rain wash over him, it came with a mild sense of respite.

It took some time before he realized he wasn't alone.

"I was supposed to save it," he said without looking back. "It was all I ever wanted."

"You did," Lark replied as she joined him. "You helped recover the Hymnflute. Sought my father. Requested aid for Kolmar. Without that aid, maybe no one could have escaped. Most of your village's people reached safety in Amrochan because of your effort. Isn't that enough?"

"Not when they don't have a home to go back to."

She was quiet for a time, though she stared into the trees with a thoughtful frown. The forest on the other side of the grassy hill was where they first met. From the distant look in the rich blue of her eyes, she thought of it, too.

When she spoke again, she kept her words cool and formal. "Resia has completed the ritual necessary to restore the magic barrier that protects the Kolmari valley. She anchored it to the temple, as it was before, but elected to make the spring of power the anchor, instead of the Vale Hymnflute. She feels the artifact is too valuable a tool at this point in time to leave it behind."

"She's practical like that," Zaide said, unsure what it had to do with him.

"The barrier will expand over time until the entirety of the valley is under its protection once more. Unfortunately, until it reaches its full potential, it's necessary for her to stay here. She will need guards."

Ah. That was the point. "You want me to stay?"

"No," Lark said. "I want you to let Aren stay. And Murk, perhaps, if she feels it's necessary. I need you to come with me."

His eyes traveled to the sword still in his hand. Water collected at its tip and fell off at regular intervals. The sheen of colors on its surface never changed, yet it was never the same. Ever present, constantly shifting.

The princess nodded as if to confirm his thoughts. "As the Bladebearer, you'll be needed in Amrochan. Once we drive Gadranus's armies back from the city, you may escort your people back to Kolmar if you wish. Should they choose to return."

Whether or not they would seemed a big question. The forest was all any of them had, but rebuilding from nothing—while the valley was still right beside the front lines, no less—wouldn't appeal to many. Or was it beside the front lines? The goborrins had pushed through, made camps elsewhere in Amroch, reached Amrochan with a force the city already struggled to hold at bay. They'd reclaimed Kolmar, but the Vale made it a sheltered bubble within a greater storm.

Troubled, Zaide lifted a hand to rub his brow.

"I can't make you come," Lark continued when he did not speak. "All I can do is inform you that you are needed and let you choose for yourself. I trust you'll make the right decision."

"How do you decide?" he asked softly.

"That's the hardest part. But it comes down to deciding if you can commit to heroism, I suppose. We all come in with our own desires, with ideas of how we think it ought to work out. Often, that just isn't the way." Her wistful gaze settled on the Spectrum Blade in his hand. "But being a hero isn't charging in with courage or being the one to strike a final blow. It's being able to put your wants—your needs—aside for the sake of a greater good." She turned back toward the village, where the heavy rain had dimmed the fires.

Zaide watched her descend the hill, her golden hair plastered to her back and shoulders. She looked small, defeated, nothing like the princess he'd come to know, and in that moment, he understood why.

The Spectrum Blade shimmered in his hand when he tilted it toward the sky. That was her goal; her dream, her need.

The blade that had chosen him to wield it and sparked against her hand.

It was her struggle. Her failure. And one she'd accepted graciously, presenting him with the choice to take her place while he sulked atop a rainy hill.

After everything they'd been through, the desire to sulk was an embarrassment. He squeezed his eyes closed as shame crept up to his ears.

He was Kolmari. The Elder's apprentice. And today, it seemed, he'd get to be a hero as well.

Zaide jogged down the hill to catch up with the princess and fell in stride beside her.

Lark turned her head, curious, but with a tentative light of hope in her eyes.

"All right," he sighed as he shifted the sword to his right hand and rested it against his shoulder, as had already come to be habit. The sword was his. That meant its responsibilities were, too, and he wasn't one to shirk.

He met her gaze and nodded. "Let's do this."

GLOSSARY

Addare – (uh-dare) – An oasis city on the western coast of Amroch.

Amroch – (AM-roke) – The Allied Kingdoms ruled by King Sendassian. Originally a number of smaller kingdoms, unified as an empire for defense purposes.

Amrochan – (am-ROW-kan) – The capital city of Amroch.

Andriun – (AN-dree-un) – The Desheni Shaman's son.

Aren – A soldier stationed at the garrison outside Kolmar. Friend of Zaide and Resia.

Beshnai – (besh-NIGH) – An isolated city on the northern coast of Amroch.

Broken-born – People born in the western kingdoms destroyed by Gadranus. Many seek refuge in Amroch, but face difficulty integrating due to their history in the war.

GLOSSARY

Bugrak – (BUG-rack) – Small, flat-faced and ugly gray creatures. Hunt in packs and use primitive weapons.

Captured Spring – One of the three artifacts. A vial that contains a self-replenishing healing tonic.

Chithal – (chee-thal) – A large port city and trade hub

Dasienna – (das-EE-en-uh) – The princess. King Sendassian's daughter.

Desheni – (duh-SHEN-nee) – A settlement named after the race of aquatic people who live there. The Desheni people bear blue-tinged skin, fin-like ears, webbed fingers, and gills on their necks.

Elder – Kolmar's chief overseer and most skilled mage. Zaide and Resia's mentor. Also known as the Paragon of Forest.

Elsanna – (el-san-nuh) – Chief of the Magister's guardswomen.

Estkel – (est-KELL) – A marshy city at the edge of the Ellean Sea.

Gadranus – (guh-DRA-nuss) – Breaker of the Shattered Lands, leader of the army that threatens to destroy Amroch. According to legend, he has been cursed to be reborn a thousand times as a punishment for his misdeeds.

Ganede – (gan-NEED) – Jadora's sister city. A port of trade on one of the peninsulas that frame the Ellean Sea.

Goborrin – (guh-BOR-rin) – Bipedal man-like monsters with pig-like faces and tusks. The smallest of the goborrins are the size of an adult man.

Jadora – (jah-DOR-ah) – Ganede's sister city. Referred to as The Watcher. A fortress atop a desert plateau.

Kolmar – (coal-mar) – A small forest village in the southwestern region of Amroch.

Lark – The name Dasienna uses while traveling to protect her identity.

Magister – The leader of the fortress city of Jadora. Also known as the Paragon of Fire.

Molten Dagger – One of the three artifacts. An obsidian dagger that appears to have veins of magma trapped within it. Contains fire magic.

Murk – A soldier from the garrison outside Kolmar.

Paragons – Leaders entrusted with the protection of the three magic artifacts.

Parral – (puh-rawl) – A port city at the southernmost tip of Amroch.

Plain – A soldier from the garrison outside Kolmar.

Raddan – A lieutenant and medic in Amroch's army. Stationed at the garrison outside Kolmar.

Resia – (ree-see-uh) – Zaide's foster sister and the Elder's preferred apprentice. Bears a strong magical bond with the forest and wields earth magic.

Sarma – Resia's mother and Zaide's foster mother.

Sast – A fortress outpost on an island in the Ellean sea. Unfriendly to visitors. Little is known about the city.

Sendassian – (sin-das-see-an) – King of Amroch.

Shaman – The leader of the Desheni. Entrusted with the protection of the Captured Spring.

Shattered Lands – The western kingdoms destroyed by Gadranus.

Spectrum Blade – The fourth artifact. A legendary weapon said to be the only thing that can strike down the cursed knight Gadranus.

Tinith – (ten-nith) – A marketplace large enough to be its own city.

Tula – (too-lah) – An apprentice librarian at the Great Library in Jadora. Fancies herself an archaeologist and adventurer.

Valla – (vah-lah) – A high-ranking Jadoran guardswoman. One of Elsanna's most trusted soldiers.

Verlin – Resia's father and Zaide's foster father.

Vale Hymnflute – One of the three artifacts. A set of wooden pan pipes that serves as anchor for Kolmar's Vale magic. It bears power over earth and wind.

Vale magic – A spiritual shield that lays over Kolmar's valley and protects the forest from evil.

Yithel – (yee-THEL) – A trade city along the river north of Amrochan.

GLOSSARY

Zaide – (zayd) – A broken-born refugee fostered in Kolmar after his mother's death. Accidentally involved in helping the princess recover the artifacts and saving Amroch.